What's Bred in the Bone

By GRANT ALLEN, *author of* "*In all Shades*," *etc.* . . . .

NEW YORK AND LONDON
STREET & SMITH, PUBLISHERS

WHAT'S BRED IN THE BONE.

CHAPTER I.

It was late when Elma reached the station. Her pony had jibbed on the way down hill, and the train was just on the point of moving off as she hurried upon the platform. Old Matthews, the stout and chubby-cheeked station-master, seized her most unceremoniously by the left arm, and bundled her into a carriage. He had known her from a child, so he could venture upon such liberties.

"Second class, miss? Yes, miss. Here y'are. Look sharp, please! Any more goin' on? All right, Tom! Go ahead there!" And lifting his left hand, he whistled a shrill signal to the guard to start her.

As for Elma, somewhat hot in the face with the wild rush for her ticket, and grasping her uncounted change, pence and all, in her little gloved hand, she found herself thrust haphazard, at the very last moment, into the last compartment of the last carriage—alone—with an artist.

Now, you and I, to be sure, most proverbially courteous and intelligent reader, might never have guessed at first sight, from the young man's outer aspect, the nature of his occupation. The gross and clumsy male intellect, which works in accordance with the stupid laws of inductive logic, has a queer habit of requiring something or other, in the way of definite evidence, before it commits itself offhand to the distinct conclusion. But Elma Clifford was a woman; and therefore she knew a more excellent

way. *Her* habit was, rather to look things once fairly
and squarely in the face, and then, with the unerring
intuition of her sex, to make up her mind about them
firmly, at once and forever. That's one of the many
glorious advantages of being born a woman. You don't
need to learn in order to know. You know instinctively.
And yet our girls want to go to Girton, and train themselves up to be senior wranglers!

Elma Clifford, however, had *not* been to Girton, so, as she
stumbled into her place, she snatched one hurried look
at Cyril Waring's face, and knew at a glance he was a
landscape painter.

Now this was clever of her, even in a woman, for Cyril
Waring, as he fondly imagined, was travelling that line
that day disguised as a stock-broker. In other words,
there was none of the brown velveteen affectation about
his easy get-up. He was an artist, to be sure, but he hadn't
assiduously and obtrusively dressed his character. Instead of cutting his beard to a Vandyke point, or enduing
his body in a Titianesque coat, or wearing on his head a
slouched Rembrandt hat, stuck carelessly just a trifle on
one side in artistic disorder, he was habited for all the
world like anybody else, in the gray tweed suit of the
common British tourist, surmounted by the light felt
hat (or bowler) to match, of the modern English country
gentleman. Even the soft silk necktie of a delicate
æsthetic hue that adorned his open throat didn't proclaim
him at once a painter by trade. It showed him merely
as a man of taste, with a decided eye for harmonies of
color.

So when Elma pronounced her fellow-traveller immediately, in her own mind, a landscape artist, she was exer-
cising the familiar feminine prerogative of jumping as
if by magic to a correct conclusion. It's a provoking
way they have, those inscrutable women, which no mere
male human being can ever conceivably fathom.

She was just about to drop down, as propriety demands
into the corner seat diagonally opposite to (and therefore
as far as possible away from) her handsome companion,
when the stranger rose, and with a very flushed face,
said in a hasty, though markedly deferential and apologetic
tone :—

" I beg your pardon, but—excuse me for mentioning it
—I think you're going to sit down upon—ur—pray don't
be frightened—a rather large snake of mine."

There was something so comically alarmed in the ring
of his tone—as of a naughty schoolboy detected in a piece
of mischief—that propriety to the contrary notwith-
standing, Elma couldn't for the life of her repress a
smile. She lookeddown at the seat where the stranger
pointed, and there, sure enough, coiled up in huge folds,
with his glossy head in attitude to spring at her, a great
banded snake lay alert and open-eyed.

"Dear me," Elma cried, drawing back a little in surprise, but not at all in horror, as she felt she ought to do.
"A snake! How curious! I hope he's not dangerous."

" Not at all," the young man answered, still in the same
half-guilty tone of voice as before. " He's of a poisonous
kind, you know ; but his fangs have been extracted. He
won't do you any injury. He's perfectly harmless. Aren't
you, Sardanapalus ? Eh, eh, my beauty ? But I oughtn't
to have let him loose in the carriage, of course," he added,
after a short pause. " It's calculated to alarm a nervous
passenger. Only I thought I was alone, and nobody
would come in ; so I let him out for a bit of a run between
the stations. It's so dull for him, poor fellow, being shut
up in his box all the time when he's travelling."

Elma looked down at the beautiful, glossy creature
with genuine admiration. His skin was like enamel ; his
banded scales shone bright and silvery. She didn't know
why, but somehow she felt she wasn't in the least afraid
of him. " I suppose one ought to be repelled at once by
a snake," she said, taking the opposite seat, and keeping
her glance fixed firmly upom the reptile's eye ; " but then,
this is such a handsome one! I can't say why, but I
don't feel afraid of him at all as I ought to do. Every
right-minded person detests snakes, don't they ? And
yet, how exquisitely flexible and beautiful he is! Oh,
pray don't put him back in his box for me. He's basking
in the sun here. I should be sorry to disturb him."

Cyril Waring looked at her in considerable surprise.
He caught the creature in his hands as he spoke, and
transferred it at once to a tin box with a perforated lid
that lay beside him. " Go back, Sardanapalus," he said

in a very musical and pleasant voice, forcing the huge
beast into the lair with gentle but masterful hands. "Go
back, and go to sleep, sir. It's time for your nap. . . .
Oh, no I couldn't think of letting him out any more in
the carriage to the annoyance of others. I'm ashamed
enough as it is of having unintentionally alarmed you.
But you came in so unexpectedly, you see, I hadn't time
to put my queer pet away; and, when the door opened, I
was afraid he might slip out, or get under the seats, so
all I could do was just to soothe him with my hand, and
keep him quiet till the door was shut to again."

"Indeed, I wasn't at all afraid of him," Elma answered,
slipping her change into her pocket and looking prettier
through her blush than even her usual self. "On the
contrary, I really liked to see him. He's such a glorious
snake! The lights and shades on his back are so glancing and so wonderful! He's a perfect model. Of course,
you're painting him."

The stranger started.

"I'm painting him—yes, that's true," he replied, with
a look of sudden surprise; "but why 'of course,' please?
How on earth could you tell I was an artist even?"

Elma glanced back in his face, and wondered to herself,
too. Now she came to think of it, *how* did she know
that handsome young man, with the charming features,
and the expressive eyes, and the neatly cut brown beard,
and the attractive manner, was an artist at all, or anything like it? And how did she know the snake was his
model? For the life of her, she couldn't have answered
those questions herself.

"I suppose I just guessed it," she answered, after a
short pause, blushing still more deeply at the sudden
way she had thus been dragged into conversaton with
the good-looking stranger. Elma's skin was dark—a
clear and creamy olive-brown complexion, such as one
sometimes sees in Southern Europe, though rarely in
England; and the effect of the blush through it didn't
pass unnoticed by Cyril Waring's artistic eye. He would
have given something for the chance of transferring that
delicious effect to canvas. The delicate transparency of
the blush threw up those piercing dark eyes, and reflected
lustre even on the glossy black hair that fringed her fore-

head. Not an English type of beauty at all, Elma Clifford's he thought to himself as he eyed her closely; rather Spanish or Italian, or say even Hungarian.

"Well, you guessed right at any rate," he went on, settling down in his seat once more, after boxing his snake, but this time face to face with her.

"I'm working at a beautiful bit of fern and foliage—quite tropical in its way—in a wood hereabout; and I've introduced Sardanapalus, coiled up in the foreground, just to give life to the scene, don't you know, and an excuse for a title. I mean to call it 'The Rajah's Rest.' Behind, great ferns and a mossy bank; in front, Sardanapalus, after tiffin, rolled spirally round, and taking his siesta."

This meeting was a long-wished-for occasion. Elma had never before met a real live painter. Now, it was the cherished idea of her youth to see something some day of that wonderful, non-existent, fantastic world which we still hope for, and dream about, and call Bohemia. She longed to move in literary and artistic circles. She had fashioned to herself, like many other romantic girls, a rose-colored picture of Bohemian existence; not knowing, indeed, that Bohemia is now, alas! an extinct province, since Belgravia and Kensington swallowed it bodily down, digested and assimilated it. So this casual talk with the handsome young artist in the second-class carriage, on the Great Southern line, was to Elma as a charming and delightful glimpse of an enchanted region she could never enter. It was Paradise to the Peri. She turned the conversation at once, therefore, with resolute intent, upon art and artists, determined to make the most while it lasted of this unique opportunity. And since the subject of self, with an attentive listener is always an attractive one, even to modest young men like Cyril Waring—especially when it's a pretty girl who encourages you to dilate upon it—why, the consequence was that before many minutes were over, the handsome young man was discoursing from his full heart to a sympathetic soul about his chosen art, its hopes and its ideals, accompanied by a running fire of thumb-nail illustrations. He had even got so far in the course of their intimacy as to take out the portfolio, which lay hidden under the seat (out of deference to his disguise as a stock-broker, no doubt), and to display before Elma's delighted eyes, with many explanatory comments as to light and shade, or perspective and foreshortening, the studies for the picture he had just then engaged upon.

By and by, as his enthusiasm warmed under Elma's encouragement, the young artist produced Sardanapalus himself once more from his box, and, with deftly persuasive fingers, coiled him gracefully round on the opposite seat into the precise attitude he was expected to take up when he sat for his portrait in the mossy foreground.

Elma couldn't say why, but that creature fascinated her. The longer she looked at him the more intensely he interested her. Not that she was one bit afraid of him, as she might reasonably have expected to be, according to all womanly precedent. On the contrary, she felt an overwhelming desire to take him up in her own hands and stroke and fondle him. He was so lithe and beautiful; his scales so glistened! At last she stretched out one dainty gloved hand to pet the spotted neck.

"Take care," the painter cried in a warning voice; "don't be frightened if he springs at you. He's vicious at times. But his fangs are drawn; he can't possibly hurt you."

The warning, however, was quite unnecessary. Sardanapalus, instead of springing, seemed to recognize a friend. He darted out his forked tongue in rapid vibration, and licked her neat gray glove respectfully. Then, lifting his flattened head with serpentine deliberation, he coiled his great folds slowly, slowly, with sinuous curves, round the girl's soft arm till he reached her neck in long, winding convolutions. There he held up his face, and trilled his swift, sibilant tongue once more with evident pleasure. He knew his place. He was perfectly at home at once with the pretty, olive-skinned lady. His master looked on in profound surprise.

"Why, you're a perfect snake-charmer," he cried at last, regarding her with open eyes of wonder. "I never saw Sardanapalus behave like that with a stranger before. He's generally by no means fond of new acquaintances. You must be used to snakes. Perhaps you've kept one? You're accustomed of old to their ways and manners?"

"No, indeed," Elma cried, laughing, in spite of herself, a clear little laugh of feminine triumph; for she had made a conquest, she saw, of Sardanapalus; "I never so much as touched one in all my life before; and I thought I should hate them. But this one seems quite tame and tractable I'm not in the least afraid of him. He is so soft and smooth, and his movements are all so perfectly gentle."

"Ah, that's the way with snakes always," Cyril Waring put in, with an admiring glance at the pretty, fearless brunette and her strange companion.

"They know at once whether people like them or not, and they govern themselves accordingly. I suppose it's instinct. When they see you're afraid of them, they spring and hiss; but when they see you take to them by nature, they make themselves perfectly at home in a moment. They don't wait to be asked. They've no false modesty. Well, then, you see," he went on, drawing imaginary lines with his ticket on the sketch he was holding up, "I shall work in Sardanapalus just there, like that, coiled round in a spire. You catch the idea, don't you?"

As he spoke, Elma's eye, following his hand while it moved, chanced to fall suddenly on the name of the station printed on the ticket with which he was pointing. She gave a sharp little start.

"Warnworth!" she cried, flushing up, with some slight embarrassment in her voice; "why, that's ever so far back. We're long past Warnworth. We ran by it three or four stations behind; in fact, it's the next place to Chetwood, where I got in at."

Cyril Waring looked up with a half-guilty smile as embarrassed as her own.

"Oh, yes," he said, quietly; "I knew that quite well. I'm down here often. It's half way between Chetwood and Warnworth I'm painting. But I thought—well, if you'll excuse me saying it, I thought I was so comfortable and so happy where I was that I might just as well go on a station or two more, and then pay the difference, and take the next train back to Warnworth. You see,"

he added, after a pause, with a still more apologetic
and penitent air, " I saw you were so interested in—
well, in snakes you know, and pictures."

Gentle as he was, and courteous, and perfectly frank
with her, Elma, nevertheless, felt really half inclined to
be angry at this queer avowal. That is to say, at least,
she knew it was her bounden duty, as an English lady,
to seem so; and she seemed so, accordingly, with most
Britannic severity. She drew herself up in a very stiff
style, and stared fixedly at him, while she began slowly
and steadily to uncoil Sardanapalus from her imprisoned
arm with profound dignity.

" I'm sorry I should have brought you so far out of
your way," she said, in a studied, cold voice (though
that was quite untrue, for, as a matter of fact, she had
enjoyed their talk together immensely); "and besides,
you've been wasting your valuable time when you ought
to have been painting. You'll hardly get any work done
now at all this morning. I must ask you to get out at
the very next station."

The young man bowed with a crestfallen air. " No
time could possibly be wasted," he began, with native
politeness—"that was spent"—then he broke off quite
suddenly. " I shall certainly get out wherever you
wish," he went on, more slowly, in an altered voice;
"and I sincerely regret if I've unwittingly done anything
to annoy you in any way. The fact is, the talk carried
me away. It was art that misled me. I didn't mean,
I'm sure, to obtrude myself upon you."

And even as he spoke, they whisked, unawares, into
the darkness of a tunnel.

CHAPTER II.

TWO'S COMPANY.

ELMA was just engaged in debating with herself internally how a young lady of perfect manners and impeccable breeding, travelling without a chaperon, ought to behave under such trying circumstances, after having allowed herself to be drawn unawares into familiar conversation with a most attractive young artist, when all of a sudden a rapid jerk of the carriage succeeded in extricating her perforce, and against her will, from this awkward dilemma. Something sharp pulled up their train unexpectedly. She was aware of a loud noise and a crash in front, almost instantaneously followed by a thrilling jar—a low, dull thud—a sound of broken glass —a quick, blank stoppage. Next instant she found herself flung wildly forward into her neighbor's arms, while the artist for his part, with outstretched hands, was vainly endeavoring to break the force of the fall for her.

All she knew•for the first few minutes was merely that there had been an accident to the train, and they were standing still now in the darkness of the tunnel.

For some seconds she paused, and gasped hard for breath, and tried in vain to recall her scattered senses. Then slowly she sank back on the seat once more, vaguely conscious that something terrible had happened to the train, but that neither she nor her companion were seriously injured.

As she sank back in her place, Cyril Waring bent forward towards her with sympathetic kindliness.

"You're not hurt, I hope," he said, holding out one hand to help her rise. "Stand up for a minute, and see if you're anything worse than severely shaken. No?

That's right, then! That's well, as far as it goes. But I'm afraid the nervous shock must have been very rough on you."

Elma stood up, with tears gathering fast in her eyes. She'd have given the world to be able to cry now, for the jar had half stunned her and shaken her brain; but before the artist's face she was ashamed to give free play to her feelings. So she only answered in a careless sort of tone:—

"Oh, it's nothing much, I think. My head feels rather queer; but I've no bones broken. A collision, I suppose; oughtn't we to get out at once and see what's happened to the other people?"

Cyril Waring moved hastily to the door, and, letting down the window, tried with a violent effort to turn the handle from the outside. But the door wouldn't open. As often happens in such accidents, the jar had jammed it. He tried the other side, and with some difficulty at last succeeded in forcing it open. Then he descended cautiously on to the six-foot-way, and held out his hand to help Elma from the carriage.

It was no collision, he saw at once, but a far more curious and unusual accident.

Looking ahead through the tunnel, all was black as night. A dense wall of earth seemed to block and fill in the whole space in front of them. Part of one broken and shattered carriage lay tossed about in wild confusion on the ground close by. Their own had escaped. All the rest was darkness.

In a moment, Cyril rightly divined what must have happened to the train. The roof of the tunnel had caved in on top of it. At least one carriage—the one immediately in front of them—had been crushed and shattered by the force of its fall. Their own was the last, and it had been saved as if by a miracle. It lay just outside the scene of the subsidence.

One thought rose instinctively at once in the young man's mind. They must first see if any one was injured in the other compartments, or among the *débris* of the broken carriage; and then they must make for the open mouth of the tunnel, through which the light of day still gleamed bright behind them.

He peered in hastily at the other three windows. Not
a soul in any one of the remaining compartments! It
was a very empty train, he had noticed himself, when he
got in at Tilgate; the one solitary occupant of the front
compartment of their carriage, a fat old lady with a big
black bag, had bundled out at Chetwood. They were
alone in the tunnel, at this end of the train at least;
their sole duty now was to make haste and save themselves.

He gazed overhead. The tunnel was bricked in with
an arch on top. The way through in front was blocked,
of course, by the fallen mass of water-logged sandstone.
He glanced back towards the open mouth. A curious
circumstance, half way down to the opening, attracted at
once his keen and practised eye.

Strange to say, the roof at one spot was not a true arc
of a circle. It bulged slightly downwards, in a flattened
arch, as if some superincumbent weight were pressing
hard upon it. Great heavens! what was this? Another
trouble in store! He looked again, still more earnestly,
and started with horror.

In the twinkling of an eye his reason told him, beyond
the shadow of a doubt, what was happening at the bulge.
A second fall was just about to take place close by them.
Clearly, there were *two* weak points in the roof of the
tunnel. One had already given way in front; the other
was on the very eve of giving way behind them. If it
fell, they were imprisoned between two impassable walls
of sand and earth. Without one instant's delay, he
turned and seized his companion's hand hastily.

"Quick! quick!" he cried, in a voice of eager warning.
"Run, run for your life to the mouth of the tunnel!
Here, come! You've only just time! It's going, it's
going!"

But Elma's feminine instinct worked quicker and truer
than even Cyril Waring's manly reason. She didn't
know why; she couldn't say how; but in that one invis-
ible moment of time she had taken in and grasped to the
full all the varying terrors of the situation. Instead of
running, however, she held back her companion with a
nervous force she could never before have imagined herself capable of exerting.

"Stop here," she cried, authoritatively, wrenching his arm in her haste. "If you go, you'll be killed. There's no time to run past. It'll be down before you're there. See, see, it's falling!"

Even before the words were well out of her mouth, another great crash shook the ground behind them. With a deafening roar, the tunnel gave way in a second place beyond. Dust and sand filled the air confusedly. For a minute or two all was noise and smoke and darkness. What exactly had happened neither of them could see. But now the mouth of the tunnel was blocked at either end alike, and no daylight was visible. So far as Cyril could judge, they two stood alone, in the dark and gloom, as in a narrow cell, shut in with their carriage between two solid walls of fallen earth and crumbling sandstone.

At this fresh misfortune, Elma sat down on the footboard with her face in her hands and began to sob bitterly. The artist leaned over her and let her cry for awhile in quiet despair. The poor girl's nerves, it was clear, were now wholly unstrung. She was brave, as women go, undoubtedly brave; but the shock and the terror of such a position as this were more than enough to terrify the bravest. At last Cyril ventured on a single remark.

"How lucky," he said in an undertone, "I didn't get out at Warnworth after all. It would have been dreadful if you'd been left all alone in this position."

Elma glanced up at him with a sudden rush of gratitude. By the dim light of the oil lamp that still flickered feebly in the carriage overhead, she could see his face; and she knew by the look in those truthful eyes that he really meant it. He really meant he was glad he'd come on and exposed himself to this risk, which he might otherwise have avoided, because he would be sorry to think a helpless woman should be left alone by herself in the dark to face it. And, frightened as she was, she was glad of it too. To be alone would be awful. This was pre-eminently one of those many positions in life in which a woman prefers to have a man beside her.

And yet, most men, she knew, would have thought to themselves at once, "What a fool I was to come   beyond my proper station, and let myself in for this beastly scrape, just because I'd go a few miles further with a pretty girl I never saw in my life before, and will probably never see in my life again, if I once get well out of this precious predicament."

But that they would ever get out of it at all seemed to both of them now in the highest degree improbable. Cyril, by reason, Elma, by instinct, argued out the whole situation at once, and correctly. There had been much rain lately. The sandstone was water-logged. It had caved in bodily before them and behind them. A little isthmus of archway still held out in isolation just above their heads. At any moment that isthmus might give way too, and, falling on their carriage, might crush them beneath its weight. Their lives depended upon the continued resisting power of some fifteen yards or so of dislocated masonry.

Appalled at the thought, Cyril moved from his place for a minute, and went forward to examine the fallen block in front. Then he paced his way back with groping steps to the equally ruinous mass behind them. Elma's eyes, growing gradually accustomed to the darkness and the faint glimmer of the oil lamps, followed his action with vague and tearful interest.

" If the roof doesn't give way," he said, calmly, at last, when he returned once more to her, " and if we can only let them know we're alive in the tunnel, they may possibly dig us out before we choke. There's air enough here for eighteen hours for us."

He spoke very quietly and reassuringly, as if being shut up in a fallen tunnel between two masses of earth were a matter that needn't cause one the slightest uneasiness ; but his words suggested to Elma's mind a fresh and hitherto unthought-of danger.

" Eighteen hours ! " she cried, horror-struck. " Do you mean to say we may have to stop here, all alone, for eighteen hours together ? Oh, how very dreadful ! How long ! How frightening ! And if they don't dig us out before eighteen hours are over, do you mean to say we shall die of choking ? "

Cyril gazed down at her with a very regretful and sympathetic face.

"I didn't mean to frighten you," he said; "at least, not more than you're frightened already; but, of course, there's only a certain amount of oxygen in the space that's left us; and as we're using it up at every breath, it'll naturally hold out for a limited time only. It can't be much more than eighteen hours. Still, I don't doubt they'll begin digging us out at once; and if they dig through fast, they may yet be in time, even so, to save us."

Elma bent forward with her face in her hands again, and, rocking herself to and fro in an agony of despair, gave herself up to a paroxysm of utter misery. This was too, too terrible! To think of eighteen hours in that gloom and suspense; and then to die at last, gasping hard for breath, in the poisonous air of that pestilential tunnel.

For nearly an hour she sat there, broken down and speechless; while Cyril Waring, taking a seat in silence by her side, tried at first with mute sympathy to comfort and console her. Then he turned to examine the roof and the block at either end, to see if perchance any hope remained of opening by main force an exit anywhere. He even began by removing a little of the sand at the side of the line with a piece of shattered board from the broken carriage in front; but that was clearly no use. More sand tumbled in as fast as he removed it. He saw there was nothing left for it but patience or despair; and of the two, his own temperament dictated rather patience.

He returned at last, wearied out, to Elma's side. Elma, still sitting disconsolate on the footboard, rocking herself up and down, and moaning low and piteously, looked up as he came with a mute glance of inquiry. She was very pretty; that struck him even now. It made his heart bleed to think she should be so cowed and terrified.

"I'm sorry to bother you," he said, after a pause, half afraid to speak, "but there are four lamps all burning hard in these four compartments, and using up the air we may need by and by for our own breathing. If I were to climb to the top of the carriage—which I can easily do—I could put them all out, and economize our oxygen.

It would leave us in the dark, but it'd give us one more chance of life. Don't you think I'd better get up and turn them off, or squash them?"

Elma clasped her hands in horror at the bare suggestion.

"Oh, dear, no!" she cried, hastily. "Please, *please* don't do that. It's bad enough to choke slowly, like this, in the gloom. But to die in the dark—that would be ten times more terrible. Why, it's a perfect Black Hole of Calcutta, even now. If you were to turn out the lights, I could never stand it."

Cyril give a respectful little nod of assent.

"Very well," he answered, as calm as ever; "that's just as you will. I only meant to suggest it to you. My one wish is to do the best I can for you. Perhaps"—and he hesitated—"perhaps I'd better let it go on for an hour or two more, and then, whenever the air begins to get very oppressive—I mean when one begins to feel it's really failing us—one person, you know, could live on so much longer than two . . . it would be a pity not to let you stand every chance. Perhaps I might—"

Elma gazed at him aghast in the utmost horror. She knew what he meant at once. She didn't even need that he should finish his sentence.

"Never!" she said, firmly clenching her small hand hard. "It's so wrong of you to think of it even. I could never permit it. It's your duty to keep yourself alive at all hazards as long as ever you can. You should remember your mother, your sisters, your family."

"Why, that's just it," Cyril answered, a little crestfallen, and feeling he had done quite a wicked thing in venturing to suggest that his companion should have every chance for her own life, "I've got no mother, you see, no sisters, no family. Nobody on earth would ever be one penny the worse if *I* were to die, except my twin brother; he's the only relation I ever had in my life; and even *he*, I daresay, would very soon get over it. Whereas *you*"—he paused, and glanced at her compassionately— "there are probably many to whom the loss would be a very serious one. If I could do anything to save you—" He broke off suddenly, for Elma looked up at him once more with a little burst of despair.

"If you talk like that," she cried, with a familiarity
that comes of association in a very great danger, "I don't
know what I shall do ; I don't know what I shall say to
you.   Why, I couldn't bear to be left alone here to die
by myself.   If only for my sake, now we're boxed up here
together, I think you ought to wait and do the best you
can for yourself."

"Very well," Cyril answered once more, in a most
obedient tone.   "If you wish me to live to keep you company in the tunnel, I'll live while I may.   You have only
to say what you wish ; I'm here to wait upon you."

In any other circumstances, such a phrase would have
been a mere piece of conversational politeness.   At that
critical moment, Elma knew it for just what it was—a
simple expression of his real feeling.

CHAPTER III.

CYRIL WARING'S BROTH

IT was nine o'clock that self-same night, and two men sat together in a comfortable sitting-room under the gabled roofs of Staple Inn, Holborn. It was as cosy a nook as any to be found within the four-mile radius, and artistic withal in its furniture and decorations.

It the biggest arm-chair by the empty grate, a young man with a flute paused for a moment, irresolute. He was a handsome young man, with expressive eyes and a neatly cut brown beard—for all the world like Cyril Waring's. Indeed, if Elma Clifford could that moment have been transported from her gloomy prison in the Lavington tunnel to that cosy room at Staple Inn, Holborn, she would have started with surprise to find the young man who sat in the arm-chair was to all outer appearance the self-same person as the painter she had just left at the scene of the accident. For the two Warings were truly "as like as two peas"; a photograph of one might almost have done duty for the photograph of the other.

The other occupant of the room, who leaned carelessly against the mantleshelf, was taller and older; though he, too, was handsome, but with the somewhat cynical and unprepossessing handsomeness of a man of the world. His forehead was high; his lips were thin; his nose inclined toward the Roman pattern; his black moustache was carefully curled and twisted at the extremities. Moreover, he was musical; for he held in one hand the bow of a violin, having just laid down the instrument itself on the sofa after a plaintive duet with Guy Waring.

"Seen this evening's paper, by the way, Guy?" he asked, after a pause, in a voice that was all honeyed charm and seductiveness. "I brought the *St. James's Gazette* for you, but forgot to give you it; I was so full of this new piece of mine. Been an accident this morning, I see, on the Great Southern line. Somewhere down Cyril's way, too; he's painting near Chetwood; wonder whether he could possibly, by any chance, have been in it?"

He drew the paper carelessly from his pocket as he spoke, and handed it with a graceful air of inborn courtesy to his younger companion. Everything that Montague Nevitt did, indeed, was naturally graceful and courteous.

Guy Waring took the printed sheet from his hands without attaching much importance to his words, and glanced over it lightly.

"At ten o'clock this morning," the telegram said, "a singular catastrophe occurred in a portion of the Lavington tunnel on the Great Southern Railway. As the 9.15 way-train from Tilgate Junction to Guildford was passing through, a segment of the roof of the tunnel collapsed, under pressure of the dislocated rock on top, and bore down with enormous weight upon the carriages beneath it. The engine, tender, and four front wagons escaped unhurt; but the two hindmost, it is feared, were crushed by the falling mass of earth. It is not yet known how many passengers, if any, may have been occupying the wrecked compartments; but every effort is now being made to dig out the *débris.*"

Guy read the paragraph through unmoved, to the outer eye, though with a whitening face, and then took the dog-eared "Bradshaw" that lay close by upon the little oak writing-table. His hand trembled. One glance at the map, however, set his mind at rest.

"I thought so," he said, quietly. "Cyril wouldn't be there. It's beyond his beat. Lavington's the fourth station this way on the up-line from Chetwood. Cyril's stopping at Tilgate town, you know—I heard from him on Saturday—and the bit he's now working at's in Chetwood forest. He couldn't get lodgings at Chetwood itself, so he's put up for the present at the White Lion, at Tilgate, and runs over by train every day to Warnworth. It's three stations away—four off Lavington. He'd have been daubing for an hour in the wood by that time."

"Well, I didn't attach any great importance to it myself," Nevitt went on, unconcerned. "I thought most likely Cyril wouldn't be there. But still I felt you'd like, at any rate, to know about it."

"Oh, of course," Guy answered, still scanning the map in "Bradshaw" close. "He couldn't have been there; but one likes to know. I think, indeed, to make sure, I'll telegraph to Tilgate. Naturally, when a man's got only one relation in the whole wide world—without being a sentimentalist—that one relation means a good deal in life to him. And Cyril and I are more to one another, of course, than most ordinary brothers." He bit his thumb. "Still, I can't imagine how he could possibly be there," he went on, glancing at "Bradshaw" once more. "You see, if he went to work, he'd have got out at Warnworth; and if he meant to come to town to consult his dentist, he'd have taken the 9.30 express straight through from Tilgate, which gets up to London twenty-five minutes earlier."

"Well, but why to consult his dentist in particular?" Nevitt asked with a smile. He had very white teeth, and he smiled accordingly perhaps a little oftener than was quite inevitable. "You Warings are so absolute. I never knew any such fellows in my life as you are. You decide things so beforehand. Why mightn't he have been coming up to town, for example, to see a friend, or get himself fresh colors?"

"Oh, I said ' to consult his dentist,' " Guy answered in the most matter-of-fact voice on earth, suppressing a tremor, "because you know I've had toothache off and on myself, one day with another, for the whole last fortnight. And it's a tooth that never ached with either of us before—this one you see,"—he lifted his lip with his forefinger,—"the second on the left after the one we've lost. If Cyril was coming up to town at all, I'm pretty sure it'd be his tooth he was coming up to see about. I went to Eskell about mine myself last Wednesday."

The elder man seated himself and leaned back in his chair, with his violin in his lap; then he surveyed his friend long and curiously.

"It must be awfully odd, Guy," he said at last, after a good hard stare, "to lead such a queer sort of duplicate life as Cyril and you do! Just fancy being the counter-

foil to some other man's cheek! Just fancy being bound
to do, and think, and speak, and wish as he does! Just
fancy having to get a toothache in the very same tooth
and on the very same day! Just fancy having to consult the identical dentist that he consults simultaneously!
It'd drive *me* mad. Why, it's clean rideeklous!"

Guy Waring looked up hastily from the telegraph
form he was already filling in, and answered, with
some warmth :—

"No, no; not quite so. It isn't like that. You mistake the stituation. We're both checks equally, and
neither is a counterfoil. Cyril and I depend for our
characters, as everybody else does, upon our father and
mother and our remoter progenitors. Only being twins,
and twins cast in very much the same sort of mould,
we're naturally the product of the same two parents, at
the same precise point in their joint life history; and
therefore we're practically all but indentical."

As he rose from his desk, with the telegram in his
hand, the porter appeared at the door with letters. Guy
seized them at once, with some little impatience. The
first was from Cyril. He tore it open in haste, and
skimmed it through rapidly. Montague Nevitt meanwhile sat languid in his chair, striking a pensive note
now and again on his violin, with his eyes half closed
and his lips parted. Guy drew a sigh of relief as he
skimmed his note.

"Just what I expected," he said, slowly, "Cyril
couldn't have been there. He writes last night—the
letter's marked 'Delayed in transmission'; no doubt
by the accident—' I shall come up to town on Friday or
Saturday morning to see the dentist. One of my teeth
is troublesome; I suppose you've had the same; the
second on the left from the one we've lost; been aching
a fortnight. I want it stopped. But to-morrow I
really *can't* leave work. I've got well into the swing of
such a lovely bit of fern, with Sardanapalus just gleaming
like gold in the foreground.' So that settles matters
somewhat. He can't have been there. Though, I
think, even so, I'll just telegraph for safety's sake and
make things certain."

Nevitt struck a chord twice with a sweep of his hand,

listened to it dreamily for a minute with far-away eyes, and then remarked once more, without even looking up, "The same tooth lost, he says! You both had it drawn! And now another one aches in both of you alike! How very remarkable! How very, very curious!"

"Well, that *was* queer," Guy replied, relaxing into a smile; "queer even for us; I won't deny it; for it happened this way. I was over in Brussels at the time, as correspondent for the *Sphere* at the International Workmen's Congress, and Cyril was away by himself just then on his holiday in the Orkneys. We both got toothache in the self-same tooth on the self-same night; and we both lay awake for hours in misery. Early in the morning we each of us got up—five hundred miles away from one another, remember, and as soon as we were dressed, *I* went into a dentist's in the Montagne de la Cour, and Cyril to a local doctor's at Lerwick; and we each of us had it out, instanter. The dentists both declared they could save them if we wished; but we each preferred the lose of a tooth to another such night of abject misery."

Nevitt stroked his mustache with a reflective air. This was almost miraculous. "Well, I should think," he said at last, after close reflection, "where such sympathy as that exists between two brothers, if Cyril had really been hurt in this accident, you must surely in some way have been dimly conscious of it."

Guy Waring, standing there, telegram in hand, looked down at his companion with a somewhat contemptuous smile.

"Oh, dear, no," he answered, with common-sense confidence; for he loved not mysteries. "You don't believe any nonsense of that sort, do you? There's nothing in the least mystical in the kind of sympathy that exists between Cyril and myself. It's all purely physical. We're very like one another. But that's all. There's none of the Corsican Brothers sort of hocus-pocus about us in any way. The whole thing is a simple case of natural causation."

"Then you don't believe in brain-waves?" Nevitt suggested, with a gracefully appropriate undulation of his small, white hand.

Guy laughed incredulously.

"All rubbish, my dear fellow," he answered, "all utter rubbish. If any man knows, it's myself and Cyril. We're as near one another as any two men on earth could possibly be; but when we want to communicate our ideas, each to each, we have to speak or write, just like the rest of you. Every man is like a clock wound up to strike certain hours. Accidents may happen, events may intervene, the clock may get smashed and all may be prevented. But, bar accident, it'll strike all right under ordinary circumstances, when the hour arrives for it. Well, Cyril and I, as I always say, are like two clocks wound up at the same time to strike together, and we strike with very unusual regularity. But that's the whole mystery. If *I* get smashed by accident, there's no reason on earth why Cyril shouldn't run on for years yet as usual; and if Cyril got smashed, there's no reason on earth why I should ever know anything about it except from the newspapers."

CHAPTER IV.

INSIDE THE TUNNEL.

AND, indeed, if brain-waves had been in question at all, they ought, without a doubt, to have informed Guy Waring that at the very moment when he was going out to send off his telegram, his brother Cyril was sitting disconsolate, with dark blue lips and swollen eyelids, on the footboard of the railway carriage in Lavington tunnel. Cyril was worn out with digging by this time, for he had done his best once more to clear away the sand towards the front of the train, in the vague hope that he might succeed in letting in a little more air to their narrow prison through the chinks and interstices of the fallen sandstone. Besides, a man in an emergency must do something, if only to justify his claim to manliness—especially when a lady is looking on at his efforts.

So Cyril Waring had toiled and moiled in that deadly atmosphere for some hours in vain, and now sat, wearied out and faint from foul vapors, by Elma's side on the damp, cold footboard. By this time the air had almost failed them. They gasped for breath, their heads swam vaguely. A terrible weight seemed to oppress their bosoms. Even the lamps in the carriages flickered low and burned blue. The atmosphere of the tunnel, loaded from the very beginning with sulphurous smoke, was now all but exhausted. Death stared them in the face without hope of respite—a ghastly, slow death by gradual stifling.

"You *must* take a little water," Elma murmured, pouring out the last few drops for him into the tin cup, for Cyril had brought a small bottleful that morning for his painting, as well as a packet of sandwiches for lunch. "You're dreadfully tired. I can see your lips are parched and dry with digging."

She was deathly pale herself, and her own eyes were livid, for by this time she had fairly given up all hope of rescue, and, besides, the air in the tunnel was so foul and stupefying she could hardly speak ; indeed, her tongue clung to her palate. But she poured out the last few drops into the cup for Cyril and held them up imploringly, with a gesture of supplication. These two were no strangers to one another now. They had begun to know ˴ach other well in those twelve long hours of deadly peril shared in common.

Cyril waved the cup aside with a firm air of dissent.

"No, no," he said, faintly, "you must drink it yourself. Your need is greater far than mine."

Elma tried to put it away in turn, but Cyril would not allow her. So she moistened her mouth with those scanty last drops, and turned towards him gratefully.

"There's no hope left now," she said in a very resigned voice. "We must make up our minds to die where we stand. But I thank you, oh, I thank you so much, so earnestly."

Cyril, for his part, could hardly find breath to speak.

"Thank you," he gasped out, in one last, despairing effort. "Things look very black ; but, while there's life, there's hope. They may even still, perhaps, come up with us."

As he spoke, a sound broke unexpectedly on the silence of their prison. A dull thud seemed to make itself faintly heard from beyond the thick wall of sand that cut them off from the daylight. Cyril stared with surprise. It was a noise like a pick-axe. Stooping hastily down, he laid his ear against the rail beside the shattered carriage.

"They're digging!" he cried, earnestly, finding words in his joy. "They're digging to reach us! I can hear them! I can hear them!"

Elma glanced up at him with a certain tinge of half-incredulous surprise.

"Yes, they're digging, of course," she said, quickly. "I knew they'd dig for us, naturally, as soon as they missed us. But how far off are they yet? That's the real question. Will they reach us in time? Are they near or distant?"

Cyril knelt down on the ground as before, in an agony of suspense, and struck the rail three times distinctly with his walking-stick. Then he put his ear to it and listened, and waited. In less than half a minute three answering knocks rang, dim but unmistakable, along the buried rail. He could even feel the vibration on the iron with his face.

"They hear us! They hear us!" he cried once more, in a tremor of excitement. "I don't think they're far off. They're coming rapidly towards us."

At the words Elma rose from her seat, still paler than ever, but strangely resolute, and took the stick from his hand with a gesture of despair. She was almost stifled. But she raised it with method. Knocking the rail twice, she bent down her head and listened in turn. One more two answering knocks rang sharp along the connecting line of metal. Elma shook her head ominously.

"No, no, they're a very long way off still," she murmured in a faltering tone, "I can hear it quite well. They can never reach us!"

She seated herself on a fragment of the broken car, and buried her face in her hands once more in silence. Her heart was full. Her head was very heavy. She gasped and struggled. Then a sudden intuition seized her, after her kind. If the rail could carry the sound of a tap, surely it might carry the human voice as well. Inspired with the idea, she rose again and leant forward.

A second time she knocked two quick little taps, ringing sharp on the rail, as if to bespeak attention; then, putting her mouth close to the metals, she shouted aloud along them with all the voice that was left her :—

"Hallo, there, do you hear? Come soon, come fast! We're alive, but choking!"

Quick as lightning an answer rang back as if by magic, along the conducting line of the rail—a strange, unexpected answer.

"Break the pipe of the wires," it said, and then subsided instantly.

Cyril, who was leaning down at her side at the moment with his ear to the rail, couldn't make out one word of it. But Elma's sharp senses, now quickened by the crisis, were acute as an Oriental's and keen as a beagle's.

"'Break the pipe of the wires,' they say," she exclaimed starting back and pondering. "What on earth can they mean by that? What on earth can they be driving at? 'Break the pipe of the wires.' I don't understand them."

Hardly had she spoken, when another sharp tap resounded still more clearly along the rail at her feet. She bent down her head once more, and laid her eager ear beside it in terrible suspense. A rough man's voice —a navvy's, no doubt, or a fireman's—came speeding along the metal; and it said in thick accents : —

"Do you hear what I say? If you want to breathe freer, break the pipe of the wires, and you'll get fresh air from outside right through it."

Cyril this time had caught the words, and jumped up with a sudden air of profound conviction. It was very dark, and the lamps were going out, but he took his fusee-box from his pocket and struck a light hastily. Sure enough, on the lefthand side of the tunnel, half buried in rubbish, an earthenware pipe ran along by the edge near the wall of the archway. Cyril raised his foot and brought his heel down upon it sharply with all the strength and force he had still left in him. The pipe broke short, and Cyril saw within it a number of tele- graph wires for the railway service. The tube com- municated directly with the air outside. They were saved! They were saved! Air would come through the pipe! He saw it all now! He dimly understood it!

At the self-same moment, another sound of breaking was heard more distinctly at the opposite end, some thirty or forty feet off through the tunnel. Then a voice rang far clearer, as if issuing from the tube, in short, sharp sentences :—

"We'll pump you in air. How many of you are there? Are you all alive? Is any one injured?"

Cyril leant down and shouted back in reply :—

"We're two. Both alive. Not hurt. But sick and half dead with stifling. Send us air as soon as ever you can. And if possible pass us a bottle of water."

Some minutes elapsed—three long, slow minutes of

intense anxiety. Elma, now broken down with terror and want of oxygen, fell half fainting forward towards the shattered tube. Cyril held her up in his supporting arms, and watched the pipe eagerly. It seemed an age; but, after a time, he became conscious of a gust of air blowing cold on his face. The keen freshness revived him.

He looked about him and drew a deep breath. Cool air was streaming in through the broken place. Quick as thought, he laid Elma's mouth as close as he could lay it to the reviving current. Her eyes were closed. After a painful interval, she opened them languidly. Cyril chafed her hands with his, but his chafing seemed to produce very little effect. She lay motionless now with her eyelids half shut, and the whites of her eyes alone showing through them. The close, foul air of that damp and confined spot had worked its worst, and had almost asphyxiated her. Cyril began to fear the slight relief had arrived five minutes too late. And it must still in all probability be some hours at least before they could be actually disentombed from that living vault or restored to the open air of heaven.

As he bent over her and held his breath in speechless suspense, the voice called out again more loudly than ever:—

" Look out for the ball in the tube. We're sending you water! "

Cyril watched the pipe closely and struck another light. In a minute, a big glass marble came rattling through, with a string attached to it.

" Pull the string! " the voice cried; and Cyril pulled with a will. Now and again, the object attached to it struck against some projecting ledge or angle where the pipes overlapped. But at last, with a little humoring, it came through in safety. At the end was a large india-rubber bottle, full of fresh water, and a flask of brandy. The young man seized them both with delight and avidity, and bathed Elma's temples over and over again with the refreshing spirit. Then he poured a little into the cup, and filling it up with water, held it to her lips with all a woman's tenderness. Elma gulped the draught down unconsciously, and opened her eyes at once. For a moment she stared about her with a wild stare of surprise.

Then, of a sudden, she recollected were she was, and why, and seizing Cyril's hand pressed it long and eagerly.

" If only we can hold out for three hours more," she cried, with fresh hope returning, " I'm sure they'll reach us ; I'm sure they'll reach us ! "

CHAPTER V.

GRATITUDE.

"THERE were only two of you, then, in the last carriage?" Guy asked with deep interest, the very next morning, as Cyril, none the worse for his long imprison-ment, sat quietly in their joint chambers at Staple Inn, recounting the previous day's adventures.

"Yes. Only two of us. It was awfully fortunate. And the carriage that was smashed had nobody at all, except in the first compartment, which escaped being buried. So there were no lives lost, by a miracle, you may say. But several of the people in the front part of the train got terribly shaken."

"And you and the other man were shut up in the tunnel there for fifteen hours at a stretch?" Guy went on reflectively.

"At least fifteen hours," Cyril echoed, without attempt-ing to correct the slight error of sex, for no man, he thought, is bound to criminate himself, ever in a flirtation. "It was two in the morning before they dug us quite out. And my companion by that time was more dead then alive, I can tell you, with watching and terror."

"Was he, poor fellow?" Guy murmured, with a sympathetic face; for Cyril had always alluded casually to his fellow-traveller in such general terms that Guy was as yet unaware there was a lady in the case. "And is he all right again now, do you know? Have you heard anything more about him?"

But before Cyril could answer there come a knock at the door, and the next moment Mr. Montague Nevitt, without his violin, entered the room in some haste, all agog with excitement. His face was eager and his manner cordial. It was clear he was full of some important tidings.

"Why, Cyril, my dear fellow," he cried, grasping the painter's hand with much demonstration of friendly warmth, and wringing it hard two or three times over; "how delighted I am to see you restored to us alive and well once more. This is really too happy. What a marvellous escape! And what a romantic story! All the clubs are buzzing with it. A charming girl! You'll have to marry her of course, that's the necessary climax. You and the young lady are the staple of news, I see, in very big print, in all the evening papers!"

Guy drew back at the words with a little start of surprise. "Young lady!" he cried, aghast. "A charming girl, Nevitt! Then the person who was shut up with you for fifteen hours in the tunnel was a *girl, Cyril!*"

Cyril's handsome face flushed slightly before his brother's scrutinizing gaze; but he answered with a certain little ill-concealed embarrassment:—

"Oh, I didn't say so, did I? Well, she *was* a girl then, of course; a certain Miss Clifford. She got in at Chetwood. Her people live somewhere down there near Tilgate. At least, so I gathered from what she told me."

Nevitt stared hard at the painter's eyes, which tried (without success) to look unconscious.

"A romance!" he said, slowly, scanning his man with deep interest. "A romance, I can see. Young, rich, and beautiful. My dear Cyril, I only wish I'd had half your luck. What a splendid chance, and what a magnificent introduction! Beauty in distress! A lady in trouble! You console her alone in a tunnel for fifteen hours by yourself at a stretch. Heavens, what a *tête-à-tête!* Did British propriety ever before allow a man such a glorious opportunity for chivalrous devotion to a lady of family, face, and fortune?"

"Was she pretty?" Guy asked, coming down at once to a more realistic platform.

Cyril hesitated a moment. "Well, yes," he answered, somewhat curtly, after a short pause. "She's distinctly good-looking." And he shut his mouth sharp. But he had said quite enough.

When a man says that of a girl, and nothing more, in an unconcerned voice, as if it didn't matter twopence to him, you may be perfectly sure in your own mind he's very deeply and seriously smitten.

" And young ? " Guy continued.

" I should say about twenty."

" And rich beyond the utmost dreams of avarice ? " Montague Nevitt put in, with a faintly cynical smile.

" Well, I don't know about that," Cyril answered, truthfully. " I haven't the lest idea who she is, even. She and I had other things to think about, you may be sure, boxed up there so long in that narrow space, and choking for want of air, than minute investigations into one another's pedigrees."

" *We've* got no pedigree," Guy interposed with a bitter smile. " So the less she investigated about that the better."

" But *she* has, I expect," Nevitt put in hastily · " and if I were you, Cyril, I'd hunt her up forthwith, while the iron's hot, and find out all there is to find out about her. Clifford—Clifford ? I wonder whether by any chance she's one of the Devonshie Cliffords, now ? For if so, she might really be worth a man's serious attention. They're very good business. They bank at our place; and they're by no means paupers." For Nevitt was a clerk in the well-known banking firm of Drummond, Coutts, and Barclay, Limited; and being a man who didn't mean, as he himself said, " to throw himself away on any girl for nothing," he kept a sharp look-out on the current account of every wealthy client with an only daughter.

Ten minutes later, as the talk ran on, some further light was unexpectedly thrown upon this interesting topic by the entrance of the porter with a letter for Cyril. The painter tore it open, and glanced over it, as Nevitt observed, with evident eagerness. It was short and curt, but in its own way courteous.

" ' Mr. Reginald Clifford, C. M. G., desires to thank Mr. Cyril Waring for his kindness and consideration to Miss Clifford during her temporary incarceration—'

" Incarceration's good, isn't it ? How much does he charge a thousand for that sort, I wonder ?—

" 'During her temporary incarceration in the Lavington tunnel yesterday. Mrs. and Miss Clifford wish also to express at the same time their deep gratitude to Mr. Waring for his friendly efforts, and trust he has experienced no further ill effects from the unfortunate accident to which he was subjected.

" 'Craighton, Tilgate, Thursday morning.'

"She *might* have written herself," Cyril murmured half aloud. He was evidently disappointed at this very short measure of correspondence on the subject.

But Montague Nevitt took a more cheerful view. "Oh, Reginald Clifford of Craighton!" he cried with a smile, his invariable smile. "I know all about *him*. He's a friend of Colonel Kelmscott's down at Tilgate Park. C. M. G., indeed! What a ridiculous old peacock. He was administrator of St. Kitts once upon a time, I believe, or was it Nevis or Antigua? I don't quite recollect, I'm afraid; but anyhow, some comical little speck of a sugary, niggery, West Indian Island; and he was made a Companion of St. Michael and St. George when his term was up, just to keep him quiet, don't you know, for he wanted a knighthood, so to shelve him from being appointed to a first-class post like Barbadoes or Trinidad. If it's Elma Clifford you were shut up with in the tunnel, Cyril, you might do worse, there's no doubt, and you might do better. She's an only daughter, and there's a little money at the back of the family, I expect; but I fancy the Companion of the Fighting Saints lives mainly on his pension, which, of course, is purely personal, and so dies with him."

Cyril folded up the note without noticing Nevitt's words and put it in his pocket, somewhat carefully and obtrusively. "Thank you," he said, in a very quiet tone, "I didn't ask you about Miss Clifford's fortune. When I want information on that point I'll apply for it plainly. But meanwhile I don't think any lady's name should be dragged into conversation and bandied about like that, by an absolute stranger."

"Oh, now, you needn't be huffy," Nevitt answered, with a still sweeter smile, showing all those pearly teeth of his to the greatest advantage. "I didn't mean to put your back up, and I'll tell you what I'll do for you, I'll

heap coals of fire on your head, you ungrateful man. I'll
return good for evil. You shall have an invitation to
Mrs. Holker's garden party on Saturday week at Chetwood Court, and there you'll be almost sure to meet the
beautiful stranger."

But at that very moment, at Craighton Tilgate, Mr.
Reginald Clifford, C. M. G., a stiff little withered-up
official Briton, half mummified by long exposure to tropical suns, was sitting in his drawing-room with Mrs.
Clifford, his wife, and discussing—what subject of all
others on earth but the personality of Cyril Waring?

"Well, it was an awkward situation for Elma, of course,
I admit," he was chirping out cheerfully, with his back
turned by pure force of habit to the empty grate, and his
hands crossed behind him. "I don't deny it was an
awkward situation. Still, there's no harm done, I hope
and trust. Elma's happily not a fanciful or foolishly
susceptible sort of girl. She sees it's a case for mere
ordinary gratitude. And gratitude, in my opinion,
towards a person in his position, is sufficiently expressed
once for all—by letter. There's no reason on earth she
should ever again see or hear any more of him."

"But girls are so romantic," Mrs. Clifford put in
doubtfully, with an anxious air. She herself was by no
means romantic to look at, being, indeed, a person of a
certain age, with a plump, matronly figure, and very
staid of countenance; yet there was something in her
eye, for all that, that recalled at times the vivid keenness
of Elma's, and her cheek had once been as delicate and
creamy a brown as her pretty daughter's. "Girls are so
romantic," Mrs. Clifford repeated once more, in a dreamy
way, "and she was evidently impressed by him."

"Well, I'm glad I made inquiries at once about these
two young men, anyhow," the Companion of St. Michael
and St. George responded with fervor, clasping his
wizened little hands contentedly over his narrow waistcoat. "It's a precious odd story, and a doubtful story,
and not at all the sort of story one likes one's girl to be
any way mixed up with. For my part, I shall give them
a very wide berth indeed in future; and there's no reason
why Elma should ever knock up against them."

"Who told you they were nobodies?" Mrs. Clifford inquired, drawing a wistful sigh.

"Oh, Tom Clark was at school with them," the ex-administrator continued, with a very cunning air, "and he knows all about them—has heard the whole circumstances. Very odd, very odd; never met anything so queer in all my life; most mysterious and uncanny, They never had a father; they never had a mother; they never had anybody on earth they could call their own; they dropped from the clouds as it were, one rainy day, without a friend in the world, plump down into the Charterhouse. There they were well supplied with money, and spent their holidays with a person at Brighton, who wasn't even supposed to be their lawful guardian. Looks fishy, doesn't it? Their names are Cyril and Guy Waring—and that's all they know of themselves. They were educated like gentlemen till they were twenty-one years old; and then they were turned loose upon the world, like a pair of young bears, with a couple of hundred pounds of capital apiece, to shift for themselves with. Uncanny, very; I don't like the look of it. Not at all the sort of people an impressionable girl like our Elma should ever be allowed to see too much of."

"I don't think she was very much impressed by him," Mrs. Clifford said with confidence. "I've watched her to see, and I don't think she's in love with him. But by to-morrow, Reginald, I shall be able, I'm sure, to tell you for certain."

The Companion of the Militant Saints glanced rather uneasily across the hearthrug at his wife. "It's a marvellous gift, to be sure, this intuition of yours, Louisa," he said, shaking his head sagely, and swaying himself gently to and fro on the stone curb of the fender. "I frankly confess, my dear, I don't quite understand it. And Elma's got it too, every bit as bad as you have. Runs in the family, I suppose—runs somehow in the family. After living with you now for twenty-two years—yes, twenty-two last April—in every part of the world and every grade of the service, I'm compelled to admit that your intuition in these matters is really remarkable—simply remarkable."

Mrs. Clifford colored through her olive-brown skin,

exactly like Elma, and rose with a somewhat embarrassed and half-guilty air, avoiding her husband's eyes as if afraid to meet them.

Elma had gone to bed early, wearied out as she was with her long agony in the tunnel. Mrs. Clifford crept up to her daughter's room with a silent tread, like some noiseless Oriental, and, putting her ear to the keyhole, listened outside the door in profound suspense for several minutes.

Not a sound from within; not a gentle footfall on the carpeted floor. For a moment she hesitated; then she turned the handle slowly, and, peering before her, peeped into the room. Thank heaven! no snake signs. Elma lay asleep, with one arm above her head, as peacefully as a child, after her terrible adventure. Her bosom heaved, but slowly and regularly. The mother drew a deep breath and crept down the stairs with a palpitating heart to the drawing-room again.

"Reginald," she said, with perfect confidence, relapsing once more at a bound into the ordinary every-day British matron, "there's no harm done, I'm sure. She doesn't think of this young man at all. You may dismiss him from your mind at once and forever. She's sleeping like a baby."

CHAPTER VI.

TWO STRANGE MEETINGS.

"MRS. HUGH HOLKER, at home, Saturday, May 29th, 3 to 6:30, Chetwood Court; tennis."

Cyril Waring read it out with a little thrill of triumph. To be sure, it was by no means certain that Elma would be there; but still, Chetwood Court was well within range of Tilgate town, and Montague Nevitt felt convinced, he said, the Holkers were friends of the Cliffords and the Kelmscotts.

"For my part," Guy remarked, balancing a fragment of fried sole on his fork as he spoke, "I'm not going all that way down to Chetwood merely to swell Mrs. Holker's triumph."

"I wouldn't if I were you," Cyril answered, with quiet incisiveness. He hadn't exactly fallen in love with Elma at first sight, but he was very much interested in her, and it struck him at once that what interested him was likely also to interest his twin brother. And this is just one of those rare cases in life where a man prefers that his interest in a subject should not be shared by any other person.

Before Saturday, the 29th, arrived, however, Guy had so far changed his mind in the matter, that he presented himself duly with Nevitt at Waterloo to catch the same train to Chetwood station that Cyril went down by.

"After all," he said to Nevitt, as they walked together from the club in Piccadilly, "I may as well see what the girl's like anyhow. If she's got to be my sister-in-law—which seems not unlikely now—I'd better have a look at her beforehand, so to speak, on approbation."

The Holkers' grounds were large and well planted, with velvety lawns on the slope of a well-wooded hill overlooking the boundless blue weald of Surrey. Nevitt and the Warings were late to arrive, and found most of the guests already assembled before them.

After a time Guy found himself, to his intense chagrin, told off by his hostess to do the honors to an amiable old lady of high tonnage and great conversational powers, who rattled on uninterruptedly in one silvery stream about everybody on the ground, their histories and their pedigrees. She took the talking so completely off his hands, however, that after a very few minutes, Guy, who was by nature of a lazy and contemplative disposition, had almost ceased to trouble himself about what she said, interposing "indeeds" and "reallys" with automatic politeness at measured intervals ; when suddenly, the old lady, coming upon a bench where a mother and daughter were seated in the shade, settled down by their sides in a fervor of welcome, and shook hands with them both effusively in a most demonstrative fashion.

The daughter was pretty—yes, distinctly pretty. She attracted Guy's attention at once by the piercing keenness of her lustrous dark eyes, and the delicate olive-brown of her transparent complexion. Her expression was merry, but with a strange and attractive undertone, he thought, of some mysterious charm. A more taking girl, indeed, now he came to look close, he hadn't seen for months. He congratulated himself on his garrulous old lady's choice of a bench to sit upon, if it helped him to an introduction to the beautiful stranger.

But before he could even be introduced, the pretty girl with the olive-brown complexion had held out her hand to him frankly, and exclaimed, in a voice as sunny as her face:

"I don't need to be told your friend's name, I'm sure, Mrs. Godfrey. He's so awfully like him. I should have known him anywhere. Of course, you're Mr. Waring's brother, aren't you?"

Guy smiled, and bowed gracefully ; he was always graceful.

"I refuse to be merely *Mr. Waring's brother*," he answered, with some amusement, as he took the proffered hand in his own warmly. "If it comes to that, I'm Mr.

Waring myself; and Cyril, whom you seem to know
already, is only my brother."

"Ah, but *my* Mr. Waring isn't here to-day, is he?"
the olive-brown girl put in, looking around with quite an
eager interest at the crowd in the distance. "Naturally,
to me, he's *the* Mr. Waring, of course, and you are only
my Mr. Waring's brother."

"Elma, my dear, what on earth will Mr. Waring think
of you?" her mother put in, with the conventional
shocked face of British propriety. "You know," she
went on, turning round quickly to Guy, "we're all so
grateful to your brother for his kindness to our girl in
that dreadful accident the other day at Lavington that
we can't help thinking and talking of him all the time as
our Mr. Waring. I'm sorry he isn't here himself this
afternoon to receive our thanks. It would be such a
pleasure to all of us to give them to him in person."

"Oh, he is about, somewhere," Guy answered, carelessly, still keeping his eye fixed hard on the pretty girl.
"I'll fetch him round by and by to pay his respects in
due form. He'll be only too glad. And this, I suppose,
must be Miss Clifford, that I've heard so much about."

As he said those words, a little gleam of pleasure shot
through Elma's eyes. Her painter hadn't forgotten her,
then. He had talked much about her.

"Yes, I knew who you must be the very first moment
I saw you," she answered, blushing; "you're so much
like him in some ways, though not in all. . . . And he
told me that day he had a twin brother."

"So much like him in some ways," Guy repeated,
much amused. "Why, I wonder you don't take me for
Cyril himself at once. You're the very first person I
ever knew in my life, except a few old and very intimate
friends, who could tell at all the difference between us."

Elma drew back, almost as if shocked and hurt, at the
bare suggestion.

"Oh, dear, no," she cried, quickly, scanning him over
at once with those piercing, keen eyes of hers; "you're
like him, of course—I don't deny the likeness—as
brothers may be like one another. Your features are
the same, and the color of your hair and eyes, and all
that sort of thing; but still, I knew at a glance you

weren't my Mr. Waring. I could never mistake you for
him. The expression and the look are so utterly different."

"You must be a very subtle judge of faces," the young
man answered, still smiling, "if you knew us apart at
first sight; for I never before in my life met anybody
who'd seen my brother once or twice, and who didn't
take me for him, or him for me, the very first time he
saw us apart. But then," he added, after a short pause,
with a quick dart of his eyes," "you were with him in
the tunnel for a whole long day; and in that time, of
course, you saw a good deal of him."

Elma blushed again, and Guy noticed in passing that
she blushed very prettily.

"And how's Sardanapalus?" she asked, in a somewhat
hurried voice, making an inartistic attempt to change
the subject.

"Oh, Sardanapalus is all right," Guy answered, laughing. "Cyril told me you had made friends with him,
and weren't one bit afraid of him. Most people are so
dreadfully frightened of the poor old creature."

"But he isn't old," Elma exclaimed, interrupting him
with some wrath. "He's in the prime of life. He's so
glossy and beautiful. I quite fell in love with him."

"And who is Sardanapalus?" Mrs. Clifford asked,
with a vague maternal sense of discomfort and doubt.
"A dog or a monkey?"

"Oh, Sardanapalus, mother—didn't I tell you about
him?" Elma cried, enthusiastically. "Why, he's just
lovely and beautiful. He's such a glorious green and
yellow banded snake; and he coiled around my arm as
if he'd always known me."

Mrs. Clifford drew back with a horror-stricken face,
darting across at her daughter the same stealthy sort of
look she had given her husband the night after Elma's
adventure.

"A snake?" she repeated, aghast; "a snake! Oh,
Elma! Why, you never told me that. And he coiled
round your arm. How horrible!"

But Elma wasn't to be put down by exclamations of
horror.

"Why, you're not afraid of snakes yourself, you know,

mother," she went on, undismayed. "I remember papa
saying that when you were at St. Kitts with him you
never minded them a bit, but caught them in your hands
like an Indian juggler, and treated them as playthings,
so I wasn't afraid either. I suppose it's hereditary."

Mrs. Clifford gazed at her fixedly for a few seconds
with a very pale face.

"I suppose it is," she said, slowly and stiffly, with an
evident effort. "Most things are, in fact, in this world
we live in. But I didn't know *you*, at least, had inherited it, Elma."

Just at that moment they were relieved from the temporary embarrassment which the mention of Sardanapalus seemed to have caused the party, by the approach of
a tall and very handsome man, who came forward with
a smile towards where their group was standing. He
was military in bearing, and had dark brown hair, with a
white moustache ; but he hardly looked more than fifty
for all that, as Guy judged at once from his erect carriage and the singular youthfulness of both face and figure.
That he was a born aristocrat one could see in every
motion of his well-built limbs. His mien had that ineffable air of grace and breeding which sometimes marks
the members of our old English families. Very much
like Cyril, too, Guy thought to himself, in a flash of intuition ; very much like Cyril, the way he raised his hat
and then smiled urbanely on Mrs. Clifford and Elma. But
it was Cyril grown old, and prematurely white, and filled
full with the grave haughtiness of an honored aristocrat.

"Why, here's Colonel Kelmscott ! " Mrs. Clifford exclaimed, with a sigh of relief, not a little set at ease by
the timely diversion. "We're so glad you've come, Colonel. And Lady Emily too, she's over yonder, is she ?

"Ah, well, I'll look out for her. We heard you were to be
here. Oh, how kind of you; thank you. No, Elma's
none the worse for her adventure, thank heaven ! just a
little shaken, that's all, but not otherwise injured. And
this gentleman's the brother of the kind friend who was
so good to her in the tunnel. I'm not quite sure of the
name. I think it's—"

"Guy Waring," the young man interposed, blandly.
Hardly any one who looked at Colonel Kelmscott's eyes

could even have perceived the profound surprise this announcement caused him. He bowed without moving a muscle of that military face. Guy himself never noticed the intense emotion the introduction aroused 'n the distinguished stranger. But Mrs. Clifford and Elma, each scanning him closely with those keen gray eyes of theirs observed at once that, unmoved as he appeared, a thunderbolt falling at Colonel Kelmscott's feet could not more thoroughly or completely have stunned him. For a second or two he gazed in the young man's face uneasily, his color came and went, his bosom heaved in silence ; then he roped his moustache with his trembling fingers, and tried in vain to pump up some harmless remark appropriate to the occasion. But no remark came to him. Mrs. Clifford darted a furtive glance at Elma, and Elma darted back a furtive glance at Mrs. Clifford. Neither said a word, and each let her eyes drop to the ground at once as they met the other's. But each knew in her heart that something passing strange had astonished Colonel Kelmscott ; and each knew, too, that the other had observed it.

Mother and daughter, indeed, needed no spoken words to tell these things plainly to one another. The deep intuition that descended to both was enough to put them in sympathy at once without the need of articulate language.

" Yes, Mr. Guy Waring," Mrs. Clifford repeated at last, breaking the awkward silence that supervened upon the group. " The brother of Mr. Cyril Waring, who was so kind the other day to my daughter in the tunnel."

The Colonel started, imperceptibly to the naked eye again.

" Oh,' indeed," he said, forcing himself with an effort to speak at last. " I've read about it, of course ; it was in all the papers. . . . And — eh — is your brother here, too, this afternoon, Mr. Waring ? "

CHAPTER VII.

KELMSCOTT OF TILGATE.

To both Elma and her mother this meeting between
Colonel Kelmscott and Guy Waring was full of mystery.
For the Kelmscotts of Tilgate Park were the oldest county
family in all that part of Surrey; and Colonel Kelmscott
himself passed as the proudest man of that haughtiest
house in Southern England. What, therefore, could have
made him give so curious and almost imperceptible a
start the moment Guy Waring's name was mentioned in
conversation? Not a word that he said, to be sure, implied to Guy himself the depth of his surprise; but Elma,
with her marvellous insight, could see at once, for all
that, by the very haze in his eyes, that he was fascinated
by Guy's personality, somewhat as she herself had been
fascinated the other day in the train by Sardanapalus.
Nay, more; he seemed to wish with all his heart to leave
the young man's presence, and yet to be glued to the spot,
in spite of himself, by some strange compulsion.

It was with a dreamy, far-away tone in his voice that
the Colonel uttered those seemingly simple words, " And
is your brother here, too, this afternoon, Mr. Waring?"

" Yes, he's somewhere about," Guy answered, carelessly.
" He'll turn up by and by, no doubt. He's pretty sure to
find out, sooner or later, Miss Clifford's here, and then
he'll come round this way to speak to her."

For some time they stood talking in a little group by
the bench, Colonel Kelmscott meanwhile thawing by degrees and growing gradually interested in what Guy had
to say, while Elma looked on with a devouring curiosity.

" Your brother's a painter, you say," the Colonel murmured once under that heavy white moustache of his;
" yes, I think I remember. A rising painter. Had a

capital landscape in the Grosvenor last year, I recollect, and another in the Academy this spring, if I don't mistake—skied—skied, unfairly; yet a very pretty thing, too; ' At the Home of the Curlews.' "

" He's painting a sweet one now," Elma put in quickly, " down here, close by, in Chetwood forest. He told me about it; it must be simply lovely—all fern and mosses, with, oh! such a beautiful big snake in the foreground."

" I should like to see it " Colonel Kelmscott said, slowly, not without a pang. " If it's painted in the forest—and by your brother, Mr. Waring,—that would give it, to me, a certain personal value."

He paused a moment; then he added in a little explanatory undertone, " I'm lord of the manor, you know, at Chetwood; and I shoot the forest."

" Cyril would be delighted to let you see the piece when it's finished," Guy answered, lightly. " If you're ever up in town our way—we've rooms in Staple Inn. I dare say you know it—that quaint, old-fashioned looking place, with big lattice windows, that overhangs Holborn."

Colonel Kelmscott started, and drew himself up still taller and stiffer than before.

" I may have some opportunity of seeing it some day in one of the galleries," he answered, coldly, as if not to commit himself. To tell you the truth, I seldom have time to lounge about in studios. It was merely the coincidence of the picture being painted in Chetwood forest that made me fancy for a moment I might like to see it. But I'm no connoisseur. Mrs. Clifford, may I take you to get a cup of tea? Tea, I think, is laid out in the tent behind the shrubbery."

It was said in a tone to dismiss Guy politely; and Guy, taking the hint, accepted it as such, and fell back a pace or two to his garrulous old lady. But before Colonel Kelmscott could walk off Mrs. Clifford and her daughter to the marquee for refreshments, Elma gave a sudden start, and blushed faintly pink through that olive-brown skin of hers.

" Why, there's *my* Mr. Waring ! " she exclaimed in a very pleased tone, holding out her hand with a delicious smile; and as she said it, Cyril and Montague Nevitt strolled up from behind a great clump of lilacs beside them.

Two pairs of eyes watched those young folks closely as they shook hands once more—Guy's and Mrs. Clifford's. Guy observed that a little red spot rose on Cyril's cheek he had rarely seen there, and that his voice trembled slightly as he said, " How do you do ? " to his pretty fellow-traveller of the famous adventure. Mrs. Clifford observed that the faint pink faded out of the olive-brown skin as Elma took Cyril Waring's hand in hers, and that her face grew pale for three minutes afterwards. And Colonel Kelmscott, looking on with a quietly observant eye, remarked to himself that Cyril Waring was a very creditable young man indeed, as handsome as Guy, and as like as two peas, but if anything perhaps even a trifle more pleasing.

For the rest of that afternoon those six kept constantly together.

Elma noted that Colonel Kelmscott was evidently ill at ease ; a thing most unusual with that proud, self-reliant aristocrat. He held himself, to be sure, as straight and erect as ever, and moved about the grounds with that same haughty air of perfect supremacy, as of one who was monarch of all he surveyed in the county of Surrey. But Elma could see, for all that, that he was absent-minded and self-contained ; he answered all questions in a distant, unthinking way ; some inner trouble was undoubtedly consuming him. His eyes were all for the two Warings. They glanced nervously right and left every minute in haste, but returned after each excursion straight to Guy and Cyril. The Colonel noted narrowly all they said and did, and Elma was sure he was very much pleased at least with her painter. How could he fail to be, indeed ?—for Mr. Waring was charming. Elma wished she could have strolled off with him about the lawn alone, were it only ten paces in front of her mother. But somehow the fates that day were unpropitious. The party held together as by some magnetic bond, and Mrs. Clifford's eye never for one moment deserted her.

The Colonel glowered. The Colonel was moody. His speech was curt. He occupied himself mainly in listening to Guy and Cyril. A sort of mesmeric influence seemed to draw him towards the two young men.

He drew them out deliberately. Yet the start he had given as either young man came up towards his side was a start, not of mere natural surprise, but of positive disinclination and regret at the meeting. Nay, even now he was angling hard, with all the skill of a strategist, to keep the Warings out of Lady Emily's way. But the more he talked to them, the more interested he seemed. It was clear he meant to make the most of this passing chance—and never again, if he could help it, Elma felt certain, to see them.

Once, and once only, Granville Kelmscott, his son, strolled casually up and joined the group by pure chance for a few short minutes. The heir of Tilgate Park was tall and handsome, though less so then his father; and Mrs. Clifford was not wholly indisposed to throw him and Elma together as much as possible. Younger by a full year than the two Warings, Granville Kelmscott was not wholly unlike them in face and manner. As a rule, his father was proud of him, with a passing great pride, as he was proud of every other Kelmscott possession. But to-day Elma's keen eye observed that the Colonel's glance moved quickly in a rapid dart from Cyril and Guy to his son Granville, and back again from his son Granville to Guy and Cyril. What was odder still, the hasty comparison seemed to redound not altogether to Granville's credit. The Colonel paused, and stifled a sigh as he looked; then in spite of Mrs. Clifford's profound attempts to retain the heir by her side, he sent the young man off at a moment's notice to hunt up Lady Emily. Now why on earth did he want to keep Granville and the Warings apart? Mrs. Clifford and Elma racked their brains in vain; they could make nothing of the mystery.

It was a long afternoon, and Elma enjoyed it, though she never got her *tête-à-tête* after all with Cyril Waring. Just a rapid look, a dart from the eyes, a faint pressure of her hands at parting—that was all the romance she was able to extract from it, so closely did Mrs. Clifford play her part as chaperon. But as the two young men and Montague Nevitt hurried off at last to catch their

train back to town, the Colonel turned to Mrs. Clifford
with a sigh of relief.

"Splendid young fellows, those," he exclaimed, looking
after them. "I'm not sorry I met them. Ought to have
gone into a cavalry regiment early in life; what fine lead-
ers they'd have made, to be sure, in a dash for the guns
or a charge against a battery! But they seem to have
done well for themselves in their own way : carved out
their own fortunes, each after his fashion. Very plucky
young fellows. One of them's a painter, and one's a
jornalist; and both of them are making their mark in
their own world. I really admire them."

And on the way to the station, that moment, Mr. Montague Nevitt, as he lit his cigarette, was saying to Cyril,
with an approving smile, "Your Miss Clifford's pretty."

"Yes," Cyril answered, dryly, "she's not bad looking.
She looked her best to-day. And she's capital company."

But Guy broke out unabashed into a sudden burst of
speech. "Not bad looking!" he cried, contemptuously.

"Is that all you have to say of her? And you a painter,
too! Why, she's beautiful! She's charming! If Cyril
was shut up in a tunnel with *her*—"

He broke off suddenly.

And for the rest of the way home he spoke but seldom.
It was all too true. The two Warings were cast in the
self-same mould. What attracted one, it was clear, no
less surely and certainly attracted the other.

As they went to their separate rooms in Staple Inn that
night, Guy paused for a moment, candle in hand, by his
door, and looked straight at Cyril.

"You needn't fear *me*," he said in a very low tone.
"She's yours. You found her. I wouldn't be mean enough
for a minute to interfere with your find. But I'm not
surprised at you. I would do the same myself, it I could
have seen her first. I won't see her again. I couldn't
stand it. She's too beautiful to see and not to fall in
love with."

CHAPTER VIII.

ELMA BREAKS OUT.

MRS. CLIFFORD returned from Chetwood Court that day in by no means such high spirits as when she went there. In the first place, she hadn't succeeded in throwing Elma and Granville Kelmscott into one another's company at all, and in the second place, Elma had talked much under her very nose, for half an hour at a stretch, with the unknown young painter fellow. When Elma was asked out anywhere else in the country for the next six weeks or so, Mrs. Clifford made up her mind strictly to inquire in private, before committing herself to an acceptance, whether that dangerous young man was likely or not to be included in the party.

For Mrs. Clifford admitted frankly to herself that Cyril was dangerous; as dangerous as they made them. He was just the right age; he was handsome, he was clever; his tawny brown beard had the faintest little touch of artistic redness, and was trimmed and dressed with provoking nicety. He was an artist, too; and girls nowadays, you know, have such an unaccountable way of falling in love with men who can paint, or write verses, or play the violin, or do something foolish of that sort, instead of sticking fast to the solid attractions of the London Stock Exchange or of ancestral acres.

Mrs. Clifford confided her fears that very night to the sympathetic ear of the Companion of the Militant and Guardian Saints of the British Empire.

"Reginald," she said, solemnly, "I told you the other day, when you asked about it, Elma wasn't in love. And at the time I was right or very near it. But this afternoon I've had an opportunity of watching them both together, and I've half changed my mind. Elma thinks a great deal too much altogether, I'm afraid, about this young Mr. Waring."

" How do you know ? " Mr. Clifford asked, staring her hard in the face, and nodding solemnly.

The British matron hesitated.

" How do I know anything ? " she answered at. last, driven to bay by the question. " I never know how. I only know I know it. But whatever we do we must be careful not to let Elma and the young man get thrown together again. I should say myself it wouldn't be a bad plan if we were to send her away somewhere for the rest of the summer, but I can tell you better about all this to-morrow."

Elma, for her part, had come home from Chetwood Court more full then ever of Cyril Waring. He looked so handsome and so manly that afternoon at the Holkers'. Elma hoped she'd be asked out where he was going to be again.

She sat long in her own bedroom, thinking it over with herself, while the candle burnt down in its socket very low, and the house was still, and the rain pattered hard on the roof overhead, and her father and mother were discussing her by themselves downstairs in the drawing-room.

She sat long on her chair without caring to begin undressing. She sat and mused with her hands crossed on her lap. She sat and thought, and her thoughts, were all about Cyril Waring.

For more then an hour she sat there dreamily, and told herself over, one by one, in long order, the afternoon's events from beginning to the end of them. She repeated every word Cyril had spoken in her ear. She remembered every glance, every look he had darted at her. She thought of that faint pressure of his hand as he said farewell. The tender blush came back to her brown cheek once more with maidenly shame as she told it all over. He was so handsome and so nice, and so very, very kind, and, perhaps, after this, she might never again meet him. Her bosom heaved. She was conscious of a new sense just aroused within her.

Presently her heart began to beat more violently. She didn't know why. It had never beaten in her life that way before-not even in the tunnel, nor yet when Cyril came up to-day and spoke first to her. Slowly, slowly, she rose from her seat. The fit was upon her. Could this be a dream? Some strange impulse made her glide forward and stand for a minute or two irresolute, in the middle of the room. Then she turned round, once, twice, thrice, half unconsciously. She turned round, wondering to herself all the while what this strange thing could mean; faster, faster, faster, her heart within her beating at each turn with more frantic haste and speed then ever. For some minutes she turned, glowing with red shame, yet unable to stop, and still more unable to say to herself why or wherefore.

At first that was all. She merely turned and panted. But as she whirled, new moods and figures seemed to force themselves upon her. She lifted her hands and swayed them about above her head gracefully. She was posturing she knew, but why she had no idea. It all came upon her as suddenly and as uncontrollably as a blush. She was whirling around the room, now slow, now fast, but always with her arms held out lissom like a dancing-girl. Sometimes her body bent this way, and sometimes that, her hands keeping time to her movements meanwhile in long, graceful curves, but all as if compelled by some extrinsic necessity.

It was an instinct within her over which she had no control. Surely, surely, she must be possessed. A spirit that was not her seemed to be catching her around the waist, and twisting her about, and making her spin headlong over the floor through this wild, fierce dance. It was terrible, terrible. Yet she could not prevent it. A force not her own seemed to sustain and impel her.

And all the time, as she whirled, she was conscious also of some strange, dim need. A sense of discomfort oppressed her arms. She hadn't everything she required for this solitary orgy. Something more was lacking her. Something essential, vital. But what on earth it could be she knew not; she knew not.

By and by she paused, and, as she glanced right and left, the sense of discomfort grew clearer and more vivid. It was her hands that were wrong. Her hands were empty. She must have something to fill them. Some-

thing alive, lithe, curling, sinuous. These wavings and
swayings, to this side and to that, seemed so meaningless
and void—without some life to guide them. There was
nothing for her to hold ; nothing to tame and subdue ;
nothing to cling and writhe and give point to her movements. Oh, heavens ! how terrible !

She drew herself up suddenly and, by dint of a fierce
brief effort of will, repressed for a while the mad dance
that overmastered her. The spirit within her, if spirit it
were, kept quiet for a moment, awed and subdued by her
proud determination. Then it began once more and led
her resistlessly forward. She moved over to the chest of
drawers still rhythmically and with set steps, but to the
phantom strain of some unheard, low music. The music
was running vaguely through her head all the time—wild
Eolian music—it sounded like a rude tune on a harp or
zither. And surely the cymbals clashed now and again
overhead ; and the timbrel rang clear ; and the castanets
tinkled, keeping time with the measure. She stood still
and listened. No, no, not a sound save the rain on the
roof. It was music of her own heart, beating irregularly
and fiercely to an intermittent lilt, like a Hungarian waltz
or a Roumanian tarantella.

By this time Elma was throughly frightened. Was she
going mad ? she asked herself, or had some evil spirit taken
up his abode within her ? What made her spin and twirl
about like this—irresponsibly, unintentionally, irrepres-
sibly, meaninglessly ? Oh, what would her mother say, if
only she knew all ? And what on earth would Cyril Waring think of her ?

Cyril Waring ! Cyril Waring ! It was all Cyril Waring. And yet, if he knew—oh, mercy, mercy !

Still, in spite of these doubts, misgivings, fears, she
walked over towards the chest of drawers with a firm and
rhythmical tread, to the bars of internal music that
rang loud through her brain, and began opening one
drawer after another in an aimless fashion. She was
looking for something—she didn't know what ; and she
never could rest now until she'd found it.

Drawer upon drawer she opened and shut wearily, but
nothing that her eyes fell upon seemed to suit her mood.
Dresses and jackets and underlinen were there ; she

glanced at them all with a deep sense of profound contempt; none of these gewgaws of civilized life could be of
any use to supply the vague want her soul felt so dimly
and yet so acutely. They were dead, dead, dead, so close
and clinging! Go further! Go further! And last she
opened the bottom drawer of all, and her eye fell askance
upon a feather boa, curled up at the bottom—soft, smooth,
and long; a winding, coiling, serpentine boa. In a second
she had fallen upon it bodily with greedy hands, and was
twisting it round her waist, and holding it high and low,
and fighting fiercely at times, and figuring with it like a
posturant. Some dormant impulse of her race seemed to
stir in her blood, with frantic leaps and bounds, at its
first conscious awakening. She gave herself up to it
wildly now. She was mad. She was mad. She was
glad. She was happy.

Then she began to turn round again, slowly, slowly,
slowly. As she turned, she raised the boa now high
above her head; now held it low on one side, now stooped
down and caressed it. At times, as she played with it,
the lifeless thing seemed to glide from her grasp in curling folds and elude her; at others, she caught it round
the neck like a snake, and twisted it about her arm, or
let it twine and encircle her writhing body. Like a
snake! Like a snake! That idea ran like wildfire
through her burning veins. It was a snake, indeed,
she wanted; a real, live snake; what would she not have
given if it were only Sardanapalus!

Sardanapalus, so glossy, so beautiful, supple; that
glorious green serpent, with his large, smooth coils, and
his silvery scales, and his darting, red tongue, and his
long, lithe movements; Sardanapalus, Sardanapalus, Sardanapalus! The very name seemed to link itself with
the music in her head. It coursed with her blood. It
rang through her brain; and another as well. Cyril
Waring, Cyril Waring, Cyril Waring, Cyril Waring! Oh,
great heavens! what would Cyril Waring say now, if only
he could see her in her mad mood that moment!

And yet it was not she, not she, not she, but some spirit,
some weird, some unseen power within her. It was no
more she than that boa there was a snake. A real, live
snake. Oh, for a real, live snake! And then she could

dance—tarantel, tarantella—as the spirit within her prompted her to dance it. " Faster, faster ! " said the spirit; and she answered him back, "Faster ! "

Faster, faster, faster, faster she whirled round the room; the boa grew alive; it coiled about her; it strangled her Her candle failed; the wick in the socket flickered and died; but Elma danced on, unheeding, in the darkness. Dance, dance, dance, dance; never mind for the light! Oh! what madness was this? What insanity had come over her? Would her feet never stop? Must she go on till she dropped? Must she go on forever?

Ashamed and terrified, with her maidenly sense overawed and obscured by this hateful charm, yet unable to stay herself, unable to resist it, in a transport of fear and remorse, she danced on irresponsibly. Check herself she couldn't, let her do what she would. Her whole being seemed to go forth into that weird, wild dance. She trembled and shook. She stood aghast at her own shame. She had hard work to restrain herself from crying aloud in her horror.

At last a lull, a stillness, a recess. Her limbs seemed to yield and give way beneath her. She half fainted with fatigue. She staggered and fell. Too weary to undress, she flung herself upon the bed, just as she was, clothes and all. Her overwrought nerves lost consciousness at once. In three minutes she was asleep, breathing fast but peacefully.

CHAPTER IX.

AND AFTER?

WHEN Elma woke up next morning, it was broad day-light. She woke with a start to find herself lying upon the bed where she had flung herself. For a minute or two she couldn't recollect or recall to herself how it had all come about. It was too remote from anything in her previous waking thought, too dreamlike, too impossible. Then an unspeakable horror flashed over her unawares. Her face flushed hot. Shame and terror overcame her. She buried her head in her hands in an agony of awe. Her own self respect was literally outraged. It wasn't exactly remorse; it wasn't exactly fear; it was a strange, creeping feeling of ineffable disgust and incredulous astonishment.

There could be but one explanation of this impossible episode. She must have gone mad all at once! She must be a frantic lunatic!

A single thought usurped her whole soul. If she was going mad—if this was really mania—she could never, never, never marry Cyril Waring.

For in a flash of intuition she knew that now. She knew she was in love. She knew he loved her.

In that wild moment of awakening all the rest mattered nothing. The solitary idea that ran now through her head, as the impulse to dance had run through it last night, was the idea that she could never marry Cyril. Waring. And if Cyril Waring could have seen her just then! Her cheeks burned yet a brighter scarlet at that thought than even before. One virginal blush suffused her face from chin to forehead. The maidenly sense of shame consumed and devoured her.

Was she mad? Was she mad? And was this a lucid interval?

Presently, as she lay still on her bed all dressed, and with her face in her hands, trembling for very shame, a little knock sounded tentatively at the door of her bedroom. It was a timid, small knock, very low and soft, and, as it were, inquiring. It seemed to say in an apologetic sort of undertone, " I don't know whether you're awake or not just yet ; and if you're still asleep, pray don't let me for a moment disturb or arouse you."

"Who's there ? " Elma mustered up courage to ask, in a hushed voice of terror, hiding her head under the bedclothes.

" It's me, darling," Mrs. Clifford answered, very softly and sweetly. Elma had never heard her mother speak in so tender and gentle a tone before, though they loved one another well, and were far more sympathetic then most mothers and daughters. And besides, that knock was so unlike mamma's. Why so soft and low ?

Had mamma discovered her ? With a despairing sense of being caught, she looked down at her tell-tale clothes and the unslept-in bed.

"Oh, what shall I ever do?" she thought to herself, confusedly. " I can't let mamma come in and catch me like this. She'll ask why on earth I didn't undress last night. And then what could I ever say? How could I ever explain to her ? "

The awful sense of shame-facedness grew upon her still more deeply then ever. She jumped up, and whispered through the door, in a very penitent voice, " Oh, mother, I can't let you in just yet! Do you mind waiting five minutes? Come again by and by. I—I—I'm so awfully tired and queer this morning somehow."

Mrs. Clifford's voice had an answering little ring of terror in it, as she replied at once in the same soft tone : —

" Very well, darling. That's all right. Stay as long as you like. Don't trouble to get up if you'd rather have your breakfast in bed. And don't hurry yourself at all. I'll come back by and by, and see what's the matter."

Elma didn't know why, but by the very tone of her mother's voice she felt dimly conscious something strange had happened. Mrs. Clifford spoke with unusual gentleness, yet with an unwonted tremor.

" Thank you, dear," Elma answered through the door

going back to the bedside and beginning to undress in a
tumult of shame. " Come again by and by. In just five
minutes." It would do her good, she knew, in spite of her
shyness, to talk with her mother. Then she folded her
clothes neatly one by one on a chair ; hid the peccant
boa away in its own lower drawer ; buttoned her neat
little embroidered night-dress tightly round her throat ;
arranged her front hair into a careless disorder ; and tried
to cool down her fiery red cheeks with copious bathing
in cold water. When Mrs. Clifford came back five minutes later, everything looked to the outer eye of a mere
casual observer exactly as if Elma had laid in bed all
night, curled up between the sheets, in the most ortho-
dox fashion.

But all these elaborate preparations didn't for one moment deceive the mother's watchful glance, or the keen
intuition shared by all the women of the Clifford family.
She looked tenderly at Elma—Elma with her face half
buried in the pillows, and the tell-tale flush still crimson-
ing her cheek in a single round spot; then she turned for
a second to the clothes, too neatly folded on the chair by
the bedside, as she murmured low : —

" You're not well this morning, my child. You'd better
not get up. I'll bring you a cup of tea and some toast myself. You don't feel hungry, of course. Ah, no, I thought
not ! Just a slice of dry toast—yes, yes, I have been
there. Some *eau de Cologne* on your forehead, dear ?
There, there, don't cry, Elma. You'll be better by and
by. Stop in bed till lunch-time. I won't let Lucy come
up with the tea, of course. You'd rather be alone. You
were tired last night. Don't be afraid, my darling. It'll
soon pass off. There's nothing on earth, nothing at all
to be alarmed at."

She laid her hand nervously on Elma's arm. Half
dead with shame as she was, Elma noticed it tremble.
She noticed, too, that mamma seemed almost afraid to
catch her eye. When their glance met for an instant
her mother's eyelids fell, and her cheek, too, burned bright
red, almost as red, Elma felt, as her own that nestled hot
so deep in the pillow. Neither said a word to the other
of what she thought or felt. But their mute sympathy
itself made them more shame-faced than ever. In some

dim, indefinite, instinctive fashion, Elma knew her mother was vaguely aware what she had done last night. Her gaze fell half unconsciously on the bottom drawer. With quick insight Mrs. Clifford's eye followed her daughter's. Then it fell as before. Elma looked up at her terrified, and burst into a sudden flood of tears. Her mother stooped down, and caught her wildly in her arms. " Cry, cry, my darling," she murmured, clasping her hard to her breast. "Cry, cry; it'll do you good; there's safety in crying. Nobody but I shall come near you to-day. Nobody else shall know! Don't be afraid of me! Have not I been there, too? It's nothing, nothing! "

With a burst of despair, Elma laid her face in her mother's bosom. Some minutes later, Mrs. Clifford went down to meet her husband in the breakfast-room.

" Well ? " the father asked, shortly, looking hard at his wife's face, which told its own tale at once, for it was white and pallid.

" Well! " Mrs. Clifford answered with a preoccupied air. " Elma's not herself this morning at all. Had a nervous turn after she went to her room last night. I know what it is. I suffered from them myself when I was about her age." Her eyes fell quickly, and she shrank from her husband's searching glance. She was a plump-faced and well-favored British matron now; but once, many years before, as a slim, young girl, she had been in love with somebody—somebody whom by superior parental wisdom she was never allowed to marry, being put off instead with a well-connected match, young Mr. Clifford of the Colonial Office. That was all. No more romance than that. The common romance of every woman's heart. A forgotten love. Yet she tingled to remember it.

" And you think ? " Mr. Clifford asked, laying down his newspaper and looking very grave.

" I don't think. I know," his wife answered, hastily. " I was wrong the other day, and Elma's in love with that young man, Cyril Waring. I know more than that, Reginald; I know you may crush her; I know you may kill her; but if you don't want to do that, I know she must marry him. Whether we wish it, or whether we don't, there's nothing else to be done. As things stand now, it's inevitable, unavoidable. She'll never be happy with anybody else—she must have *him*—and I, for one, won't try to prevent her."

Mr Reginald Clifford, C.M.G., sometime administrator of the island of St. Kitts, gazed at his wife in blank astonishment. She spoke decidedly; he had never heard her speak with such firmness in his life before. It fairly took his breath away. He gazed at his wife blankly as he repeated to himself in very slow and solemn tones, each word distinct, "You for one won't try to prevent her!"

"No, I won't," Mrs Clifford retorted, defiantly, assured in her own mind she was acting right. "Elma's really in love with him; and I won't let Elma's life be wrecked —as some lives have been wrecked, and as some mothers would wreck it."

Mr. Clifford leaned back in his chair, one mass of astonishment, and let the Japanese paper-knife he was holding in his right hand drop clattering from his fingers. "If I hadn't heard you say it yourself, Louisa," he answered with a gasp, "I could never have believed it. I could—never—have—believed it I don't believe it even now. It's impossible, incredible."

"But it's true," Mrs. Clifford reported. "Elma must marry the man she's in love with."

Meanwhile poor Elma lay alone in her bedroom up stairs, that awful sense of remorse and shame still making her cheeks tingle with unspeakable horror. Mrs. Clifford brought up her cup of tea herself. Elma took it with gratitude, but still never dared to look her mother in the face. Mrs. Clifford, too, kept her own eyes averted. It made Elma's self-abasement even profounder than before to feel that her mother instinctively knew everything.

The poor child lay there long, with a burning face and tingling ears, too ashamed to get up and dress herself and face the outer world, too ashamed to go down before her father's eyes, till long after lunch-time. Then there came a noise at the door once more, the rustling of a dress, a retreating footstep. Somebody pushed an envelope stealthily under the door. Elma picked it up, and examined it curiously. It bore a penny stamp, and the local postmark. It must have come, then, by the two o'clock delivery, without a doubt; but the address, why, the address was written in some unknown hand, and in printing capitals! Elma tore it open with a beating heart, and read the one line of manuscript it contained, which was also written in the same print-like letters.

"Don't be afraid," the letter said. "It will do you no harm. Resist it when it comes. If you do, you will get the better of it."

Elma looked at the letter over and over again in a fever of dismay. She was certain it was her mother had written that note. But she read it with tears, only half reassured—and then burnt it to ashes, and proceeded to dress herself.

When she went down to the drawing-room, Mrs. Clifford rose from her seat, and took her hand in her own, and kissed her on one cheek as if nothing out of the common had happened in any way. The talk between them was obtrusively commonplace. But all that day long, Elma noticed her mother was far tenderer to her than usual; and when she went up to bed, Mrs. Clifford held her fingers for a moment with a gentle pressure, and kissed her twice upon her eyes, and stifled a sigh, and then broke from the room as if afraid to speak to her.

CHAPTER X.

COLONEL KELMSCOTT'S REPENTANCE.

ELMA CLIFFORD wasn't the only person who passed a terrible night, and suffered a painful awakening on the morning after the Holkers' garden party. Colonel Kelmscott, too, had his bad half hour or so before he finally fell asleep; and he woke up next day to a sense of shame and remorse far more definite, and, therefore, more poignant and more real, than Elma's.

Hour after hour, indeed, he lay there on his bed, afraid to toss or turn lest he should wake Lady Emily, but with his limbs all fevered and his throat all parched, thinking over the strange chance that had thus brought him face to face, on the threshold of his honored age, with the two lads he had wronged so long and so cruelly.

The shock of meeting them had been a sudden and a painful one. To be sure, the Colonel had always felt the time might come when his two eldest sons would cross his path in the intricate maze of London society. He had steeled himself, as he thought, to meet them there with dignity and with stoical reserve. He had made up his mind that if ever the names he had imposed upon them were to fall upon his startled ears, no human being that stood by and looked on should note for one second a single tremor of his lips, a faint shudder of surprise, an almost imperceptible flush or pallor on his impassive countenance. And when the shock came, indeed, he had borne it, as he meant to bear it, with military calmness. Not even Mrs. Clifford, he thought, could have discovered from any undertone of his voice or manner that the two lads he received with such well-bred unconcern were his own twin sons, the true heirs and inheritors of the Tilgate Park property.

And yet, the actual crisis had taken him quite by surprise, and shaken him far more than he could ever have conceived possible. For one thing, though he quite expected that some day he would run up unawares against Guy and Cyril, he did *not* expect it would be down in the country, and still less within a few miles' drive of Tilgate. In London, of course, all things are possible. Sooner or later, there, everybody hustles and clashes against everybody. For that reason he had tried to suggest, by indirect means, when he launched them on the world, that the twins should tempt their fortune in India or the colonies. He would have liked to think they were well out of his way, and out of Granville's too. But, against his advice, they had stayed on in England. So he expected to meet them some day, at the Academy private view, perhaps, or in Mrs. Bouverie Barton's literary saloon, but certainly *not* on the close sward of the Holkers' lawn, within a few short miles of his own home at Tilgate.

And now he had met them, his conscience, that had lain asleep so long, woke up of a sudden with a terrible start, and began to prick him fiercely.

If only they had been ugly, misshapen, vulgar ; if only they had spoken with coarse, rough voices, or irritated him by their inferior social tone, or shown themselves unworthy to be the heirs of Tilgate,—why, then the Colonel might possibly have forgiven himself ! But to see his own two sons, the sons he had never set eyes on for twenty-five years or more, grown up into such handsome, well-set, noble-looking fellows,—so clever, so bright, so able, so charming,—to feel they were in every way as much gentlemen born as Granville himself, and to know he had done all three an irreparable wrong,—oh, *that* was too much for him ! For he had kept two of his sons out of their own all these years, only in order to make the position and prospects of the third, at last, certainly doubtful, and perhaps wretched.

There was much to excuse him to himself, no doubt, he cried to his own soul piteously in the night watches. Proud man as he was, he could not so wholly abase himself even to his inmost self as to admit he had sinned without deep provocation. He thought it all over in his heart, just there, exactly as it all happened, that simple and natural tale of a common wrong, that terrible secret of a lifetime that he was still to repent in sackcloth and ashes.

It was so long before—all those twenty-six years, or was it twenty-eight?—since his regiment had been quartered away down in Devonshire. He was a handsome subaltern then, with a frank, open face,—Harry Kelmscott, of the Grays,—just such another man, he said to himself in his remorse, as his son Granville now—or rather, perhaps, as Guy and Cyril Waring. For he couldn't conceal from himself any longer the patent fact that Lucy Waring's sons were like his own old self, and sturdier, handsomer young fellows into the bargain than Lady Emily Kelmscott's boy Granville, whom he had made into the heir of the Tilgate manors. The moor, where the Grays were quartered that summer, was as dull as ditch water. No society, no dances, no hunting, no sport; what wonder a man of his tastes, spoiling for want of a drawing-room to conquer, should have kept his hand in with pretty Lucy Waring?

But he married her—he married her. He did her no wrong in the end. He hadn't that sin at least to lay to his conscience.

Ah, well, poor Lucy! he had really been fond of her, as fond as a Kelmscott of Tilgate could reasonably be expected ever to prove towards the daughter of a simple Dartmoor farmer. It began in flirtation, of course, as such things will begin; and it ended, as they will end, too, in love, at least on poor Lucy's side, for what can you expect from a Kelmscott of Tilgate? And, indeed, indeed, he said to himself earnestly, he meant her no harm, though he seemed at times to be cruel to her. As soon as he gathered how deeply she was entangled—how seriously she took it all—how much she was in love with him —he tried hard to break it off, he tried hard to put matters to her in their proper light ; he tried to show her that an officer and a gentleman, a Kelmscott of Tilgate, could never really have dreamed of marrying the half-educated, half-peasant daughter of a Devonshire farmer. Though, to be sure, she was a lady in her way, too, poor Lucy, as much of a lady in manner and in heart as Emily herself, whose father was an earl, and whose mother was a marquis's eldest daughter.

So much a lady in her way, in deed, in thought, and all that—one of nature's gentlewomen—that when Lucy cried and broke her heart at his halting explanations, he was unmanned by her sobs, and did a thing no Kelmscott of Tilgate should ever have stooped to do—yes, promised to marry her. Of course, he didn't attempt in his own heart to justify that initial folly, as he thought it to himself. He didn't pretend to condone it. He only allowed he had acted like a fool. A Kelmscott of Tilgate should have drawn back long before, or else, having gone so far, should have told the girl plainly (at whatever cost —to her) he could go no further, and have no more to say to her.

To be sure, that would have killed the poor thing outright. But a Kelmscott, you know, should respect his order, and shouldn't shrink for a moment from these trifling sacrifices !

However, his own heart was better (in those days) than his class philosophy. He couldn't trample on poor Lucy Waring. So he made a fool of himself in the end —and married Lucy. Ah, well! ah, well! every man makes a fool of himself once or twice in his life; and though the Colonel was ashamed now of having so far bemeaned his order as to marry the girl, why, if the truth must out, he would have been more ashamed still, in his heart of hearts, even then, if he hadn't married her. He was better than his creed. He could never have crushed her.

Married her, yes; but not publicly, of course. At least, he respected public decency. He married her under his own name, to be sure, but by special license, and at a remote little village on the far side of the moor, where nobody knew either himself or Lucy. In those days, he hadn't yet come into possession of the Tilgate estates ; and if his father had known of it—well, the Admiral was such a despotic old man that he'd have insisted on his son's selling out at once, and going off to Australia or heaven knows where, on a journey round the world, and breaking poor Lucy's heart by his absence. Partly for her sake, the Colonel said to himself now in the silent night, and partly for his own, he had concealed the marriage—for the time being—from the Admiral.

And then came that horrible embroilment—oh, how well he remembered it! Ah, me! ah, me! it seemed but yesterday—when his father insisted he was to marry Lady Emily Croke, Lord Aldeburgh's daughter; and he dared not marry her, of course, having a wife already, and he dared not tell his father, on the other hand, why he couldn't marry her. It was a hateful time. He shrank from recalling it. He was keeping Lucy, then his own wedded wife, as Mrs. Waring, in small rooms in Plymouth; and yet he was running up to town now and again, on leave, as the gay, young bachelor, the heir of Tilgate Park—and meeting Emily Croke at every party he went to in London—and braving the Admiral's wrath by refusing to propose to her. What he would ever have done if Lucy had lived, he couldn't imagine. But, there! Lucy *didn't* live; so he was saved that bother. Poor child! it brought tears to his eyes even now to think of her. He brushed them furtively away, lest he should waken Lady Emily.

And yet it was a shock to him, the night Lucy died. Just then, he could hardly realize how lucky was the accident. He sat there by her side, the day the twins were born, to see her safely through her trouble; for he had always done his duty, after a fashion, by Lucy. When a girl of that class marries a gentleman (don't you see), and consents, too, mind you, to marry him privately, she can't expect to share much of her husband's company. She can't expect he should stultify himself by acknowledging her publicly before his own class. And, indeed, he always meant to acknowledge her in the end—after his father's death, when there was no fear of the Admiral's cutting off his allowance.

But how curiously events often turn out of themselves. The twins were born on a Friday morning, and by the Saturday night, poor Lucy was lying dead, a pale, sweet corpse, in her own little room, near the Hoe, at Plymouth. It was a happy release for him, though he really loved her. But still, when a man's fool enough to love a girl below his own station in life—the Colonel paused and broke off. It was twenty-seven years ago now, yet he really loved her. He couldn't find it in his heart even then to indorse to the full the common philosophy of his own order.

So there he was left with the two boys on his hands, but free, if he liked, to marry Lady Emily. No reason on earth, of course, why he shouldn't marry her now. So, naturally, he married her—after a fortnight's interval. The Admiral was all smiles and paternal blessings at this sudden change of front on his son's part. Why the dickens Harry hadn't wanted to marry the girl before, to be sure, he couldn't conceive ; hankering after some missy in the country, he supposed, that silly rot about what they call love, no doubt; but now that Harry had come to his senses at last, and taken the earl's lass, why, the Admiral was indulgence and munificence itself ; the young people should have an ample. allowance, and my daughter-in-law, Lady Emily, should live on the best that Tilgate and Chetwood could possibly afford her.

What would you have ? the Colonel asked, piteously, in the dead of night, of his own conscience. How else could he have acted ? He said nothing. That was all, mind you, he declared to himself more than once in his own soul. He told no lies. He made no complications. While the Admiral lived, he brought up Lucy's sons, quite privately, at Plymouth. And as soon as ever the Admiral died, he really and truly meant to acknowledge them.

But fathers never die—in entailed estates. The Admiral lived so long—quite, quite too long for Guy and Cyril. Granville was born, and grew to be a big boy, and was treated by everybody as the heir to Tilgate. And now the Colonel's difficulties gathered thicker around him. At last, in the fulness of time, the Admiral died, and slept with his fathers, whose Elizabethan ruffs were the honor and glory of the chancel at Tilgate ; and then the day of reckoning was fairly upon him. How well he remembered that awful hour. He couldn't, he couldn't. He knew it was his duty to acknowledge his rightful sons and heirs, but he hadn't the courage. Things had all altered so much.

Meanwhile, Guy and Cyril had gone to Charterhouse as nobody's wards, and been brought up in the expectation of earning their own livelihood ; so no wrong, he said casuistically, had been done to *them*, at any rate. And Granville had been brought up as the heir of Tilgate.

Lady Emily naturally expected her son to succeed his father. He had gone too far to turn back at last. And yet—

And yet, in his own heart, disguise it as he might, he knew he was keeping his lawful sons out of their own in the end, and it was his duty to acknowledge them as the heirs of Tilgate.

CHAPTER XI.

A FAMILY JAR.

HOUR after hour the unhappy man lay still as death on his bed, and reasoned in vain with his accusing conscience. To be sure, he said to himself, no man was bound by the law of England to name his heir. It is for the eldest son himself to come forward and make his claim. If Guy and Cyril could prove their title to the Tilgate estates when he himself was dead, that was their private business. He wasn't bound to do anything special to make the way easy for them beforehand.

But still, when he saw them, his heart arose and smote him. His very class prejudices fought hard on their behalf. These men were gentlemen, the eldest sons of a Kelmscott of Tilgate,—true Kelmscotts to the core,—handsome, courtly, erect of bearing. Guy was the very image of the Kelmscott of Tilgate Park who bled for King Charles at Marston Moor; Cyril had the exactmien of Sir Rupert Kelmscott, Knight of Chetwood, the ablest of their race, whose portrait, by Kneller, hung in the great hall between his father, the Admiral, and his uncle, Sir Frederick. They had all the qualities the Colonel himself associated with the Kelmscott name. They were strong, brave, vigorous, able to hold their own against all comers. To leave them out in the cold was not only wrong—it was also, he felt in his heart of hearts, a treason to his order.

At last, after long watching, he fell asleep. But he slept uneasily. When he woke, it was with a start. He found himself murmuring to himself in his troubled sleep, "Break the entail, and settle a sum on the two that will quiet them."

It was the only way left to prevent public scandal, and

to save Lady Emily and his son Granville from a painful disclosure; while, at the same time, it would to some extent satisfy the claims of his conscience.

Compromise, compromise; there's nothing like compromise. Colonel Kelmscott had always had by temperament a truly British love of compromise.

To carry out his plan, indeed, it would be necessary to break the entail twice—once formally, and once again really. He must begin by getting Granville's consent to the proposed arrangement, so as to raise ready money with which to bribe the young men; and as soon as Granville's consent was obtained, he must put it plainly to Guy and Cyril, as an anonymous benefactor, that if they would consent to accept a fixed sum in lieu of all contingencies, then the secret of their birth would be revealed to them at last, and they would be asked to break the entail on the estates as eldest sons of a gentleman of property.

It was a hard bargain; a very hard bargain; but then these boys would jump at it, no doubt; expecting nothing, as they did, they'd certainly jump at it. It's a great point, you see, to come in suddenly, when you expect nothing, to a nice lump sum of five or six thousand!

So much so, indeed, that the real difficulty, he thought, would rather lie in approaching Granville.

After breakfast that morning, however, he tapped his son on the shoulder as he was leaving the table, and said to him, in his distinctly business tone, " Granville, will you step with me into the library for ten minutes' talk ? There's a small matter of the estate I desire to discuss with you."

Granville looked back at him with a curiously amused air.

" Why, yes," he said, shortly. " It's a very odd coincidence. But do you know, I was going this morning myself to ask for a chance of ten minutes' talk with you."

He rose, and followed his father into the oak-panelled library. The Colonel sat down on one of the uncomfortable library chairs, especially designed, with their knobs and excrescences, to prevent the bare possibility of serious study. Granville took a seat opposite him, across the formal oak table. Colonel Kelmscott paused, and cleared his throat nervously. Then, with military promptitude, he darted straight into the very thick of the fray.

"Granville," he said, abruptly, "I want to speak with you about a rather big affair. The fact of it is, I'm going to break the entail. I want to raise some money."

The son gave a little start of surprise and amusement.

"Why, this is very odd," he exclaimed once more, in an astonished tone. "That's just the precise thing I wanted to talk about with you."

Colonel Kelmscott eyed him with an answering start.

"Not debts!" he said, slowly. "My boy, my boy, this is bad. Not debts, surely, Granville; I never suspected it."

"Oh, dear, no!" Granville answered, frankly. "No debts, you may be sure. But I wanted to feel myself on a satisfactory basis—as to income, and so forth; and I was prepared to pay for my freedom well. To tell you the truth outright, I want to marry."

Colonel Kelmscott eyed him closely, with a very puzzled look.

"Not Elma Clifford, my boy," he said again, quickly. "For of course, if it is her, Granville, I need hardly say—"

The young man cut him short with a hasty little laugh.

"Elma Clifford," he repeated, with some scorn in his musical voice; "oh, dear, no; not *her*. If it had been her, you may be sure there'd be no reason of any sort for breaking the entail. But the fact is this : I dislike allowances one way or the other. I want to feel once for all I'm my own master. I want to marry—not this girl or that, but whomever I will. I don't care to come to you with my hat in my hand, asking how much you'll be kind enough to allow me if I venture to take Miss So-and-so or What-you-may-call-it. And as I know you want money yourself for this new wing you're thinking of, why, I'm prepared to break the entail at once, and sell whatever building land you think right and proper."

The father held his breath. What on earth could this mean? "And who is the girl, Granville?" he asked, with unconcealed interest.

"You won't care to hear," his son answered, carelessly.

Colonel Kelmscott looked across at him with a very

red face. "Not some girl who'll bring disgrace upon your mother, I hope?" he said, with a half-pang of remorse, remembering Lucy. "Not some young woman beneath your own station in life? For to that, you may be sure, I'll never consent under any circumstances."

Granville drew himself up proudly, with a haughty smile. He was a Kelmscott, too, as arrogant as the best of them.

"No, that's not the difficulty," he answered, looking rather *amused* than annoyed or frightened. "My tastes are *not* low. I hope I know better than to disgrace my family. The lady I want to marry, and for whose sake I wish you to make some arrangement beforehand, is— don't be surprised—well, Gwendoline Gildersleeve."

"Gwendoline Gildersleeve!" his father echoed, astonished, for there was a feud between the families. "That rascally, land-grabbing barrister's daughter! Why, how on earth do you come to know anything of her, Granville? Nobody in Surrey ever had the impertinence yet to ask me or mine to meet the Gildersleeves anywhere, since that disgraceful behavior of his about the boundary fences. And I didn't suppose you'd ever even seen her."

"Nobody in Surrey ever did ask me to meet her," Granville answered, somewhat curtly. "But you can't expect every one in London society to keep watch over the quarrels of every country parish in provincial England. It wouldn't be reasonable. I met Gwendoline, if you want to know, at the Bertrams', in Berkeley Square, and she and I got on so well together that we've—well, we've met from time to time in the park, since our return from town, and we think by this time we may consider ourselves informally engaged to one another."

Colonel Kelmscott gazed at his son in a perfect access of indignant amazement. Gilbert Gildersleeve's daughter! That rascally Q. C.'s! At any other moment such a proposal would have driven him forthwith into open hostilities. If Granville chose to marry a girl like that, why, Granville might have lived on what his father would allow him.

Just now, however, with this keen fit of remorse quite fresh upon his soul about poor Lucy's sons, Colonel Kelmscott was almost disposed to accept the opening thus laid before him by Granville's proposal.

So he temporized for a while, nursing his chin with his hand, and then, after much discussion, yielded at last a conditional consent—conditional upon their mutual agreement as to the terms on which the entail was to be finally broken.

" And what sort of arrangment do you propose I should make for your personal maintenance, and this Gildersleeve girl's household?" the Colonel asked at length, with a very red face, descending to details.

His son, without appearing to notice the implied slight to Gwendoline, named the terms that he thought would satisfy him.

" That's a very stiff sum," the master of Tilgate retorted; " but perhaps I could manage it; per—haps I could manage it. We must sell the Dowland farm at once, that's certain, and I must take the twelve thousand or so the land will fetch for my own use, absolutely and without restriction."

" To build the new wing with?" the son put in, with a gesture of assent.

" To build the new wing with? Why, certainly not," his father answered, angrily. "Am I to bargain with my son what use I'm to make of my own property? Mark my words, I won't submit to interference. To do precisely as I choose with, sir. To roll in, if I like! To fling into the sea, if the fancy takes me!"

Granville Kelmscott stared hard at him. Twelve thousand pounds! What on earth could his father mean by this whim? he wondered. "Twelve thousand pounds is a very big sum to fling away from the estate without a question asked," he retorted, growing hot. "It seems to me you too closely resemble our ancestors who came over from Holland. In matters of business, you know, the fault of the Dutch is giving too little and asking too much."

His father glared at him. That's the worst of this huckstering and higgling with your own flesh and blood. You have to put up with such intolerable insults. But he controlled himself, and continued. The longer he talked, however, the hotter and angrier he became by degrees. And what made him the hottest and angriest of all was the knowledge meanwhile that he was doing it every bit for Granville's own sake; nay, more, that consideration for Granville alone had brought him originally into this peck of trouble.

At last he could contain himself with indignation no longer. His temper broke down. He flared up and out with it. "Take care what you do!" he cried. "Take care what you say, Granville! I'm not going to be bearded with impunity in my den. If you press me too hard, remember, I'll ruin all. I can cut you off with a shilling, sir, if I choose—cut you off with a shilling! Yes; and do justice to others I've wronged for your sake! Don't provoke me too far, I say! If you do, you'll repent it!"

"Cut me off with a shilling, sir!" his son answered, angrily, rising, and staring hard at him. "Why, what do you mean by that? You know you can't do it. My interest in the estate's as good as your own. I'm the eldest son—"

He broke off suddenly; for at those fatal words Colonel Kelmscott's face, fiery red till then, grew instantly blanched and white with terror. "Oh, what have I done?" the unhappy man cried, seeing his son's eyes read some glimpse of the truth too clearly in his look. "Oh, what have I said? Forget it, Granny, forget it! I didn't mean to go so far as I did in my anger. I was a fool— a fool! I gave way too much. For heaven's sake, my boy, forget it, forget it!"

The young man looked across at him with a dazed and puzzled look, yet very full of meaning. "I shall never forget it," he said, slowly. "I shall learn what it means. I don't know how things stand; but I see you meant it. Do as you like about the entail. It's no business of mine. Take your pound of flesh, your twelve thousand down, and pay your hush-money! I don't know whom you bribe, and I have nothing to say to it. I never dragged the honor of the Kelmscotts in the dust. I won't drag it now. I wash my hands clean from it. I ask no questions. I demand no explanations. I only say this: Until I know what you mean—know whether I am lawful heir to Tilgate Park or not—I won't marry the girl I meant to marry. I have too much regard for her, and for the honor of our house, to take her on what may prove to be false expectations. Break the entail, I say! Raise your twelve thousand! Pay off your bloodhounds! But never expect me to touch a penny of your money, henceforth and forever, till I know whether it was yours and mine at all to deal with."

Colonel Kelmscott bent down his proud head meekly. "As you will, Granville," he answered, quite broken with remorse and silenced by shame. "My boy, my boy, I only wanted to save you!"

CHAPTER XII.

IN SILENCE AND TEARS.

WHEN he had time to think, Colonel Kelmscott determined in his own mind that he would still do his best to save Granville, whether Granville himself wished it or otherwise. So he proceeded to take all the necessary steps for breaking the entail, and raising the money he needed for Guy and Cyril.

In all this Granville neither acquiesced nor dissented. He signed mechanically whatever documents his father presented to him, and he stood by his bargain with a certain sullen, undeviating, hard-featured loyalty; but he never forgot those few angry words in which his father had half let out his long-guarded life secret.

Thinking the matter over continually with himself, however, he came in the end to the natural conclusion that one explanation alone would fit all the facts. He was not his father's eldest son at all. Colonel Kelmscott must have been married to someone else before his marriage with Lady Emily. That someone else's son was the real heir of Tilgate. And it was to him that his father, in his passionate penitence, proposed after many years to do one-sided justice. Now Granville Kelmscott, though a haughty and somewhat headstrong fellow, after the fashion of his race, was a young man of principle and of honor. The moment this hideous doubt occurred to his mind he couldn't rest in his bed till he had cleared it all up and settled it forever, one way or the other. If Tilgate wasn't his by law and right, he wanted none of it. If his father was trying to buy off the real heir to the estate with a pitiful pittance, in order to preserve the ill-gotten remainder for Lady Emily's son, why, Granville for his part would be no active party to such a miserable compromise. If some other man was the Colonel's law-

ful heir, let that other man take the property and enjoy
it; but he, Granville Kelmscott would go forth upon the
world, an honest adventurer, to seek his fortune with his
own right hand wherever he might find it.

Still, he could take no active step, on the other hand,
to hunt up the truth about the Colonel's real or supposed
first marriage, for here an awful dilemma blocked the
way before him. If the Colonel had married before, and
if by that former marriage he had a son or sons, how
could Granville be sure the supposed first wife was dead
before the second was married? And supposing, for a
moment, she was not dead—supposing his father had been
even more criminal and more unjust than he at first imagined—how could he take the initiative himself in showing that his own mother, Lady Emily Kelmscott, was no
wife at all in the sight of the law? that some other
woman was his father's lawful consort? The bare possibility of such an issue was too horrible for any son on
earth to face undismayed. So, tortured and distracted
by his divided duty, Granville Kelmscott shrank alike
from action or inaction.

In the midst of such doubts and difficulties, however,
one duty shone out clear as day before him. Till the
mystery was cleared up, till the problem was solved, he
must see no more of Gwendoline Gildersleeve. He had
engaged himself to her as the heir of Tilgate. She had
accepted him under that guise, and looked forward to an
early and happy marriage. Now all was changed. He
was, or might be, a beggar and an outcast. To be sure,
he knew Gwendoline loved him for himself; but how
could he marry her if he didn't even know he had anything of his own in the world to marry upon? The park
and fallow deer had been a part of himself; without them
he felt he was hardly even a Kelmscott. It was his plain
duty, now, for Gwendoline's sake, to release her from her
promise to a man who might perhaps be penniless, and
who couldn't even feel sure he was the lawful son of his
own father. And yet—for Lady Emily's sake—he mustn't
hint, even to Gwendoline, the real reason which moved
him to offer her this release. He must throw himself
upon her mercy, without cause assigned, and ask her
for the time being to have faith in him and to believe him,

So a day or two after the interview with his father in the library, the self-disinherited heir of Tilgate took the path through the glade that led into the dell beyond the boundary fence, that dell which once had been accounted a component part of Tilgate Park, but which Gilbert Gildersleeve, had proved, in his cold-blooded, documentary, legal way to belong in reality to the grounds of Woodlands. It was in the dell that Granville sometimes ran up against Gwendoline. He sat down on the broken ledge of ironstone that overhung the little brook. It was eleven o'clock gone. By eleven o'clock, three mornings in the week, chance—pure chance—the patron god of lovers, brought Gwendoline into the dell to meet him. Presently a light footfall rang soft upon the path, and next moment a tall and beautiful girl, with a wealth of auburn hair, and a bright color in her cheeks, tripped lightly down the slope, as if strolling through the wood in maiden meditation, fancy free, unexpecting any one.

"What, you here, Mr Kelmscott?" she exclaimed, as she saw him, her pink cheek deepening as she spoke to a still profounder crimson.

"Yes, I'm here, Gwendoline," Granville Kelmscott answered, with a smile of recognition at her maidenly pretence of an undesigned coincidence. "And I'm here, to say the truth, because I quite expected this morning to meet you."

He took her hand gravely. Gwendoline let her eyes fall modestly on the ground, as if some warmer greeting were more often bestowed between them. The young man blushed with a certain manly shame. "No, not to-day, dear," he said with an effort, as she held her cheek aside, half courting and half deprecating the expected kiss. "O Gwendoline, I don't know how to begin I don't know how to say it. But I've got very sad news for you—news that I can't bear to break—that I can't venture to explain—that I don't even properly understand myself. I must throw myself upon your faith. I must just ask you to trust me."

Gwendoline let him seat her, unresisting, upon the ledge by his side, and her cheek grew suddenly ashy pale as she answered with a gasp, forgetting the "Mr. Kelmscott" at this sudden leap into the stern realities of life,

" Why, Granville, what do you mean? You know I can
trust you. You know, whatever it may be, I believe you
implicitly."

The young man took her hand in his with a tender
pressure. It was a terrible message to have to deliver. He
bungled and blundered on, with many twists and turns,
through some inarticulate attempt at an indefinite explanation. It wasn't that he didn't love her—oh, devotedly, eternally! she must know that well; she never
could doubt it. It wasn't that any shadow had arisen
between him and her ; it wasn't anything he could speak
about, or anything she must say to any soul on earth
—oh, for his mother's sake, he hoped and trusted she
would religiously keep his secret inviolate! But something had happened to him within the last few days—
something unspeakable, indefinite, uncertain, vague, yet
very full of the most dreadful possibilities ; something that
might make him unable to support a wife ; something that
at least must delay or postpone for an unknown time the
long-hoped-for prospect of his claiming her and marrying
her. Some day, perhaps—he broke off suddenly, and
looked with a wistful look into her deep gray eyes. His
resolution failed him.   " One kiss," he said, " Gwendoline,"
His voice was choking. The beautiful girl, turning towards
him with a wild sob, fell, yielding herself on his breast,
and cried hot tears of joy at that evident sign that, in
spite of all he said, he still really loved her.

They sat there long, hand in hand, and eye on eye, talking
it all over, as lovers will, with infinite delays, yet getting
no nearer towards a solution either way.   Gwendoline,
for her part, didn't care, of course (what true woman
does ?), whether Granville was the heir of Tilgate or not;
she would marry him all the more, she said, if he were a
penniless nobody.   All she wanted was to love him and
be near him.   Let him marry her now, marry her to-
day, and then go where he would in the world to seek
his livelihood.   But Granville, poor fellow, alarmed at the
bare suggestion (for his mother's sake) that Tilgate might
really not be his, checked her at once in her outburst with
a grave, silent look ; he was still, he said calmly, the
inheritor of Tilgate.   It wasn't that.   At least, not as
she took it.   He didn't know precisely what it was him-

self. She must have faith in him and trust him. She must wait and see. In the end, he hoped, he would come back and marry her.

And Gwendoline made answer, with many tears, that she knew it was so, and that she loved him and trusted him. So after sitting there long, hand locked in hand, and heart intent on heart, the two young people rose at last to go, protesting and vowing their mutual love on either side, as happy and as miserable in their divided lives as any two young people in all England that moment. Over and over again they kissed and said good-bye; then they stood with one another's fingers clasped hard in their own, unwilling to part, and unable to loose them. After that they kissed again, and declared once more they were broken-hearted, and could never leave one another. But still, Granville added, half aside, he must make up his mind not to see Gwendoline again—honor demanded that sacrifice—till he could come at last a rich man to claim her. Meanwhile, she was free; and he—he was ever hers, devotedly, whole-souledly. But they were no longer engaged. He was hers in heart only. Let her try to forget him. He could never forget her.

And Gwendoline, sobbing and tearful, but believing him implicitly, retreated with slow steps, looking back at each turn of the zigzag path and sending the ghosts of dead kisses from her finger-tips to greet him.

Below in the dell Granville stood still and watched her depart in breathless silence. Then in an agony of despair he flung himself down on the ground and burst into tears and sobbed like a child over his broken day-dream.

Gwendoline, coming back to make sure, saw him lying and sobbing so; and woman-like, felt compelled to step down just one minute to comfort him. Granville in turn refused her proffered comfort—it was better so; he mustn't listen to her any more; he must steel himself to say no; he must remember it was dishonorable of him to drag a delicately nurtured girl into a penniless marriage. Then they kissed once more and made it all up again; and they sobbed and wept as before, and broke it off forever; and they said good-bye for the very last time; and they decided they must never meet till Gran-

ville came back; and they hoped they would sometimes
catch just a glimpse of one another in the outer world,
and whatever the other one said or did, they would each
in their hearts be always true to their first great love;
and they were more miserable still, and they were hap-
pier than they had ever been in their lives before; and
they parted at last, with a desperate effort, each perfectly
sure of the other's love, and each vowing in soul they
would never, never see one another again, but each, for
all that, perfectly certain that some day or other they
would be husband and wife, though Tilgate and the
wretched little fallow deer should sink, unwept, to the
bottom of the ocean.

CHAPTER XIII.

BUSINESS FIRST.

THE manager at Messrs, Drummond, Coutts, and Barclay's, Limited, received Colonel Kelmscott with distinguished consideration. A courteous, conciliatory sort of man, that manager, with his close-shaven face and his spotless shirt-front.

"Five minutes, my dear sir?" he exclaimed with warmth, motioning his visitor blandly into the leather-covered chair. "Half an hour if you wish it. We always have leisure to receive our clients. Any service we can render them, we're only too happy.'

"But this is a very peculiar bit of business," Colonel Kelmscott answered, humming and hawing with obvious hesitation. "It isn't quite in the regular way of banking, I believe. Perhaps, indeed, I ought rather to have put it into the hands of my solicitor. But even if you can't manage the thing yourself, you may be able to put me in the way of finding out how best I can get it managed elsewhere."

The manager bowed. His smile was a smile of genuine satisfaction. Colonel Kelmscott of Tilgate was in a most gracious humor. The manager, with deference, held himself wholly at his client's disposition.

So the Colonel proceeded to unfold his business. There were two young men, now knocking about town, of the names of Guy and Cyril Waring,—the one a journalist, the other a painter,—and they had rooms in Staple Inn, Holborn, which would doubtless form a sufficient clue by which to identify them. Colonel Kelmscott desired unobtrusively to know where these young men banked —if, indeed, they were in a position to keep an account; and when that was found out, he wished Messrs. Drum-

mond, Coutts, and Barclay, Limited, to place a sum of
money at their bankers to their credit, without mentioning the name of the person so placing it, as well as to
transmit to them a sealed envelope, containing instructions as to the use to be made of the money in question.

The manager nodded a cautious acquiescence. To
place the money to the credit of the two young men,
indeed, would be quite in their way; but to send the
sealed envelope, without being aware of its contents or
the nature of the business on which it was despatched,
would be much less regular. Perhaps the Colonel might
find some other means of managing without their aid
that portion of the business arrangement.

The Colonel, for his part, fell in readily enough with
this modest point of view. It amply sufficed for him if
the money were paid to the young men's credit, and a
receipt forwarded to him in due course, under cover of a
number, to the care of the bankers.

" Very well," the manager answered, rubbing his hands
contentedly. " Our confidential clerk will settle all that
for you. A most sagacious person, our confidential clerk.
No eyes, no ears, no tongue for anything but our clients'
interests."

The Colonel smiled, and sat a little longer, giving further details as to the precise amount he wished sent, and
the particular way he wished to send it,—the whole sum
to be, in fact, twelve thousand pounds, amount of the
purchase money of the Dowlands farms, whereof only six
thousand had as yet been paid down; and that six thousand he wished to place forthwith to the credit of Cyril
Waring, the painter. The remaining six thousand, to be
settled, as agreed, in five weeks' time, he would then
make over under the self-same conditions to the other
brother, Guy Waring, the journalist. It had gone a trifle
too cheap, that land at Dowlands, the Colonel opined;
but still, in days like these he was very glad, indeed, to
find a purchaser for the place at anything like its value.

" I think a Miss Ewes was the fortunate bidder, wasn't
she ? " the manager asked, just to make a certain decent
show of interest in his client's estate.

" Yes, Miss Elma Ewes of Kenilworth," the Colonel
answered, letting loose for a moment his tongue, that un-

ruly member. " She's the composer, you know,—writes songs and dances; remotely connected with Reginald Clifford, the man who was governor of some West Indian Dutch-oven—St. Kitts, I think, or Antigua. He lives down our way, and he's a neighbor of mine at Tilgate. Or, rather, she's connected with Mrs. Clifford, the governor's wife, who was one of the younger branch, a Miss Ewes of Worthing, daughter of the Ewes who was Dean of Dorchester. Elma's been a family name for years with all the lot of Eweses, good, bad, or indifferent. Came down to them, don't you know, from that Roumanian ancestress."

" Indeed," the manager answered, now beginning to be really interested; for the Cliffords were clients too, and it behoves a banker to know everything about everybody's business. " So Mrs. Clifford had an ancestress who was a Roumanian, had she? Well, I've noticed at times her complexion looked very southern and gypsy-like—distinctly un-English."

" Oh! they call it Roumanian," Colonel Kelmscott went on in a confidential tone, roping his white moustache and growing more and more conversational; " they call it Roumanian, because it sounds more respectable; but I believe, if you go right down to the very bottom of the thing, it was much more like some kind of Oriental gypsy. Sir Michael Ewes, the founder of the house, in George the Second's time, was ambassador for awhile at Constantinople. He began life, indeed, I believe, as a Turkey merchant. Well, at Pera one day, so the story goes,— you'll find it all in Horace Walpole's diary,—he picked up with this dark-skinned gypsy woman, who was a wonderful creature in her way, a sort of mesmeric sorceress, who belonged to some tribe of far-Eastern serpent-charmers. It seems that women of this particular tribe were regularly trained by the men to be capering priestesses —or fortune-tellers if you like—who performed some extraordinary sacred antics of a mystical kind, much after the fashion of the howling dervishes. However that may be, Sir Michael, at any rate, pacing the streets of Pera, saw the woman that she was passing fair, and fell in love with her outright at some dervish entertainment. But being a very well-behaved old man, combining a liking for Orientals with a British taste for the highest respectability, he had the girl baptized and made into a proper Christian first; and then he married her off-hand, and brought her home with him as my Lady Ewes to England. She was presented at Court to George the Second; and Lady Mary Wortley Montague stood her sponsor on the occasion.

"But how did it all turn out?" the manager asked, with an air of intelligent historical interest.

"Turn out? Well, it turned out in a thumping big family of thirteen children," the Colonel answered, "most of whom, happily for the father, died young. But the five who survived, and who married at last into very good connections, all had one peculiarity, which they transmitted to all their female descendants. Very odd these hereditary traits, to be sure. Very singular! Very singular!"

"Ah! to be sure," the manager answered, turning over a pile of letters. "And what was the hereditary trait handed down, as you say, in the family of the Roumanian lady?"

"Why, in the first place," the Colonel continued, leaning back in his chair and making himself perfectly comfortable, "all the girls of the Ewes connection, to the third and fourth generation, have olive-brown complexions, creamy and soft, but clear as crystal. Then again, they've all got most extraordinary intuition—a perfectly marvellous gift of reading faces. By George, sir," the Colonel exclaimed, growing hot and red at the memory of that afternoon on the Holkers' lawn, "I don't like to see those women's eyes fixed upon my cheek when there's anything going on I don't want them to know. A man's transparent like glass before them. They see into his very soul. They look right through him."

"If the lady who founded the family habits was a fortune-teller," the manager interposed, with a scientific air, "that's not so remarkable; for fortune-tellers must always be quickwitted people, keen to perceive the changes of countenance in the dupes who employ them, and prompt at humoring all the fads and fancies of their customers, mustn't they?"

"Quite so," the Colonel echoed. "You've hit it on

the nail. And this particular lady, — Esmeralda they called her, so that Elma, which is short for Esmeralda, understand, has come to be the regular Christian name among all her woman descendants,— this particular lady belonged to what you might call a caste or priestly family, as it were, of hereditary fortune-tellers, every one of whose ancestors had been specially selected for generations for the work, till a kind of transmissible mesmeric habit got developed among them. And they do say," the Colonel went on, lowering his voice a little more to a confidential whisper, " that all the girls descended from Madame Esmeralda—Lady Ewes of Charlwood, as she was in England — retain to this day another still odder and un-cannier mark of their peculiar origin ; but, of course, it's a story that would be hard to substantiate, though I've heard it discussed more than once among the friends of the family."

" Dear me ! What's *that ?* " the manager asked in a tone of marked curiosity.

" Why, they do say," the Colonel went on, now fairly launched upon a piece of after-dinner gossip, " that the Eastern snake-dance of Madame Esmeralda's people is hereditary even still among the women of the family, and that, sooner or later, it breaks out unexpectedly in every one of them. When the fit comes on, they shut them-selves up in their own rooms, I've been told, and twirl round and round for hours like dancing dervishes, with anything they can get in their hands to represent a serpent, till they fall exhausted with the hysterical effort. Even if a woman of Esmeralda's blood escapes it at all other times it's sure to break out when she first sees a real live snake, or falls in love for the first time. Then the dor-mant instincts of the race come over her with a rush, at the very dawn of womanhood, all quickened and aroused, as it were, in the general awakening."

‘ That's very curious," the manager said, leaning back in his chair in turn, and twirling his thumbs, " very curious indeed ; and yet, in its way, very probable, very probable. For habits like those must set themselves deep in the very core of the system, don't you think, Colonel? If this woman, now, was descended from a whole line of ancestresses who had all been trained for their work into a sort of ecstatic fervor, the ecstasy and all that went with it must have got so deeply ingrained—"

" I beg your pardon," the Colonel interrupted, consulting his watch and seizing his hat hastily, — for, as a Kelmscott he refused point-blank to be lectured, — " I've an appointment at my club at half-past three, and I must not wait any longer. Well, you'll get these young men's address for me, then, at the very earliest possible opportunity ? "

The manager pocketed the snub, and bowed his farewell. " Oh, certainly ! " he answered, trying to look as pleased and gracious as his features would permit. " Our confidential clerk will hunt them up immediately. We're delighted to be of use to you. Good morning, good morning."

And as soon as the Colonel's back was turned, the manager rang on his sharp little bell for the confidential clerk to receive his orders.

Mr. Montague Nevitt immediately presented himself in answer to the summons.

" Mr. Nevitt," the manager said, with a dry, small cough, " here's a bit of business of the most domestic kind—strict seal of secrecy ; not a word on any account. Colonel Kelmscott of Tilgate wants to know where two young men, named Guy and Cyril Waring, keep their banking account, if any ; and, as soon as he knows, he wishes to pay in a substantial sum, quite privately, to their credit."

Mr. Montague Nevitt bowed a bow of assent, without the faintest sign of passing recognition. " Guy and Cyril Waring," he repeated to himself, looking close at the scrap of paper his chief had handed him ; " Guy and Cyril Waring, Staple Inn, Holborn. I can find out to-day, sir, if you attach any special and pressing importance to promptitude in the matter."

CHAPTER XIV.

MUSIC HATH POWER.

FOR Mr. Montague Nevitt was a cautious, cool, and calculating person. He knew better than most of us that
knowledge is power. So when the manager mentioned
to him casually in the way of business the names of
Guy and Cyril Waring, Mr. Montague Nevitt didn't
respond at once : "Oh, dear, yes ; one of them's my most
intimate personal friend, and the other's his brother," as
a man of less discretion might have been tempted to do.
For, in the first place, by finding out, or seeming to find
out, the facts about the Warings that very afternoon, he
could increase his character with his employers for zeal
and ability. And, in the second place, if he had let out
too soon that he knew the Warings personally, he might
most likely on that very account have been no further
employed in carrying into execution this delicate little
piece of family business.

So Nevitt held his peace discreetly, like a wise man
that he was, and answered merely, in a most submissive
voice, "I'll do my best to ascertain where they bank at
once," as if he had never before in his life heard the
name of Waring.

For the self-same reason, Mr. Montague Nevitt didn't
hint that evening to Guy that he had become possessed
during the course of the day of a secret of the first
importance to Guy's fortune and future. Of course, a
man so astute as Montague Nevitt jumped at once at the
correct conclusion that Colonel Kelmscott must be the
two Warings' father. But he wasn't going to be fool
enough to chuck his chance away by sharing that information with any second person. A secret is far too
valuable a lever in life to be carelessly flung aside by a

man of ambition : and Montague Nevitt saw this secret
in particular was doubly valuable to him. He could use
it, wedgewise, with both the, Warings in all his future
dealings, by promising to reveal to one or other of them
a matter of importance and probable money-value, and
he could use it also as a perpetual threat to hold over
Colonel Kelmscott, if ever it should be needful to extort
blackmail from the possessor of Tilgate, or to thwart his
schemes by some active interference.

So when Nevitt strolled round about nine o'clock that
night to Saple Inn, violin case in hand and cigarette in
mouth, he gave not a sign of the curious information he
had that day acquired to the person most interested in
learning the truth as to the precise genealogy of the
Waring family.

There was no great underlying community of interests
between the clever young journalist and his banking
companion ; a common love for music was the main bond
of union between the two men. Yet Montague Nevitt
exercised over Guy a strange and fatal fascination which
Cyril always found positively unaccountable. And on
this particular evening, as Nevitt stood swaying himself
to and fro upon the hearth-rug before the empty grate,
with his eyes half closed, drawing low, weird music
with his enchanted bow from those submissive strings,
Guy leaned back on the sofa and listened, entranced,
with a hopeless feeling of utter inability ever to approach
the wizard-like and supreme execution of that masterly
hand and those superhuman fingers. How he twisted
and turned them as though his bones were india-rubber.
His palms were all joints and his eyes all ecstasy. He
seemed able to do what he liked with his violin. He
played on his instrument, indeed, as he played on Guy—
with the consummate art of a skilful executant.

"That's marvellous, Nevitt," Guy broke out at last.
"Never heard even Sarasate himself do anything quite
so wild and weird as that. What's the piece called? It
seems to have something almost impish or sprite-like in
its wailing music. It's Hungarian, of course, or Polish,
or Greek ; I detect at once the Oriental tinge in it."

"Wrong for once, my dear boy," Nevitt answered,
smiling. "It's English, pure English, and by a lady,

what's more—one of the Eweses of Kenilworth. She's
a distant relation of Cyril's Miss Clifford, I believe. An
Elma, too, name runs in the family. But she composes
wonderfully. Everything she writes is in that mystic
key. It sounds like a reminiscence of some dim and
lamp-lit Eastern temple. The sort of thing a nautch
girl might be supposed to compose to sing to the clash
and clang of cymbals, while she was performing the
snake-dance before some Juggernaut idol."

" Exactly," Guy answered, shutting his eyes dreamily;
"that's just the very picture it brings up before my
mind's eye—as you render it, Nevitt. I seem to see
vague visions of some vast and dimly lighted rockhewn
cavern, with long vistas of pillars cut from the solid stone,
while dark-limbed priestesses, clad in white muslin robes,
swing censers in the foreground to solemn music. Upon
my word, the power of sound is something simply wonderful. There's almost nothing, I believe, good music
wouldn't drive me to—or rather lead me to; for it sways
one and guides even more than it impels one.

" And yet," Nevitt mused in slow tones to himself, taking up his violin again, and drawing his bow over the
chords with half-closed eyes in a seemingly listless, aimless manner, "I don't believe music's your real first love,
Guy. You took it up only to be different from Cyril.
The artistic impulse in both of you is the same at bottom.
If you'd let it have its own way you'd have taken, not to
this I'm sure, but to painting. But Cyril painted, so, to
make yourself different, you went in for music. That's
you all over! You always have such a hankering after
being what you are not!"

" Well, hang it all, a man wants to have *some* individuality," Guy answered, apologetically. "He doesn't like
to be a mere copy or repetition of his brother."

Nevitt reflected quietly to himself that Cyril never
wanted to be different from Guy; his was by far the
stronger nature of the two; he was content to be himself,
without regard to his brother. But Nevitt didn't say so
indeed, why should he? He merely went on playing a
few disconnected bars of a very lively, hopeful, Utopian
sort of a tune—a tune all youth and health, and go and
gayety—as he interjected from time to time some brief

financial remarks on the numerous good strokes he'd
pulled off of late in his transactions in the city

" Can't do them in my own name, you know," he observed, lightly, at last laying down his bow, and replacing
the dainty white rose in his left top button-hole. " Not
official for a bank employee to operate on the Stock Exchange ; the chiefs object to it. so I do my little ventures
in Tom's name instead—my brother-in-law, Tom Whit-
leys. Those Cedulas went up another eighth yesterday
Well hit again ! I'm always lucky. And that was a good
thing I put you on last week, too, wasn't it ? Did you
sell out to-day ? They're up at ninety-six, and you bought
in at eighty."

" No, I didn't sell to-day," Guy answered with a yawn.
" I'm holding on still for a further rise. I thought I'd
sell out when they reached the even hundred."

" My dear fellow, you're wrong," Nevitt put in eagerly.
" You ought to have sold to-day. It's the top of the mar-
ket. They'll begin to decline soon, and when once they
begin they'll come down with a crash, as P. L.'s did on
Saturday. You take my advice, and sell out first thing
to-morrow morning. You'll clear sixteen pounds on each
of your shares ; that's enough for any man. You bought
ten shares, I think, didn't you ? Well, there you are, you
see—a hundred and sixty off-hand for you on your bargain."

Guy paused and reflected a doubtful moment. " Yes,
I'll sell out to-morrow, Nevitt," he said after a struggle,
" or what comes to the same thing, you can sell out for
me. But, do you know, my dear fellow, I sometimes
fancy I'm a fool for my pains, going in for all this silly
speculation. Better stick to my guinea a column in the
Morning Mail. The risks are so great, and the gains so
small. I don't believe outsiders ought to back their luck
at all like this on the Stock Exchange."

Montague Nevitt acquiesced with cheerful promptitude. " I agree with you down to the ground," he said,
lighting a cigarette, and puffing away at it vigorously.
" Outsiders ought not to back their luck on the Stock Exchange. That, I take it, is a self-evident proposition.
But the point is, here, that you're not an outsider ; and
you don't back your luck, which alters the case, you'll

admit, somewhat. You embark on speculations on my advice only, and I'm in a position to judge, as well as any other expert in the city of London, what things are genuine, and what things are not worth a wise man's attention."

He stretched himself on the sofa with a lazy, luxurious air, and continued to puff away in silence at his cigarette for another ten minutes. Then he drew unostentatiously from his pocket a folded sheet of foolscap paper, printed after the fashion of the common company prospectus. For a second or two he read it over to himself in silence, till Guy's curiosity was sufficiently roused by his mute proceeding.

" What have you got there?" the journalist asked at last, eying it inquiringly, as the fly eyes the cobweb.

" Oh, nothing," Nevitt answered, folding the paper up neatly, and returning it to his pocket. " You've sworn off now, so it does not concern you. Just the prospectus of a little fresh thing coming out next week,—a very exceptional chance,—but you don't want to go in for it. I mean to apply for three hundred shares myself, I'm so certain of its success ; and I had thought of advising you to take a hundred and fifty on your own account as well, with that hundred and fifty you cleared over the Cordova Cattle bonds. They're ten-pound shares, at a merely nominal price—ten bob on application and ten on allotment—so you could take a hundred and fifty as easy as look at it. No further calls will ever be made. It's really a most remarkable investment."

" Let me see the prospectus," Guy murmured, faltering, the fever of speculation once more getting the better of him.

Nevitt pretended to hang back like a man with fine scruples. "It's the Rio Negro Diamond and Sapphire Mine, Limited," he said, with a deprecatory air. " But you'd better not go in for it. I expect to make a pot out of the thing myself. It's a unique occasion. Still, no doubt you're right, and I don't like the responsibility of advising any other fellow. Though you can see for yourself what the promoters say. Very first-class names. And Klink thinks most highly of it."

He handed Guy a paper and took up his violin as if by pure accident, while Guy scanned it closely.

The journalist bent over the prospectus with eager eyes, and Nevitt poured forth strange music as he read, music like the murmur of the stream of Pactolus. It was an inspiring strain; the violin seemed to possess the true Midas touch; gold flowed like water in liquid. rills from its catgut. Guy finished, and rose, and dipped a pen in the ink-pot. "All right," he said low, half hesitating still. "I'll give you an order to sell out at once, and I'll fill up this application for three hundred shares—why not three hundred? I may as well go as many as you do. If it's really such a good thing as you say, why shouldn't I profit by it? Send this to Klink to-morrow early; strike while the iron's hot, and get the thing finished."

Nevitt looked at the paper with an attentive eye "How curious it is," he said, regarding the signature narrowly, " that you and Cyril, who are so much alike in everything else, should write so differently. I should have expected your hands to be almost identical."

" Oh, don't you know why that is?" Guy answered, with an innocent smile. "I do it on purpose. Cyril writes sloping forwards, the ordinary way, so I slope backward just to prevent confusion. And I form all my letters as unlike his as I can, though if I follow my own bent they turn out the same ; his way is more natural to me, in fact, than the way I write myself. But I must do something to keep our letters apart. That's why we always bank at a different banker's. If I like I could write exactly like Cyril. See, here's his own signature to his letter this morning, and here's my imitation of it, written off-hand, in my own natural manner. No forger on earth could ever need anything more absolutely identical."

Montague Nevitt took it up, and examined it with interest." " Well, this is wonderful," he said, comparing the two, stroke for stroke, with the practised eye of an expert. " The signatures are as if written by the self-same hand. Any cashier in England would accept your check at sight for Cyril's."

He didn't add aloud that such similarity was very convenient. But none the less, in his own mind he thought so.

CHAPER XV.

THE PATH OF DUTY.

Down at Tilgate, meanwhile, Elma Clifford had met more than once with Cyril Waring at friends' houses around ; for, ever since the accident, Society had made up its mind that Elma ought to marry her companion of the tunnel; and, when Society once makes up its mind on a question of this sort, why, it does its level best in the long run to insure the fulfilment of its own prediction.

Wherever Elma had met her painter, however, during those few short weeks, she had seen him only before the quizzing eyes of all the world ; and though she admitted to herself that she liked him very much, she was nevertheless so thoroughly frightened by her own performance after the Holkers' party, that she almost avoided him, in spite of officious friends—partly, it is true, from a pure feeling of maidenly shame, but partly, also, from a deeper-seated and profoundly moral belief that, with this fierce, mad taint upon her, as she naturally thought, it would be nothing short of wrong in her even to marry. She couldn't meet Cyril now without thinking at once of that irresistible impulse which had seized her by the throat, as it were, and bent her to its wild will in her own room after their interview at the Holkers' ; and the thought did far more than bring a deep blush into her rich brown cheek—it made her feel most acutely she must never dream of burdening him with that terrible uncertainty and all it might enclose in it of sinister import.

For Elma felt sure she was mad that night. And if so, oh, how could she poison Cyril Waring's life with so unspeakable an inheritance for himself and his children?

She didn't know, what any psychologist might at once have told her, that no one with the fatal taint of madness in her blood could ever even have thought of that righteous self-denial. Such scruples have no place in the selfish insane temperament; they belong only to the highest and purest types of moral nature.

One morning, however, a few weeks later, Elma had strolled off by herself into Chetwood forest, without any intention of going anywhere in particular, save for a solitary walk, when suddenly, a turn round the corner of a devious path brought her face to face, all at once, with a piece of white canvas, stretched opposite her on an easel; at the other side of which, to her profound dismay, an artist in a gray tweed suit was busily working.

The artist, as it happened, didn't see her at once, for the canvas stretched between them, shutting her out from his eyes, and Elma's light footstep on the mossy ground hadn't aroused his attention. So the girl's first impulse was to retrace her way unobtrusively without exchanging a word, and retire round the corner again before Cyril could recognize her. But somehow, when she came to try, she couldn't. Her feet refused point blank to obey her will. And this time, in her own heart, she knew very well why. For there in the background, coiled up against the dense wall of rock and fern, Sardanapalus lay knotted in sleepy folds, with his great ringed back shining blue in the sunlight that struggled in round patches through the shimmering foliage. More consciously now than even in the train, the beautiful, deadly creature seemed to fascinate Elma, and bind her to the spot. For a moment she hesitated, unable to resist the strange, inexplicable attraction that ran in her blood. That brief interval settled it. Even as she paused, Cyril glanced round at the snake to note the passing effect of a gleam of light that fell slantwise through the leaves to dapple his spotty back, and caught sight of Elma. The poor girl gave a start. It was too late now to retreat. She stood there rooted.

Cyril moved forward to meet her, with a frankly outstretched hand. "Good morning, Miss Clifford," he said, in his cheery, manly voice. "So you've dropped down by accident upon my lair here, have you? Well, I'm glad you've happened to pass by to-day; for this, do you know, is my very last morning. I'm putting the finishing touches upon my picture now, before I take it back to town. I go away to-morrow, perhaps to North Wales, perhaps to Scotland."

Elma trembled a little at those words, in spite of resolution; for though she could never, never, never marry him, it was nice, of course, to feel he was near at hand, and to have the chance of seeing him, and avoiding him as far as possible, on other people's lawns at garden parties. She trembled and turned pale. She could never *marry* him, to be sure; but then she could never marry any one else either; and, that being so, she liked to *see* him now and again, on neutral ground, as it were, and to know he was somewhere that she could meet him occasionally Wales and Scotland are so far distant from Surrey. Elma showed in her face at once that she thought them both unpleasantly remote from Craighton, Tilgate.

With timid and shrinking steps she came in front of the picture, and gazed at it in detail long and attentively. Never before did she know how fond she was of art.

"It's beautiful," she said after a pause; " I like it immensely. That moss is so soft, and the ferns are so delicate. And how lovely that patch of rich golden light is on Sardanapalus's shoulder."

The painter stepped back a pace or two and examined his own handicraft, with his head on one side, in a very critical attitude. "I don't know that I'm quite satisfied, after all, with the color-scheme," he said, glancing askance at Elma. "I fancy it's perhaps just a trifle too green. It looks all right, of course, out here in the open; but the question is, when it's hung in the Academy, surrounded by warm reds, and purples and blues, won't it look, by comparison, much too cabbagey and grassy?"

Elma drew a deep breath.

"Oh, Mr. Waring!" she cried in a deprecating tone, holding her breath for awe.

It pained her that anybody—even Cyril himself—should speak so lightly about so beautiful a picture.

"Then you like it?" Cyril asked, turning round to her full face and fronting her as she stood there, all beautiful blushes through her creamy white skin.

"Like it? I love it," Elma answered, enthusiastically. "Apart from its being yours, I think it simply beautiful."

"And you like *me*, too, then?" the painter asked, once more, making a sudden dash at the question that was nearest to both their hearts, after all, that moment. He was going away to-morrow, and this was a last opportunity. Who could tell how soon somebody might come up through the woods and interrupt their interview? He must make the best use of his time. He must make haste to ask her.

Elma let her eyes drop, and her heart beat hard. She laid her hand upon the easel to steady herself, as she answered slowly, "You know I like you, Mr. Waring; I like you very, very much indeed. You were so kind to me in the tunnel. And I felt your kindness. You could see that day I was — very, very grateful to you."

"When I asked you if you liked my picture, Elma," the young man said reproachfully, her other hand in his, and looking straight into her eyes, "you said, 'Like it? I love it.' But when I ask you if you like me,—ask you if you will take me,—you only say you're very, very grateful."

Elma let him take her hand, all trembling, in his. She let him call her by her name. She let him lean forward and gaze at her, lover-like. Her heart throbbed high. She couldn't refuse him. She knew she loved him. But to marry him—oh, no! That was quite another thing. There duty interposed. It would be cruel, unworthy, disgraceful, wicked.

She drew herself back a little with maidenly dignity, as she answered low, "Mr. Waring, we two saw into one another's hearts so deep in the tunnel that day we spent together, that it would be foolish for us now to make false barriers between us. I'll tell you the plain truth."

She trembled like an aspen-leaf. "I love you, I think; but I can never marry you."

She said it so simply, yet with such an earnestness of despair, that Cyril knew with a pang she really meant it.

"Why not?" he cried, eagerly, raising her hand to his lips, and kissing it with fervor. "If you tell me you love me, Elma, all the rest must come. Say that, and you say all. So long as I've gained your heart, I don't care for anything."

Elma drew her hand away with stately reserve. "I mean it, Mr. Waring," she said, slowly, sitting down on the bank and gasping a little for air, just as she had done in the tunnel. "I really mean it. I *liked* you in the train that day; I was *grateful* to you in the accident; I know I *loved* you the afternoon we met at the Holkers'."

There, I've told you that plainly—more plainly than I thought I ever could tell it to any man on earth—because we knew one another so well when we thought we were dying side by side, and because—because I can see you really love me. . . . Well, it can never be. I can never marry you."

She gazed at him wistfully. Cyril sat down by her side, and talked it all over with her from a hundred points of view. He pressed his suit hard, till Elma felt, if words could win, her painter would have won her. But she couldn't yield, she said; for *his* sake a thousand times more than for her own, she must never marry. As the man grew more earnest the girl in turn grew more frank and confiding. She could never marry *him*, to be sure, she said fervently, but then she could never, never, never marry any one else. If she married at all, she would marry Cyril. He took her hand again. Without one shadow of resistance she let him take it and hold it.

Yes, yes, he might love her, if he liked, no harm at all in that; and *she*, she would always, always love him.

All her life through, she cried, letting her passionate southern nature get the better of her at last, she would love him every hour of every day in the year, and love him only. But she could never marry him. Why, she must never say. It was no use his trying to read her secret. He must never find it out; never, never, never! But she, for her part, could never forget it.

So Cyril, eagerly pressing his suit with every art he knew, was forced in the end to content himself with that scanty measure. She would love him, she would write to him, even; but she would never marry him.

At last the time came when they must really part, or she would be late for lunch, and mamma would know all; mamma would read everything. He looked her wistfully in the face. Elma held out her lips, obedient to that

mute demand, with remorseful blush of maidenly shame
on her cheek. "Only once," she murmured. "Just to
seal our compact. For the first and last time. You go
away to-morrow."

"That was *before* you said you loved me," Cyril cried
with delight, emboldened by success. "Mayn't I stay on
now, just one little week longer?"

At the proposal Elma drew back her face in haste
before he had time to kiss it, and answered in a very
serious voice: —

"Oh, no, don't ask me. After this, I daren't stand
the strain of seeing you again—at least not just now—
not so very, very soon. Please, please don't ask me. Go
to-morrow, as you said. If you don't, I can't let you,"
she blushed, and held up her blushing face once more.

"Only if you promise me to go to-morrow, mind," she
said, with a half coquettish, half tearful smile at him.

Cyril hesitated for a second. He was inclined to tem-
porize. "Those are very hard terms," he said. Then
impulse proved too much for him. He bent forward and
pressed his lips just once on that olive-brown cheek.

"But I may come back again very soon," he murmured,
pushing home his advantage.

Elma seized his hand in hers, wrung it hard and tremu-
lously, and then turned and ran like a frightened fawn,
without pausing to look back, down the path homeward.
Yet she whispered one broken sentence through her
tears, for all that, before she went.

"I shall love you always, but spare me, spare me."

And Cyril was left behind by himself in the wood, completely mystified.

CHAPTER XVI.

STRUGGLE AND VICTORY.

ELMA hurried home full of intense misgivings. She dreaded having to meet her mother's eye. How on earth could she hide from that searching glance the whole truth as to what had happened in the wood that morning? When she reached home, however, she learned to her relief, from the maid who opened the door to her, that their neighbor, Mr. Gilbert Gildersleeve, the distinguished Q.C., had dropped in for lunch; and this chance diversion supplied Elma with a little fresh courage to face the inevitable. She went straight up to her own room the moment she entered the house, without seeing her mother, and there she waited, bathing her face copiously, till some minutes after the lunch bell had rung. For she felt sure she would blush crimson when she met her mother; but as she blushed habitually when strangers came in, the cause of it might thus, perhaps, she vainly flattered herself, escape even those lynx-like eyes of Mrs. Clifford's.

The great Q.C., a big, overbearing man, with a pair of huge, burly hands that somehow seemed to form his chief feature, was a little bit blustering in his talk, as usual; the more so because he had just learned incidentally that something had gone wrong between his daughter Gwendoline and Granville Kelmscott. For though that little episode of private wooing had run its course nominally without the knowledge or consent of either family, Mr. Gilbert Gildersleeve, at least, had none the less been aware for many weeks past of the frequent meetings between Gwendoline and Granville in the dell just beyond the disputed boundary line. And as Mr Gildersleeve disliked Colonel Kelmscott of Tilgate Park, for a pigheaded esquire, almost as cordially as Colonel Kelmscott disliked Mr. Gildersleeve in return, for a rascally lawyer, it had given the great Q.C., no little secret satisfaction in his own soul to learn that his daughter Gwendoline was likely to marry the Colonel's son and heir, directly against the wishes and consent of his father.

Only that very morning, however, poor Mrs. Gildersleeve, that tired, crushed wife, had imparted to her lord and master, in fear and trembling, the unpleasant intelligence that, so far as she could make out, there was something wrong between Granville and Gwendoline. And this something wrong, she ventured to suggest, was no mere lover's tiff of the ordinary kiss-and-make-it-up description, but a really serious difficulty in the way of their marriage. So Mr. Gildersleeve, thus suddenly deprived of his expected triumph, took it out another way by more than even his wonted boisterousness of manner in talking about the fortunes of the Kelmscott family.

"I fancy, myself, you know, Mrs. Clifford," he was saying, very loud, as Elma entered, "there's a screw loose just now in the Kelmscott affairs—something rotten somewhere in the state of Denmark. That young fellow, Granville, who's by no means such a bad lot as his father all round—too good for the family, in fact; too good for the family—Granville's been accustomed of late to come over into my grounds, beyond the boundary wall; and, being anxious above all things to cultivate friendly relations with all my neighbors in the county, I've allowed him to come—I've allowed him, and I may even say to a certain extent I've encouraged him. There, at times, he's met by accident my daughter Gwendoline. Oh, dear, no!" with uplifted hand and deprecating lips, "I assure you, nothing of *that* sort, my dear Mrs. Clifford. Gwendoline's far too young, and I couldn't dream of allowing her to marry into Colonel Kelmscott's family. But however, be that as it may, he's been in the habit of coming there, till very recently, when all of a sudden, only a week or ten days back, to my immense surprise he ceased at once, and ever since has dropped into the defensive, exactly as he used to do. And I interpret it to mean——"

Elma heard no more of that pompous speech. Her

knees shook under her. For she was aware only of Mrs. Clifford's eyes, fixed mildly and calmly upon her face, not in anger, as she feared, or reproach. but rather in infinite pity. For a second their glances met in mute intercourse of soul, then each dropped their eyelashes as suddenly as before. Through the rest of that lunch Elma sat as in a maze, hearing and seeing nothing. What she ate, or drank, or talked about, she knew not. Mr. Gildersleeve's pungent and embellished anecdotes of the Kelmscott family and their unneighborly pride went in at one ear and out at the other. All she was conscious of was her mother's sympathetic yet unerring eye; she felt sure that at one glance that wonderful thought-reader had divined everything, and seen through and through their interview that morning.

After lunch, the two men strolled upon the lawn to enjoy their cigars, and Elma and her mother were left alone in the drawing-room.

For some minutes neither could make up her mind to break the ice and speak. They sat shame-faced beside one another on the sofa, like a pair of shy and frightened maidens. At last Mrs. Clifford braced herself up to interrupt the awkward silence. "You've been in Chetwood forest, Elma," she murmured low, looking down and averting her eyes carefully from her trembling daughter.

"Yes, mother," Elma answered, all aglow with conscious blushes. "In Chetwood forest."

"And you met him, dear?" The mother spoke tenderly and sympathetically.

Elma's heart stood still. "Yes, mother, I met him."

"And he had the snake there?"

Elma started in surprise. Why dwell upon that seemingly unimportant detail? "Oh, yes," she answered, still redder and hotter than ever. "He had it there. He was painting it."

Mrs. Clifford paused a minute. Then she went on with pain. "And he asked you, Elma?"

Elma bowed her head. "Yes, he asked me—and I refused him," she answered, with a terrible wrench.

"Oh, darling, I know it!" Mrs. Clifford cried, seizing both cold hands in hers. "And I know why, too. But,

Elma, believe me, you needn't have done it. **My**
daughter, my daughter, you might just as well have taken
him!"

"No, never," Elma cried, rising from her seat and
moving towards the door in an agony of shame. "I
couldn't. I daren't. It would be wrong. It would be
cruel. But, mother, don't speak to me of it. Don't mention it again. Even before you, it makes me more
wretched and ashamed than I can say to allude to it."

She rushed from the room, with cheeks burning like
fire. Come what might, she never could talk to any
living soul again about that awful episode.

But Mrs. Clifford sat on, on the sofa where Elma left
her, and cried to herself silently, silently, silently.
What a mother should do in these hateful circumstances
she could hardly even guess. She only knew she could
never speak it out, and even if she did, Elma would never
have the courage or the heart to listen to her.

That same evening, when Elma went up to bed, a
strange longing came across her to sit up late, and think
over to herself again all the painful details of the morning's
interview. She seated herself by her bedside in her
evening dress, and began to think it all out again, exactly
as it happened. As she did so, the picture of Sardanapalus, on his bed of fern, came up clear in her mind.
just as he lay coiled round in Cyril Waring's landscape.
Beautiful Sardanapalus, so sleek and smooth and glossy,
if only she had him here now—she paused and hesitated.
In a moment the wild impulse rushed upon her once
more. It clutched her by the throat; it held her fast as
in a vice. She must get up and dance, she must obey
the mandate: she must whirl till she fell in that mystical ecstasy.

She rose, and seemed for a moment as though she
must yield to the temptation. The boa—the boa was in
the lower drawer. Reluctantly, remorsefully, she opened
the drawer and took it out in her hands Fluff and
feathers, fluff and feathers—nothing more than that!
But oh, how soft, how smooth, how yielding, how serpentine! With a violent effort she steadied herself, and
looked round for her scissors. They lay on the dress-
ing-table. She took them up with a fixed and determined

air. " If thy right hand offend thee, cut it off," she thought to herself. Then she began ruthlessly hacking the boa into short little lengths of a few inches each, which she gathered up in her hands as soon as she had finished, and replaced with care in the drawer where she had originally found them. After that her mind felt somewhat more at ease and a trifle less turbulent. She loved Cyril Waring—oh, yes, she loved him with all her heart; it was hard to give him up; hard not to yield to that pressing impulse in such a moment of doubt and despondency. The boa had said to her as it were, "Come, dance, go mad, and forget your trouble!" But she had resisted the temptation. And now —

Why, now, she would undress, and creep into bed, like any other good English girl under similar circumstances, and cry herself asleep with thoughts of Cyril.

And so she did in truth. She let her emotion take its natural outlet. She lay awake for an hour or two, till her eyes were red and sore and swollen. Then at last she dropped off, for very weariness, and slept soundly an unbroken sleep till morning.

At eight o'clock Mrs. Clifford knocked her tentative little knock at the door. " Come in, mother," Elma cried, starting up in her surprise; and her mother, much wondering, turned the handle and entered.

When she reached the bed, she gave a little cry of amazement. " Why, Elma, she exclaimed, staring her hard and long in the face; "my darling, what's this? Your eyes are red! How strange! You've been crying!"

" Yes, mother," Elma answered, turning her face to the wall, but a thousand times less ashamed than she had been the day before, when her mother spoke to her. " I couldn't help it, dearest " She took that soft, white hand in hers and pressed it hard in silence. " It's no wonder, you know," she said at last, after a long, deep pause. " He's going away from Chetwood to-day—and it was so very, very hard to say good bye to him forever "

" Oh, yes, I know, darling," Mrs. Clifford answered, eying her harder than ever now, with a half incredulous look. " I know all that. But—you've had a good night in spite of everything, Elma."

Elma guessed what she meant. They two could converse together quite plainly without words. "Well, yes, a better night," she answered, hesitating, and shutting her eyes under the bedclothes for very shame. "A little disturbed—don't you know—just at first; but I had a good cry very soon and then that mended every thing."

Her mother still looked at her, half doubting and half delighted. "A good cry's the right thing," she said, slowly, in a very low voice. "The exact right thing. perfectly proper and normal. A good cry never did any girl on this earth one atom of harm. It's the best safety-valve. You're lucky, Elma, my child, in being able to get one."

"Yes, dear," Elma answered, with her head still buried. "Very lucky indeed. So I think, too, mother."

Mrs. Clifford's eye fell aimlessly upon certain tiny bits of feathery fluff that flecked the floor here and there like floating fragments of thistle-down. In a second, her keen instinct divined what they meant. Without one word she rose silently and noiselessly, and opened the lower drawer, where the boa usually reposed among the furs and feathers. One glimpse of those mangled morsels showed her the truth at a glance. She shut the drawer again noiselessly and silently as she had opened it. But Elma, lying still with her eyes closed tight, yet knew perfectly well how her mother had been occupied.

Mrs. Clifford came back, and stooping over her daughter's bed, kissed her forehead tenderly. "Elma, darling," she said, while a hot tear or two fell silently upon the girl's burning cheek, "you're very, very brave. I'm so pleased with you, so proud of you! I couldn't have done it myself. You're stronger-minded than I am. My child, he kissed you for good-bye, yesterday. You needn't say yes, you needn't say no. I read it in your face. No need for you to tell me of it. Well, darling, it wasn't good-bye after all, I'm certain of that. Believe me, my child, he'll come back some day, and you'll know you can marry him."

"Never!" Elma cried, hiding her face still more passionately and wildly than before beneath great folds of the bed-clothes. "Don't speak to me of him any more, mother! Never! Never! Never!"

CHAPTER XVII.

VISIONS OF WEALTH.

CYRIL WARING, thus dismissed, and as in honor bound, hurried up to London, with a mind preoccupied by many pressing doubts and misgivings. He thought much of Elma, but he thought much, too, of sundry strange events that had happened of late to his own private fortues. For one thing, he had sold, and sold mysteriously, at a very good price, the picture of Sardanapalus in the glade at Chetwood. A well-know London dealer had witten down to him at Tilgate, making an excellent offer for the unfinished work, as soon as it should be ready, on behalf ot a customer whose name he didn't happen to mention. And who could that customer be, Cyril thought to himself, but Colonel Kelmscott? But that wasn't all. The dealer, who had offered him a round sum down for " The Rajah's Rest," had also at the same time commissioned him to go over to the Belgian Ardennes to paint a picture or two, at a specified price, of certain selected scenes upon the Meuse and its tributaries. The price offered for the work was a very respectable one, and yet—he had some internal misgivings, somehow, about this mysterious commission. Could it be to get rid of him? He had an uncomfortable suspicion in the back chambers of his mind, that whoever had commissioned the pictures might be more anxious to send him well away from Tilgate than to possess a series of picturesque sketches on the Meuse and its tributaries.

And who could have an interest in keeping him far from Tilgate? That was the question. Was there anybody whom his presence there could in any way incommode? Could it be Elma's father who wanted to send him so quickly away from England?

And what was the meaning of Elma's profound resolution, so strangely and strongly expressed, never, never to marry him?

A painful idea flitted across the young man's puzzled brain. Had the Cliffords alone discovered the secret of his birth, and was that secret of such a disgraceful sort that Elma's father shrank from owning him as a prospective son-in-law, while even Elma herself could not bring herself to accept him as her future husband? If so, what could that ghastly secret be? Were he and Guy the inheritors of some deadly crime? Had their origin been concealed from them, more in mercy than in cruelty, only lest some hideous taint of murder or of madness might mar their future, and make their whole lives miserable?

When he reached Staple Inn, he found Guy and Montague Nevitt already in their joint rooms, and arrears of three days' correspondence awaiting him.

A close observer, like Elma Clifford, might perhaps have noted in Montague Nevitt's eye certain well-restrained symptoms of suppressed curiosity. But Cyril Waring, in his straightforward, simple English manliness, was not sharp enough to perceive that Nevitt watched him close while he broke the envelopes and glanced over his letters; or that Nevitt's keen anxiety grew at once far deeper and more carefully concealed as Cyril turned to one big missive with an official-looking seal and a distinctly important legal aspect. On the contrary, to the outer eye or ear all that could be observed in Montague Nevitt's manner was the nervous way he went on tightening his violin strings with a tremulous hand and whistling low to himself a few soft and tender bars of some melancholy scrap from Miss Ewes's repertory.

As Cyril read through that letter, however, his breath came and went in short little gasps, and his cheek flushed hotly with a sudden and overpowering flood of emotion.

"What's the matter?" Guy asked, looking over his shoulder curiously. And Cyril, almost faint with the innumerable ideas and suspicions that the tidings conjured up in his brain at once, said with an evident effort. "Read it, Guy; read it."

Guy took the letter and read, Montague Nevitt gazing at it by his side meanwhile, with profound interest.

As soon as they had glanced through its carefully worded sentences, each drew a long breath and stared hard at the other. Then Cyril added, in a whirl. "And here's a letter from my own bankers, saying they've duly received the six thousand pounds and put it to my credit."

Guy's face was pale, but he faltered out, none the less, with ashy lips, staring hard at the words all the time, "It isn't only the money, of course, one thinks about. Cyril; but the clue it seems to promise us to our father and mother."

"Exactly," Cyril answered, with a responsive nod. "The money I won't take. I don't know what it means. But the clue I'll follow up till I've run to earth the whole truth about who we are and where we come from."

Montague Nevitt glanced quickly from one to the other with an incredulous air. "Not take the money!" he exclaimed, in cynical surprise. "Why, of course you'll take it! Twelve thousand pounds isn't to be sneezed at in these days, I can tell you. And as for the clue,—why, there isn't any clue. Not a jot or a tittle, a ghost or a shadow of it. The unnatural parent, whoever he may be—for I take it for granted the unnatural parent's the person at the bottom of the offer—takes jolly good care not to let you know who on earth he is. He wraps himself up in a double cloak of mystery. Drummonds' pay in the money to your account at your own bank, you see, and while they're authorized to receive your acknowledgment of the sum remitted, they are clearly *not* authorized to receive to the sender's credit any return check for the amount, or cash in repayment. The unnatural parent evidently intends to remain, for the present at least, strictly anonymous."

"Couldn't you find out for us at Drummond, Coutts, and Barclay's who the sender is?" Guy asked, with some hesitation, still turning over in his hand the mysterious letter.

Nevitt shook his head with prompt decision. "No; certainly not," he answered, assuming an air of the severest probity. "It would be absolutely impossible. The secrets of a bank are secrets of honor. We are the depositories of tales that might ruin thousands, and we never say a word about one of them to anybody."

As for Cyril, he felt himself almost too astonished for words. It was long before he could even discuss the matter quietly. The whole episode seemed so strange, so mysterious, so uncanny. And no wonder he hesitated; for the unknown writer of the letter with the legal seal had proposed a most curious and unsatisfactory arrangement. Six thousand pounds down on the nail to Cyril, six thousand more in a few weeks to Guy. But not for nothing. As in all law business, " valuable consideration" loomed large in the background. They were both to repair, on a given day, at a given hour, to a given office, in a given street, where they were to sign without inquiry, and even without perusal, whatever documents might then and there be presented to them. This course, the writer pointed out, with perspicuous plainness, was all in the end to their own greater advantage. For unless they signed, they would get nothing more, and it would be useless for them to attempt the unravelling of the mystery. But if they consented to sign, then, the writer declared, the annonymous benefactor, at whose instigation he wrote, would leave them by his will a further substantial sum, not one penny of which would ever otherwise come to them.

And Montague Nevitt, as a man of business, looking the facts in the face, without sentiment or nonsense, advised them to sign, and make the best of a good bargain.

For Montague Nevitt saw at once in his own mind that this course would prove the most useful in the end for his own interests, both as regards the Warings and Colonel Kelmscott.

The two persons most concerned, however, viewed the matter in a very different light. To them this letter, with its obscure half-hints, opened up a chance of solving at last the mystery of their position, which had so long oppressed them. They might now perhaps find out who they really were, if only they could follow up this pregnant clue; and the clue itself suggested so many things.

" Whatever else it shows," Guy said, emphatically, " it

shows we must be the lawful sons of some person of property, or else why should he want us to sign away our rights like this, all blindfold? And whatever the rights themselves may be, they must be very considerable, or else why should he bribe us so heavily to sign ourselves out of them? Depend upon it, Nevitt, it's an entailed estate, and the man who dictated that letter is in possession of the property which ought to belong to Cyril and me. For my part, I'm opposed to all bargaining in the dark. I'll sign nothing, and I'll give away nothing, without knowing what it is. And that's what I advise Cyril to write back and tell him."

Cyril, however, was revolving in his own mind meanwhile a still more painful question. Could it be any blood relationship between himself and Elma, unknown to him but just made known to her, that gave rise to her firm and obviously recent determination never to marry him? And a week or two since, he was sure, Elma knew of no cause or just impediment why they should not be joined together in holy matrimony. Could she have learned it meanwhile, before she met him in the wood, and could the fact of her so learning it have thus pricked the slumbering conscience of their unknown kinsman or their supposed supplanter?

They sat there long and late, discussing the question from all possible standpoints—save the one thus silently started in his own mind by Cyril. But in the end, Cyril's resolution remained unshaken. He would leave the six thousand pounds in the bank, untouched; but he would write back at once to the unknown sender, declining plainly, once for all, to have anything to do with it or with the proposed transactions. If anything was his by right, he would take it as of right, but he would be no party to such hole-and-corner renunciations of unknown contingencies as the writer suggested. If the writer was willing to state at once all the facts of the case, in clear and succinct language, and to come to terms thus openly with himself and his brother, why then, Cyril averred, he was ready to promise they would deal with his claims in a spirit of the utmost generosity and consideration. But if this was an attempt to do them out of their rights by a fraudulent bribe, he, for one, would have nothing to say to it. He would therefore hold the six thousand pounds paid in to his account entirely at his anonymous correspondent's disposition.

"And as there isn't any use in my wasting the summer, Guy," he said, in conclusion, "I won't let this red herring, trailed across my path, prevent me from going over at once, as I originally intended, to Dinant and Spa, and fulfilling the commission for those pictures of Dale and Norton's. You and Nevitt can see meanwhile what it's possible for us to do in the matter of hunting up this family mystery. Yon can telegraph, if you want me, and I'll come back at once. But more than ever now I feel the need of redeeming the time and working as hard as I can go at my profession."

"Well, yes," Guy answered, as if both their thoughts ran naturally in the self-same channel, "I agree with you there. She's been accustomed to luxury. No man has a right to marry any girl if he can't provide for her in the comfort and style she's always been used to. And from that point of view, when one looks it in the face, Cyril, six thousand pounds would come in handy."

CHAPTER XVIII.

GENTLE WOOER.

Mr. Montague Nevitt rubbed his hands with delight in the sacred privacy of his own aparment. Mr. Nevitt, indeed, had laid his plans deep. He had everybody's secrets all round in his hands, and he meant to make everybody pay dear in the end for his information.

Mr. Nevitt was free. His holidays were on at Drummond, Coutts, and Barclay's, Limited. He loved the sea, the sun, and the summer. He was off that day on a projected series of short country runs, in which it was his intention strictly to combine business and pleasure. Dartmoor, for example, as everybody knows, is a most delightful and bracing tourist district; but what more amusing to a man of taste than to go a round of the moor with its heather-clad tors, and at the same time hunt up the parish registers of the neighborhood for the purpose of discovering, if possible, the supposed marriage record of Colonel Kelmscott of Tilgate with the Warings' mother? For that there *was* a marriage Montague Nevitt felt certain in his own wise mind; and, having early arrived at that correct conclusion, why, he had quietly offered forthwith, in the Plymouth papers, a considerable reward to parish clerks and others who would supply him with any information as to the births, marriages, or deaths of any person or persons of the name of Waring for some eighteen months or so before or after the reputed date when Guy and Cyril began their earthly pilgrimage.

For deaths, Nevitt said to himself, with a sinister smile, were every bit as important to him as births or marriages. He knew the date of Colonel Kelmscott's wedding with Lady Emily Croke, and if at that date wife number one was not yet dead, when the Colonel took to himself wife number two, who now did the honors of Tilgate Park for him, why, there you had as clear and convincing a case of bigamy as any man could wish to find out against another, and to utilize some day for his own good purposes.

As he thought these thoughts, Montague Nevitt gave the last delicate twirl, and final touch of art, to the wire-like ends of his waxed mustache, in front of his mirror, and after surveying the result in the glass with considerable satisfaction, proceeded to set out, on very good terms with himself, for his summer holiday.

Devonshire, however, wasn't his first destination. Montague Nevitt, besides being a man of business and a man of taste, was also in due season a man of feeling. A heart beat beneath that white rosebud in his left top button-hole. All his thoughts were not thoughts of greed and of gain. He was bound to Tilgate to-day, and to see a lady.

It isn't so easy in England to see a lady alone. But fortune favors the brave. Luck always attended Mr. Montague Nevitt's most unimportant schemes. Hardly had he got into the field path across the meadows between Tilgate station and the grounds of Woodland, than, at the seat by the bend, what should he see but a lady sitting down, in an airy, white summer dress, her head leaning on her hand, most pensive and melancholy. Montague Nevitt's heart gave a sudden bound. In luck once more! It was Gwendoline Gildersleeve.

"Good-morning!" he said, briskly, coming up before Gwendoline had time to perceive him—and fly. "This is really most fortunate. I've run down from town to-day on purpose to see you, but hardly hoped I should have the good fortune to get a *tête-à-tête* with you—at least so easily. I'm glad I'm in time. Now, don't look so cross. You must at any rate admit, you know, my persistence is flattering."

"I don't feel flattered by it, Mr. Nevitt," Gwendoline answered, coldly, holding out her gloved hands to him with marked disinclination. "I thought last time I had said good-by to you for good and forever."

Nevitt took her hand, and held it in his own a trifle

longer than was strictly necessary. "Now don't talk like that, Gwendoline," he said, coaxingly. "Don't crush me quite flat. Remember at least that you *once* were kind to me. It isn't my fault, surely, if *I* still recollect it."

Gwendoline withdrew her hand from his with yet more evident coolness. "Circumstances alter cases," she said, severely. "That was before I really knew you."

"That was before you knew Granville Kelmscott, you mean," Nevitt responded, with an unpleasantly knowing air. "Oh, yes; you needn't wince. I've heard all about that. It's my business to hear and find out everything. But circumstances alter cases, as you justly say, Gwendoline. And I've discovered some circumstances about Granville Kelmscott that may alter the case as regards your opinion of that rich young man, whose estate weighed down a poor fellow like me in what you're graciously pleased to call your affections."

Gwendoline rose, and looked down at the man contemptuously. "Mr. Nevitt," she said in a chilling voice, "you've no right to call me Gwendoline any longer now. You've no right to speak to me of Mr. Granville Kelmscott. I refused your advances, not for any one else's sake, or any one else's estate, but simply and solely because I came to know you better than I knew you at first; and the more I knew of you the less I liked you. I am *not* engaged to Mr. Granville Kelmscott. I don't mean to see him again. I don't mean to marry him."

Nevitt took his cue at once, like a clever hand that he was, and followed it up remorselessly. "Well I'm glad to hear that anyhow," he answered, assuming a careless air of unconcern, "for your sake as well as for his, Miss Gildersleeve; for Granville Kelmscott, as I happen to know in the course of business, is a ruined man—a ruined man this moment. He isn't, and never was, the heir of Tilgate. And I'm sure it was very honorable of him, the minute he found he was a penniless beggar, to release you from such an unequal engagement."

He had played his card well. He had delivered his shot neatly. Gwendoline, though anxious to withdraw from his hateful presence, couldn't help but stay and learn

more about this terrible hint of his. A light broke in
upon her even as the fellow spoke. Was it this, then, that
had made Granville talk so strangely to her that morning
by the dell in the Woodlands? Was it this which, as
he told her, rendered their marriage impossible? Why,
if *that* were all—Gwendoline drew a deep breath, and
clasped her hands together in a sudden access of mingled
hope and despair. "Oh, what do you mean, Mr. Nevitt?"
she cried, eagerly. "What can Granville have done?
Don't keep me in suspense. Do tell me what you mean
by it."

Montague Nevitt, still seated, looked up at her with a
smile of quiet satisfaction. He played with her for a
moment, as a cat plays with a mouse. She was such a
beautiful creature, so tall and fair and graceful, and she
was so awfully afraid, and he was so awfully fond of her,
that he loved to torture her thus, and hold her dangling in
his power. "No, Gwendoline," he said, slowly, drawing his
words out by driblets, so as to prolong her suspense; "I
oughtn't to have mentioned it at all. It's a professional
secret. I retract what I said. Forget that I said it. Excuse me on the ground of my natural reluctance to see a
woman I still love so deeply and so purely—whatever she
may happen to think of *me*—throw herself away on a
man without a name or a penny. However, as Kelmscott
seems to have done the honorable thing of his own accord, and given you up the minute he knew he couldn't
keep you in the way you've been accustomed to—why,
there's no need, of course, of any warning from me. I'll
say no more on the subject."

His studied air of mystery piqued and drew on his
victim. Gwendoline knew in her own heart she ought to
go at once; her own dignity demanded it, and she should
consult her dignity. But still, she couldn't help longing
to know what Nevitt's half-hints and innuendoes might
mean. After all, she was a woman! "Oh, do tell me,"
she cried, clasping her hands in suspense once more;
"what have you heard about Mr. Kelmscott? I'm not engaged to him; I don't want to know for that, but——"

She broke down, blushing crimson, and Montague
Nevitt, gazing fixedly at her delicate, peach-like cheek,

remarked to himself how extremely well that blush became her.

"No; but remember," he said, in a very grave voice, in
his favorite impersonation of the man of honor, "whatever I tell you—if I give way at all, and tell you anything—you must hear in confidence, and must repeat to
nobody. If you do repeat it, you'll get me into very serious trouble. And not only so, but, as nobody knows it
except myself, you'll as good as proclaim to all the world
that you heard it from *me.* If I tell you what I know,
will you promise me this—not to breath a syllable of
what I say to anybody?"

Gwendoline, glancing down, and thoroughly ashamed
of herself, yet answered, in a very low and trembling
voice, "I'll promise, Mr. Nevitt."

"Then, the facts are these," the man of feeling went on,
with an undercurrent of malicious triumph in his musical
voice: "Kelmscott is *not* his father's eldest son. He's
not, and never was, the heir of Tilgate. More than that,
nobody knows these facts but myself. And I know the
true heirs, and I can prove their title. Well, now, Miss
Gildersleeve—if it's to be Miss Gildersleeve still—this
is the circumstance that alters the case as regards Granville Kelmscott. I have it in my hands to ruin Kelmscott.
And what I've taken the trouble to come down and say
to you to-day is simply this—for your own advantage,
beware, at least, how you throw yourself away upon a
penniless man, with neither name nor fortune! When
you've quite got over that dream, you'll be glad to return to the man you threw overboard for the rich squire's
son. No circumstances have ever altered him. He loved
you from the first, and he will always love you."

Gwendoline looked him back in the face again, as pale
as death. "Mr. Nevitt," she said, scornfully, unmoved
by his tale, "I do not love, and I never will love you.
You have no right to say such things to me as these. I'm
glad you've told me; for I know now what Mr. Kelmscott
meant. And if he were as poor as a church mouse, I'd
marry him to-morrow. I said just now I didn't mean to
marry him. I retract that word. Circumstances alter
cases, and what you've just told me alters this one. I

withdraw what I said. I'll marry Granville Kelmscott
to-morrow if he asks me."

She looked down at him so proudly, so defiantly, so
haughtily, that Montague Nevitt, sitting there, with his
cynical smile on his thin, red lips, flinched and wavered
before her. He saw in a moment the game was up. He
had played the wrong card; he had mistaken his woman,
and tried false tactics. It was too late now to retreat.
An empty revenge was all that remained to him. "Very
well," he said, sullenly, looking her back in the face, with
a nasty scowl—for, indeed, he loved that girl, and was
loath to lose her—"remember your promise, and say nothing to anybody. You'll find it best so, for your own
reputation in the end. But mark my words; be sure I
won't spare Granville Kelmscott now. I'll play my own
game. I'll ruin him ruthlessly. He's in my power, I
tell you, and I'll crush him under my heel. Well, that's
settled at last. I'm off to Devonshire to-morrow on the
hunt of the records—to the skirts of Dartmoor—to a place
in the wilds by the name of Mambury."

He raised his hat, and, curling his lip maliciously,
walked away without even so much as shaking hands
with her. He knew it was all up. That game was lost.
And, being a man of feeling, he regretted it bitterly.

Gwendoline, for her part, hurried home, all aglow with
remorse and excitement. When she reached the house
she went straight up in haste to her own bedroom. In
spite of her promise, all woman that she was, she couldn't
resist sitting down at once and inditing a hurried note to
Granville Kelmscott.

"Dearest Granville," it said, in a very shaky hand, not
unblurred by tears, "I know all now, and I wonder you
thought it could ever matter. I know you're not the
eldest son, and that somebody else is the heir of Tilgate.
And I care for all that a great deal less than nothing. I
love you ten thousand times too dearly to mind one pin
whether you're rich or poor. And, rich or poor, whenever you like I'll marry you.

"Yours ever devotedly and unalterably,

"GWENDOLINE."

She sealed it up in haste, and ran out with it, all tremors, to the post by herself. Her hands were hot. She was in a high fever. But Mr. Montague Nevitt, that man of feeling, thus balked of his game, walked off his disappointment as well as he could by a long, smart tramp across the springy downs, lunching at a wayside inn on bread and cheese and beer, and descending as the evening shades drew in on the Guilford station. Thence he ran up to town by the first fast train, and sauntered sulkily across Waterloo Bridge to his rooms on the Embankment. As he went a poster caught his eye on the bridge. It riveted his attention by one fatal phrase. *"Financial News.* Collapse of the Rio Negro Diamond and Sapphire Mines!"

He stared at the placard with a dim sense of disaster. What on earth could this mean? It fairly took his breath away. The mines were the best things out this season. He held three hundred shares on his own account. If this rumor were true, he had let himself in for a loss of a clear three thousand!

But, being a person of restricted sympathies, he didn't reflect till several minutes had passed that he must at the same time have let Guy Waring in for three thousand also.

CHAPTER XIX.

SELF OR BEARER.

AT Charing Cross station Montague Nevitt bought a
Financial News, and proceeded forthwith to his own
rooms to read of the sudden collapse of his pet speculation. It was only too true. The Rio Negro Diamond
and Sapphire Mines had gone entirely in one of the peri-
odical South American crashes, which involved them in
the liabilities of several other companies. A call would
be made at once to the full extent of the nominal capital.

And he would have to find three thousand pounds
down to meet the demand on his credit immediately.

Nevitt hadn't three thousand pounds in the world to
pay. The little he possessed beyond his salary was locked
up, here and there, in speculative undertakings, where he
couldn't touch it except at long notice. It was a crushing blow. He had need of steadying. Some men would
have flown, in such a plight, to brandy. Montague
Nevitt flew, instead, to the consolations of music.

For some minutes, indeed, he paced his room up and
down in solemn silence. Then his eye fell by accident
on the violin case in the corner. Ah, that would do!

That beloved violin would inspire him with ideas; was
it suicide or fraud, or some honest way out; be it this
plan or that, the violin would help him. Screwing up
the strings for a minute with those deft, long, double-
jointed fingers of his, he took the bow in his right hand,
and, still pacing the room with great strides, like a wild
beast in its cage, began to discourse low, passionate music
to himself from one of those serpentine pieces of Miss
Ewes of Leamington.

As he played and played, his whole soul in his fingers,
a plan began to frame itself, vaguely, dimly at first, then

more and more definitely by slow degrees—shape, form, and features—as it grew and developed. A beautiful chord, that last! Oh, how subtle, how beautiful! It seemed to curl and glide on like a serpent through the grass, leaving strange trails behind as of a flowing signature; a flowing signature with bold twirls and flourishes—twirls and flourishes—twirls and flourishes—twirls, twirls, twirls and flourishes; the signature to a check; to a check for money; three thousand pounds at Drummond, Coutts, and Barclay's.

It ran through his head, keeping time with the bars. Four thousand pounds; five thousand; six thousand.

The longer he played the clearer and sharper the plan stood out. He saw his way now as clear as daylight. And his way, too, to make a deal more in the end by it.

"Pay self or bearer six thousand pounds! Six thousand pounds; signed, Cyril Waring!"

For hours he paced up and down there, playing long and low. Oh, music, how he loved it! It seemed to set everything straight all at once in his head. With bow in hand, and violin at rest, he surpassed himself that evening in ingenuity of fingering. He trembled to think of his own cleverness and skill. What a miracle of device! What a triumph of cunning! Not an element was overlooked. It was "safe as houses." He could go to bed now, and drop off like a child; having arranged before he went to make Guy Waring his cat's-paw, and turn this sad stroke of ill-luck, in the end, to his own ultimate greater and wider advantage.

And he was quite right, too. He did sleep as he expected. Next morning he woke in a very good humor, and proceeded at once to Guy Waring's rooms the moment after breakfast.

He found Guy, as he expected, in a tumult of excitement, having only just that moment received by post the final call for the Rio Negro capital.

When other men are excited the wise man takes care to be perfectly calm. Montague Nevitt was calm under this crushing blow. He pointed out blandly that everything would yet go well. All was not lost. They had other irons in the fire. And even the Rio Negros themselves were not an absolute failure. The diamonds, the

diamonds themselves, he insisted, were still there, and
the sapphires also. They studded the soil; they were to
be had for the picking. Every bit of their money would
come back to them in the end. It was a question of
meeting an immediate emergency only.

"But I haven't three thousand pounds in the world to
meet it with," Guy exclaimed in despair. "I shall be
ruined, of course. I don't mind about that; but I never
shall be able to make good my liabilities."

Nevitt lighted a cigarette with a philosophical smile.
The hotter Guy waxed, the faster did he cool down.

"Neither have I, my dear boy," he said, in his most
careless voice, puffing out rings of smoke in the interval
between his clauses, "but I don't, therefore, go mad. I
don't tear my hair over it, though, to be sure, I'm a deal
worse off than you. My position's at stake. If Drummond were to hear of it—sack—sack instanter. As to
making yourself responsible for what you don't possess,
that's simply speculation. Everybody on the Stock Exchange always does it. If they didn't there'd be no such
thing as enterprise at all. You can't make a fortune by
risking a ha'penny."

"But what am I to do?" Guy cried, wildly. "However am I to raise three thousand pound? I should be
ashamed to let Cyril know I'd defaulted like this. If
I can't find the money I shall go mad or kill myself."

Montague Nevitt played him gently, as an experienced
angler plays a plunging trout, before proceeding to land
him. At last, after offering Guy much sympathetic advice, and suggesting several intentionally feeble schemes,
only to quash them instantly, he observed, with a certain
apologetic air of unobtrusive friendliness, "Well, if the
worst comes to the worst, you've one thing to fall back
upon. There's that six thousand, of course, coming in by
and by from the unknown benefactor."

Guy flung himself down in his easy-chair with a look
of utter despondency upon his handsome face. "But I
promised Cyril," he exclaimed with a groan, "I'd never
touch that. If I were to spend it I don't know how I
could ever face Cyril.

"I was told yesterday," Nevitt answered, with a bitter
little smile, "and by a lady, too, many times over, that

circumstances alter cases till I began to believe it. When you promised Cyril you weren't face to face with a financial crisis. If you were to use the money temporarily—mind, I say only temporarily, for to my certain knowledge Rio Negros will pull through all right in the end—if you were to use it temporarily in such an emergency as this, no blame of any sort could possibly attach to you. The unknown benefactor won't mind whether your money's at your banker's, or employed for the time being in paying your debts. Your creditors will. If I were you, therefore, I'd use it up in paying them."

" You would?" Guy inquired, glancing across at him with a faint gleam of hope in his eye.

Nevitt fixed him at once with his strange, cold stare. He had caught his man now. He could play upon him as readily as he could play his violin.

" Why, certainly I would," he answered with confidence, striking the new chord full. " Cyril himself would do the same in your place, I'll bet you. And the proof that he would is simply this—you yourself will do it. Depend upon it, if you can do anything, under given circumstances, Cyril would do it too, in the same set of conditions. And if ever Cyril feels inclined to criticise what you've done, you can answer him back, ' I know your heart as you know mine. In my place, I know you'd have acted as I did.' "

Cyril and I are not absolutely identical," Guy answered, slowly, his eyes still fixed on Montague Nevitt's. " Sometimes I feel he does things I wouldn't do."

" He has more initiative than you," Nevitt answered, as if carelessly, though with deep design in his heart. " He acts where you debate. You're often afraid to take a serious step. Cyril never hesitates. You draw back and falter ; Cyril goes straight ahead. But all the more reason, accordingly, that Cyril should admit the rightness of whatever you do ; for if you do anything—anything in the nature of a definite step, mean—why far more readily, then would Cyril, in like case, have done it."

" You think he has more initiative ?" Guy asked, with a somewhat nettled air. He hated to be thought less individual than Cyril.

" Of course he has, my dear boy," Nevitt answered,

smiling. "He'd use the money at once, without a second's hesitation. But I haven't got the money to use," Guy continued, after a short pause.

"Cyril has, though," Nevitt responded, with a significant nod.

Guy perused his boots, and made no immediate answer. Nevitt wanted none just then; he waited some seconds, humming all the while an appropriate tune. Then he caught Guy's eye again, and fixed him a second time.

"It's a pity we don't know Cyril's address in Belgium," he said in a musing tone. "We might telegraph across for leave to use his money meanwhile. Remember I'm just as deeply compromised as you, or even more so. It's a pity we should both be ruined, with six thousand pounds standing this very moment to Cyril's account at the London and West County. But it can't be helped. There's no time to lose. The money must be paid in sharp by this evening."

"By this evening!" Guy exclaimed, starting up excitedly. Nevitt nodded assent. "Yes, by this evening, of course," he answered, unperturbed, "or we become *ipso factor* defaulters and bankrupts."

That was a lie, to be sure, but it served his purpose. Guy was a child at business, and believed whatever nonsense Nevitt chose to foist upon him.

The journalist rose and paced the room twice or thrice with a frantic air of unspeakable misery.

"I shall lose my place at our bank, no doubt," Nevitt went on, in a resigned tone. "But that doesn't much matter. Though a temporary loan—I could pay every penny in six weeks if I'd time—a temporary loan would set things all straight again."

"I wish to heaven Cyril was here," Guy exclaimed, in piteous tones.

"He is, practically, when you're here," Nevitt answered with a knowing smile. "You can act as his deputy."

"How do you mean?" Guy asked, turning round upon him open-mouthed.

Nevitt paused, and smiled sweetly.

"This is his check-book, I think," he replied, in the oblique retort, picking it up and looking at it. He tore out a check, as if pensively and by accident.

"That's a precious odd thing," he went on, "that you showed me the other day, don't you know, about your signature and Cyril's being so absolutely identical."

Guy gazed at him in horror. "Oh, don't talk about that!" he cried, running his hand through his hair. "If I were even to entertain such an idea for a moment my self-respect would be gone forever."

"Exactly so," Nevitt put in with a satirical smile. "I said so just now. You've no initiative. Cyril wouldn't be afraid. Knowing the interests at stake, he'd take a firm stand and act off-hand on his own discretion."

"Do you think so?" Guy faltered, in a hesitating voice.

Nevitt held him with his eye.

"Do I think so?" he echoed, "do I think so? I know it. Look here, Guy; you and Cyril are practically one. If Cyril were here we'd ask him at once to lend us the money. If we knew where Cyril was we'd telegraph across and get his leave like a bird. But as he isn't here, and as we don't know where he is, we must show some initiative; we must act for once on our own responsibility, exactly as Cyril would. It's only for six weeks. At the end of that time the unknown benefactor stumps up your share. You needn't even tell Cyril, if you don't like, of this little transaction. See, here's his check. You fill it in and sign it. Nobody can tell the signature isn't Cyril's. You take the money and release us both. In six weeks' time you get your own share of the unnatural parent's bribe. You pay it in to his credit, and not a living soul on earth but ourselves need ever be one penny the wiser."

Guy tried to look away, but he couldn't. He couldn't. Nevitt held him fixed with his penetrating gaze. Guy moved uneasily. He felt as if he had a stiff neck, so hard was it to turn. Nevitt took a pen and dipped it quick in the ink.

"Just as an experiment," he said, firmly, yet in a coaxing voice; "sit down and sign. Let me see what it looks like. There. Write it just here. Write 'Cyril Waring.'"

Guy sat down as in a maze, and took the pen from his hand like an obedient schoolboy. For a second the pen

trembled in his vacillating fingers; then he wrote on the
check, in a free and flowing hand, where the signature
ought to be, his brother's name. He wrote it without
stopping.

"Capital! Capital!" Nevitt cried in delight, looking
over his shoulder. "It's a splendid fac-simile! Now
date and amount, if you please. Six thousand pounds.
It's your own natural hand, after all. Ah, capital,
capital!"

As he spoke, Guy framed the fatal words like one
dreaming or entranced, on the slip of paper before him.
"Pay Self or Bearer Six Thousand Pounds (£6000), Cyril
Waring."

Nevitt looked at it critically. "That'll do all right,"
he said, with his eye still fixed in between whiles on
Guy's bloodless face. "Now the only one thing you have
still left to do is to take it to the bank and get it cashed
instanter."

CHAPTER XX.

MONTAGUE NEVITT FINESSES.

GUY rose mechanically, and followed him to the door. Nevitt still held the forged check in his hand. Guy thought of it so to himself, in plain terms, as the forgery. Yet somehow, he knew not why, he followed that sinister figure through the passage and down the stairs like one irresistibly and magnetically drawn forward. Why, he couldn't let any one go forth upon the streets of London, with the check he himself had forged, in his hands, unwatched and unshadowed!

Nevitt called a cab, and jumped in and beckoned him. Guy, still as in a dream, jumped after him hastily.

" To the London and West County Bank, in Lombard Street," Nevitt called through the flap.

The cab drove off, and Guy Waring leaned back, all trembling and irresolute, with his head on the cushions. At last, after a short drive, during which Guy's head seemed to be swimming most dreamily, they reached the bank—that crowded bank in Lombard Street. Nevitt thrust the check bodily into his companion's hand.

" Take it in now, and cash it," he said, with an authoritative air. " Do you hear what I say ? Take it in— and cash it."

Guy, as if impelled by some superior power, walked inside the door, and presented it timidly.

The cashier glanced at the sum inscribed on the check with no little surprise.

" It's a rather large amount, Mr. Waring," he said, scanning his face closely. " How will you take it ? "

Guy trembled violently from head to foot as he

answered, in a voice half choked with terror, "Bank of England hundreds, if you please. It *is* a large sum as you say, but I'm placing it elsewhere."

The cashier retired for a few minutes; then he re-turned once more, bringing a big roll of notes, and a second clerk by his side (just to prevent mistake) stared hard at the customer.

"All square," the second clerk said, in a half-whispered aside. "It's him right enough."

And the cashier proceeded to count out the notes with oft-wetted fingers.

Guy took them up mechanically, like a drunken man, counted them over, one by one, in a strange, dazed way, and staggered out at last to the cab to Nevitt.

Nevitt leaned forward and took the bundle from his hands. Guy stood on the pavement and looked vacantly in at him. "That's right," Nevitt said, clasping the bundle tight. "Rio Negro Diamond and Sapphire Mines, cabby, 127 Knatchbull Street, Cheapside."

The cabman whipped up his horse and disappeared round the corner, leaving Guy Waring alone—like a fool —on the pavement.

For a minute or two the dazed and dazzled journalist stood there, awaking by degrees, as from some trance or stupefaction. At first he could only stand still and gaze vacantly down the street after the disappearing cab; but as his brain cleared slowly, and the mist that hung over his mind dispelled itself bit by bit, he was able to walk a few steps at a time towards the nearest shops, where he looked in at the windows intently, with a hollow stare, and tried to collect his scattered wits for a great effort at understanding this strange transaction.

All at once, as he looked, the full folly of his deed burst, in its true light, upon his muddled brain. He had handed Nevitt six thousand pounds in Bank of England notes, to waste, or lose, or speculate, or run away with.

Six—thousand—pounds of Cyril's money! Not that for one moment he suspected Nevitt. Guy Waring was too innocent to suspect anybody. But as he woke up more fully now to the nature of his own act, a horrible sense of guilt and pollution crept slowly over him. He put his hand to his forehead. Cold sweat stood in clammy, small drops upon his brow. Bit by bit the hateful truth dawned clearly upon him. Nevitt had lured him by strange means, he knew not how, into hateful crime —into a disgraceful conspiracy. Word by word the self-accusing sentence framed itself upon his lips.

He spoke it out aloud : " Why—this—is forgery ! "

Dazzled and stunned by the intensity of that awful awaking from some weird possession or suggestion of evil by a stronger mind, Guy Waring began to walk on in a feverish fashion, fast, fast, oh, so fast, not knowing where he went, but conscious only that he must keep moving, lest an accusing conscience should gnaw his very heart out.

Whither, he hadn't as yet the faintest idea. His whole being, for the moment, was centred and summed up in that unspeakable remorse. He had done a great wrong. He had made himself a felon. And now, in the first re-coil of his revolted nature, he must go after the man who held the evidences of his guilt, and by force or persua-sion demand them at once from him. Those notes were Cyril's. He must get them. He must get them.

Possessed by this one idea, with devouring force, but still in a very nebulous and hazy form, Guy began walk-ing towards the Strand and the Embankment, at the hot top of his speed, to get the notes back—at Montague Nevitt's chambers. He had walked with fiery zeal in that wrong direction for nearly a mile, his heart burning within him all the way, and his brain in a whirl, before it began to strike him, in a flash of common sense, that Montague Nevitt wouldn't be there at all. He had driven off to the office. Guy clapped his hand to his forehead once more, in an agony of remorse. Great heavens, what folly ! He had heard him tell the cabman the address himself—" 127 Knatchbull Street, Cheap-side."

Even now he hadn't sense enough to hail a cab and go after him. His faculties were still numbed and entranced by that horrible spell of Montague Nevitt's eye. He had but one thought—to walk on, walk hastily. He tramped along the streets in the direction of Cheapside, straining every muscle to arrive at the office before Nevitt had parted with Cyril's six thousand ; but he never even thought of saving the precious moments by driving the distance between instead of walking it. Montague Nevitt's personality still weighed down half his brain, and rendered his mind almost childish or imbecile.

Hurrying on so through the crowded streets, now walking, now running, now pausing, now panting, knocking up here against a little knot of wayfarers, and delayed again there by an untimely block at some crowded crossing, he turned the corner at last, with a beating heart, into the narrow pavement of an alley marked up as Knatchbull Street. Number 127 was visible from afar.

A mob of excited people marked its site by loitering about the door. Two policemen held off the angrier spirits among the shareholders, But, nothing daunted by the press, Guy forced his way in and looked around the room, trembling, for Montague Nevitt. Too late! Too late! Nevitt wasn't there. The unhappy dupe turned to the clerk in charge.

" Has Mr. Montague Nevitt been here ? " he asked, in a voice all tremulous with emotion.

" Mr. Montague Nevitt ? " the clerk responded. " Just gone ten minutes ago. Came to settle Mr. Whitley's call—his brother-in-law's. Went off in a cab. Can I do anything for you ? "

" He's paid in six thousand pounds ? " Guy gasped out interrogatively.

The clerk gazed at him hard with a suspicious glance. "Are you a shareholder ? " he asked, with one eye on the policeman. " What do you want to know for ? "

" Yes, I'm a shareholder, unfortunately," Guy answered, still in a maze. " I hold three hundred original shares. My name's Guy Waring. You've got me on your books. Mr. Nevitt has paid three thousand in Mr. Whitley's name, and three thousand for me. That was our arrangement."

The clerk glanced hard at him again. " Waring!" he repeated, turning ever the leaves of his big book for further verification. " Waring! Waring! Waring! Ah, here it is. Waring, Guy; journalist; 22 Staple Inn; 300 shares. Three hundred pounds paid. Then we call up to three thousand. No, Mr. Nevitt didn't settle for you, sir. He paid Mr. Whitley's call in full. That was all. Nothing else. You're still our debtor."

"He didn't pay up!" Guy exclaimed, clapping his hanks to Lis head, all the black guile and treachery of the man coming home to him at once, at one fell blow. "He didn't pay up for me! Oh, this is too, too terrible!"

He paused for a moment. Floods of feeling rushed over him. He knew now that he had committed that forgery for nothing. Cyril's money was gone. And Montague Nevitt had stolen the three thousand Guy intrusted to him at the bank for the second payment. Yet Guy knew he had no legal remedy save by acknowledging the forgery. This was almost more than human nature could stand. If Montague Nevitt had been by his side that moment Guy would have leapt at his throat, and it would have gone hard with him if he had left the villain living.

He clapped his hands to his ears in the horror and agony of that hideous disclosure.

"The thief!" he cried aloud in a choking voice. "Did he pay what he from a big roll of notes, and did he take the rest of the notes in the roll away with him?"

"Yes, just so," the clerk answered, calmly. "He didn't mention your name. But perhaps he's coming back by and by to settle for you."

Guy knew better. He saw through the man's whole black nature at once.

"I've been robbed," he said, slowly. "I've been robbed and deserted. I must follow the man and compel him to disgorge. When I've got the cash back I'll return and pay you. . . No I won't, though. I forgot. I'll take it home to the bank for Cyril."

The clerk gazed at him with a smile of pitying contempt. Mad, mad; quite mad! The loss of his fortune had, no doubt, unhinged this shareholder's reason. But Guy, never heeding him, rushed out into the street and hailed a passing cab.

"Temple Flats," he cried aloud, and drove to Nevitt's chambers. Too late, once more! The housekeeper told him Mr. Nevitt was out. He'd just started off, portmanteau and all, as hard as a hansom could drive, to Waterloo station.

"Waterloo, then," Guy shouted in wild despair to the cabman. "We must follow this man post haste. Alive or dead, I won't rest till I catch him!"

It was an unhappy phrase. In the **events that** came after, it **was** remembered against him.

CHAPTER XXI.

COLONEL KELMSCOTT'S PUNISHMENT.

WHILE Montague Nevitt was thus congenially engaged in pulling off his treble coup of settling his own share in the Rio Negro deficit, pocketing three thousand pounds, *pro tem.*, for incidental expenses, and getting Guy Waring thoroughly into his power by his knowledge of a forgery, two other events were taking place elsewhere, which were destined to prove of no small importance to the future of the twins and their immediate surroundings. Things generally were converging towards a crisis in their affairs. Colonel Kelmscott's wrong-doing was bearing first fruit abundantly.

For as soon as Granville Kelmscott received that strangely worded note from Gwendoline Gildersleeve, he proceeded, as was natural, straight down, in his doubt, to his father's library. There, bursting into the room, with Gwendoline's letter still crushed in his hand in the side pocket of his coat, and a face like thunder, he stood in the attitude of avenging fate before his father's chair, and gazed down upon him angrily.

" What does *this* mean?" he asked, in a low but fuming voice, brandishing the note before his eyes as he spoke. " Is every one in the country to be told it but I? Is everybody else to hear my business before you tell me a word of it? A letter comes to me this morning,—no matter from whom,—and here's what it says: 'I know you're not the eldest son, and that somebody else is the heir of Tilgate.' Surely, if anybody was to know, *I* should have known it first. Surely, if I'm to be turned adrift on the world after being brought up to think myself a man of means so long, I should, at least, be turned adrift with my eyes open."

Colonel Kelmscott gazed at him open-mouthed with horror.

"Did Gwendoline Gildersleeve write that to you?" he cried, overpowered at once by remorse and awe. "Did Gwendoline Gildersleeve write that to you? Well, if Gwendoline Gildersleeve knows it, it's all up with the scheme! That rascally lawyer, her father, has found out everything. These two young men must have put their case in the fellow's hands. He must be hunting up the facts. He must be preparing to contest it. My boy, my boy! we're ruined, we're ruined!"

"These two young men," Granville repeated with a puzzled air of surprise, "*What* two young men? I don't know them. I never heard of them." Then suddenly one of those flashes of intuition burst in upon him that bursts in upon us all at moments of critical importance to our lives. "Father, father," he cried, leaning forward in his anguish, and clutching the oak chair, "you don't mean to tell me those fellows, the Warings, that we met at Chetwood Court, are your lawful sons—and that *that* was why you bought the landscape with the snake in it?"

Kelmscott of Tilgate bent his proud head down to the table unchecked. "My son, my son!" he cried in his despair, "you have said it yourself. Your own mouth has suggested it. What use my trying to keep it from you any longer? These lads—are Kelmscotts."

"And—my mother?" Granville Kelmscott burst out in a very tremulous voice. The question was almost more than a man dare ask. But he asked it in the first bitterness of a terrible awakening.

"Your mother," Colonel Kelmscott answered, lifting his head once more, with a terrible effort, and looking his son point-blank in the face, "your mother is just what I have always called her—my lawful wife—Lady Emily Kelmscott. The mother of these lads, to whom I was also once duly married, died before my marriage with my present wife—thank God, I can say so! I may have acted foolishly, cruelly, criminally; but at least I never acted quite so basely and so ill as you impute to me, Granville"

"Thank heaven for that!" his son answered, fervently, with one hand on his breast, drawing a deep sigh as he

spoke. "You're my father, sir, and it isn't for me to
reproach you, but if you had only done *that*—oh, my
mother! my mother! I don't know, sir, I'm sure, how I
could ever have forgiven you; I don't know how I could
ever have kept my hands off you."

Colonel Kelmscott straightened himself up, and looked
hard at his son. A terrible pathos gleamed in his proud
brown eyes. His white mustache had more dignity than
ever.

"Granville," he said, slowly, like a broken man, "I
don't ask you to forgive me: you can never forgive me;
I don't ask you to sympathize with me ; a father knows
better than to accept sympathy from a son; but I do ask
you to bear with me while I try to explain myself."

He braced himself up, and with many long pauses, and
many inarticulate attempts to set forth the facts in the
least unfavorable aspect, told his story all through, in
minute detail, to that hardest of all critics, his own dispossessed and disinherited boy.

"If you're hard upon me, Granville," he cried at last
as he finished, looking wistfully for pity into his son's
face, "you should remember, at least, it was for *your*
sake I did it, my boy; it was for your sake I did it—
yours, yours, and your mother's."

Granville let him relate his whole story in full to the
bitter end, though it was with difficulty at times that that
proud and gray-haired man nerved himself up to tell it.
Then, as soon as all was told, he looked in his father's
face once more, and said slowly with the pitilessness of
sons in general towards the faults and failings of their
erring parents:—

"It's not my place to blame you, I know. You did it,
I suppose, as you say so, for me and my mother. But it
is my place to tell you plainly, father, that I, for one, will
have nothing at all to do with the fruits of your decep-
tion. I was no party to the fraud; I will be no party
either to its results or its clearing up. I, too, have to
think, as you say, of my mother. For her sake, I won't
urge you to break her heart at once by disinheriting her
son, now and here, too openly. You can make what
arrangements you like with these blood-sucking Warings.
You can do as you will in providing them with hush-

money. Let them take their blackmail! You've handed them over half the sum you got for Dowlands already, I suppose. You can buy them off for awhile by handing them over the remainder. Twelve thousand will do. Leeches as they are, that will surely content them, at least for the present."

Colonel Kelmscott raised one hand and tried hard to interrupt him; but Granville would not be interrupted.

"No, no," he went on sternly, shaking his head and frowning. "I'll have my say for once, and then forever keep silence. This is the first and last time as long as we both live I will speak with you on the subject. So we may as well understand one another, once and forever. For my mother's sake, as i said, there need be just at present no open disclosure. You have years to live yet; and as long as you live, these Waring people have no claim upon the estate in any way. You've given them as much as they've any right to expect. Let them wait for the rest till, in the course of nature, they come into possession. As for me, I will go to carve out for myself a place in the world elsewhere by my own exertions. Perhaps, before my mother need know her son was left a beggar by the father who brought him up like the heir to a large estate, I may have been able to carve out that place for myself so well that she need never really feel the difference. I'm a Kelmscott, and can fight the world on my own account. But in any case, I must go. Tilgate's no longer a fit home for me. I leave it to those who have a better right to it."

He rose as if to depart, with the air of a man who sets forth upon the world to seek his fortune. Colonel Kelmscott rose too, and faced him, all broken.

"Granville," he said, in a voice scarcely audible through the stifled sobs he was too proud to give vent too, "you're not going like this! You're not going without at least shaking hands with your father! You're not going without saying good-bye to your mother!"

Granville turned, with hot tears standing dim in his eyes,—like his father, he was too proud to let them trickle down his cheek,—and taking the Colonel's weather-beaten hand in his, wrung it silently for some minutes with profound emotion.

Then he looked at the white moustache, the grizzled hair, the bright brown eyes suffused with answering dimness, and said almost remorsefully, " Father, good-bye. You meant me well, no doubt. You thought you were befriending me. But I wish to heaven in my soul you had meant me worse. It would have been easier for me to bear in the end. If you'd brought me up as a nobody —as a younger son's accustomed—" he paused and drew back, for he could see his words were too cruel for that proud man's heart. Then he broke off suddenly.

" But I *can't* say good-bye to my mother," he went on, with a piteous look. " If I tried to say good-bye to her, I must tell her all. I'd break down in the attempt. I'll write to her from the Cape. It'll be easier so. She won't feel it so much then."

" From the Cape ! " Colonel Kelmscott exclaimed, drawing back in horror. " Oh, Granville, don't tell me you're going away from us to Africa ! "

" Where else ? " his son asked, looking him back in the face steadily. " Africa it is ! That's the only opening left nowadays for a man of spirit. There I may be able to hew out a place for myself at last, worthy of Lady Emily Kelmscott's son. I won't come back till I come back able to hold my own in the world with the best of them. These Warings sha'n't crow over the younger son. Good-bye once more, father." He wrung his hand hard " Think kindly of me when I'm gone ; and don't forget altogether I once loved Tilgate."

He opened the door and went up to his own room again. His mind was resolved. He wouldn't even say good-bye to Gwendoline Gildersleeve. He'd pack a few belongings in a portmanteau in haste, and go forth upon the world to seek his fortune in the South African diamond fields.

But Colonel Kelmscott sat still in the library, bowed down in his chair, with his head between his hands, in abject misery A strange feeling seemed to throb through his weary brain ; he had a sensation as though his skull were opening and shutting. Great veins on his forehead beat black and swollen. The pressure was almost more than the vessels could stand. He held his temples between his two palms as if to keep them from bursting.

All ahead looked dark as night; the ground was cut from under him.   The punishment of his sin was too heavy for him to bear.   How could he ever tell Emily now that Granville was gone?   A horrible numbness oppressed his brain.   Oh, mercy! mercy! his head was flooded.

CHAPTER XXII.

CROSS PURPOSES.

At the Gildersleeves, too, the house that day was alive
with excitement.

Gwendoline had thrown herself into a fever of alarm
as soon as she had posted her letter to Granville Kelmscott. She went up to her own room, flung herself wildly
on the bed, and sobbed herself into a half hysterical, half
delirious state, long before dinner-time. She hardly
knew herself at first how really ill she was. Her hands
were hot and her forehead burning. But she disregarded
such mere physical and mental details as those by the
side of a heart too full for utterance. She thought only
of Granville, and of that horrid man who had threatened
with such evident spite and rancor to ruin him.

She lay there some hours alone, in a high fever, before
her mother came up to her room to fetch her. Mrs. Gildersleeve was a subdued and soft-voiced woman, utterly
crushed, so people said, by the stronger individuality of
that blustering, domineering, headstrong man, her husband. And to say the truth, the eminent Q.C. had taken
all the will out of her in twenty-three years of obedient
slavery. She was pretty still, to be sure, in a certain
faded, jaded, unassuming way; but her patient face wore
a constant expression of suppressed terror, as if she expected every moment to be the victim of some terrible
and unexplained exposure. And that feature at least, in
her idiosyncrasy, could hardly be put down to Gilbert
Gildersleeve's account; for hectoring and strong-minded
as the successful Q.C. was known to be, nobody could
for a moment accuse him in any definite way of deliberate unkindness to his wife or daughter. On the contrary,
he was tender and indulgent to them to the last degree,
as he understood those virtues. It was only by constant

assertion of his own individuality, and constant repression or disregard of theirs, that he had broken his wife's spirit and was breaking his daughter's. He treated them as considerately as one treats a pet dog, doing everything for them that care and money could effect, except to admit for a moment their claim to independent opinions and actions of their own, or to allow the possibility of their thinking and feeling on any subject on earth one nail's breadth otherwise than as he himself did.

At sight of Gwendoline Mrs. Gildersleeve came over to the bed with a scared and startled air, felt her daughter's face tenderly with her hands for a moment, and then cried in alarm, " Why, Gwennie, what's this? Your cheeks are burning. Who on earth has been here? Has that horrid man come down again from London to worry you? '

Gwendoline looked up and tried to prevaricate. But conscience was too strong for her; the truth would out for all that. " Yes, mother," she cried, after a pause, " and he said, oh, he said—I could never tell you what dreadful things he said. But he's so wicked, so cruel! You never knew such a man! He thinks I want to marry Granville Kelmscott, and so he told me "—she broke off, of a sudden, unable to proceed, and buried her face in her hands, sobbing long and bitterly.

" Well, what did he tell you, dear? " Mrs. Gildersleeve asked, with that frightened air, as of a startled wild thing, growing deeper than ever upon her countenance as she uttered the question.

" He told me—oh, he told me—I can't tell you what he told me ; but he threatened to ruin us—he threatened it so dreadfully. It was a hateful threat. He seemed to have found out something that he knew would be our ruin. He frightened me to death. I never heard any one say such things as he did."

Mrs. Gildersleeve drew back in profound agitation. " Found out something that would be our ruin!" she cried, with white face all aghast. " Oh, Gwennie, what do you mean? Didn't he tell you what it was? Didn't he try to explain to you? He's a wicked, wicked man —so cruel, so unscrupulous! He get's one's secrets into his hands by underhand means, and then uses them to make one do whatever he chooses. I see how it is. He wants to force us into letting him marry you—into making you marry him! Oh, Gwennie, this is hard! Didn't he tell you at all what it was he knew? Didn't he give you a hint what sort of secret he was driving at?"

Gwendoline looked up once more and murmured low through her sobs, "No, he didn't say what it was. He's too cunning for that. But I think—I think it was something about Granville. Mother, I never told you, but you know I love him! I think it was something about *him*, though I can't quite make sure. Some secret about something body not being properly married, or something of that sort. I didn't quite understand. You see he was so discreetly vague and reticent."

Mrs Gildersleeve drew back her face all aghast with horror. "Some secret—about somebody—not being properly married!" she repeated, slowly, with wild terror in her eyes.

"Yes, mother," Gwendoline gasped out with an effort once more. "It was about somebody not being really the proper heir; he made me promise I wouldn't tell, but I don't know how to keep it. He was immensely full of it; it was an awful secret; and he said he would ruin us—ruin us ruthlessly. He said we were in his power, and he'd crush us under his heel. And oh, when he said it, you should have seen his face! It was horrible, horrible! I've seen nothing else since. It dogs me —it haunts me!"

Mrs. Gildersleeve sat down by the bedside, wringing her hands in silence. "It's too late to-night," she said at last, after a long, deep pause, and in a voice like a woman condemned to death, "too late to do anything; but to-morrow your father must go up to town and try to see him. At all costs we must buy him off. He knows everything—that's clear. He'll ruin us! He'll ruin us!"

"It's no use papa going up to town thcugh," Gwendoline answered, half dreamily. "That dreadful man said he was going away for his holiday to the country at once. He'll be gone to-morrow."

"Gone? Gone where?" Mrs. Gildersleeve cried in the same awe-struck voice.

"To Devonshire," Gwendoline replied, shutting her eyes hard and still seeing him.

Mrs. Gildersleeve echoed the phrase in a startled cry. "To Devonshire, Gwendoline! To Devonshire! Did he say to Devonshire?"

"Yes," Gwendoline went on slowly, trying to recall his very words. "To the skirts of Dartmoor, I think he said; to a place in the wilds by the name of Mambury."

"Mambury!"

The terror and horror that frail and faded woman threw into the one word fairly startled Gwendoline. She opened her eyes and stared aghast at her mother. And well she might, for the effect was electrical. Mrs. Gildersleeve was sitting there, transfixed with awe and some unspeakable alarm; her figure was rigid; her face was dead white; her mouth was drawn down with a convulsive twitch; she clasped her bloodless hands on her knees in mute agony. For a moment she sat there like a statue of flesh. Then, as sense and feeling came back to her by slow degrees, she could but rock her body up and down in her chair with a short swaying motion, and mutter over and over again to herself in that same appalled and terrified voice, " Mambury—Mambury— Mambury—Mambury."

"That was the name, I'm sure," Gwendoline went on, almost equally alarmed. "On a hunt after records, he said; on a hunt after records. Whatever it was he wanted to prove, I suppose he knew that was the place to prove it."

Mrs. Gildersleeve rose, or to speak with more truth, staggered slowly to her feet, and steadying herself with an effort, made blindly for the door, groping her way as she went like some faint and wounded creature. She said not a word to Gwendoline. She had no tongue left for speech or comment. She merely stepped on, pale and white, like one who walks in her sleep, and clutched the door-handle hard to keep her from falling. Gwendoline, now thoroughly alarmed, followed her close on her way to the top of the stairs. There Mrs. Gildersleeve paused, turned round to her daughter with a mute look of anguish, and, held up one hand, palm outward, appealingly, as

as if on purpose to forbid her from following further.
At the gesture, Gwendoline fell back, and looked after
her mother with straining eyes. Mrs. Gildersleeve staggered on, erect, yet to all appearance almost incapable of
motion, and stumbled down the stairs, and across the
hall, and into the drawing-room opposite. The rest
Gwendoline neither saw, nor heard, nor guessed at.
She crept back into her own room, and flinging herself
on her bed alone as she stood, cried still more piteously
and miserably than ever.

Down in the drawing-room, however, Mrs. Gildersleeve found the famous Q. C. absorbed in the perusal of
that day's paper. She came across towards him, pale as
a ghost, and with ashen lips. "Gilbert," she said
slowly, blurting it all out in her horror, without one word
of warning, "that dreadful man, Nevitt, has seen Gwennie again, and he's told her he knows all, and he means
to ruin us, and he's heard of the marriage, and he's gone
down to Mambury to hunt up the records!"

The eminent Q. C. let the paper drop from his huge
red hands in the intensity of his surprise, while his jaw
fell in unison at so startling and almost incredible a piece
of intelligence. "Nevitt knows all!" he exclaimed, half
incredulous. "He means to ruin us! And he told this
to Gwendoline! Gone down to Mambury! Oh, no
Minnie, impossible! You must have made some mistake. What did she say exactly? Did she mention
Mambury?"

"She said it exactly as I've said it now to you," Mrs.
Gildersleeve persisted, with a stony stare. "He's gone
down to Devonshire, she said; to the borders of Dartmoor, on a hunt after the records; to a place in the wilds
by the name of Mambury. Those were her very words.
I could stake my life on each syllable. I give them to
you precisely as she gave them to me."

Mr. Gildersleeve gazed across at her with the countenance which had made so many a nervous witness quake
at the Old Bailey. "Are you *quite* sure of that, Minnie?"
he asked, in his best cross-examining tone. "Quite
sure she said Mambury, all of her own accord? Quite
sure you didn't suggest it to her, or supply the name, or
give her a hint of its whereabouts, or put her a leading
question?"

" Is it likely I'd suggest it to her?" the meekest of women answered, aroused to retort for once, and with her face like a sheet. "Is it likely I'd tell her? Is it likely I'd give my own girl the clue? She said it all of herself, I tell you, without one word of prompting. She said it just as I repeated it—to a place in the wilds by the name of Mambury."

Gilbert Gildersleeve whistled inaudibly to himself, 'Twas his way when he felt himself utterly nonplussed. This was very strange news. He didn't really understand it. But he rose and confronted his wife anxiously. That overbearing, big man was evidently stirred by this untoward event to the very depths of his nature.

" Then Gwennie knows all!" he cried, the blood rushing purple into his ruddy, flushed cheeks. "The wretch! The brute! He must have told her everything."

" O Gilbert!" his wife answered, sinking into a chair in her horror; " even *he* couldn't do that—not to my own very daughter! And he didn't do it, I'm sure; he didn't dare. Coward as he is, he couldn't be quite so cowardly. She doesn't guess what it means. She thinks it's something, I believe, about Granville Kelmscott. She's in love with young Kelmscott, as I told you long ago, and everything to her mind takes some color from that fancy. I don't think it ever, occurred to her, from what she says that this anything at all to do with you or me, Gilbert."

The Q.C. reflected. He saw at once he was in a tight corner. That boisterous man, with the burly big hands, looked quite subdued and crestfallen now. He could hardly have snubbed the most unassuming junior. This was a terrible thing, indeed, for a man so unscrupulous and clever as Montague Nevitt to have wormed out of the registers. How he could ever have wormed it out Gilbert Gildersleeve hadn't the faintest idea. Why, who on earth could have shown him the entry of that fatal marriage—Minnie's first marriage—the marriage with that wretch who died in Portland prison—the marriage that was celebrated at St. Mary's at Mambury? He couldn't for a moment conceive, for nobody but themselves, he fondly imagined, had ever identified Mrs.

Gilbert Gildersleeve, the wife of the eminent Q. C. with that unhappy Mrs. Read, the convict's widow. The convict's widow—ah, there was the rub! For she was really a widow in name alone when Gilbert Gildersleeve marrried her.

And Montague Nevitt, that human ferret, with his keen, sharp eyes, and his sleek, polite ways, had found it all out in spite of them—had hunted up the date of Read's death and their marriage, and had bragged how he was going down to Mambury to prove it!

All the Warings and Reads always got married at Widdicombe or Mambury. There were lots of them on the books there, that was one comfort, anyhow. He'd have a good search to find his needle in such a pottle of hay. But to think the fellow should have had the doubled-dyed cruelty to break the shameful secret first of all to Gwendoline! That was his vile way of trying to force a poor girl into an unwilling consent. Gilbert Gildersleeve lifted his burly big hands in front of his capacious waistcoat, and pressed them together angrily. If only he had that rascal's throat well between them at that moment! He'd crush the fellow's windpipe till he choked him on the spot, though he answered for it before the judges of assize to-morrow!

"There's only one thing possible for it, Minnie," he said at last, drawing a long, deep breath. "I must go down to Mambury to-morrow to be beforehand with him. And I must either buy him off—or else, if that won't do——"

"Or else what, Gilbert?"

She trembled like an aspen-leaf.

"Or else get at the books in the vestry myself," the Q C muttered low between his clenched teeth, "before the fellow has time to see them and prove it."

CHAPTER XXIII.

GUY IN LUCK.

GUY WARING reached Waterloo ten minutes too late. Nevitt had gone on by the West of England express. The porter at the labelling place " minded the gentleman well." He was a sharp-looking gentleman, with a queer look about the eyes, and a dark moustache curled round at the corners.

" Yes, yes," Guy cried, eagerly, " that's him right enough. The eyes mark the man. And where was he going to?"

" He had his things labelled," the porter said, " for Plymouth."

" And when does the next train start?" Guy inquired, all on fire.

The porter, consulting the time-table in the muddle-headed way peculiar to railway porters, and stroking his chin with his hand to assist cerebration, announced, after a severe internal struggle, that the 3.45 down, slow, was the earliest train available.

There was nothing for it then, Guy perceived, but to run home to his rooms, possessing his soul in patience, pack up a few things in his Gladstone bag, and return at his leisure to catch the down train thus unfavorably introduced to his critical notice.

If Guy had dared, to be sure he might have gone straight to a police station, and got an inspector to telegraph along the line to stop the thief with his booty at Basingstoke or Salisbury. But Guy didn't dare. For to interfere with Nevitt now by legal means would be to risk the discovery of his own share in the forgery. And from that risk the startled and awakened young man shrank for a thousand reasons; though the chief among them all was certainly one that never would have occurred to any one but himself as even probable.

He didn't wish Elma Clifford to know that the man she loved, and the man who loved her, had become that day a forger's brother.

To be sure, he had only seen Elma once—that afternoon at the Holkers' garden party. But, as Cyril himself knew, he had fallen in love with her at first sight—far more immediately, indeed, then even Cyril himself had done. Blood, as usual, was thicker then water. The points that appealed to one brother appealed also to the other, but with this characteristic difference, that Guy, who was the more emotional and less strong-willed of the two, yielded himself up at the very first glance to the beautiful stranger, while Cyril required some further acquaintance before quite giving way and losing his heart outright to her. And from that first meeting forward, Guy had carried Elma Clifford's image engraved upon his memory—as he would carry it, he believed, to his dying day. Not, to be sure, that he ever thought for a moment of endeavoring to win her away from his brother. She was Cyril's discovery, and to Cyril, therefore, he yielded her up as of prior right, though with a pang of reluctance. But now that he stood face to face at last with his own accomplished crime, the first thought that rose in his mind spontaneously was for Elma's happiness. He must never let Elma Clifford know that the man she loved, and would doubtless marry, was now by *his* act—a forger's brother.

Three forty-five arrived at last, and Guy set off, all trembling, on his fatal quest. As he sped along, indignant at heart with Nevitt's black treachery, on the line to Plymouth, he had plenty of time to revolve these things abundantly in his own soul. And when, after a long and dusty drive, he reached Plymouth, late at night, he could learn nothing for the moment about Montague Nevitt's movements. So he was forced to go quietly for the evening to the Duke of Devonshire Hotel, and there wait as best he might to see how events would next develop themselves.

A day passed away—two days—but nothing turned up. Guy wasted much time in Plymouth making various in-

quiries before he learnt at last that a man with a queer
look about the eyes and a moustache with waxed ends
had gone down a night or so earlier by the other line to
a station at the foot of Dartmoor, by the name of Mambury.

No sooner, however, had he learnt this promising
news, than he set off at once, hot at heart as ever, to pursue the robber That wretch shouldn't get away scot
free with his booty Guy would follow him and denounce
him to the other end of the universe ! When he reached
Mambury, he went direct to the village inn and asked,
with trembling lips, if Mr. Montague Nevitt was at present staying there. The landlord shook his head with a
stubborn, rustic negative. "No, we arn't a-got no
gentleman o' thik there name in the house," he said ;
" fact is, zur, to tell 'ee the truth, we arn't a-had nobody
stoppin' in the Arms at all lately, 'sep' it might be a
gentleman come down from London, an' it was day afore
yesterday as he did come, an' he do call 'unself Mc-
Gregor."

Quick as lightning, Guy suspected Nevitt might be
passing under a false name. What more likely, indeed,
seeing he had made off with Guy's three thousand
pounds ?

"And what sort of a man is this McGregor ? " he asked,
hastily, putting his suspicion in shape. "What age ?
What height ? What kind of a person to look at ? "

" Wull, he's a vine upstandin' zart of a gentleman,"
the landlord answered glibly in his own dialect; " as
proper a gentleman as you'd wish to zee in a day's
march ; med be about your height, zur or a trifle more,
has his moustaches curled round zame as if it med be a
bellick's harns ; an' a strange zart o' a look about his eyes,
too, as if ur could zee right drew an' drew' ee."

" That's him ! " Guy exclaimed, with a start, in profound excitement. " That's the fellow, sure enough. I
know him, I know him. And where is he now, landlord ? Is he in the house ? Can I see him ? "

"Well, no, 'ee can't zee him. zur," the landlord answered, eying the stranger askance; " he be out, jest
at present. He do go vur a walk, mostly, down yonner
in the bottom alongside the brook. Mebbe if you was to

vollow by river bank you med come up wi' him by an
by. . . . and mebbe, again, you medn't."

"I'll follow him," Guy exclaimed, growing more excited than ever, now his quarry was almost well within
sight; "I'll follow him till I find him, the confounded
rascal. I'll follow him to his grave! He shan't get
away from me!"

The landlord looked at him with a dubious frown.
That one could smile and smile and be a villain didn't
enter into his simple rustic philosophy.

"He's a pleasant-spoken gentleman is Maister Mc-
Gregor," the honest Devonian said, with a tinge of disapprobation in his thick voice. "What vur do 'ee want
to find 'un? That's what *I* wants to know. He don't
look like one as did ever hurt a mice. Such a soft zart
of voice. An' he do play on the viddle that beautiful
—that beautiful, why, 'tis the zame if he war a angel from
heaven. Viddler Moore, he wur up here wi' his music
last night: and Maister McGregor, he took the instrument vrom un' an' 'Let *me* have a try, my vrend,' says he,
all modest and unassoomin; and wi' that, he wounded 't
up, an' he begun to play. Lard, how he did play.
Never heard nothing like it in all my barn days. It is
the zame, vor all the world, as you do hear they viddler
chaps that plays by themselves in the Albert Hall up to
London. Depend upon it, zur, there ain't no harm in
him. A vullow as can play on the viddle like thik there,
why, he couldn't do no hurt, not to child nor chicken."

Guy turned away from the door, fretting and fuming
inwardly. He knew better than that. Nevitt's consummate mastery of his chosen instrument was but of a
piece, after all, with the way he could play on all the
world, as on a familiar gamut. It was the very skill of
the man that made him so dangerous and so devilish.
Guy felt that under the spell of Nevitt' eye he himself
was but as clay in the hands of the potter.

But Nevitt should never so trick him and twist him
again. To that his mind was now fully made up. He
would never let that cold eye hold him fixed as of yore
by its steely glance. Once for all, Nevitt had proved his
power too well. Guy would take good care he never
subjected himself in future to that uncanny influence,

One forgery was enough. Henceforth he was adamant.

And yet? And yet he was going to seek out Nevitt; going to stand face to face with that smiling villain again; going to tax him with his crime; going to ask him what he meant by this double-dyed treachery.

The landlord had told him where Nevitt was most likely to be found. He followed that direction. At a gate that turned by the river-bank, twenty minutes from the inn, a small boy was seated. He was a Devonshire boy of the poorest moorland type, short, squat, and thick set. As Guy reached the gate, the boy rose and opened it, pulling his forelock twice or thrice, expectant of a ha'penny. "Has anybody gone down here?" Guy asked, in an excited voice.

And the boy answered promptly, "Yes, thik there gentleman, what's stoppin' at the Talbot Arms. And another gentleman, too; o'ny t'other one come after and went t'other way round. A big zart o' a gentleman wi', 'ands vit vor two. He axed me the zame question, had anybody gone by. This is dree of 'ee 'as has come zince I've bin a zitting here."

Guy paid no attention to the second-named gentleman, with the hands fit for two, or to his inquiries after who might have gone before him. He fastened at once on the really important and serious information that the person who was stopping at the Talbot Arms had shortly before turned down the side foot-path.

"All right, my boy," he said, tossing the lad a sixpence, the first coin he came across in his waistcoat pocket. The boy opened his eyes wide, and pocketed it with a grin. So unexpected a largess sufficed to impress the handsome stranger firmly on his memory. He didn't forget him when a few days later he was called on to give evidence—at a coroner's inquest.

But Guy, unsuspicious of the harm he had done himself, walked on, all on fire, down the woodland path. It was a shady path, and it led through a deep dell arched with hazels on every side, while a little brawling brook ran along hard by, more heard than seen, in the bottom of the dingle. Thick bramble obscured the petty rapids from view and half trailed their lush shoots here and there across the pathway. It was just such a mossy spot as Cyril would have loved to paint; and Guy, himself half an artist by nature, would in any other mood have paused to gaze delighted on its tangled greenery.

As it was, however, he was in no mood to loiter long over ferns and mosses. He walked down that narrow way, where luxuriant branches of fresh, green blackberry bushes encroached upon the track, still seething in soul, and full of the bitter wrong inflicted upon him by the man he had till lately considered his dearest friend. At each bend of the footpath, as it threaded its way through the tortuous dell, following close the elbows of the bickering little stream, he expected to come full in sight of Nevitt. But gaze as he would, no Nevitt appeared. He must have gone on, Guy thought, and come out at the other end, into the upland road of which the porters at Mambury station had told him.

At last he arrived at a delicious green nook, where the shade of the trees overhead was exceptionally dense, and where the ferns by the side were somewhat torn and trodden. Casting his eye on the ground to the left, a metal clasp, gleaming silvery among the bracken, happened to attract his cursory attention. Something about that clasp looked strangely familiar. He paused and stared hard at it. Surely, surely he had seen those metal knobs before. A flash of recognition ran electric through his brain. Why, yes; it was the fastener of Montague Nevitt's pocket-book—the pocket-book in which he carried his most private documents; the pocket-book that must have held Cyril's stolen six thousand. Guy stooped down to pick it up with a whirling sense of surprise. Great heavens? what was this? Not only the clasp, but the pocket-book itself—the pocket-book filled full and crammed to bursting with papers. Ah, mercy, what papers? Yes, incredible—the money! Hundred-pound notes! Not a doubt upon earth of it. The whole of the stolen and re-stolen three thousand.

For a minute or two Guy stood there, unable to believe his own swimming eyes. What on earth could have happened? Was it chance or design. Had Nevitt deliberately thrown away his ill-gotten gains? Were detectives on the track? Was he anxious to conceal his

part in the theft? Had remorse got the better of him?
Or was he frightened at last, thinking Guy was on his way
to recover and restore Cyril's stolen property?

But no, the pocket-book was neither hidden in the ferns
nor yet studiously thrown away. From the place where
it lay, Guy felt confident at once it had fallen unperceived
from Nevitt's pocket, and been trodden by his heel unawares into the yielding leaf-mould.

Had he pulled it out accidentally with his handkerchief? Very likely, Guy thought. But then, how strange
and improbable that a man so methodical and calculating
as Nevitt should carry such valuable belongings as those
in the self-same pocket. It was certainly most singular.
However, Guy congratulated himself after a moment's
pause that so much at least of the stolen property was
duly recovered. He could pay back one-half of the purloined sum now to Cyril's credit. So he went on his
way through the rest of the wood in a somewhat calmer
and easier frame of mind. To be sure, he had still to
hunt down that villain Nevitt, and to tax him to his face
with his double-dyed treachery. But it was something,
nevertheless, to have recovered a part, at any rate, of the
stolen money. And Nevitt himself need never know by
what fortunate accident he had happened to recover it.

He emerged on the upland road, and struck back towards Mambury. All the way round, he never saw his
man. Weary with walking, he returned in the end to the
Talbot Arms. Had Mr. McGregor come back? No, not
yet; but he was sure to be home for dinner. Then Guy
would wait, and dine at the inn as well. He might have
to stop all night, but he must see McGregor.

As the day wore on, however, it became gradually clear
to him that Montague Nevitt didn't mean to return at
all. Hour after hour passed by, but nothing was heard
of him. The landlord, good man, began to express his
doubts and fears most freely. He hoped no harm hadn't
come to the gentleman in the parlor: he had a powerful
zight o' money on un for a man to carry about; the landlord had zeen it when he took out his book from his
pocket to pay the porter. Volks didn't ought to go about
with two or dree hundred pounds or more in the lonely
lanes on the edge of the moorland.

But Guy, for his part, put a different interpretation on the affair at once. In some way or other Montague Nevitt, he thought, must have found out that he was being tracked, and fearing for his safety, must have dropped the pocket-book and made off, without note or notice given, on his own sound legs, for some other part of the country.

So Guy made up his mind to return next morning by the very first train direct to Plymouth, and there inquire once more whether anything further had been seen of the noticeable stranger.

CHAPTER XXIV.

A SLIGHT MISUNDERSTANDING.

On the very same day Guy Waring visited Mambury, where his mother was married, Montague Nevitt had hunted up the entry of Colonel Kelmscott's wedding in the church register.

Nevitt's behavior, to say the truth, wasn't quite so black as Guy Waring painted it. He had gone off with the extra three thousand in his pocket, to be sure; but he didn't intend to appropriate it outright to his own uses. He merely meant to give Guy a thoroughly good fright, as it wasn't really necessary the call should be met for another fortnight; and then, as soon as he'd found out the truth about Colonel Kelmscott and his unacknowledged sons, he proposed to use his knowledge of the forgery as a lever with Guy, so as to force him to come to advantageous terms with his supposed father. Nevitt's idea was that Guy and Cyril should drive a hard bargain on their own account with the colonel, and that he himself should then receive a handsome commission on the transaction from both the brothers, under penalty of disclosing the true facts about the check by whose aid Guy had met their joint liability to the Rio Negro Diamond Mines.

It was with no small joy, therefore, that Nevitt saw at last in the parish register of St. Mary's at Mambury the interesting announcement, "June 27, Henry Lucius Kelmscott of the parish of Plymouth, bachelor, private in the Regiment of Scots Greys, to Lucy Waring, spinster, of this parish."

He saw at a glance, of course, why Kelmscott of Tilgate had chosen to describe himself in this case as a private soldier. But he also saw that the entry was an official document, and that here he had one firm hold the more on

Colonel Kelmscott, who must falsely have sworn to that incorrect description. The great point of all, however, was the signature to the books; and though nearly thirty years had elapsed since those words were written, it was clear to Nevitt, when he compared the autograph in the ·register with one of Colonel Kelmscott's recent business letters, brought with him for the purpose, that both had been penned by one and the same person.

He chuckled to himself with delight to think how great a benefactor he had proved himself unawares to Guy and Cyril. At that very moment, no doubt, his misguided young friend, whom he had compelled to assist him with the sinews of war for this important campaign, was reviling and objurgating him in revengeful terms as the blackest and most infamous of double-dyed traitors. Ah, well! ah, well! the good are inured to gross ingratitude. Guy little knew, as he, Montague Nevitt, stood there triumphant in the vestry, blandly rewarding the expectant clerk for his pains with a whole Bank of England five-pound note—the largest sum that functionary had ever in his life received all at once in a single payment—Guy little knew that Nevitt was really the chief friend and founder of the family fortunes, and was prepared to compel the "unknown benefactor" [for a moderate commision] to recognize his unacknowledged first-born sons before all the world as the heirs of Tilgate. But yesterday, they were nameless waifs and strays, of uncertain origin, ashamed of their birth, and ignorant even whether they had been duly begotten in lawful wedlock; to-day, they were the legal inheritors of an honored name and a great estate, the first and foremost among the landed gentry of a wealthy and beautiful English county.

He smiled to think what a good turn he had done unawares to those ungrateful youths—and how little credit, as yet, they were prepared to give him for it. In such a mood he returned to the inn to lunch. His spirits were high. This was a good day's work, and he could afford, indeed, to make merry with his host over it. He ordered in a bottle of wine—such wine as the little country cellar could produce—and invited that honest man, the landlord, to step in and share it with him. He had tasted worse sherry on London dinner tables, and he told his

host so. An affable man with inferiors, Mr. Montague
Nevitt! Then he strolled out by himself down the path
by the brook. It was a pleasant walk, with the water
making music in little trickles by its side, and Montague
Nevitt, as a man of taste, found it suited exactly with
his temper for the moment. He noted an undercurrent
of rejoicing and triumphant cheeriness in the tone of the
stream as it splashed among the pebbles on its precipitous
bed that suggested to his mind some bars of a symphony
which he determined to compose as soon as he got home
again to his beloved fiddle.

So he walked along by himself, elate, and with a
springy step, on thoughts of ambition intent, till he came
at last to a cool and shadowy place, where as yet the ferns
were *not* broken down and trampled under foot, though
Guy Waring found them so some twenty minutes later.

At that spot he looped up, and saw advancing along
the path in the opposite direction the burly figure of a
man, in a light tourist suit, whom he hadn't yet observed
since he came to Mambury. The very first point he noticed about the man, long before he recognized him, was
a pair of overgrown, obtrusive hands, held somewhat
awkwardly in front of him—just like Gilbert Gildersleeve's. The likeness, indeed, was so ridiculously close
that Montague Nevitt smiled quietly to himself to observe
it. If he'd been in the Tilgate district now, he'd have
declared, without the slightest hesitation, that the man on
the path *was* Gilbert Gildersleeve.

One second later, he pulled himself up with a jerk in
alarmed surprise. "Great heavens!" he cried to himself,
a weird sense of awe creeping over him piecemeal,
"either this is a dream, or else it *is*, it must be Gilbert
Gildersleeve."

And so, indeed, it was. Gilbert Gildersleeve himself,
in his proper person. But the eminent Q. C., better versed
in the wiles of time and place than Guy Waring in his
innocence, had not come obtrusively to Mambury village,
or asked point-blank at the Talbot Arms by his own right
name for the man he was in search of. Such simplicity
of procedure would never even have occurred to that prac-
ticed hand at the Old Bailey. Mr. Gilbert Gildersleeve
appeared on that woodland path in the general guise of

the common pedestrian tourist with his headquarters at Ivybridge, walking about on the congenial outskirts of the moor in search of the picturesque, and coming and going by mere accident through Mambury. He had hovered around the neighborhood for two days, off and on, in search of his man; and now, by careful watching like an amateur detective, he had run his prey to earth by a a dexterous flank movement, and secured an interview with him where he couldn't shirk or avoid it.

To Montague Nevitt, however, the meeting seemed at first sight but the purest accident. He had no reason to suppose, indeed, that Gilbert Gildersleeve had any special interest in his visit to Mambury, further than might be implied in its possible connection with Granville Kelmscott's affairs; and he didn't believe Gwendoline, in her fear of her father, that blustering man, would ever have communicated to him the personal facts of their interview at Tilgate. So he advanced to meet his old acquaintance the barrister, with frankly outstretched hand.

" Mr. Gildersleeve! " he exclaimed, in some surprise. " No, it can't be you. Well, this *is* indeed an unexpected pleasure."

Gilbert Gildersleeve gazed down upon him from the towering elevation of his six feet four. Montague Nevitt was tall enough, as men go in England, but with his slim, tailor-made form, and his waxed mustaches, he looked by the side of that big-built giant like a Bond-Street exquisite before some prize-fighting Goliath. The barrister didn't hold out his huge hand in return. On the contrary he concealed it, as far as was posible, behind his burly back, and looking down from the full height of his contempt, upon the sinister, smirking creature who advanced to greet him with that false smile on his face, he asked, severely :—

" What are *you* doing here ? That's what I have to ask. What foxy ferreting have you come down to Mambury for ? "

" Foxy ferreting,'' Montague Nevitt repeated, drawing back as if stung, and profoundly astonished. " Why, what do you mean by that, Mr. Gildersleeve ? I don't understand you." The home-thrust was too true (after the great cross-examiner's well-known bullying manner) not to pierce him to the quick. "Who dares to say I go anywhere ferreting?"

"*I* do," Gilbert Gildersleeve answered, with assured confidence. "I say it, and I know it. You pitiful sneak, don't deny it to *me.* You were in the vestry this morning looking up the registers. Even *you,* with your false eyes, sir, daren't look me in the face and tell me you weren't. I saw you there myself. And I know you found in the books what you wanted, for you paid the clerk an extravagant fee. . . . What's that? You rat! Don't try to interrupt me. Don't try to bully me. It never succeeds. Montague Nevitt, I tell you I *won't* be bullied." And the great Q. C. put his foot down on the path with an elephantine solidity that made the prospect of bullying him seem tolerably unlikely. "I know the facts, and I'll stand no prevarication. Now, tell me, what vile use did you mean to make of your discovery this morning?"

Montague Nevitt drew back, fairly nonplussed for the moment by such a vigorous and unexpected attack on his flank. Resourceful as he was, even his cunning mind came wholly unprepared to this sudden cross-questioning. He felt his own physical inferiority to the big Q. C. more keenly just then, than he could ever have conceived it possible for a man of his type to feel it. After all, mind doesn't always trample over matter. Montague Nevitt was aware that that mountain of a man, with his six feet four of muscular humanity, fairly cowed and over-awed him at such very close quarters.

"I don't see what business it is of yours, Mr. Gildersleeve," he murmured, in a somewhat apologetic voice. "I may surely be allowed to hunt up questions of pedigree, of service in the end to myself and my friends, without *your* interference."

Gilbert Gildersleeve glared at him, and flared up all at once with righteous indignation.

"Of service in the end to yourself and your friends!" he cried, with unfeigned scorn, putting his own interpretation, as was natural, on the words. "Why, you cur! you reptile! you unblushing sneak! Do you mean to say openly you avow your intention of threatening and backmailing me, here—alone—to my face! You extortionate wretch! I wouldn't have believed even *you* in your heart would descend to such meanness."

Montague Nevitt, flurried and taken aback as he was, yet reflected vaguely with some wonder, as he listened and looked, what this sudden passion of disinterested zeal could betoken. Why such burning solicitude for Colonel Kelmscott's estate on the part of a man who was his avowed enemy? Even if Gwendoline meant to marry the young fellow Granville, with her father's consent, how could Nevitt himself levy blackmail upon Gilbert Gildersleeve by his knowledge of the two Warings' claim to the property? A complication, surely. Was there not some unexpected intricacy here which the cunning schemer himself didn't yet understand, but which might redound, if unraveled, to his greater advantage?

"Blackmail *you*, Mr. Gildersleeve," he cried, with a righteously indignant air. "That's an ugly word. I blackmail nobody, and least of all, the father of a lady whom I still regard, in spite of all she can say or do to make my life a blank, with affection and respect as profound as ever. How can my inquiries into the two Warings' affairs——"

Gilbert Gildersleeve crushed him with a sudden outburst of indignant wrath.

"You cad!" he cried, growing red in the face with horror and disgust. "You dare to speak so to me, and to urge such motives! But you've mistaken your man. I won't be bullied. If what you want is to use this vile knowledge you've so vilely ferreted out, as a lever to compel me to marry my daughter to you against her will, I can only tell you, you sneak, you're on the wrong tack. I will never consent to it. You may do your worst, but you will never bend me. I'm not a man to be bent or bullied—I won't be put down. I'll withstand you and defy you. You may ruin me, if you like, but you'll never break me. I stand here firm. Expose me, and I'll fight you to the bitter end; I'll fight you, and I'll conquer you."

He spoke with a fiery earnestness that Nevitt was only just beginning to understand. There was something in this. Here was a clew, indeed, to follow up and investigate. Surely, a menace to Granville Kelmscott's prospects could never have moved that heavy, phlegmatic, pachydermatous man to such an outburst of anger and suppressed fear.

"Expose *you* ?" Nevitt repeated, in a dazed and startled voice. "Expose *you*, my dear sir! I assure you, in truth, I don't understand you."

The barrister gazed down upon him with immeasurable scorn. "You liar!" he broke forth, almost choking at the words. "How dare you so pretend and prevaricate to my face? I *know* it's not true. My own daughter told me. She told me what you said to her—every word of your vile threats. You had the incredible meanness to terrify a poor helpless, and innocent girl by threatening to expose her mother's disgrace publicly. Only *you* could have done it; but you did it, you abject thing, you did it. She told me with her own lips you threatened to come down to Mambury, to hunt up the records. And she told me the truth; for I've seen you doing it."

A light broke slowly upon Montague Nevitt's mind. He drew a deep breath. This was good luck incredible. What Gilbert Gildersleeve meant he hadn't as yet, to be sure, the faintest conception. But it was clear they two were at cross-questions with one another. The secret Gilbert Gildersleeve thought he had come down to Mambury to discover was not the secret he had actually found out in the register that morning. It was nothing about the Kelmscotts or Guy and Cyril Waring; it was something about the great Q. C. and his wife themselves—presumably some unknown and disgraceful fact in Mrs. Gilbert Gildersleeve's early history.

And here was the cleverest lawyer at the English criminal bar just giving himself away—giving himself away unawares and telling him the secret, bit by bit, unconsciously.

This chance was too valuable for Mr. Montague Nevitt to lose. At all risks he must worm it out. He paused and temporized. His cue was now not to let Gilbert Gildersleeve see he didn't know his secret. He must draw on the Q. C. by obscure half-hints till he was inextricably entangled in a complete confession.

"I had no intention of terrifying Miss Gildersleeve, I'm sure," he said, in his blandest voice, with his best

,ompany smile, now recovering his equanimity exactly
in proportion as the barrister grew angrier. "I merely
desired to satisfy myself as to the salient facts, and to
learn their true bearing upon the family history. If I
spoke to her at all as to any knowledge I might possess
with regard to any other lady's early antecedents——"

Gilbert Gildersleeve's brow was black as night. His
great hands trembled and twitched convulsively. Was
ever blackguard so cynically candid in his avowal of the
basest crimes as this fine-spoken specimen of the culture
of Pall Mall in his open confession of that disgusting
insult to a young girl's innocence? Gilbert Gildersleeve,
who was at heart an honest man, loathed, and despised,
and scorned, and detested him.

"Do you dare to hint to me, then," he cried, every muscle
of his body quivering with just horror, "that you told
my own daughter you thought you had reason to suspect
her own mother's early antecedents?"

Montague Nevitt looked up at him with a quietly
sarcastic smile. "All's fair in love and war, you know,"
he said, not caring to commit himself.

That smile sealed his fate. With an irrepressible
impulse, Gilbert Gildersleeve sprang upon him. He
didn't mean to hurt the man : he sprang upon him merely
as the sole outlet for his own incensed and outraged
feelings. Those great hands seized him for a second by
the dainty white throat, and flung him back in anger.
Montague Nevitt fell heavily on a thick mass of bracken.
There was a gurgle, a gasp ; then his head lolled senseless.
He was very much hurt. That at least was certain.
The barrister stood over him for a minute, still purple in
the face. Montague Nevitt was white—very white and
deathlike. All at once it occurred to the big, strong man
that his hands—those great hands—were very fierce and
powerful. He had clutched Nevitt by the throat, half
unconsciously, with all his might, just to give him a
purchase as he flung the man from him. He looked at
him again. Great Heavens—what was this? It burst
over him at once. He woke to it with a wild start. The
fellow was dead! And the case was clearly manslaughter!

Justifiable homicide, if the jury knew all. But no
ury now could ever know all. And he had killed him

unawares . A great horror came over him. The man was dead—the man was dead; and he, Gilbert Gildersleeve, had unconsciously choked him.

He had no time to think. He had no time to calculate. His wrath was still hot, though rapidly cooling down before this awful discovery. Hide it! Hide it! Hide it! That was all he could think. He lifted the body in his arms as easily as most men would lift a baby. Then he laid it down among the brambles close beside the stream. Something heavy fell out of the pocket as he carried it. The barrister took no heed. Little matter for that. He laid it down in fear and trembling. As soon as it was hidden, he fled for his life. By trackless ways he walked over the moor, and returned to Ivybridge unseen very late in the evening. Ten minutes after he left the spot Guy Waring passed by and picked up the pocket-book.

CHAPTER XXV.

LEAD TRUMPS.

NATURALLY, under these circumstances, it was all in vain that Guy Waring pursued his investigations into Montague Nevitt's whereabouts. Neither at Plymouth nor anywhere else along the skirts of Dartmoor could he learn that anything more had been seen or heard of the man who called himself " Mr. McGregor." And yet Guy felt sure Nevitt wouldn't go far from Mambnry as things stood just then; for as soon as he missed the pocket-book containing the three thousand pounds, he would surely take some steps to recover it.

Two days later, however, Gilbert Gildersleeve sat in the hotel at Plymouth, where he had moved from Ivy-bridge after—well, as he phrased it to himself, after that unfortunate accident. The blustering Q. C. was like another man now. For the first time in his life he knew what it meant to be nervous and timid. Every sound made him suppress an involuntary start; for as yet he had heard no whisper of the body being discovered. He couldn't leave the neighborhood, however, till the murder was out. Dangerous as he felt it to be to remain on the spot, some strange spell seemed to bind him against his will to Dartmoor. He must stop and hear what local gossip had to say when the body came to light. And above all, for the present, he hadn't the courage to go home; he dared not face his own wife and daughter.

So he stayed on and lounged, and pretended to interest himself with walks over the hills and up the Tamar valley.

As he sat there in the billiard-room that day, a young fellow entered whom he remembered to have seen once or twice in London, at evening parties, with Montague

Nevitt. He turned pale at the sight—Gilbert **Gildersleeve** turned pale, that great red man. At first he
didn't even remember the young fellow's name; but it
came back to him in time that he was one Guy Waring.
It was a hard ordeal to meet him, but Gilbert Gildersleeve felt he must brazen it out. To slink away from
the young man would be to rouse suspicion. So they sat
and talked for a minute or two together, on indifferent
subjects, neither to say the truth, being very well pleased
to see the other under such peculiar circumstances. Then
Guy, who had the least reason for concealment of the two,
sauntered out for a stroll, with his heart still full of that
villain Nevitt, whose name, of course, he had never
mentioned to Gilbert Gildersleeve. And Gilbert Gildersleeve, for his part, had had equal cause for a correspond-
ing reticence as to their common acquaintance.

Just as Guy left the room, the landlord dropped in, and
began to talk with his guest about the latest new sensation.

"Heard the news, sir, this morning?" he asked, with
an important air. "Inspector's just told me. A case
very much in your line of business. Dead body's been
discovered at Mambury, choked and then thrown down
among the brake by the river. Name of McGregor—a
visitor from London. And they do say the police have a
clue to the murderer. Person who did it—"

Gilbert Gildersleeeve's heart gave a great bound within
him, and then stood stock-still; but by an iron effect of
will he suppressed all outer sign of his profound emotion.
He seemed to the observant eye merely interested and
curious, as the landlord finished his sentence carelessly
—"Person who did it's supposed to be a young man who
was at Mambury this week, of the name of Waring."

Gilbert Gildersleeve's heart gave another bound, still
more violent than before. But again he repressed with
difficulty all external symptoms of his profound agitation. This was very strange news. Then somebody
else was suspected instead of himself. In one way that
was bad; for Gilbert Gildersleeve had a conscience and
a sense of justice. But in another way, why, it would
save time for the moment, and divert attention from his
own personality. Better anything now than immediate

suspicion. In a week or two more every trace would be lost of his presence at Mambury.

" Waring," he said, thoughtfully, turning over the name to himself, as if he attached it to no particular individual, " Waring—Waring—Waring."

He paused and looked hard. Ha! so far good! It was clear the landlord didn't know Waring was the name of the young man who had just left the billiard-room. This was lucky, indeed, for if he *had* known it now, and had taxed Guy then and there, before his very own face, with being the murderer of this unknown person at Mambury, Gilbert Gildersleeve felt no course would have been open for him save to tell the whole truth on the spot unreservedly. Try as he would, he *couldn't* see another man arrested before his very eyes for the crime he himself had really, though almost unwittingly, committed.

" Waring," he repeated slowly, like one who endeavored to collect his scattered thoughts; " what sort of person was he, do you know? And how did the police come to get a clue to him?"

The landlord, nothing loth, went off into a long and circumstantial story of the discovery of the body, with minute details of how the innkeeper at Mambury had traced the supposed murderer (who gave no name) by an envelope which he'd left in his bedroom that evening. The county was up in arms about the affair to-day. All Dartmoor was being searched, and it was supposed the fellow was in hiding somewhere in the neighborhood of Tavistock or Oakhampton. They'd catch him by to-night. The landlord wouldn't be surprised, indeed, now he came to think of it, if his guest himself—here a very long long pause—were retained by and by for the prosecution.

Gilbert Gildersleeve drew a deep breath, unperceived. That was all, was it? The pause had unnerved him. He talked some minutes, as unconcernedly as he could, though trembling inwardly all the while, about the murder and the murderer. The landlord listened with profound respect to the words of legal wisdom as they dropped from his lips; for he knew Mr. Gildersleeve by common repute as one of the ablest and acutest of crim-

inal lawyers in all England. Then, after a short interval, the big, burly man, moving his guilty fingers nervously over the seal on his watch-chain, and assuming as
much as possible his ordinary air of blustering self-
assertion, asked in an off-hand fashion, "By the way,
let me see, I've some business to arrange ; what's the
number of my friend Mr. Billington's bedroom ?"

The landlord looked up with a little start of surprise. "Mr. Billington?" he said, hesitating. "We've
got no Mr. Billington."

Gilbert Gildersleeve smiled a sickly smile. It was neck
or nothing now. He must go right through with it.
"Oh, yes," he answered, with prompt conviction, playing
a dangerous card well—for how could he know what
name this young man Waring might possibly be passing
under? "The gentleman who was talking to me when
you came in just now. His name's Billington—though,
perhaps," he added after a pause, with a reflective air,
"he may have given you another one. Young men will
be young men. They've often some reason, when travelling, for concealing their names. Though Billington's
not the sort of fellow, to be sure, who's likely to be knocking about anywhere incognito."

The landlord laughed. "Oh we've plenty of that
sort," he replied, good-humoredly. "Both ladies and
gentlemen. It all makes trade. But your friend ain't
one of 'em. To tell you the truth, he didn't give any
name at all when he came to the hotel ; and we didn't ask
any. Billington, is it? Ah. Billington, Billington. I
knew a Billington myself once, a trainer at Newmarket.
Well he's a very pleasant young man, nice-spoken, and
that ; but I don't fancy he's quite right in his head,
somehow."

With instinctive cleverness, Gilbert Gildersleeve
snatched at the opening at once. "Ah, no, poor fellow,"
he said, shaking his head sympathetically, "youv'e found
that out already, have you? Well, he's subject to delusions a bit; mere harmless delusions ; but he's not at all
dangerous. Excitable, very when anything odd turns
up; he'll be calling himself Waring and giving himself
in charge for this murder, I dare say, when he comes to
hear of it. But as good-hearted a fellow as ever lived

though only a trifle obstinate. If you've any difficulty
with him at any time, just send for me. I've known him
from a boy. He'll do anything I tell him."

It was a critical game, but Gilbert Gildersleeve saw
something definite must be done, and he trusted to bluster
and a well-known name to carry him through with it.
And, indeed, he had said enough. From that moment
forth the landlord's suspicions were never even so much
as aroused by the innocent young man with the preoccupied manner who knew Mr. Gildersleeve. The great
Q. C.'s word was guarantee enough—for any one but
himself. And the great Q. C. himself knew it. Why, a
chance word from his lips was enough to protect Guy
Waring from suspicion. Who would ever believe, then,
anything so preposterously improbable as that the great
Q. C. himself was the murderer?

Not the police, you may be sure; nor the Plymouth
landlord.

He went out into the town, with his mind now filled
full of a curious scheme. A plan of campaign loomed
up visibly before him. Waring was suspected. Therefore Waring must somehow have given cause for suspicion. Well, Waring was a friend of Montague Nevitt's,
and had evidently been at Mambury, either with him or
without him, immediately before the—h'm—the unfortunate accident. But as soon as Waring came to learn
of the discovery of the body, which he would be sure to
do from the papers that evening at latest, he would see
at once the full strength of whatever suspicions might
tell against him. Now Gilbert Gildersleeve's experience
of criminal cases had abundantly shown him that a suspected person, even when innocent, always has one fixed
desire in his head—to gain time, anyhow. So Waring
would naturally wish to gain time, at whatever cost.
There were evidently circumstances connecting Waring
with the crime; there were none at all, known to the
outer world, connecting the eminent lawyer. Therefore,
the eminent lawyer argued to himself, as coolly almost
as if it had been somebody else's case, not his own, he
was conducting—therefore, if an immediate means of
escape is provided for Waring, Waring will almost undoubtedly fall blindfold into it.

Not that he meant to let Guy pay the penalty in the
end for his own rash crime. He was no hardened villain.
He had still a conscience.   If the worst came to the
worst, he said to himself, he would tell all, openly, rather
than let an innocent man suffer.   But, like everything
else, in accordance with his own inference from his ob-
servation of others, he, too, wanted to gain time, anyhow; and if he could but gain time by kindly helping Guy
to escape for the present, why, he would gladly do so.
An innocent man may be suspected for the moment, Gilbert Gildersleeve thought to himself, with a lawyer's
blind confidence; but under our English law he need
never at least fear that the suspicion will be permanent.
For lawyers repeat their own incredible commonplaces
about the absolute perfection of English law so often that
at last, by a sort of retributive nemesis, they really almost come to believe him.

Filled with these ideas, then, which rose naturally up
in his mind without his taking the trouble, as it were,
definitely to prove them, Gilbert Gildersleeve hurried on
through the crowded streets of Plymouth town, till he
reached the office of the London and South Africa
Steamship Company.   There he entered with an air of
decided business, and asked to take a passage to Cape
Town at once by the steamer *Cetewayo,* due to call at
Plymouth, outward bound that evening.   He had looked
up particulars of sailing in the papers at the hotel, and
asked now, as if for himself, for a large and roomy berth,
with all his usual self-possession and boldness of manner.   The clerk gazed at him carelessly; that big and
burly man with the great awkward hands raised no picture in his brain of the supposed murderer of McGregor
in the wood at Mambury as that murderer had been described to him by the police that morning, from a verbal
portrait after the landlord of the Talbot Arms.   This
colossal, red-faced, loud-spoken person, who required a
large and roomy berth, was certainly not the rather slim
young man, a little above the medium height, with a
dark mustache and a gentle, musical voice, whom the
innkeeper had seen in an excited mood on the hunt for
McGregor along the slopes of Dartmoor.

"What name?" the clerk asked, briskly, after Gilbert

Gildersleeve had selected his stateroom from the plan,
with some show of interest as to its being well amidships
and not too near the noise of the engines.

"Billington," the barrister answered, without a glimmer of hesitation. "Arthur Standish Billington, if you
want the full name. Thirty-two will suit me very well,
I think, and I'll pay for it now. Go aboard when she's
sighted, I suppose; nine o'clock or thereabouts."

The clerk made out the ticket in the name he was told.
"Yes, nine o'clock," he said, curtly. "All luggage to be
on board the tender by eight sharp. You've left taking
your passage very late, Mr. Billington. Lucky we've a
room that'll suit you, I'm sure. It isn't often we have
berths left amidships like this on the day of sailing."

Gilbert Gildersleeve pretended to look unconcerned
once more. "No, I suppose not," he answered, in a careless voice. "People generally know their own minds
rather longer beforehand. But I'd a telegram from the
Cape this morning that calls me over immediately."

He folded up his ticket, and put it in his pocket. Then
he pulled out a roll of notes, and paid the amount in full.
The clerk gave him change promptly. Nobody could
ever have suspected so solid a man as the great Q. C. of
any more serious crime or misdemeanor than shirking
the second service on Sunday evening. There was a
ponderous respectability about his portly build that defied
detection. The agents of all the steamboat companies
had been warned that morning that the slim young man
of the name of Waring might try to escape at the last
moment. But who could ever suspect this colossal pile,
in the British churchwarden style of human architecture,
of aiding and abetting the escape of the young man
Waring from the pervasive myrmidons of English justice? The very idea was absurd. Gilbert Gildersleeve's
waistcoat was above suspicion.

And when Guy Waring returned to his room at the
Duke of Devonshire Hotel half an hour later, in complete
ignorance as yet of the bare fact of the murder, he found
on his table an envelope addressed in an unknown hand,
"Guy Waring, Esq.," while below, in the corner, twice
underlined were the importunate words, *"Immediate!
Important!"*

Guy tore it open in wonder. What on earth could this mean? He trembled as he read. Could Cyril have learnt all? Or had Nevitt, that double-dyed traitor, now trebled his treachery by informing against the man whom he had driven into a crime? Guy couldn't imagine what it all could be driving at, for there, before his eyes, in a round, schoolboy hand, very carefully formed, without the faintest trace of anything like character, were the words of this strange and startling message, whose origin and intent were alike a mystery to him.

" Guy Waring, a warrant is out for your apprehension. Fly at once, or things may be worse for you. It is something always to gain time for the moment. You will avoid suspicion, public scandal, trial. Enclosed find a ticket for Cape Town by the *Cetewayo* to-night. She sails at nine. Luggage to be on board the tender by eight, sharp If you go, all can yet be satisfactorily cleared up. If you stay, the danger is great, and may be very serious Ticket is taken (and paid for) in the name of Arthur Standish Billington. Settle your account at the hotel in that name and go.

" Yours, in frantic haste,
" A SINCERE WELL-WISHER."

Guy gazed at the strange missive long and dubiously. " A warrant is out." He scarcely knew what to do Oh, for time, time, time! Had Cyril sent this? Or was it some final device of that fiend Nevitt?

CHAPTER XXVI.

A CHANCE MEETING.

THERE wasn't much time left, however, for Guy to make up his mind in. He must decide at once. Should he accept this mysterious warning or not? Pure fate decided it. As he hesitated he heard a boy crying in the street. It was the special-edition fiend calling his evening paper. The words the boy said Guy didn't altogether catch; but the last sentence of all fell on his ear distinctly. He started in horror. It was an awful sound: "Warrant issued to-day for the apprehension of Waring."

Then the letter, whoever wrote it, was not all a lie. The forgery was out. Cyril or the bankers had learnt the whole truth. He was to be arrested to-day as a common felon. All the world knew his shame. He hid his face in his hands. Come what might, he must accept the mysterious warning now. He would take the ticket, and go off to South Africa.

In a moment a whole policy had arisen like a cloud and framed itself in his mind. He was a forger, he knew, and by this time Cyril too most probably knew it. But he had the three thousand pounds safe and sound in his pocket, and those at least he could send back to Cyril. With them he could send a check on his own banker for three thousand more; not that there were funds there at present to meet the demand; but if the unknown benefactor should pay in the six thousand he promised within the next few weeks, then Cyril could repay himself from that hypothetical fortune. On the other hand, Guy didn't disguise from himself the strong possibility that the unknown benefactor might now refuse to pay in the six thousand. In that case, Guy said to himself with a groan, he would take to the diamond fields, and never rest day or night in his self-imposed task till he had made enough to repay Cyril in full the missing three thousand, and to make up the other three thousand he still owed the creditors of the Rio Negro Company. After which, he would return and give himself up like a man, to stand his trial voluntarily for the crime he had committed.

It was a young man's scheme, very fond and youthful; but with the full confidence of his age he proceeded at once to put it in practice. Indeed, now he came to think upon it, he fancied to himself he saw something like a solution of the mystery in the presence of the great Q. C. at Plymouth that morning. Cyril had found out all, and had determined to save time. The bankers had found out all, and had determined to prosecute. They had consulted Gildersleeve. Gildersleeve had come down on a holiday trip, and had run up against him at Plymouth by pure accident. Indeed, Guy remembered now that the great Q. C. looked not a little surprised and excited at meeting him. Clearly Gildersleeve had communicated with the police at once; hence the issue of the warrant. At the same time the writer of the letter, whoever he might be —and Guy now believed he was sent down by Cyril, or in Cyril's interest—the writer had found out the facts betimes, and had taken a passage for him in the name of Billington. Uncertain as he felt about the minor details, Guy was sure this interpretation must be right in the main. For Elma's sake—for the honor of the family— Cyril wished him for the present to disappear. Cyril's wish was sacred. He would go to South Africa.

The great point was now to avoid meeting Gildersleeve before the ship sailed. So he would pay his bill quietly, put his things in his portmanteau, stop in his room till dusk, and then drive off in a closed cab to the landing-stage.

But, first of all, he must send the three thousand direct to Cyril.

He sat down in a fit of profound penitence, and penned a heartbroken letter of confession to his brother.

It was vague, of course; such letters are always vague; no man, even in confessing, likes to allude in plain terms to the exact nature of the crime he has committed; and besides, Guy took it for granted that Cyril knew all

about the main features of the case already. He didn't
ask his brother to forgive him, he said; he didn't try to
explain, for explanation would be impossible. How he
came to do it, he had no idea himself. A sudden suggestion—a strange, unaccountable impulse—a minute or
two of indecision—and almost before he knew it, under
the spell of that strange eye the thing was done, irre-
trievably done forever. The best he could offer now
was to express his profound and undying regret at the
wrong he had committed, and by which he had never
profited himself a single farthing. Nevitt had deceived
him with incredible meanness; he could never have be
lieved any man would act as Nevitt had acted. Nevitt
had stolen three thousand pounds of the sum, and applied
them to paying off his own debt to the Rio Negro
creditors. The remaining three thousand, sent herewith, Guy had recovered, almost by a miracle, from that
false creature's grasp, and he returned them now, in
proof of the fact, in Montague Nevitt's own pocket-book,
which Cyril will no doubt immediately recognize. For
himself, he meant to leave England at once, at least for
the present. Where he was going he wouldn't as yet
let Cyril know. He hoped in a new country to recover
his honor and rehabilitate his name. Meanwhile, it was
mainly for Cyril's sake that he fled—and for one other
person's too—to avoid a scandal. He hoped Cyril would
be happy with the woman of his choice; for it was to
insure their joint happiness that he was accepting the
offer of escape so unexpectedly tendered him.

He sealed up the letter—that incriminating letter,
that might mean so much more than he ever put to it—
and took it out to the post, with the three thousand
pounds and Montague Nevitt's pocket-book in a separated
packet. Proud Kelmscott as he was by birth and nature,
he slunk through the streets like a guilty man, fancying
all eyes were fixed suspiciously upon him. Then he
returned to the hotel in a burning heat, went into the
smoking-room on purpose like an honest man, and rang
the bell for the servant boldly.

"Bring my bill, please," he said to the waiter who
answered it. "I go at seven o'clock."

"Yes, sir," the waiter replied, with official promptitude. "Directly, sir. What number?"

"I forgot the number," Guy answered, with a beating heart; "but the name's Billington."

"Yes, sir," the waiter responded once more in the self-same, unvaried tone, and went off to the office.

Guy waited in profound suspense, half expecting the waiter to come back for the number again; but, to his immense surprise and mystification, the fellow didn't. Instead of that, he returned some minutes later, all respectful attention, bringing the bill on a salver, duly headed and lettered, "Mr. Billington, number 40." In unspeakable trepidation, Guy paid it and walked away. Never before in all his life had he been surrounded so close on every side by a thick hedge of impenetrable and inexplicable mystery.

Then a new terror seized him. Was he running his head into a noose, blindfold? Who was the Billington he was thus made to personate, and who must really be staying at the very same time in the Duke of Devonshire? Was this just another of Nevitt's wily tricks? Had he induced his victim to accept without question the name and character of some still more open criminal?

There was no time now, however, to draw back or to hesitate. The die was cast; he must stand by its arbitrament. He had decided to go, and on that hasty decision had acted in a way that was practically irrevocable. He put his things together with trembling hands, called a cab by the porter, and drove off alone in a turmoil of doubt, to the landing-stage in the harbor.

Policemen not a few were standing about on the pier and in the streets as he drove past openly. But in spite of the fact that a warrant had been issued for his apprehension, none of them took the slightest apparent notice of him. He wondered much at this. But there was really no just cause for wonder. For at least an hour earlier the police had ceased to look out any longer for Nevitt's murderer. And the reason they had done so was simply this: a telegram had come down from Scotland Yard in the most positive terms, "Waring arrested this afternoon at Dover. The murdered man

McGregor is now certainly known to be Montague Nevitt, a bank clerk in London. Endeavor to trace Waring's line of retreat from Mambury to Dover by inquiry of the railway officials. We are sure of our man. Photographs will be forwarded you by post immediately."

And as a matter of fact, at the very moment when Guy was driving down to the tender, in order to escape from an imaginary charge of forgery, his brother Cyril, to his own immense astonishment, was being conveyed from Dover pier to Tavistock, under close police escort, on a warrant charging him with the wilful murder of Montague Nevitt, two days before, at Mambury, in Devon.

If Guy had only known that, he would never have fled. But he didn't know it. How could he, indeed, in his turmoil and hurry? He didn't even know Montague Nevitt was dead. He had been too busy that day to look at the papers. And the few facts he knew from the boy's crying in the street he naturally misinterpreted, by the light of his own fears and personal dangers. He thought he was " wanted " for the yet undiscovered forgery, not for the murder, of which he was wholly ignorant.

Nevertheless, we can never in this world entirely escape our own personality. As Guy went on board, believing himself to have left his identity on shore, he heard somebody, in a voice that he fancied he knew, ask a newsboy on the tender for an evening paper. Guy was the only passenger who embarked at Plymouth ; and this person unseen was the newsboy's one customer.

Guy couldn't discover who he was at the moment, for the call for a paper came from the upper deck ; he only heard the voice, and wasn't certain at first that he recognized even that any more than as a vague and indeterminate reminiscence. No doubt the sense of guilt made him preternaturally suspicious. But he began to fear that somebody might possibly recognize him. And he had bought the paper with news about the warrant. That was bad ; but 'twas too late to draw back again now. The tender lay alongside a while, discharging her mails, and then cast loose to go. The *Cetewayo's* screw began to move through the water. With a dim sense of horror Guy knew they were off. He was well under way for far distant South Africa.

But he did *not* know or reflect that while he ploughed his path on over that trackless sea, day after day, without news from England, there would be ample time for Cyril to be tried, and found guilty, and perhaps hanged as well, for the crime that neither of them had really committed.

The great ship steamed out, cutting the waves with her prow, and left the harbor lights far behind her. Guy stood on deck and watched them disappearing with very mingled feelings. Everything had been so hurried, he hardly knew himself as yet how his flight affected all the active and passive characters in this painful drama. He only knew he was irrevocably committed to the voyage now. There would be no chance of turning till they reached Cape Town, or at the very least Madeira.

He stood on deck and looked back. Somebody else in an ulster stood not far off, near a light by the saloon, conversing with an officer. Guy recognized at once the voice of the man who had asked in the harbor for an evening paper. At that moment a steward came up as he stood there, on the look-out for the new passenger they'd just taken in. "You're in thirty-two, sir, I think," he said, "and your name—"

"Is Billington," Guy answered, with a faint tremor of shame at the continued falsehood.

The man who had bought the paper turned round sharply and stared at him. Their eyes met in one quick flash of unexpected recognition. Guy started in horror. This was an awful meeting. He had seen the man but once before in his life, yet he knew him at a glance. It was Granville Kelmscott.

For a minute or two they stood and stared at one another blankly, those unacknowledged half-brothers, of whom one now knew, while the other did not guess, the real relationship that existed between them. Then Granville Kelmscott turned away without one word of greeting. Guy trembled in his shame. He knew he was discovered. But before his very eyes, Granville took the paper he had been reading by that uncertain light, and raising it high in his hand, flung it over into the sea

with spasmodic energy. It was the special edition containing the account of the man McGregor's death and
Guy Waring's supposed connection with the murder.
Granville Kelmscott, indeed, couldn't bring himself to
denounce his own half-brother. He stared at him coldly
for a second with a horrified face.

Then he said in a very low and distant voice, "I know
your identity, Mr. Billington," with a profoundly sarcastic accent on the assumed name, "and I will not betray
it. I know your secret, too; and I will keep that inviolate. Only, during the rest of this voyage, do me the
honor, I beg of you, not to recognize me or speak to me
in any way at any time."

Guy slunk away in silence to his own cabin. Never
before in his life had he known such shame. He felt
that his punishment was indeed too heavy for him.

CHAPTER XXVII.

SOMETHING TO THEIR ADVANTAGE.

A<small>T</small> Tilgate and Chetwood next morning two distin·
guished households were thrown into confusion by the
news in the papers. To Colonel Kelmscott and to Elma
Clifford alike that news came with crushing force and
horror. A murder, said the *Times*, had been committed
in Devonshire, in a romantic dell, on the skirts of Dartmoor. No element of dramatic interest was wanting to
the case; persons, place, and time were all equally remarkable. The victim of the outrage was Mr. Montague Nevitt, confidential clerk to Messrs. Drummond,
Coutts, and Barclay, the well-known bankers, and himself a familiar figure in musica. society in London. The
murderer was presumably a young journalist, Mr. Guy
Waring, not unknown himself in musical circles, and
brother of that rising landscape painter, Mr. Cyril Waring, whose pictures of wild life in forest scenery had
lately attracted considerable attention at the Academy
and the Grosvenor. Mr. Guy Waring had been arrested the day before on the pier at Dover, where he had
just arrived by the Ostend packet. It was supposed by
the police that he had hastily crossed the Channel from
Plymouth to Cherbourg, soon after the murder, to escape detection, and after journeying by cross-country
routes through France and Belgium, had returned *via*
Ostend to the shores of England. It was a triumphant
vindication of our much-maligned English detective system that within a few hours after the discovery of the
body on Dartmoor, the supposed criminal should have
been recognized, arrested, and detained among a thousand
others, in a busy port, at the very opposite extremity of
Southern England.

Colonel Kelmscott that day was strangely touched, even before he took up his morning paper. A letter from Granville, posted at Plymouth, had just reached him by the early mail, to tell him that the only son he had ever really loved or cared for on earth had sailed the day before, a disinherited outcast, to seek his fortune in the wild wastes of Africa. How he could break the news to Lady Emily he couldn't imagine. The Colonel, twisting his white moustache with a quivering hand on his tremulous lips, hardly dared to realize what their future would seem like. And then—he turned to the paper, and saw to his horror this awful tale of a cold-blooded and cowardly murder, committed on a friend by one who, however little he might choose to acknowledge it, was after all his own eldest son, a Kelmscott of Tilgate, as much as Granville himself, in lawful wedlock duly begotten.

The proud but broken man gazed at the deadly announcement in blank amaze and agony. His Nemesis had come. Guy Waring was his own son; and Guy Waring was a murderer.

He tried to argue with himself at first that this tragic result in some strange way justified him, after the event, for his own long neglect of his paternal responsibilities. The young man was no true Kelmscott at heart, he was sure, or such an act as that would have revolted and appalled him. He was no true son in reality; his order disowned him. Base blood flowed in his veins, and made crimes like these conceivable.

"I was right after all," the Colonel thought, "not to acknowledge these half low-born lads as the heirs of Tilgate. Bad blood will out in the end—and *this* is the result of it."

And then, with sudden revulsion he thought once more—God help him! How could he say such things in his heart even now of *her*, his pure, trustful Lucy? She was better than him in her soul, he knew—ten thousand times better. If bad blood came in anywhere it came in from himself, not from that simple-hearted, innocent little country-bred angel.

And perhaps if he'd treated these lads as he ought and brought them up to their own, and made them Kelmscotts indeed, instead of nameless adventures, they

might never have fallen into such abysses of turpitude.
But he had let them grow up in ignorance of their own
origin, with the vague stain of a possible illegitimacy
hanging over their heads; and what wonder if they forgot
in the end that *noblesse oblige*, and sank at last into foul
depths of vice and criminality?

As he read on, his head swam with the cumulative
evidence of that deliberately planned and cruelly ex-
ecuted yet brutal murder. The details of the crime gave
him a sickening sense of loathing and incredulity. Impossible that his own son could have schemed and carried
out so vile an attack upon a helpless person, who had
once been his nearest and dearest companion. And yet,
the account in the paper gave him no alternative but to
believe it. Nevitt and Guy Waring had been in-
separable friends. They had dined together, supped
together, played duets in their own rooms, gone out to
the same parties, belonged to the same club, in all things
been closer than even the two twin brothers. Some
quarrel seemed to have arisen about a matter of speculations in which both had suffered. They separated at once
—separated in anger. Nevitt went down to Devonshire
by himself for his holiday. Then Waring followed
him, without any pretence at concealment; inquired
for him at the village inn with expressions of deadly
hate; tracked him to a lonely place in the adjacent woods;
choked him, apparently with some form of garrotte or
twisted rope,—for the injuries seemed greater than even
the most powerful man could possibly inflict with the
hands alone,—and hid the body of his murdered friend
at last in a mossy dell by the bank of the streamlet.
Nor was that all; for with callous effrontery he had returned to the inn, still inquiring after his victim; and
had gone off next morning early with a lie on his lips,
pretending even then to nurse his undying wrath and to
be bent on following up with coarse threats of revenge
his stark and silent enemy.

So far the *Times*. But to Colonel Kelmscott, reading
in between the lines as he went, there was more in it
than even that. He saw, though dimly, some hint of a
motive. For it was at Mambury that all these things
had taken place; and it was at Mambury that the secret

of Guy Waring's descent lay buried, as he thought, in the parish registers. What it all meant, Colonel Kelmscott couldn't indeed wholly understand; but many things he knew which the writer of the account in the *Times* knew not. He knew that Nevitt was a clerk in the bank where he himself kept his account, and to which he had given orders to pay in the six thousand to Cyril's credit at Cyril's banker's. He knew, therefore, that Nevitt might thus have been led to suspect the real truth of the case as to the two so-called Warings. He knew that Cyril had just received the six thousand. Trying to put these facts together and understand their meaning, he utterly failed; but this much at least was clear to him, he thought—the reason for the murder was something connected with a search for the entry of his own clandestine marriage.

He looked down at the paper again. Great heavens! what was this? "It is rumored that a further inducement to the crime may perhaps be sought in the fact that the deceased gentleman had a large sum of money in his possession in Bank of England notes at the time of his death. These notes he carried in a pocket-book about his person, where they were seen by the landlord of the Talbot Arms at Mambury, the night before the supposed murder. When the body was discovered by the side of the brook two days later, the notes were gone. The pockets were carefully searched by order of the police, but no trace of the missing money could be discovered. It is now conjectured that Mr. Guy Waring, who is known to have lost heavily in the Rio Negro Diamond Mines, may have committed the crime from purely pecuniary motives, in order to release himself from his considerable and very pressing financial embarrassments."

The paper dropped from Colonel Kelmscott's hands. His eyes ceased to see. His arm fell rigid. This last horrible suggesstion proved too much for him to bear. He shrank from it like poison. That a son of his own, unacknowledged or not, should be a criminal—a murderer—was terrible enough; but that he should even be suspected of having committed murder for such base and vulgar motives as mere thirst of gain was more than the blood of the Kelmscotts could put up with. The unhappy father had said to himself in his agony at first that if Guy really killed that prying bank clerk at all, it was no doubt in defence of his mother's honor. *That* was a reason a Kelmscott could understand. That, if not an excuse, was at least a palliation. But to be told he had killed him for a roll of bank-notes—oh, horrible, incredible! his reason drew back at it. That was a depth to which the Kelmscott idiosyncrasy could never descend. The Colonel in his horror refused to believe it.

He put his hands up feebly to his throbbing brow. This was a ghastly idea—a ghastly accusation. The men called Waring had dragged the honor of the Kelmscotts through the mud of the street. There was but one comfort left. He never bore that unsullied name. Nobody would know he was a Kelmscott of Tilgate.

The Colonel rose from his seat, and staggered across the floor. Half way to the door he reeled and stopped short. The veins of his forehead were black and swollen.

He had the same strange feeling in his head as he experienced on the day when Granville left—only a hundred times worse. The two halves of his brain were opening and shutting. His temples seemed too full; he fancied there was something wrong with his forehead somewhere. He reeled once more, like a drunken man. Then he clutched at a chair and sat down. His brain was flooded.

He collapsed all at once, mumbling to himself some inarticulate gibberish. Half an hour later, the servants came in and found him. He was seated in his chair, still doddering feebly. The house was roused. A doctor was summoned, and the Colonel put to bed. Lady Emily watched him with devoted care. But it was all in vain. The doctor shook his head the moment he examined him. " A paralytic stroke," he said, gravely; " and a very serious one. He seems to have had a slighter attack some time since, and to have wholly neglected it. A great blood-vessel in the brain must have given way with a rush. I can hold out no hope. He won't live till morning."

And indeed, as it turned out, about ten that night the Colonel's loud and stertorous breathing began to fail slowly. The intervals grew longer and longer between each recurrent gasp, and life died away at last in imperceptible struggles.

By two in the moring, Kelmscott of Tilgate lay dead on his bed ; and his two unacknowledged and unrecognized sons were the masters of his property.

But one of them was at that moment being tossed about wildly on the waves of Biscay; and the other was locked up on a charge of murder in the county jail at Tavistock, in Devonshire.

Meanwhile, at the other house at Chetwood,where these tidings were being read with almost equal interest, Elma Clifford laid down the paper on the table with a very pale face, and looked at her mother. Mrs. Clifford, all solicitous watchfulness for the effect on Elma, looked in return with searching eyes at her daughter. Then Elma, opened her lips like one who talks in her sleep, and spoke out twice in two short, disconnected sentences. The first time she said simply " He didn't do it, I know," and the second time, with all the intensity of her emotional nature, " Mother, mother, whatever turns up, I *must* go there."

" *He* will be there," Mrs. Clifford interposed after a painful pause.

And Elma answered dreamily with her great eyes far away, " Yes, of course I know he will. And I must be there, too, to see how far, if at all, I can help them."

" Yes, darling," her mother replied, stroking her hair with a caressing hand. She knew that when Elma spoke in a tone like that no power on earth could possibly restran her.

CHAPTER XXVIII.

MISTAKEN IDENTITY.

To Cyril Waring himself the arrest at Dover came as an immense surprise; rather a surprise, indeed, than a shock just at first, for he could only treat it as a mistaken identity. The man the police wanted was Guy, not himself; and that Guy should have done it was clearly incredible.

As he landed from the Ostend packet, recalled to England unexpectedly by the announcement that the Rio Negro Diamond Mines had gone with a crash—and no doubt involved Guy in the common ruin—Cyril was astonished to find himself greeted on the Admiralty Pier by a policeman, who tapped him on the shoulder with the casual remark, " I think your name's Waring."

Cyril answered at once, " yes, my name's Waring."

It didn't occur to him at the moment that the man meant to arrest him.

" Then you're wanted," the minion of authority answered, seizing his arm rather gruffly. " We've got a warrant out to-day against you, my friend. You'd better come along with me quietly to the station."

" A warrant!" Cyril repeated, amazed, shaking off the man's hand. " There must be some mistake somewhere."

The policeman smiled. " Oh, yes," he answered, briskly, with some humor in his tone. " There's always a mistake, of course, in all these arrests. You never get a hold of the right man just at first. It's sure to be a case of his twin brother. But there ain't no mistake this time, don't you fear. I knowed you at once, when I see you, by your photograph. Though we were looking out

for you, to be sure, going the other way. But it's you all
right. There ain't a doubt about that. Warrant in the
name of Guy Waring, gentleman : wanted for the wilful
murder of a man unknown, said to be one McGregor, *alias*
Montague Nevitt, on the 27th instant, at Mambury, in
Devonshire."

Cyril gave a sudden start at the conjunction of names,
which naturally increased his captor's suspicions. "But
there *is* a mistake, though," he said, angrily, "even on
your own showing. You've got the wrong man. It's not
I that am wanted. My name's Cyril Waring, and Guy
is my brother's. Though Guy can't have murdered Mr.
Nevitt, either, if it comes to that; they were most intimate friends. However, that's neither here nor there.
I'm Cyril, not Guy; I'm not your prisoner."

"Oh, yes, you are, though," the officer answered, holding his arm very tight, and calling mutely for assistance
by a glance at the other policeman. "I've got your photograph in my pocket right enough. Here's the man we've
orders to arrest at once. I suppose you won't deny,
now, that's your living image."

Cyril glanced at the photograph with another start of
surprise. Sure enough, it *was* Guy ; his last new cabinet
portrait. The police must be acting under some gross
misapprehension.

"That man's my brother," he said, confidently, brushing
the photograph aside. "I can't understand it at all.
This is extremely odd. It's impossible my brother can
even be suspected of committing murder."

The policeman smiled cynically. "Well, it ain't impossible your brother's brother can be suspected, anyhow,"
he said, with a quiet air of superior knowledge. "The
good old double trick's been tried on once too often. If
I was you, I wouldn't say too much. Whatever you say
may be used as evidence at the trial against you. You
just come along quietly to the station with me—take his
other arm, Jim ; that's right ; no violence please, prisoner
—and we'll pretty soon find out whether you're the man
we've got orders to arrest, or his twin brother." And he
winked at his ally He was proud of having effected the
catch of the season.

"But I *am* his twin brother," Cyril said, half struggling

still to release himself. " You can't take me up on that warrant, I tell you. It's not my name. I'm not the man you've orders to look for."

" Oh, that's all right," the constable answered as before, with an incredulous smile. " Don't you go trying to obstruct the police in the exercise of their duty. If I can't take you up on the warrant as it stands, well, anyhow,I can arrest you on suspicion all the same, for looking so precious like the photograph of the man as is wanted. Twin brothers ain't got any call, don't you know, to sit, turn about, for one another's photographs. It hinders the administration of justice; that's where it is. And remember, whatever you choose to say may be used as evidence at the trial against you."

Thus adjured, Cyril yielded at last to *force majeure* and walked arm in arm between the two policeman, followed by a large and admiring crowd, to the nearest station.

But the matter was far less easily arranged than at first imagined. An innocent man who knows his own innocence, taken up in mistake for a brother whom he believes to be equally incapable of the crime with which he is charged, naturally expects to find no difficulty at all in proving his identity and escaping from custody on a false charge of murder. But the result of a hasty examination at the station soon effectually removed this little delusion. His own admission that the photograph was a portrait of Guy, and his resemblance to it in every leading particular, made the authorities decide on the first blush of the thing this was really the man Scotland Yard was in search of. He was trying to escape them on the ridiculous pretext that he was in point of fact his own twin brother. The inspector declined to let him go for the night. He wasn't going to repeat the mistake that was made in the Lefroy case, he said very decidedly. He would send the suspected person under escort to Tavistock.

So to Tavistock Cyril went, uncertain as yet what all this could mean, and ignorant of the crime with which he was charged, if indeed any crime had been really committed. All the way down, an endless string of questions suggested themselves one by one to his excited mind. Was Nevitt really dead? And if so, who had killed him? Was it suicide to escape from the monetary embarrassments brought about by the failure of the Rio Negro Diamond Mines, or was it accident or mischance? Or was it in fact a murder? And in any case—strangest of all—where was Guy? Why didn't Guy come forward and court inquiry? For as yet, of course, Cyril hadn't received his brother's letter, with the incriminating pocket-book and the three thousand pounds; nor indeed, for several days after, as things turned out, was there even a possibility of his ever receiving it.

Next morning, however, when Cyril was examined before the Tavistock magistrates, he began to realize the whole strength of the case against him. The proceedings were purely formal, as the lawyers said; yet they were quite enough to make Cyril's cheek turn pale with horror. One witness after another came forward and swore to him. The station-master at Mambury gave evidence that he had made inquiries on the platform after Nevitt by name; the inn-keeper deposed as to his excited behavior when he called at the Talbot Arms, and his recognition of Mc-Gregor as the person he was in search of, the boy of whom Guy had inquired at the gate unhesitatingly set down the conversation to Cyril. None of them had the faintest doubt in his own mind (each swore) that the prisoner before the magistrates was the self-same person who went over to Mambury on that fatal day, and who followed Montague Nevitt down the path by the river.

As Cyril listened, one terrible fact dawned clearer and clearer upon his brain. Every fragment of evidence they piled up against himself made the case against Guy look blacker and blacker.

The magistrates accepted the proofs thus tendered, and Cyril, as yet unassisted by professional advice, was remanded accordingly till next morning.

Just as he was about to leave the Sessions House in a tumult of horror, fear, and suspense, somebody close by tapped him on the shoulder gravely, after a few whispered words with the chairman and the magistrates. Cyril turned round, and saw a burly man with very large hands, whom he remembered to have had pointed out to him in London, and, strange to say, by Montague Nevitt himself, as the eminent Q.C., Mr. Gilbert Gildersleeve.

The great advocate was pale, but very sincere and

earnest. Cyril noticed his manner was completely changed. It was clear some overmastering idea possessed his soul.

" Mr. Waring," he said, looking him full in the face. " I see you're unrepresented. This is a case in which I take a very deep interest. My conduct's unprofessional, I know,—point-blank against all our recognized etiquette, —but perhaps you'll excuse it. Will you allow me to undertake your defence in this matter ? "

Cyril turned round to him with truly heartfelt thanks. It was a great relief to him, alone and in doubt, and much wondering about Guy, to hear a friendly word from whatever quarter.

And Cyril knew he was safe in Gilbert Gildersleeve's hands : the greatest criminal lawyer of the day in England might surely be trusted to set right such a mere little error of mistaken identity. Though for Guy— whenever Guy gave himself up to the police—Cyril felt the position was far more dangerous. He couldn't believe indeed, that Guy was guilty ; yet the circumstances, he could no longer conceal from himself, looked terribly black against him.

" You're too good," he cried, taking the lawyer's hand in his with very fervent gratitude. " How can I thank you enough ? I'm deeply obliged to you."

" Not at all," Gilbert Gildersleeve answered, with very blanched lips. He was ashamed of his duplicity. " You've nothing to thank me for. The case is a simple one, and I'd like to see you out of it. I've met your brother ; and the moment I saw you I knew you weren't he, though you're very like him. I should know you two apart wherever I saw you."

" That's curious," Cyril cried, " for very few people know us from one another, except the most intimate friends."

The Q. C. looked at him with a very penetrating glance. " I had occasion to see your brother not long since," he answered, slowly, " and his features and expression fastened themselves indelibly on my mind's eye. I should know you from him at a glance. This case, as you say, is one of mistaken identity. That's just why I'm so anxious to help you well through it."

And, indeed, Gilbert Gildersleeve, profoundly agitated as he was, saw in the accident a marvellous chance for himself to secure a diverson of police attention from the real murderer. The fact was, he had passed twenty-four hours of supreme misery. As soon as he learned from common report that "the murderer was caught and was being brought to Tavistock," he took it for granted at first that Guy hadn't gone to Africa at all, but had left by rail for the East, and been arrested elsewhere. That belief filled him full of excruciating terrors. For Gilbert Gildersleeve, accidental manslaughterer as he was, was not by any means a depraved or wholly heartless person. Big, blustering, and gruff, he was yet in essence an honest, kind-hearted, unemotional Englishman. His one desire now was to save his wife and daughter from further misery; and if he could only save them, he was ready to sacrifice for the moment, to a certain extent, Guy Waring's reputation. But if Guy Waring himself had stood before him in the dock, he must have stepped forward to confess. The strain would have been too great for him. He couldn't have allowed an innocent man to be hanged in his place. Come what might, in that case he must let his wife and daughter go, and save the innocent by acknowledging himself guilty. So when he looked at the prisoner, it gave him a shock of joy to see that fortune had once more befriended him. Thank heaven! thank heaven! it wasn't the man they wanted at all. This was the other brother of the two—Cyril, the painter, not Guy, the journalist.

In a moment the acute and experienced criminal hand recognized that this chance told unconsciously in his own favor. Like every other suspected person, he wanted time, and time would be taken up in proving an *alibi* for Cyril, as well as showing by concurrent proof that he was not his brother. Meanwhile, suspicion would fix itself still more firmly upon Guy, whose flight would give color to the charges brought against him by the authorities.

So the great Q. C. determined to take up Cyril Waring's case as a labor of love, and didn't doubt he would succeed in finally proving it.

CHAPTER XXIX.

WOMAN'S INTUITION.

NEXT morning Cyril Waring appeared once more in
the Sessions House for the preliminary investigation on
the charge of murder. As he entered, a momentary hush
pervaded the room ; then, suddenly, from a seat beneath,
a woman's voice burst forth, quite low, yet loud enough
to be heard by all the magistrates on the bench.

" Why, mother," it said, in a very tremulous tone, " it
isn't Guy himself, at all; don't you see it's Cyril ? "

The words were so involuntarily spoken, and in such
hushed awe and amaze, that even the magistrates themselves, hard Devonshire squires, didn't turn their heads
to rebuke the speaker. As for Cyril, he had no need to
look towards a blushing face in the body of the court to
know that the voice was Elma Clifford's.

She sat there looking lovelier than he had ever before
seen her. Cyril's glance caught hers. They didn't need
to speak. He saw at once in her eye that Elma, at least,
knew instinctively he was innocent.

Next moment Gilbert Gildersleeve stood up to state
his defence, and gazed at her steadily. As he rose in his
place, Elma's eye met his. Gilbert Gildersleeve's fell.
He didn't know why, but in that second of time, the
great blustering man felt certain in his heart that Elma
Clifford suspected him.

Elma Clifford, for her part, knew still more than that.
With the swift intuition she inherited from her long line
of Oriental ancestry, she said to herself at once in categorical terms, " It was that man that did it. I know it
was he. And he sees I know it. And he knows I'm
right. And he's afraid of me accordingly." But an intuition, however valuable to its possessor, is not yet

admitted as evidence in English courts. Elma also knew it was no use in the world for her to get up in her place, and say so openly.

The great Q. C. put his case in a nutshell. "Our client," he contended, "was *not* the man against whom the warrant in this case had been duly issued; he was *not* the man named Guy Waring; he was *not* the man whom the witnesses deposed to having seen at Mambury; he was *not* the man who had loitered with evil intent around the skirts of Dartmoor; in short," the great Q. C. observed, with demonstrative eye-glass, "it was a very clear case of mistaken identity. It would take them time, no doubt, to prove the conclusive *alibi* they intended to establish; for the gentleman now charged before them, he would hope to show hereafter, was Mr. Cyril Waring, the distinguished painter, twin brother to Mr. Guy Waring, the journalist, against whom the warrant was issued; and he was away in Belgium during the whole precise time when Mr. Guy Waring— as to whose guilt or innocence he would make no definite assertion—was prowling round Dartmoor on the trail of McGregor, *alias* Montague Nevitt. Therefore, they would consent to an indefinite remand till evidence to that effect was duly forthcoming. Meanwhile—and here Gilbert Gildersleeve's eyes fell upon Elma once more with a quiet, forensic smile—he would call one witness, on the spur of the moment, whom he hadn't thought till that very morning of calling, but whom the magistrates would allow to be a very important one,—a lady from Chetwood,—Miss Elma Clifford."

Elma, taken aback, stood up in the box and gave her evidence timidly. It amounted to no more then the simple fact that the person before the magistrates was Cyril, not Guy; that the two brothers were extremely like; but that she had reason to know them easily apart, having been associated in a most painful accident in a tunnel with the brother, the present Mr. Cyril Waring. What she said gave only a presumption of mistaken identity, but didn't at all invalidate the positive identification of all the people who had seen the supposed murderer. However, from Gilbert Gildersleeve's point of view, this delay was doubly valuable. In the first place, it gave

him time to prove his *alibi* for Cyril, and bring witnesses
from Belgium; and in the second place, it succeeded
in still further fastening public suspicion on Guy, and
narrowing the question for the police to the simple issue
whether or not they had really caught the brother who
was seen at Mambury on the day of the murder.

The law's delays were as marvellous as is their wont.
It was a full fortnight before the barrister was able to
prove his point by bringing over witnesses at considerable
expense from Belgium and elsewhere, and by the aid of a
few intimate friends in London, who could speak with
certainty as to the difference between the brothers. At
the end of a fortnight, however, he did sufficiently prove
it by tracing Cyril in detail from England to the Ardennes
and back again to Dover, as well as by showing exactly
how Guy had been employed in London and elsewhere
on every day or night of the intervening period. The
magistrates at last released Cyril, convinced by his argu-
ments, and on the very same day, the coroner's inquest
on Montague Nevitt's body, after adjourning time upon
time to await the clearing up of this initial difficulty, returned a verdict of willful murder against Guy Waring.

That evening, in town, the most completely mystified
person of all was a certain cashier of the London and West
County Bank in Lombard Street, who read in his *St.
James's* this morning complete proof that Cyril had been in
Belgium through all those days when he himself distinctly
remembered cashing over the counter for him a check
for no less a sum than six thousand pounds to "self or
bearer." Had the brothers, then, been deliberately and
nefariously engaged in a deep laid scheme (the cashier
asked himself, much puzzled) to confuse one another's
identity with great care beforehand, with a distinct view
to the projected murder? For as yet, of course, nobody
on earth except Guy Waring himself on the waters of
Biscay knew or suspected anything at all about the
forgery.

Elma Clifford and her mother, had stopped on at Tavistock till Cyril was released from his close confinement.
Elma never meant to marry him, of course,—to that
prime determination she still remained firm as a rock
under all conditions,—but in such straits as those, why,

naturally she couldn't bear to be far away from him. So she remained at Tavistock quietly till the inquiry was over.

On the evening of his release Elma met him at the hotel. Her mother had gone out on purpose to leave them alone. Elma took Cyril's hand in hers with a profound trembling. She felt the moment for reserve had long gone past.

"Cyril," she said, boldly calling him by his Christian name, because she could call him only as she always thought of him, "I knew from the first you didn't do it. And just because I know you didn't, I know Guy didn't either, though everything looks now so very black against him. I can trust *you*, and I can trust *him*. All through, I've never had a doubt one moment of either of you."

Cyril held her hand in his, and raised it tenderly to his lips. Elma looked at him, half surprised. Only her hand! how strange of him! Cyril read the unspoken thought, as she would have read it herself, and answered quickly, "Never, Elma, now, till Guy has cleared himself of this deadly accusation. I couldn't bear to ask you to accept a man whom every one else would call a murderer's brother."

Elma gazed at him steadfastly. Tears stood in her eyes. Her voice trembled; but she was very firm.

"We must clear you and him from this dreadful charge," she said, slowly. "I know we must do that, Cyril. Guy didn't kill him. Guy is wholly incapable of it. But where is Guy now? That's what I don't understand. We must clear that all up. Though, even when it's cleared up, I can only love you. As I told you that day at Chetwood, —and I mean it still, —whatever comes to us two, I can never, never marry you."

"Not even if I clear this all up?" Cyril asked, with a wistful look.

"Not even if you clear this all up," Elma answered, seriously. "The difficulty's on *my* side, don't you see, not on yours at all. So far as you're concerned, Cyril, clear this up or leave it just where it is, I'd marry you to-morrow. I'd marry you at once, and proud to do it if only to show the world openly I trust you both. I half faltered just once as you stood there in court, whether I wouldn't

say *yes* to you, for nothing else but that—to let **everybody**
see how implicitly I trusted you."

"But *I* couldn't allow it," Cyril answered, all aglow.
"As things stand now, Elma, our positions are reversed.
While this cloud still hangs so black over Guy, I couldn't
find it in my conscience to ask you to marry me."

He gazed at her steadily. They were both too profoundly stirred for tears or emotions. A quiet despair
gleamed in the eyes of each. Cyril could never marry
her till he had cleared up this mystery. Elma could
never marry him, even if it were all cleared up, with
that terrible taint of madness, as she thought it, hanging threateningly forever over her and her family.

She paused for a minute or two, with her hand locked
in his. Then she said once more, very low, "No, Guy
didn't do it. But why did he run away? That baffles
me quite. That's the one point of it all that makes it so
strange and so terribly mysterious."

"Elma," Cyril answered, with a cold thrill, "I believe
in Guy. I think I know myself, and I think I know
him, well enough to say that such a thing as murder is
impossible for either of us. He's weak at times, I admit; and his will was powerless before the magnetic
force of Montague Nevitt's. But when I try to face that
inscrutable mystery of why, if he's innocent, he has run
away from this charge, I confess my faith begins to falter and tremble. He must have seen it in the papers.
He must have seen I was accused. What can he mean
by leaving me to bear it in his stead without ever coming forward to help me fairly out of it?"

Elma looked up at him with another of her sudden
flashes of superb intuition. "He *can't* have seen it in
the papers," she said. "That gives us some clue. If
he'd seen it, he *must* have come forward to help you.
But, Cyril, *my* faith never falters at all. And I tell you
why. Not only do I know Guy didn't do it, but I know
who did it. The man who murdered Montague Nevitt
is—why shouldn't I tell you?—Mr. Gilbert Glidersleeve."

Cyril started back astonished. "Oh, Elma, why do
you think so?" he cried, in amazement. "What possible reason can you have for saying so?"

"None," Elma answered, with a calmly resigned air.

"I only know it; I know it from his eyes. I looked in them once and read it like a book. But of course that's nothing. What we must do now is to try and find out the facts. I looked in his eyes and saw it at a glance. And I saw he saw it. He knows I've discovered him."

Cyril half drew away from her with a faint sense of alarm. "Elma," he said, slowly, "I believe in Guy; but really and truly, I can't quite believe *that*. You make your intuition tell you far too much. In your natural anxiety to screen my brother, you've fixed the guilt, without proof, upon another innocent man. I'm sure Mr. Gildersleeve's as incapable as Guy of any such action."

"And I'm sure of it, too," Elma answered, with the instinctive certainty of feminine conviction. "But still I know, for all that, he did it. Perhaps it was all done in a moment of haste. But at least he did it. And nothing on earth that anybody could say will ever make me believe he didn't."

"When Mrs. Clifford came back to the hotel an hour later, she scanned her daughter's face with a keen glance of inquiry.

"Well, he says he won't ask you again," she murmured, laying Elma's head on her shoulder, "till this case is cleared up, and Guy is proved innocent."

"Yes," Elma answered, nestling close and looking red as a rose. "He knows very well Guy didn't do it, but he wants all the rest of the world to acknowledge it also."

And *you* know who did it?" Mra. Clifford said, with a tentative air."

"Yes, mother. Do you?"

"Of course I do, darling. But it'll never be proved against *him*, you may be sure. I saw it at a glance. It's Mr. Gilbert Gildersleeve."

CHAPTER XXX.

FRESH DISCOVERIES.

As Cyril drove home from Waterloo next day, to his
lonely rooms in Staple Inn, Holborn, he turned aside
with his cab for a few minutes to make a passing call at
the bank in Lombard Street. He was short of ready
money, and wanted to cash a check for fifty pounds for
expenses incurred in his defence at Tavistock

The cashier stared at him hard; then, without consulting anybody, he said, in a somewhat embarrassed tone,
"I don't know whether you're aware of it, Mr. Waring,
but this overdraws your current account. We haven't
fifty pounds on our books to your credit."

He was well posted on the subject, in fact, for only
that morning he had hunted up Cyril's balance in the
ledger at his side for the gratification of his own pure
personal curiosity.

Cyril stared at him in astonishment. In this age of sur-
prises, one more surprise was thus suddenly sprung upon
him. His first impulse was to exclaim in a very amazed
voice, "Why, I've six thousand odd pounds to my credit,
surely"; but he checked himself in time with a violent
effort. How could he tell what strange things might
have happened in his absence? If the money was gone,
and Nevitt was murdered, and Guy in hiding, who could
say what fresh complications might not still be in store
for him? So he merely answered, with a strenuous endeavor to suppress his agitation, "Will you kindly let me
have my balance-sheet, if you please? I—ur—I thought
I'd more money than that still left with you."

The cashier brought out a big book and a bundle of
checks, which he handed to Cyril, with a face of profound
interest. To him, too, this little drama was pregnant

with mystery and personal implications. Cyril turned the vouchers over one by one, with close attention recognizing the signature and occasion of each, till he arrived at last at a big check which staggered him sadly for a moment. He took it up in his hands and examined it in the light. "Pay Self or Bearer, Six Thousand Pounds (£6000), Cyril Waring."

Oh, horrible, horrible! This, then, was the secret of Guy's sudden disappearance.

He didn't cry aloud He didn't say a word. He looked at the thing hard, and knew in a moment exactly what had happened. Guy had forged that check; it was Guy's natural hand, written forward like Cyril's own, instead of backward, as usual. And no one but himself could possibly have told it from his own true signature. But Cyril knew it at once for Guy's by one infallible sign,— a tiny sign that might escape the veriest expert,—some faint hesitation about the tail of the capital C, which was shorter in Guy's hand than Cyril ever made it, and which Guy had therefore deliberately lengthened, by an effort or an afterthought, to complete the imitation.

"You cashed that check yourself, sir, over the counter, you remember," the cashier said, quietly, "on the date it was drawn on."

Cyril never altered a muscle of his rigid face.

"Ah, quite so," he answered, in a very dry voice, not daring to contradict the man. He knew just what had happened. Guy must have come to get the money himself, and the cashier must have mistaken him for the proper owner of the purloined six thousand. They were so very much alike. Nobody ever distinguished them.

"And that was one of the days, I think, when you proved the *alibi* in Belgium before the Devonshire magistrates at Tavistock, yesterday," the clerk went on, with a searching glance, Cyril started this time. He saw in a second the new danger thus sprung upon him. If the cashier chose to press the matter home to the hilt, he must necessarily arrive at one or other of two results.

Either the *alibi* would break down altogether, or it would be perfectly clear that Guy had committed a forgery.

"So it seems," he answered, looking his keen interlocutor straight in the eyes. "So it seems, I should say, by the date on the face of it."

But the cashier did *not* care to press the matter home any further; and for a very good reason. It was none of his business to suggest the idea of a forgery, after a check had been presented and duly cashed, if the customer to whose account it was debited in course chose voluntarily to accept the responsibility of honoring it. The objection should come first from the customer's side. If *he* didn't care to press it, then neither did the cashier. Why should he, indeed? Why saddle his firm with six thousand pounds loss? He would only get himself into trouble for having failed to observe the discrepancy in the signatures, and the difference between the brothers. That, after all, is what a cashier is for. If he doesn't fulfil those first duties of his post, why, what on earth can be the good of him to anybody in any way?

The two men looked at one another across the counter with a strong, inscrutable stare of mutual suspicion. Then Cyril slowly tore up the check he had tendered for fifty pounds, filled in another for his real balance of twenty-two, handed it across to the clerk without another word, received the cash in white, trembling hands, and went out to his cab again in a turmoil of excitement.

All the way back to his rooms in Staple Inn, one seething idea possessed his soul. His faith in Guy was beginning to break down. And with it, his faith in himself almost went. The man was his own brother—his very counterpart, he knew; could he really believe him capable of commiting a murder? Cyril looked within, and said a thousand times *no;* he looked at that forged check, and his heart misgave him.

At Staple Inn, the housekeeper, who took care of their joint rooms, came out to greet him with no small store of tears and lamentations. "Oh, Mr. Cyril," she cried, seizing both his hands in hers with a tremulous welcome, "I'm glad to see you back, and to know you're innocent. I always said you never could have done it; no, no, not you; nor yet Mr. Guy neither. The police has been here time and again to search the rooms, but the Lord be praised, they never found anything! And I've got a letter for you, too, from Mr. Guy himself; but there—I locked it up till you come in my own cupboard at home, for fear of the detectives; and now you're back and safe in London again, I'll run home this minute, round the corner, and get it."

Cyril sat down in the familiar easy-chair, holding his face in his hands, and gazed about him blankly. Such a home-coming as this was inexpressibly terrible to him.

In a few minutes more the housekeeper came back, bringing in her hands Guy's letter from Plymouth.

Cyril sat for a minute and looked at the envelope in deadly silence. Then he motioned the housekeeper out of the room with one quivering hand. Before that good woman's face he couldn't open it and read it.

As soon as she was gone, he tore it apart, trembling. As he read and read, the suspicion within him deepened quickly into a doubt, the doubt into a conviction, the conviction into a certainty. He clapped his hand to his head. Oh, God! what was this? Guy acknowledged his own guilt! He confessed he had done it!

Cyril's last hope was gone. Guy himself admitted it!

"How I came to do it," the letter said, "I've no idea myself. A sudden suggestion,—a strange, unaccountable impulse,—a prompting, as it were, pressed upon me from without, and almost before I knew, the crime was committed."

Cyril bent his head low upon his knees with shame. He never could hold up that head henceforth. No further doubt or hesitation remained. He knew the whole truth. Guy was indeed a murderer.

He steeled himself for the worst, and read the letter through with a superhuman effort. It almost choked him to read. The very consecutiveness and coherency of the sentences seemed all but incredible under such awful circumstances. A murderer, red-handed, to speak of his crime so calmly as that! And then, too, this undying anger expressed and felt, even after death, against his victim, Nevitt! Cyril couldn't understand how any man—least of all his own brother—could write such words about the murdered man whose body was then lying all silent and cold, under the open sky, among the bracken at Mambury.

And once more, this awful clue of the dead man's

pocket-book! Those accursed notes! That hateful sum of money! How could Guy venture to speak of it all in such terms as those—the one palpable fact that indubitably linked him with that cold-blooded murder. "The three thousand sent herewith I recovered, almost by a miracle, from that false creature's grasp, under extraordinary circumstances, and I return them now, in proof of the fact, in Montague Nevitt's own pocket-book, which I'm sure you'll recognize as soon as you look at it."

Cyril saw it all now beyond the shadow of a doubt. He reconstructed the whole sad tale. He was sure he understood it. But to understand it was hardly even yet to believe it. Guy had lost heavily in the Rio Negro Mines, as the prosecution declared; in an evil hour he'd been cajoled into forging Cyril's name for six thousand. Montague Nevitt had in some way misappropriated the stolen sum. Guy had pursued him in a sudden white-heat of fury, had come up with him unawares, had killed him in his rage, and now calmly returned as much as he could recover of that fateful and twice-stolen money to Cyril. It was all too horrible, but all too true. In a wild ferment of remorse for his brother's sin, the unhappy painter sat down at once and penned a letter of abject self humiliation to Elma Clifford.

" ELMA,—I said to you last night that I could never marry you till I had clearly proved my brother Guy's innocence. Well, I said what I can never conceivably do. Since returning to town I received a letter from Guy himself. What it contained I must never tell you, for Guy's own sake. But what I *must* tell you, is this : I can never again see you. Guy and I are so nearly one, in every nerve and fibre of our being, that whatever he may have done is to me almost as if I myself had done it. You will know how terrible a thing it is for me to write these words, but for *your* sake I can't refrain from writing them. Think no more of me. I am not worthy of you. I will think of *you* as long as I live.

"Your ever devoted and heart-broken
"CYRIL."

He folded the letter and sent it off to the temporary ad-

dress at the West-End where Elma had told him that she and her mother would spend the night in London. Very late that evening a ring came at the bell. Cyril ran to the door. It was a boy with a telegram. He opened it, and read it with breathless excitement. " Whatever Guy may have said, you are quite mistaken. There's a mystery somewhere. Keep his letter and show it to me. I may perhaps be able to unravel the tangle. I'm more than ever convinced that what I said to you last night was perfectly true. We will save him yet. Unalterably,
"ELMA."

But the telegram brought little peace to Cyril. Of what value were Elma's vague intuitions now, by the side of Guy's own positive confession? With his very own hand Guy admitted that he had done it. Cyril went to bed that night, the unhappiest, loneliest man in London. What Guy was, he was. He felt himself almost like the actual murderer.

CHAPTER XXXI.

" GOLDEN JOYS."

THE voyage to the Cape was long and tedious. On the whole way out, Guy made but few friends, and talked very little to his fellow-passengers. That unhappy recognition by Granville Kelmscott, the evening he went on board the *Cetewayo*, poisoned the fugitive's mind for the entire passage. He felt himself, in fact, a moral outcast; he slunk away from his kind; he hardly dared to meet Kelmscott's eyes for shame, whenever he passed him. But for one thing at least he was truly grateful. Though Kelmscott had evidently discovered from the papers the nature of Guy's crime, and knew his real name well, it was clear he had said nothing of any sort on the subject to the other passengers. Only one man on board was aware of his guilt, Guy believed, and that one man he shunned accordingly as far as was possible within the narrow limits of the saloon and the quarter-deck.

Granville Kelmscott, of course, took a very different view of Guy Waring's position. He had read in the paper he bought at Plymouth that Guy was the murderer of Montague Nevitt. Regarding him, therefore, as a criminal of the deepest dye now flying from justice, he wasn't at all surprised at Guy's shrinking and shunning him; what astonished him rather, was the man's occasional and incredible fits of effrontery. How that fellow could ever laugh and talk at all among the ladies on deck—with the hangman at his back—simply appalled and horrified the proud soul of a Kelmscott. Granville had hard work to keep from expressing his horror openly at times. But still, with an effort, he kept his peace. With the picture of his father and Lady Emily now strong before his mind, he couldn't find it in his heart to bring his own half-

brother, however guilty and criminal the man might be,
to the foot of the gallows.

So they voyaged on together without once interchang-
ing a single word, all the way from Plymouth to the
Cape Colony. And the day they landed at Port Eliza-
beth, it was an infinite relief indeed to Guy, to think he
could now get well away forever from that fellow Kelmscott. Not being by any means overburdened with ready
cash, however, Guy determined to waste no time in the
coastwise towns, but to make his way at once boldly up
country towards Kimberley. The railway ran then only
as far as Grahamstown; the rest of his journey to the
South African Golconda was accomplished by road in a
two wheeled cart, drawn by four small horses, which rattled along with a will, up hill and down dale, over the
precarious highways of that semi-civilized upland.

To Guy, just fresh from England and the monotonous
sea, there was a certain exhilaration in this first hasty
glimpse of the infinite luxuriance of sub-tropical nature.
At times he almost forgot Montague Nevitt and the forgery in the boundless sense of freedom and novelty given
him by those vast wastes of rolling tableland, thickly
covered with grass or low, thorny acacias, and stretching
illimitably away in low range after range to the blue
mountains in the distance. It was strange, indeed, to
him on the wild plains through which they scurried in
wild haste, to see the springbok rush away from the
doubtful track at the first whirr of their wheels, or the
bolder bustard stand and gaze among the long grass with
his wary eye turned sideways to look at them. Guy
felt for the moment he had left Europe and its reminis-
cences now fairly behind him; in this free, new world,
he was free once more himself; his shame was cast aside;
he could revel like the antelopes in the immensity
of a land where nobody knew him and he knew nobody.

What added most of all, however, to this quaint, new
sense of vastness and freedom, was the occasional appearance of naked blacks, roaming at large through the
burnt-up fields of which till lately they had been undis-
puted possessors. Day after day Guy drove on along
the uncertain roads, past queer outlying towns of white

wooden houses,—Cradock, and Middelburg, and Coles-
burgh, and others,—till they crossed at last the boundary of Orange River into the Free State, and halted for
a while in the main street of Philippolis.

It was a dreary place. Guy began now to see the
other side of South Africa. Though he had left England
in autumn, it was spring-time at the Cape, and the winter
drought had parched up all the grass, leaving the bare,
red dust in the roads or streets as dry and desolate as
the sand of the desert. The town itself consisted of
some sixty melancholy and distressful houses, bare,
square, and flat-roofed, standing unenclosed along a dismal highroad, and with that congenitally shabby look,
in spite of their newness, which seems to belong by
nature to all southern buildings. Some stagnant pools
alone remained to attest the presence after rain of a roar-
ing brook, the pits in whose dried-up channel they now
occupied; over their tops hung the faded foliage of a few
dust-laden trees, struggling hard for life with the energy
of despair against depressing circumstances. It was a
picture that gave Guy a sudden attack of pessimism; if
this was the El Dorado towards which he was going, he
earnestly wished himself back again once more, forgery
or no forgery, among the breezy green fields of dear old
England.

On to Fauresmith he travelled, with less comfort than
before, in a rickety buggy of most primitive construction,
designed to meet the needs of rough mountain roads,
and as innocent of springs as Guy himself of the murder
of Montague Nevitt. It was a wretched drive. The
drought had now broken; the wet season had begun;
rain fell heavily. A piercing, cold wind blew down from
the nearer mountains: and Guy began to feel still more
acutely than ever that South Africa was by no means
an earthly paradise. As he drove on and on, this feeling deepened upon him. Huge blocks of stone obstruct-
ed the rough road, intersected as it was by deep cart-
wheel ruts, down which the rainwater now flowed in
impromptu torrents. The Dutch driver, too, anxious to
show the mettle of his coarse-limbed steeds, persisted
in dashing over the hummocky ground, at a break-neck
pace, while Guy balanced himself with difficulty on the

narrow seat, hanging on to his portmanteau for dear life among the jerks and jolts, till his fingers were numbed with cold and exposure.

They held out against it all, before the pelting rain, till man and beast were well-nigh exhausted. At last, about three-quarters of the way to Fauresmith, on the bleak, bare hill-tops, sleety snow began to fall in big flakes, and the barking of a dog to be heard in the distance. The Boer driver pricked up his ears at the sound.

" That must a house be," he remarked, in his Dutch pigeon-English to Guy; and Guy felt in his soul that the most miserable and filthy of Kaffir huts would just then be a welcome sight to his weary eyes. He would have given a sovereign, indeed, from the scanty store he possessed, for a night's lodging in a convenient dog kennel. He was agreeably surprised, therefore, to find it was a comfortable farmhouse, where the lights in the casement beamed forth a cheery welcome on the wet and draggled wayfarers from real glass windows. The farmer within received them hospitably. Business was brisk to-day. Another traveller, he said, had just gone on towards Fauresmith.

" A young man like yourself, fresh from England," the farmer observed, scanning Guy closely. " He's off for the diamond diggings. I think to Dutoitspan."

Guy rested the night there, thinking nothing of the stranger, and went on next day more quietly to Fauresmith. Thence to the diamond fields, the country became at each step more sombre and more monotonous than ever. In the afternoon they rested at Jacobsdal, another dusty, dreary, comfortless place, consisting of about five and twenty bankrupt houses scattered in bare clumps over a scorched-up desert. Then on again next day, over a drearier and ever drearier expanse of landscape. It was ghastly. It was horrible. At last, on the top of a dismal hill range, looking down on a deep dale, the driver halted. In the vast flat below, a dull, dense fog feemed to envelop the world with inscrutable mists. The driver pointed to it with his demonstrative whip.

" Down yonder," he said, encouragingly, as he put the

skid on his wheel, " down yonder's the diamond fields—
that's Dutoitspan before you."

" What makes it so gray?" Guy asked, looking in
front of him with a sinking heart. This first view of his
future home was by no means encouraging.

" Oh, the sand make it be like that," the driver answered, unconcernedly. " Diamond fields all make up of
fine, red sand; and diggers pile it about around their own
claims Then the wind comes and blows, and makes
sand-storm always around Dutoitspan."

Guy groaned inwardly. This was certainly *not* the
El Dorado of his fancy. They descended the hill, at the
same break-neck pace as before, and entered the miserable mushroom town of diamond-grubbers. Amidst the
huts in the diggings great heaps of red earth lay piled
up everywhere. Dust and sand rose high on the hot
breeze into the stifling air. As they reached the encampment— for Dutoitspan then was little more than a camp
—the blinding mists of solid, red particles drove so thick
in their eyes that Guy could hardly see a few yards
before him. Their clothes and faces were literally en-
crusted in thick coats of dust. The fine, red mist seemed
to pervade everything. It filled their eyes, their nostrils
their ears, their mouths. They breathed solid dust. The
air was laden deep with it.

And *this* was the diamond fields! This was the Golconda where Guy was to find six thousand pounds, ready
made to recover his losses and to repay Cyril. Oh, horrible, horrible! His heart sank low at it.

And still they went on, and on, and on, and on, through
the mist of dust to the place for out-spanning. Guy only
shared the common fate of all new-comers to " the fields"
in feeling much distressed and really ill. The very horses
in the cart snorted and sneezed and showed their high
displeasure by trying every now and then to jib and turn
back again. Here and there, on either side, to right and
left, where the gloom permitted it, Guy made out dimly
a few round or oblong tents, with occasional rude huts of
corrugated iron. A few uncertain figures lounged
vaguely in the back-ground. On closer inspection they
proved to be much-grimed and half-naked natives, rest-

ing their weary limbs on piles of dry dust after their
toil in the diggings.

It was an unearthly scene. Guy's heart sank lower
and lower still at every step the horses took into that
howling wilderness.

At last the driver drew up with a jolt in front of a
long, low hut of corrugated iron, somewhat larger than
the rest, but no less dull and dreary. "The hotel," he
said, briefly; and Guy jumped out to secure himself a
night's lodging or so at this place of entertainment, till
he could negotiate for a hut and a decent claim, and com-
mence his digging.

At the bar of the primitive saloon where he found
himself landed, a man in a gray tweed suit was already
seated. He was drinking something fizzy from a tall
soda-water glass. With a sudden start of horror Guy
recognized him at once. Oh, great heavens! what was
this? It was Granville Kelmscott!

Then Granville, too, was bound for the diamond fields
like himself. What an incredible coincidence! How
strange! How inexplicable! That rich man's son, the
pampered heir to Tilgate! What could he be doing here,
in this out-of-the-way spot, this last resort of poor broken-
down men, this miserable haunt of wretched, gambling
money-grubbers?

Mere curiosity, surely, must have drawn him to the
spot. He couldn't have come to dig! Guy gazed in
amazement at that gray tweed suit. He must be staying for a day or two in search of adventure. No more
than just that! He couldn't mean to *stop* here.

As he gazed and stood open-mouthed in the shadow of
the door, Granville Kelmscott, who hadn't seen him
enter, laid down his glass, wiped his lips with gusto, and
continued his conversation with the complacent barman.

"Yes, I want a hut here," he said, "and to buy a good
claim. I've been looking over the kopje down by Wat-
son's spare land, and I think I've seen a lot that's likely
to suit me."

Guy could hardly restrain his astonishment and surprise. He had come, then, to dig! Oh, incredible! Impossible!

But at any rate, this settled his own immediate move.
ments, Guy's mind was made up at once. If Granville
Kelmscott was going to dig at Dutoitspan—why, clearly,
Dutoitspan was no place for him. He could never stand
the continual presence of the one man in South Africa
who knew his deadly secret. Comes what might, he
must leave the neighborhood without a moment's delay.
He must strike out at once for the far interior. As he
paused, Granville Kelmscott turned round and saw him.
Their eyes met with a start. Each was equally astonished. Then Granville rose slowly from his seat and
murmured in a low voice, as he regarded him fixedly :

"You here again, Mr. Billington? This is once too
often. I hardly expected *this*. There's no room here for
both of us."

And he strode from the saloon, with a very black brow,
leaving Guy for the moment alone with the barman.

CHAPTER XXXII.

A NEW DEPARTURE.

A FORTNIGHT later, one sultry afternoon, Granville Kelm-scott found himself, after various strange adventures and escapes by the way, in a Koranna hut, far in the untrav-elled heart of the savage Barolong country.

The tenement where he sat, or more precisely squatted, was by no means either a commodious or sweet-scented one. Yet it was the biggest of a group on the river-bank, some five feet high from floor to roof, so that a Kelmscott couldn't possibly stand erect at full length in it; and it was roughly round in shape, like an over-grown beehive, the framework consisting of branches of trees, arranged in a rude circle, over whose arching ribs native rush mats had been thrown or sewn with irregular order. The door was a hole, through which the proud descendant of the squires of Tilgate had to creep on all fours; a hollow pit dug out in the centre served as the only fireplace; smoke and stagnant air formed the staples of the atmos-phere. A more squalid hovel Granville Kelmscott had never even conceived as possible. It was as dirty and as loathsome as the most vivid imagination could picture the hut of the lowest savages.

Yet here that delicately nurtured English gentleman was to be cooped up for an indefinite time, as it seemed, by order of the black despot who ruled over the Barolong with a rod of iron.

What had led Granville Kelmscott into this extraor-dinary scrape it would not be hard to say. The Kelm-scott nature, in all its embodiments, worked on very simple but very fixed lines. The moment Granville saw his half-brother Guy at Dutoitspan, his mind was made up at once as to his immediate procedure. He wouldn't stop one day—one hour longer than necessary—where he could see that fellow who committed the murder. Come what might, he would make his escape at once into the far interior.

As before in England, so now in Africa, both brothers were moved by the self-same impulses; and each carried them out with characteristic promptitude.

Where could Granville go, however? Well it was rumored at Dutoitspan that "pebbles" had been found far away to the north in the Barolong country. "Pebbles," of course, is good South African for diamonds; and, at this welcome news, all Kimberley and Griqualand pricked up their ears with congenial delight; for business was growing flat on the old-established diamond fields. The palmy era of great finds and lucky hits was now long past; the day of systematic and prosaic industry had set in instead for the over-stocked diggings. It was no longer possible for the luckest fresh hand to pick up pebbles lying loose on the surface; the mode of working had become highly skilled and scientific.

Machines and scaffolds, and washing-cradles and lifting apparatus, were now required to make the business a success; the simple old gambling element was rapidly going out, and the capitalist was rapidly coming up in its stead as master of the situation. So Granville Kelmscott, being an enterprising young man though destitute of cash, and utterly ignorant of South African life, determined to push on with all his might and main into the Barolong country, and to rush for the front among the first in the field in these rumored new diggings on the extreme north frontier of civilization.

He started alone, as a Kelmscott might do, and made his way adventurously, without any knowledge of the the Koranna language or manners, through many wild villages of King Khatsua's dominions. Night after night he camped out in the open; and day after day he tramped on by himself, buying food, as he went, from the natives for English silver, in search of precious stones, over that dreary tableland. At last on the fourteenth day, in a deep, alluvial hollow, near a squalid group of small Barolong huts, he saw a tiny, round stone, much rubbed and water-worn, which he picked up and examined with no little curiosity. The two days he had spent at Dutoit-span had not been wasted. He had learnt to recognize the look of the native gem. One glance told him at once what his pebble was. He recognized it at sight as one of those small but much valued diamonds of the finest water, which diggers know by the technical name of "glass-stones."

The hollow where he stood was, in fact, an ancient alluvial pit or volcanic mud-crater. Scoriac rubble filled it in to a very great depth; and in the interstices of this rubble were embedded, here and there, rude blocks of greenstone, containing almond-shaped chalcedonies, and agate, and milk-quartz, with now and then a tiny water-worn speck, which an experienced eye would have detected at once as the finest "riverstones."

Here, indeed, was a prize! The solitary Englishman recognized in a second that he was the first pioneer of a new and richer Kimberley.

But as Granville Kelmscott stood still, looking hard at his find through the little pocket-lens he had brought with him from England, with a justifiable tremor of delight at the pleasant thought that here, perhaps, he had lighted on the key to something which might restore him once more to his proper place at Tilgate, he was suddenly roused from his delightful reverie by a harsh negro voice, shrill and clear, close behind him, saying, in very tolerable African-English:—

"Hillo, you white man! what dat you got there? You come here to Barolong land, so go look for diamond?"

Granville turned sharply round, and saw standing by his side a naked and stalwart black man, smiling blandly at his discovery with broad negro amusement.

"It's a pebble," the Englishman said, pocketing it as carelessly as he could, and trying to look unconcerned, for his new acquaintance held a long, native spear in his stout, left hand, and looked by no means the sort of person to be lightly trifled with.

"Oh, dat a pebble, mistah white man!" the Barolong said, sarcastically, holding out his black right hand with a very imperious air. "Den you please hand him over dat pebble you find. Me got me orders. King Khatsua no want any diamond digging in Barolong land."

Granville tried to parley with the categorical native; but his attempts at palaver were eminently unsuccessful. The naked black man was master of the situation.

"You hand over dat stone, me friend," he said, assuming a menacing attitude, and holding out his hand once more with no very gentle air, "or me run you trew de body wit me assegai—just so! King Khatsua, him no want any diamond diggings in Barolong land."

And, indeed, Granville Kelmscott couldn't help admitting to himself, when he came to think of it, that King Khatsua was acting wisely in his generation. For the introduction of diggers into his dominions would surely have meant, as everywhere else, the speedy proclamation of a British protectorate, and the final annihilation of King Khatsua himself and his dusky fellow-countrymen.

There is nothing, to say the truth, the South African native dreads so much as being "eaten up," as he calls it, by those aggressive English. King Khatsua knew his one chance in life consisted in keeping the diggers firmly out of his dominions; and he was prepared to deny the very existence of diamonds throughout the whole of Barolong land, until the English by sheer force should come in flocks and unearth them.

In obedience to his chief's command, therefore, the naked henchman still held out his hand menacingly.

"Dis land King Khatsua's," he repeated once more, in an angry voice. "All diamonds found on it belong to King Khatsua. Just you hand dat over. No steal; no tief-ee."

The instincts of the land-owning class were too strong in Granville Kelmscott not to make him admit at once to himself the justice of this claim. The owner of the soil had a right to the diamonds. He handed over the stone with a pang of regret. The savage grinned to himself, and scanned it attentively. Then extending his spear, as one might do to a cow or a sheep, he drove Granville before him.

"You come along 'a me," he said, shortly, in a most determined voice. "You come along 'a me. King Khatsua's orders."

Granville went before him without one word of remonstrance, much wondering what was likely to happen next, till he found himself suddenly driven into that noisome hut, where he was forced to enter ignominiously on all fours like an eight month's old baby.

By the light of the fire that burned dimly in the midst of his captor's house he could see, as his eyes grew gradually accustomed to the murky gloom, a strange and savage scene such as he had never before in his life dreamt of. In the pit of the hut some embers glowed feebly, from whose midst a fleecy object was sputtering and hissing. A second glance assured him that the savory morsel was the head of an antelope in process of roasting. Two greasy black women, naked to the waist, were superintending this primitive cookery; all round, a group of unclad little imps, as black as their mothers, lounged idly about, with their eyes firmly fixed on the chance of dinner. As Granville entered, the husband and father, poking in his head, shouted a few words after him. Another native outside kept watch and ward with a spear at the door meanwhile, to prevent his escape against King Khatsua's orders.

For two long hours the Englishman waited there, fretting and fuming, in that stifling atmosphere. Meanwhile, the antelope's head was fully cooked, and the women and children falling on it like wild beasts, tore off the scorched fleece, and snatched the charred flesh from the bones with their fingers greedily. It was a hideous sight; it sickened him to see it.

By and by Granville heard a loud voice outside. He listened in surprise. It sounded as though Barolong had another prisoner. There was a pause and a scuffle. Then, all of a sudden, somebody else came bundling unceremoniously through the hole that served for a door in the same undignified fashion as he himself had done. Granville's eyes, now accustomed to the gloom, recognized the stranger at once with a thrill of astonishment. He could hardly trust his senses at the sight. It was—no, it couldn't be—yes, it was—Guy Waring.

Guy Waring, sure enough; as before, they were companions. The Kelmscott character had worked itself out exactly alike in each of them. They had come independently by the self-same road to the rumored diamond fields of the Barolong country.

It was some minutes, however, before Guy for his part recognized his fellow-prisoner in the dark and gloomy hut. Then each stared at the other in mute surprise. They found no words to speak their mutual astonishment. This was more wonderful, to be sure, than even either of their former encounters.

For another long hour the two unfriendly Englishmen huddled away from one another in opposite corners of that native hut, without speaking a word of any sort in their present straits. At the end of that time, a voice spoke at the door some guttural sentences in the Barolong language. The natives inside responded alike in their own savage clicks. Next the voice spoke in English; it was Granville's captor, he now knew well.

" White men, you come out; King Khatsua himself, him go to 'peak to you."

They crawled out, one at a time, in sorry guise, through the narrow hole. It was a pitiful exhibition. Were it not for the danger and uncertainty of the event, they could almost themselves have fairly laughed at it. King Khatsua stood before them, a tall, full-blooded black, in European costume, with a round felt hat and a crimson tie, surrounded by his naked wives and attendants. In his outstretched hand he held before their faces two incriminating diamonds. He spoke to them with much dignity at considerable length in the Barolong tongue, to a running accompaniment of laudatory exclamations— " Oh, my King! Oh, wise words !"—from the mouths of his courtiers. Neither Granville nor Guy understood, of course, a single syllable of the stately address; but that didn't in the least disturb the composure of the dusky monarch. He went right through to the end with his solemn warning, scolding them both roundly, as they guessed, in his native tongue, like a master reproving a pair of naughty schoolboys.

As he finished, their captor stood forth, with great importance, to act as interpreter. He had been to the Kimberley diamond mines himself as a laborer, and was, therefore, accounted by his own people a perfect model of English scholarship.

" King Khatsua say this," he observed, curtly. " You very bad men; you come to Barolong land. King

Khatsua say, Barolong land for Barolong. No allow white man dig here for diamonds. If white man come, him eat up Barolong. Keep white man out; keep land for King Khatsua."

"Does King Khatsua want us to leave his country, then?" Granville Kelmscott asked, with a distinct tremor in his voice, for the great chief and his followers looked decidedly hostile.

The interpreter threw back his head and laughed a loud, long laugh.

"King Khatsua not a fool!" he answered at last after a rhetorical pause. "King Khatsua no want to give up his land to white man. If you two white man go back to Kimberley, you tell plenty other people, 'Diamonds in Barolong.' You say, 'Come along o' me to Barolong land with gun; we show you where to dig 'um!' No, no, King Khatsua not a fool. King Khatsua say this. You two white men no go back to Kimberley. You spies. You stop here plenty time along o' King Khatsua. Never go back, till King Khatsua give leave. So no let any other white man come along into Barolong land."

Granville looked at Guy and Guy looked at Granville. In this last extremity, before those domineering blacks, they almost forgot everything, save that they were both English. What were they to do now? The situation was becoming truly terrible.

The interpreter went on once more, however, with genuine savage enjoyment of the consternation he was causing them.

"King Khatsua say this," he continued, in a very amused tone. "You stop here plenty days, very good, in Barolong land. King Khatsua give you hut; King Khatsua give you claim; Barolong man bring spear and guard you. No do you any harm for fear of Governor. Governor keep plenty guns in Cape Town. You two white man live in hut together, dig diamonds together; get plenty pebbles. Keep one diamond you find for yourself; give one diamond after that to King Khatsua. Barolong man bring you plenty food, plenty drink but no let you go back. You try to go, then Barolong man spear you."

The playful dig with which the savage thrust forward his assegai at that final remark showed Granville Kelmscott in a moment that this was no idle threat. It was clear, for the present, they must accept the inevitable. They must remain in Barolong land ; and he must share hut and work with that doubly hateful creature—the man who had deprived him of his patrimony at Tilgate, and whom he firmly believed to be the murderer of Montague Nevitt. This was what had come then of his journey to Africa ! Truly, adversity makes us acquainted with strange bedfellows.

CHAPTER XXXIII.

TIME FLIES.

EIGHTEEN months passed away in England, and nothing more was heard of the two fugitives to Africa. Lady Emily's cup was very full indeed. On the self-same day she learned of her husband's death and her son's mysterious and unaccountable disappearance. From that moment forth, he was to her as if dead. After Granville left, no letters or news of him, direct or indirect, ever reached Tilgate. It was almost inexplicable. He had disappeared into space, and no man knew of him.

Cyril, too, had now almost given up hoping for news of Guy. Slowly the conviction forced itself deeper and still deeper upon his mind, in spite of Elma, that Guy was really Montague Nevitt's murderer. Else how account for Guy's sudden disappearance, and for the fact that he never even wrote home his whereabouts? Nay, Guy's letter itself left no doubt upon his mind. Cyril went through life now oppressed continually with the terrible burden of being a murderer's brother.

And indeed everybody else—except Elma Clifford—implicitly shared that opinion with him. Cyril was sure the unknown benefactor shared it too, for Guy's six thousand pounds were never paid in to his credit—as indeed how could they, since Colonel Kelmscott, who had promised to pay them, died before receiving the balance of the purchase money for the Dowlands estate? Cyril slank through the world, then, weighed down by his shame; for Guy and he were each other's doubles, and he always had a deep, underlying conviction that, as Guy was in any particular, so also in the very fibre of his nature he himself was.

Everybody else except Elma Clifford; but, in spite of all,

Elma still held out firm, in her intuitive way, in favor of Guy's innocence. She knew it, she said; and there the matter dropped. And she knew quite equally, in her own firm mind, that Gilbert Gildersleeve was the real murderer.

Gilbert Gildersleeve, meanwhile, had gone up a step or two higher in the social scale. He had been promoted to the bench on the first vacancy, as all the world had long expected; but, strange to say, he took it far more modestly than all the world had ever anticipated. Indeed, before he was made a judge, everybody said he'd be intolerable in the ermine. He was blustering and bullying enough, in all conscience, as a mere Queen's Counsel; but when he came to preside in a court of his own, his insolence would surpass even the wonted insolence of our autocratic British justices. In this, however, everybody was mistaken.

A curious change had of late come over Gilbert Gildersleeve. The big, bullying lawyer was growing nervous and diffident, where of old he had been coarse and self-assertive and blustering. He was beginning at times almost to doubt his own absolute omniscience and absolute wisdom. He was prepared half to admit that under certain circumstances a prisoner might possibly be in the right, and that all crimes alike did not necessarily deserve the hardest sentence the law of the land allowed him to allot them. Habitual criminals, even, began after a while to express a fervent hope, as assizes approached, they might be tried by old Gildersleeve; "Gilly," they said, gave, a cove a chance"; he wasn't "one of these 'ere reg'lar 'anging judges, like Sir Enery Atkins."

During those eighteen months, too, Cyril tried as far as he could, from a stern sense of duty, to see as little as possible of Elma Clifford. He loved Elma still—that goes without saying—more devotedly than ever; and Elma's profound belief that Cyril's brother couldn't possibly have committed so grave a crime touched his heart to the core by its womanly confidence. There's nothing a man likes so much as being trusted. But he had declared, in the first flush of his horror and despair, that he would never again ask Elma to marry him till the cloud that hung over Guy's character had been lifted and dissipated; and now that, month after month, no news came from Guy, and all hope seemed to fade, he felt it would be wrong of him even to see her or speak with her.

On that question, however, Elma herself had a voice as well. Man proposes; woman decides. And though Elma for her part had quite equally made up her mind never to marry Cyril, with that nameless terror of expected madness hanging ever over her head, she felt, on the other hand, her very loyalty to Cyril and to Cyril's brother imperatively demanded that she should still see him often, and display marked friendship towards him as openly as possible. She wanted the world to see plainly for itself that, so far as this matter of Guy's reputation was concerned, if Cyril for his part wanted to marry her, she on her side would be quite ready to marry Cyril.

So she insisted on meeting him whenever she could, and on writing to him openly from time to time very affectionate notes—those familiar notes we all know so well and prize so dearly—full of hopeless love and unabated confidence. Yes, good Mr. Stockbroker, who do me the honor to read my simple tale, smile cynically if you will. You can pretend to care nothing for these little sentimentalities; but you know very well, in your own heart, you've a bundle of them at home, very brown and yellow, locked up in your escritoire; and you'd let New Zealand Fours sink to the bottom of the Indian Ocean, and Egyptian Unified go down to zero, before you'd part with a single faded page of them.

What can a man do, then, even under such painful circumstances, when a girl whom he loves with all his heart lets him clearly see she loves him in return quite as truly? Cyril would have been more than human if he hadn't answered those notes in an equally ardent and equally desponding strain. The burden of both their tales was always this—even if *you* would, *I* couldn't, because I love you too much to impose my own disgrace upon you.

But what Elma's mysterious trouble could be, Cyril was still unable even to hazard a guess. He only knew she had some reason of her own which seemed to her a sufficient bar to matrimony, and made her firmly determine never in any case to marry any one.

About twelve months after Guy's sudden disappearance, however, a new element entered into Elma's life. At first sight it seemed to have but little to do with the secret of her soul. It was merely that the new purchaser of the Dowlands estate had built herself a pretty little Queen Anne house on the ground, and come to live in it.

Nevertheless, from the very first day they met, Elma took most kindly to this new Miss Ewes, the strange and eccentric musical composer. The mistress of Dowlands was a distant cousin of Mrs. Clifford's own, so the family naturally had to call upon her at once; and Elma somehow seemed always to get on from the outset in a remarkable way with her mother's relations. At first, to be sure, Elma could see Mrs. Clifford was rather afraid to leave her alone with the odd new-comer, whose habits and manners were as curious and weird as the sudden twists and turns of her own wayward music. But after a time a change came over Mrs. Clifford in this respect; and instead of trying to keep Elma and Miss Ewes apart, it was evident to Elma (who never missed any of the small by-play of life) that her mother rather desired to throw them closely together. Thus it came to pass that one morning, about a month after Miss Ewes' arrival in her new home, Elma had run in with a message from her mother, and found the distinguished composer, as was often the case at that time of day, sitting dreamily at her piano, trying over on the gamut strange, fanciful chords of her own peculiar, witch-like character. The music waxed and waned to a familiar lilt.

"That's beautiful," Elma cried, enthusiastically, as the composer looked up at her with an inquiring glance. "I never heard anything in my life before that went so straight through one, with it's penetrating melody. Such a lovely, gliding sound, you know! So soft and serpentine!" And even as she said it, a deep flush rose red in the centre of her cheek. She was sorry for the words before they were out of her mouth. They recalled all at once, in some mysterious way, that horrid, persistent nightmare of the hateful snake-dance. In a second Miss Ewes caught the bright gleam in her eye, and the deep flush on her cheek that so hastily followed it. A meaning smile came over the elder woman's face all at once, not unpleas-

antly. She was a handsome woman for her age, but very
dark and gypsy-like, after the fashion of the Eweses,
with keen Italian eyes and a large, smooth expanse of
powerful forehead. Lightly she ran her hand over the
keys with a masterly touch and fixed her glance as she
did so on Elma. There was a moment's pause. Miss
Ewes eyed her closely. She was playing a tune that
seemed oddly familiar to Elma's brain somehow—to her
brain, not to her ears, for Elma felt certain, even while
she recognized it most, she had never before heard it.
It was a tune that waxed and waned and curled up and
down sinuously, and twisted in and out and—ah, yes,
now she knew it!—raised its sleek head, and darted out
its forked tongue, and vibrated with swift tremors, and
tightened and slackened, and coiled restlessly at last in
great folds all around her. Elma listened, with eager eyes
half-starting from her head, with clenched nails dug deep
into the tremulous palms, as her heart throbbed fast and
her nerves quivered fiercely. Oh, it was wrong of Miss
Ewes to tempt her like this! It was wrong, so wrong
of her! For Elma knew what it was at once—the song
she had heard running vaguely through her head the
night of the dance, the night she fell in love with Cyril
Waring.

With a throbbing heart, Elma sat down on the sofa,
and tried with all her might and main not to listen. She
clasped her hands still tighter. She refused to be
wrought up. She wouldn't give way to it. If she had
followed her own impulse, to be sure, she would have
risen on the spot and danced that mad dance once more
with all the wild abandonment of an almeh or a Zingari.
But she resisted with all her might. And she resisted
successfully,

Miss Ewes, never faltering, kept her keen eye fixed
hard on her with a searching glance, as she ran over the
keys in ever fresh combinations.

Faster, wilder, and stranger the music rose; but Elma
sat still, her breast heaving hard and her breath panting,
yet otherwise as still and motionless as a statue. She
knew Miss Ewes could tell exactly how she felt. She
knew she was trying her; she knew she was tempt-
ing her to get up and dance; and yet she was not one

bit afraid of this strange, weird woman as she'd been
afraid that sad morning at home of her own mother.

The composer went on fiercely for some minutes more,
leaning close over the keyboard, and throwing her very
soul, as Elma could plainly see, into the tips of her fingers.
Then, suddenly she rose, and came over, well pleased,
to the sofa where Elma sat. With a motherly gesture,
she took Elma's hand ; she smoothed her dark hair ; she
bent down with a tender look in those strange, gray eyes,
and printed a kiss unexpectedly on the poor girl's forehead.

" Elma," she said, leaning over her, " do you know
what that was ? That was the Naga snake-dance. It
gave you an almost irresistible longing to rise, and hold
the snake in your own hands, and coil his great folds
around you. I could see how you felt. But you were
strong enough to resist. That was very well done.
You resisted even the force of my music, didn't you ? "

Elma, trembling all over, but bursting with joy that
she could speak of it at last without restraint to somebody, answered, in a very low and tremulous voice,
" Yes, Miss Ewes, I resisted it."

Miss Ewes leant back in her place, and gazed at her
long with a very affectionate and motherly air. " Then
I'm sure I don't know," she said at last, breaking out in
a voice full of confidence, " why on earth you shouldn't
marry this young man you're in love with ! "

Elma's heart beat still harder and higher than ever.

" What young man ? " she murmured low—just to
test the enchantress.

And Miss Ewes made answer without one moment's
hesitation, " Why, of course, Cyril Waring ! "

For a minute or two, then, there was a dead silence.
After that, Miss Ewes looked up and spoke again.
" Have you felt it often ? " she asked, without one word
of explanation.

" Twice before," Elma answered, not pretending to
misunderstand. " Once I gave way. That was the very
first time, you see, and I didn't know yet exactly what
it meant. The second time I knew, and then I resisted
it."

Somehow, before Miss Ewes, she hardly ever felt shy.

She was so conscious Miss Ewes knew all about it without her telling her.

The elder woman looked at her with unfeigned admiration.

" That was brave of you," she said, quietly. " I couldn't have done it myself! I should have *had* to give way to it. Then in *you* it's dying out. That's as clear as daylight. It won't go any farther. I knew it wouldn't, of course, when I saw you resisted even the Naga dance. And for you, that's excellent. . . . For myself, I encourage it. It's that that makes my music what it is. It's that that inspires me. I composed that Naga dance I just played over to you, Elma. But not all out of my own head. I couldn't have invented it. It comes down in our blood, my dear, to you and me alike. We both inherit it from a common ancestress."

" Tell me all about it," Elma cried, nestling close to her new friend with a wild burst of relief. " I don't know why, but I'm not at all ashamed of it all before you, Miss Ewes—at least, not in the way I am before mother."

" You needn't be ashamed of it," Miss Ewes answered, kindly. " You've nothing to be ashamed of. It'll never trouble *you* in your life again. It always dies out at last, they say, in the sixth or seventh generation, and when it's dying out, it goes as it went with you, on the night you first fell in love with Cyril. If, after that, you resist, it never comes back again. Year after year the impulse grows feebler and feebler. And if you can withstand the Naga dance, you can withstand anything. Come here and take my hand, dear. I'll tell you all about it."

Late at night Elma sat, tearful but happy, in her own room at home, writing a few short lines to Cyril Waring. This was all she said : —

" There's no reason on my side now, dearest Cyril. It's all a mistake. I'll marry you whenever and wherever you will. There need be no reason on your side either. I love you and can trust you. Yours ever, ELMA."

When Cyril Waring received that note next morning

he kissed it reverently and put it away in his desk among a bundle of others. But he said to himself sternly in his own soul for all that, "Never while Guy still rests under that cloud! And how it's ever to be lifted from him is to me inconceivable."

CHAPTER XXXIV.

A STROKE FOR FREEDOM.

IN Africa, meanwhile, during those eighteen months, King Khatsua had kept his royal word. He had held his two European prisoners under close watch and ward in the Koranna hut he had assigned them for their residence.

Like most other negro princes, indeed, Khatsua was a shrewd man of business in his own way; and while he meant to prevent the English strangers from escaping seaward with news of the new El Dorado they had discovered in Barolong land, he hadn't the least idea of turning away on that account the incidental advantages to be gained for himself by permitting them to hunt freely in his dominions for diamonds. So long as they acquiesced in the rough-and-ready royalty of fifty per cent, he had proposed to them when he first decided to detain them in his own territory,—one stone for the king, and one for the explorers,—they were free to pursue their quest after gems to their hearts' content in the valleys of Barolong land. And as the two Englishmen, for their part, had nothing else to do in Africa, and as they still went on hoping against hope for some chance of escape or rescue, they dug for diamonds with a will, and secured a number of first-class stones that would have made their fortunes indeed—if only they could have got them to the sea or to England.

Of course they lived perforce in the Koranna hut assigned them by the king, in pretty much the same way as the Korannas themselves did. King Khatsua's men supplied them abundantly with grain, and fruits, and game ; and even at times procured them ready-made clothes, by exchange with Kimberley. In other respects,

they were not ill-treated; they were merely detained
"during his majesty's pleasure." But as his majesty had
no intention of killing the goose that laid the golden eggs,
or of letting them go, if he could help it, to spread the
news of their find among their greedy fellow-countrymen, it seemed to them both as if they might go on being detained like this in Barolong land for an indefinite
period.

Still, things went indifferently with them. As they
lived and worked together in their native hut by Khatsua's village, a change began slowly but irresistibly to
come over Granville Kelmscott's feelings towards his unacknowledged half-brother. At first, it was with the deepest sense of distaste and loathing that the dispossessed
heir found himself compelled to associate with Guy Waring in such close companionship. But bit by bit, as they
two saw more and more of one another, this feeling of
distaste began to wear off piecemeal. Granville Kelmscott was more than half ashamed to admit it even to
himself, but in process of time he really almost caught
himself beginning to like—well, to like the man he believed to be a murderer. It was shocking and horrible,
no doubt: but what else was he to do? Guy formed now
his only European society. By the side of those savage
Barolongs, whose chief thought nothing of perpetrating
the most nameless horrors before their very eyes, for the
gratification of mere freaks of passion or jealousy, a European murderer of the gentlemanly class seemed almost,
by comparsion, a mild and gentle personage. Granville
hardly liked to allow it in his own mind, but it was nevertheless the case; he was getting positively fond of this
man, Guy Waring.

Besides, blood is generally thicker than water. Living in such close daily communion with Guy, and talking
with him unrestrainedly at last, upon all possible points,
—save that one unapproachable one which both seemed
to instinctively avoid alluding to in any way,—Granville
began to feel that, murderer or no murderer, Guy was in
all essentials very near indeed to him. Nay, more, he
found himself at times actually arguing the point with
his own conscience that, after all, Guy was a very good
sort of fellow; and if ever he had murdered Montague

Nevitt at all—which looked very probable—he must have murdered him under considerable extenuating circumstances.

There was only one thing about Guy that Granville didn't like when he got to know him. This homicidal half-brother of his was gentle as a woman; tender, kind-hearted, truthful, affectionate; a gentleman to the core, and a jolly good fellow into the bargain; but—there's always a but—he was a terrible money-grubber! Even there in the lost heart of Africa, at such a distance from home, with so little chance of ever making any use of his hoarded wealth, the fellow used to hunt up those wretched small stones, and wear them night and day in a belt around his waist, as if he really loved them for their own mere sakes—dirty, high-priced little baubles! Granville, for his part, couldn't bear to see such ingrained love of pelf. It was miserable; it was mercenary.

To be sure, he himself hunted diamonds every day of his life, just as hard as Guy did; there was nothing else to do in this detestable place, and a man *must* find something to turn his idle hands to. Also, he carried them, like Guy, bound up in a girdle around his own waist; it was a pity they should be lost, if ever he should chance to get away safe in the end, to England. But then, don't you see, the cases were so different. Guy hoarded up his diamonds for mere wretched gain; whereas Granville valued his (he said to himself often) not for the mere worth in money of those shimmering little trinkets, but for his mother's sake, and Gwendoline's, and the credit of the family. He wanted Lady Emily to see her son filling the place in the world she had always looked forward with hope to his filling; and by heaven's help, he thought, he could still fill it. He couldn't marry Gwendoline on a beggar's pittance; and by heaven's help he hoped still to be able to marry her.

Guy, on the other hand, found himself almost equally surprised, in turn, at the rapid way he grew really to be fond of Granville Kelmscott. Though Kelmscott knew (as he thought) the terrible secret of his half-unconscious crime—for he could feel how completely he had acted under Montague Nevitt's compelling influence,—Guy was aware before long of such a profound and deep-seated sympathy existing between them, that he became exceedingly attached, in time, to his friendly fellow-prisoner. In spite of the one barrier they could never break down, he spoke freely by degrees to Granville of everything else in his whole life; and Granville in return spoke just as freely. A good fellow, Granville, when you got to know him. There was only a single trait in his character Guy couldn't endure, and that was his ingrained love of money-grubbing. For the way the man pounced down upon those dirty little stones, when he saw them in the mud, and hoarded them up in his belt, and seemed prepared to defend them with his very life-blood, Guy couldn't conceal from himself the fact that he fairly despised him. Such vulgar, commonplace, unredeemed love of pelf! Such mere *bourgeois* avarice! Of what use could those wretched pebbles be to him here in the dusty plains of far inland Africa?

Guy himself kept close count of his finds, to be sure; but then; the cases, don't you see, were so different! *He* wanted his diamonds to discharge the great debt of his life to Cyril, and to appear an honest man, rehabilitated once more, before the brother he had so deeply wronged and humiliated. Whereas Granville Kelmscott, a rich man's son, and the heir to a great estate beyond the dreams of avarice—that *he* should have come risking his life in these savage wilds for mere increase of superfluous wealth, why, it was simply despicable!

So eighteen months wore away, in mutual friendship, tempered to a certain degree by mutual contempt, and little chance of escape came to the captives in Baralong land.

At last, as the second winter came round once more, for two or three weeks the Englishmen in their huts began to perceive that much bustle and confusion was going on all around in King Khatsua's dominions. Preparations for a war on a considerable scale were clearly taking place. Men mustered daily on the dusty plain with firearms and assegais. Much pombé was drunk; many palavers took place; a constant drumming of gongs and tom-toms disturbed their ears by day and by night. The Englishmen concluded some big marauding expedition was in contemplation. And they were quite right. King Khatsua was about to concentrate his forces for an attack on a neighboring black monarch, as powerful and perhaps as cruel as himself, Montisive of the Bush Veldt.

Slowly the preparations went on all around. Then the great day came at last, and King Khatsua set forth on his mighty campaign, to the sound of big drums and the blare of native trumpets.

When the warriors had marched out of the villages on their way northward to the war, Guy saw the two prisoners' chance of escape had arrived in earnest. They were guarded as usual, of course; but not so strictly as before; and during the night, in particular, Guy noticed with pleasure, little watch was now kept upon them. The savage, indeed, can't hold two ideas in his head at once. If he's making war on his neighbor on one side, he has no room left to think of guarding his prisoners on the other.

" To-night," Guy said, one evening, as they sat together in their hut, over their native supper of mealie cakes and springbok venison, " we must make a bold stroke. We must creep out of the kraal as well as we can, and go for the sea westward, through Namaqua land to Angra Pequena."

" Westward ? " Granville answered, very dubiously. " But why westward, Waring? Surely our shortest way to the coast is down to Kimberley, and so on to the Cape. It'll take us weeks and weeks to reach the sea, won't it, by way of Namaqua land ?"

" No matter for that," Guy replied with confidence. He knew the map pretty well, and had thought it all over. " As soon as the Barolong miss us in the morning, they'll naturally think we've gone south, as you say, towards our own people. So they'll pursue us in that direction and try to take us ; and if they were to catch us after we'd once run away, you may be sure they'd kill us as soon as look at us. But it would never occur to them, don't you see, we were going away west. They won't follow us that way. So west we'll go, and strike out for the sea, as I say, at Angra Pequena."

They sat up through the night discussing plans low to

themselves in the dark, till nearly two in the morning. Then, when all was silent around, and the Barolong slept, they stole quietly out, and began their long march across the country to westward. Each man had his diamonds tied tightly round his waist, and his revolver at his belt. They were prepared to face every unknown danger. Crawling past the native huts with very cautious steps, they made for the open, and emerged from the village on to the heights that bounded the valley of the Lugura. They had proceeded in this direction for more than an hour, walking as hard as their legs would carry them, when the sound of a man running fast, but barefoot, fell on their ears from behind in a regular pit-a-pat. Guy looked back in dismay, and saw a naked Barolong just silhouetted against the pale sky on the top of a long, low ridge they had lately crossed over. At the very same instant Granville raised his revolver and pointed it at the man, who evidently had not yet perceived them. With a sudden gesture of horror, Guy knocked down his hand and prevented his taking aim.

"Don't shoot," he cried, in a voice of surprised dismay and disapproval. "We mustn't take his life. How do we know he is an enemy at all? He mayn't be pursuing us."

"Best shoot on spec anyway," Granville answered, somewhat discomposed. "All's fair in war. The fellow's after us, no doubt. And at any rate, if he sees us he may go and report our whereabouts to the village."

"What? shoot an unarmed man who shows no signs of hostility! Why, it would be sheer murder," Guy cried with some horror. "We mustn't make our retreat on *those* principles, Kelmscott; it'd be quite indefensible. I decline to fire except when we're attacked. I won't be any party, myself, to needless bloodshed."

Granville Kelmscott gazed at him, there in the gray dawn, in unspeakable surprise Not shoot at a negro! In such straits, too, as theirs! And this rebuke had come to him—from the mouth of the murderer!

Turn it over as he might, Granville couldn't understand it.

The Barolong ran along on the crest of the ridge, still at the top of his speed, without seeming to notice them in the gloom of the valley. Presently he disappeared over the edge to southward. Guy was right, after all. He wasn't in pursuit of them. More likely he was only a runaway slave, taking advantage, like themselves, of King Khatsua's absence.

CHAPTER XXXV.

PERILS BY THE WAY.

THREE weeks later, two torn and tattered, half-starved Europeans sat under a burning South African sun by the dry bed of a shrunken summer torrent. It was in the depths of Namaqua land, among the stony Karoo; and the fugitives were straggling, helplessly and hopelessly seaward, thirsty and weary, through a half hostile country, making their marches as best they could at dead of night and resting by day where the natives would permit them.

Their commissariat had indeed been a lean and hungry one. Though they carried many thousand pounds' worth of diamonds about their persons, they had nothing negotiable with which to buy food or shelter from the uncivilized Namaquas. Ivory, cloth, and beads were the currency of the country. No native thereabouts would look for a moment at their little round nobs of water-worn pebbles. The fame of the diamond fields hadn't penetrated as yet so far west in the land as to have reached to the huts of the savage Namaquas.

And now their staying power was almost worn out. Granville Kelmscott lay down on the sandy soil with a wild gesture of despair. All around were bare rocks and the dry, sweltering veldts, covered only with round stones and red sand and low, bushy vegetation.

" Waring," he said, feebly, in a very faint voice, " I wish you'd leave me and go on by yourself. I am no good any more. I'm only a drag upon you. This fever's too bad for me to stand much longer. I can never pull through to the coast alive. I've no energy left, were it even to try. I'd like to lie down here and die where I sit. Do go and leave me."

"Never!" Guy answered, resolutely. "I'll never desert you, Kelmscott, while I've a drop of blood left. If I carry you on my back to the coast, I'll get you there at last, or else we'll both die on the veldt together."

Granville held his friend's hand in his own fevered fingers as he might have held a woman's.

"Oh, Waring," he cried once more, in a voice half choked with profound emotion, "I don't know how to thank you enough for all you've done for me. You've behaved to me like a brother—like a brother indeed. It makes me ashamed to think, when I see how unselfish, and good, and kind you've been—ashamed to think I once distrusted you. You've been an angel to me all through. Without you, I don't know how I could ever have lived on through this journey at all. And I can't bear to feel now I may spoil your retreat—can't bear to know I'm a drag and burden to you."

"My dear fellow," Guy said, holding the thin and fevered hand very tenderly in his, "don't talk to me like that. I feel to you every bit as you feel to me in this matter, I was afraid of you at first, because I knew you misunderstood me. But the more I've seen of you, the better we've each of us learned to sympathize with the other. We've long been friends. I love you now, as you say, like a brother."

Granville hesitated for a moment. Should he out with it or not? Then, at last, the whole long-suppressed truth came out with a burst. He seized his companion's two hands at once in a convulsive grasp.

"That's not surprising, either," he said, "after all—for, Guy, do you know, we *are* really brothers!"

Guy gazed at him in astonishment. For a moment he thought his friend's reason was giving way. Then slowly and gradually he took it all in.

"*Are* really brothers!" he repeated, in dazed sort of way. "Do you mean it, Kelmscott? Then my father and Cyril's—"

"Was mine, too, Waring. Yes; I couldn't bear to die without telling you that. And I tell it now to you. You two are the heirs of the Tilgate estates. And the unknown person who paid six thousand pounds to Cyril, just

before you left England, was your father and mine—
Colonel Henry Kelmscott."

Guy bent over him for a few seconds in speechless
surprise. Words failed him at first. "How do you know
all this, Kelmscott?" he said at last, faintly.

Granville told him in as few words as possible—for indeed, he was desperately weak and ill—by what accident
he had discovered his father's secret. But he told him
only what he knew himself. For, of course, he was
ignorant as yet of the Colonel's seizure and sudden death
on the very day after they had sailed from England.

Guy listened to it all in profound silence. It was a
strange and for him a momentous tale. Then he said
at last, as Granville finished, "And you never told me
this all these long months, Kelmscott."

"I always meant to tell you, Guy," his half-brother answered, in a sudden fit of penitence. "I always meant
in the end you and your brothers Cyril should come into
your own at Tilgate as you ought. I was only waiting—"

"Till you'd realized enough to make good some part of
your personal loss," Guy suggested, not unkindly.

"Oh, no," Granville answered, flushing up at the
suggestion. "I wasn't waiting for that. Don't think me so
mercenary. I was waiting for *you* in your turn to
extend to *me* your own personal confidence. You know,
Guy," he went on dropping into a still more hushed and
solemn undertone "I saw an evening paper the night we
left Plymouth—"

"Oh, I know, I know," Guy cried, interrupting him,
with a very pale face. "Don't speak to me of that. I
can't bear to think of it. Kelmscott, I was mad when I
did that deed. I wasn't myself. I acted under somebody else's compulsion and influence. The man had a
sort of hypnotic power over my will, I believe. I couldn't
help doing whatever he ordered me. It was he who
suggested it. It was he that did it. And it's he who
was really and truly guilty."

"And who was that man?" Granville Kelmscott
asked, with some little curiosity.

"There's no reason I shouldn't tell you," Guy
answered, "now we've once broken the ice; and I'm glad
in my heart, I must say, that we've broken it. For a

year and a half, day and night, that barrier has been
raised between us always, and I've longed to get rid of it.
But I was afraid to speak of it to you, and you to me.
Well, the man, if you must know, was Montague Nevitt!"

Granville Kelmscott looked up at him in incredulous
surprise. But he was too ill and weak to ask the meaning of this riddle. Montague Nevitt! What on earth
could Waring mean by that? How on earth could Montague Nevitt have influenced and directed him in assault-
ing and murdering Montague Nevitt?

For a long time there was silence. Each brother was
thinking his own thoughts to himself about this double
disclosure. At last Granville lifted his head and spoke
again.

" And you'll go home to England now," he said, " under an assumed name, I suppose; and arrange with your
brother Cyril for him to claim the Kelmscott estates, and
allow you something out of them in retirement somewhere."

" Oh, no," Guy answered, manfully. " I'm going home
to England now, if I go at all, under my own proper
name that I've always borne, to repay Cyril in full every
penny I owe him, to make what reparation I can for the
wrong I've done, and to give myself up to the police for
trial."

Granville gazed at him, more surprised and more admiring than ever.

" You're a brave man, Waring," he said, slowly. " I
don't understand it at all. But I know you're right.
And I almost believe you. I almost believe it was not
your fault. I should like to get through to England,
after all, if it was only to see you safe out of your trou-
bles."

Guy looked at him fixedly.

" My dear fellow," he said, in a compassionate tone,
" you mustn't talk any more. " You've talked a great
deal too much already. I see a hut, I fancy, over yonder,
beside that dark patch of brush. Now, you must do exactly as I bid you. Don't struggle or kick. Lie as still
as you can. I'll carry you there on my back, and then
we'll see if we can get you anyhow a drop of pure water."

CHAPTER XXXVI

DESERTED.

That was almost the last thing Granville Kelmscott knew. Some strange, shadowy dreams, to be sure, disturbed the lethargy into which he fell soon after, but they were intermittent and indefinite. He was vaguely aware of being lifted with gentle care into somebody's arms, and of the somebody staggering along with him, not without considerable difficulty, over the rough, stony ground of that South African plateau. He remembered, also, as in a trance, some sound of angry voices—a loud expostulation—a hasty palaver—a long, slow pause—a gradual sense of reconciliation and friendliness—during all which, as far as he could recover the circumstances afterwards, he must have been extended on the earth, with his back propped against a great ledge of jutting rock, and his head hanging listless on his sinking breast. Thenceforward all was blank, or just dimly perceived at long intervals between delirium and unconsciousness. He was ill for many days, where or how he knew not.

In some half-dreamy way ne was aware, too, now and again, of strange voices by his side, strange faces tending him. But they were black faces, all, and the voices spoke in deep, guttural tones, unlike even the clicks and harsh Bantu jerks with which he had grown so familiar in eighteen months among the Barolong. This that he heard now, or seemed to hear in his delirium, like distant sounds of water, was a wholly different and very much harsher tongue—the tongue of the Namaquas, in fact, though Granville was far too ill and too drowsy just then to think of reasoning about it or classifying it in any way. All he knew for the moment was that sometimes, when he turned round feebly on his bed of straw, and asked for drink or help in a faltering voice, no white man appeared to answer his summons. Black faces all—black, black, and unfamiliar. Very intermittently he was conscious of a faint sense of loneliness. He knew not why. But he thought he could guess. Guy Waring had deserted him.

At last, one morning, after more days had passed than Granville could possibly count, all of a sudden, in a wild whirl, he came to himself again at once, with that instant revulsion of complete awakening which often occurs at the end of long fits of delirium in malarious fever. A light burst in upon him with a flash. In a moment his brain seemed to clear all at once, and everything to grow plain as day before him. He raised himself on one wasted elbow and gazed around him with profound awe. He saw it all now; he remembered everything, everything.

He was alone among savages in the far heart of Africa.

He lay on his back, on a heap of fresh straw, in a close and filthy mud-built hut. Under his aching neck a wooden pillow or prop of native make supported his head. Two women and a man bent over him and smiled. Their faces, though black, were far from unkindly. They were pleased to see him stare about with such meaning in his eyes. They were friendly, no doubt. They seemed really to take an interest in their patient's recovery.

But where was Guy Waring? Dead? Dead? Or run away? Had his half-brother, in this utmost need, then, so basely deserted him?

For some minutes Granville gazed around him, half dazed, and in a turmoil of surprise, yet with a vivid passion of acute inquiry. Now he was once well awake he must know all immediately. But how? Whom to ask? This was terrible, terrible! He had no means of inter-communication with the people in the hut. He knew none of their language, nor they of his. He was utterly alone, among unmitigated savages.

Meanwhile, the man and the women talked loud among themselves in their own harsh speech, evidently well pleased and satisfied at their guest's improvement. With a violent effort, Granville began to communicate with them in the language of signs which every savage knows as he

knows his native tongue, and in which the two Englishmen had already made some progress during their stay
in Barolong land.

Pointing first to himself, with one hand on his breast,
he held up two fingers before the observant Namaqua, to
indicate that at first there had been a couple of them
on the road, both white men. The latter point he still
further elaborated by showing the white skin on his own
bare wrist, and once more holding up the two fingers de-
monstratively. The Namaqua nodded. He had seized
the point well. He held up two fingers in return himself;
then looked at his own black wrist and shook his head in
dissent—they were not black men; after which he touched
Granville's fair forearm with his hand; yes, yes, just so;
he took it in; two white men.

What had become of the other one? Granville asked,
in the same fashion, by looking around him on all sides in
dumb show, inquiringly. One finger only was held up
now, pointing about the hut; one hand was laid upon his
own breast to show that a single white man alone remained. He glanced about him uneasily. What had
happened to his companion?

The Namaqua pointed with his finger to the door of
the hut, as much as to say the other man was gone. He
seized every sign at once with true savage quickness.

Then Granville tried once more. Was his companion
dead? Had he been killed in a fight? Was that the
reason of his absence? He lunged forward with his hand
holding an imaginary assegai. He pressed on upon the
foe; he drove it through a body. Then he fell, as if dead,
on the floor, with a groan and a shriek. After which,
picking himself up as well as he was able, and crawling
back to his straw, he proceeded in mute pantomime to
bury himself decently.

The Namaqua shook his head again, with a laugh of
dissent. Oh, no; not like that. It had happened quite
otherwise. The missing white man was well and vigorous,
a slap on his own chest sufficiently indicated that news.
He placed his two first fingers in the ground, astride
like legs, and made them walk along fast, one in front of
the other. The white man had gone away. He had gone
on foot. Granville nodded acquiescence. The savage

took water in a calabash and laid it on the floor. Then he walked once more with his fingers, as if on a long and weary march, to the water's brink. Granville nodded comprehension again. He understood the signs. The white man had gone away, alone, on foot—and seaward.

At that instant, with a sudden cry of terror, the invalid's hands went down to his waist, where he wore the girdle that contained those precious diamonds—the diamonds that were to be the ransom of some fraction of Tilgate. An awful sense of desertion broke over him all at once. He called aloud in his horror. It was too much to believe. The girdle was gone, and the diamonds with it!

Hypocrite! Hypocrite! Thief! Murderer! Robber! He had trusted that vile creature, that plausible wretch, in spite of all the horrible charges he knew against him. And *this* was the sequel of their talk that day! *This* was how Guy Waring had requited his confidence.

He had stolen the fruits of eighteen months' labor.

Granville turned to the Namaqua, wild with his terrible loss, and pointed angrily to his loins, where the diamonds were not. The savage nodded; looked wise and shook his head; pretended to gird himself round the waist with a cloth; then went over to Granville, who lay still in the straw, undid an imaginary belt with deliberate care, tied it round his own body above the other one with every appearance of prudence and forethought, counted the small stones in it one by one in his hand to the exact number with grotesque fidelity, and finally set his fingers to walk a second time at a rapid pace in the direction of the calabash, which represented the ocean.

Granville fell back on his wooden pillow with a horrible groan of awakened distrust. The man had gone off, that was clear, and had stolen his diamonds. This is what comes of intrusting your life and property to a discovered murderer. How could he ever have been such a fool? He would never forgive himself.

The desertion itself was bad enough, in all conscience; but it was as nothing at all in Granville's mind to the wickedness of the robbery.

He might have known it, of course. How that fellow

toiled and moiled and gloated over his wretched diamonds! How little he seemed to think of the stain of
blood on his hands, and how much of the mere chance of
making filthy lucre! Pah! Pah! it was pitiable. The
man's whole mind was distorted by a hideous fungoid
growth—the love of gain, which is the root of all evil.
For a few miserable stones he would plunder his own
brother, lying helpless and ill in that African hut, and
make off with the booty himself, saving his own skin,
seaward.

If it had not been for the unrequited kindness of these
mere savage Namaquas, Granville cried to himself in his
bitterness, he might have died of want in the open desert. And now he would go down to the coast after all, a
ruined man, penniless and friendless. It was a hard
thought indeed for a Kelmscott to think he should have
been abandoned and robbed by his own half-brother, and
should owe his life now to a heathen African. The
tender mercies of a naked barbarian in a mud-built hut
were better than the false friendship of his father's son,
the true heir of Tilgate.

It was miserable! pitiable! The shock of that discovery threw Granville back once more into a profound
fever. For several hours he relapsed into delirium. And
the worst of it was, the negroes wouldn't let him die
quietly in his own plain way. In the midst of it all, he
was dimly aware of a dose thrust down his throat. It
was the Namaqua adminstering him a pill,—some nau-
seous native decoction, no doubt,—which tasted as if it
were made of stiff, white paper.

CHAPTER XXXVII.

AUX ARMES !

For a day or two more, Granville remained seriously ill in the dirty hut. At the end of that time, weak and wasted as he was he insisted upon getting up and setting out alone on his long march seaward.

It was a wild resolve. He was utterly unfit for it. The hospitable Namaqua, whose wives had nursed him well through that almost hopeless illness, did his best to persuade the rash Englishman from so mad a course, by gestures and entreaties, in his own mute language. But, Granville was obstinate. He would *not* sit down quietly and be robbed like this of the fruit of his labors. He would not be despoiled. He would not be trampled upon. He would make for the coast, if he staggered in like a skeleton, and would confront the robber with his own vile crime, be it at Angra Pequena, or Cape Town, or London, or Tilgate.

In short, he would do much as Guy himself had done when he discovered Montague Nevitt's theft of the six thousand. He would follow the villain till he ran him to earth, and would tax him at last to his face with the open proofs of his consummate treachery. What's bred in the bone will out in the blood. The Kelmscott strain worked alike its own way in each of them.

The Namaqua, to be sure, tried in vain to explain to Granville by elaborate signs that the other white man had given orders to the contrary. The other white man had strictly enjoined upon him not to let the invalid escape from his hut on any pretext whatever. The other white man had promised him a reward, a very large reward—money, guns, ammunition—if he kept him safely and didn't allow him to escape. Granville Kelmscott

smiled to himself a bitter, cynical smile. Poor confiding
savage! He didn't know Guy as well as he, his brother,
did.

And yet, in the midst of it all, in spite of the revulsion,
Granville was conscious now and then of some little ingratitude somewhere to his half-brother's memory. After
all, Guy had shown him time and again no small kindness.
Some excuse should be made for a man who saves his
own life first in very dire extremities. But none, no,
none for one who has the incredible and inhuman meanness to rob his own brother of his hard-earned gains in
a strange, wild land, when he thinks him dying.

For it was the robbery, not the desertion, Granville
could never forgive. The man who was capable of doing
that basest of acts was capable also of murder or any
crime in the decalogue.

So the fevered white man rose at last one morning on
his shrunken limbs, and staggered as best he might from
his protector's hut in a wild impulse of resolution on his
mad journey seaward. When the Namaqua saw nothing
on earth would induce him to remain, he shouldered
his arms and went out beside him, fully equipped for
fight with matchlock and assegai. Not that the savage
made any undue pretence to a purely personal devotion
to the belated white man. On the contrary, he signified
to Granville with many ingenious signs that he was afraid
of losing the great reward he had been promised, if once
he let the invalid get out of his sight unattended.

Granville smiled once more that bitter smile of new-
born cynicism. Well, let the fellow follow him if he
liked! He would reward him himself if ever they reached
the coast in safety. And in any case, it was better to go
attended by a native. An interpreter who can communicate in their own tongue with the people through whose
territory you are going to pass, is always useful in a
savage country.

How Granville got over that terrible journey seaward
he could never tell. He crawled on and on, supported
by the faithful Namaqua with unfailing good humor, over
that endless veldt, for three long days of wretched, foot-
sore marching. And for three long nights he slept, or
lay awake, under the clear desert stars, on the open

ground of barren Namaqua land.   It was a terrible time.
Worn and weary with the fever, Granville was wholly
unfit for any kind of travelling.   Nothing but the iron
constitution of the Kelmscotts could ever have stood so
severe an ordeal.   But the son of six generations of sol-
diers, who had commanded in the fever-stricken flats of
Walcheren, or followed Wellesley through the jungles o*
tropical India, or forced their way with Napier into the
depths of Abyssinia, was not to be daunted even by the
nameless horrors of that South African desert.   Granville
still endured for three days and nights, and was ready
to march, or crawl on, once more, upon the fourth morning.

Here, however, his Namaqua guide, with every appearance of terror, made strong warnings of danger.   The
country beyond, he signified by strange gestures, lay in
the hands of a hostile tribe, hereditarily at war with his
own fellow-clansmen.   He didn't even know whether the
other white man, with the diamonds round his waist, had
got safely through, or whether the hostile tribe beyond
the frontier had assegaied him and " eaten him up," as
the picturesque native phrase goes.   It was difficult
enough for even a strong warrior to force his way through
that district with a good company of followers ; impossible for a single weak invalid like Granville, attended
only by one poor ill-armed Namaqua.

So the savage seemed to say in his ingenious pantomime.
If they went on, they'd be killed and eaten up resistlessly.
If they stopped, they might pull through.   They must
wait and camp there.   For what they were to wait Granville hadn't the faintest conception.   But the Namaqua
insisted upon it, and Granville was helpless as a child in
his hands.   The man was alarmed, apparently, for his
promised reward.   If Granville insisted, he showed in
in very frank, dumb show, why—a thrust with the assegai explained the rest most persuasively.   Granville
still had his revolver, to be sure, and a few rounds of ball
cartridge.   But he was too weak to show fight; the
savage overmastered him.

They were seated on a stony ridge or sharp hog's back
overlooking the valley of a dry summer stream.   The
watershed on which they sat separated, with its chine of

rugged rocks, the territory of the two rival tribes.   **But**
the Namaqua was evidently very little afraid that **the**
enemy might transgress the boundaries of his fellow-
tribesmen.   He dared not himself go beyond the **jagged**
crest of the ridge ; but he seemed to think it pretty certain the people of the other tribe wouldn't, for their part,
in turn come across to molest him.   He sat down there
doggedly, as if expecting something or other to turn up
in course of time; and more than once he made signs to
Granville which the Englishman interpreted to mean that
after so many days and nights from some previous event
unspecified somebody would arrive on the track from the
coast at the point of junction between the hostile races !
  Granville was gazing at the Namaqua in the vain attempt to interpret these signs more fully to himself, when,
all of a sudden, an unexpected noise in the valley below
attracted his attention.   He pricked up his ears.   Impossible ! Incredible ! It couldn't be—yes, it was—the sharp
hiss of firearms !
  At the very same moment the Namaqua leapt to his
feet in sudden alarm, and, shading his eyes with his dusky
hand, gazed intently in front of him.   For a minute or
so he stood still, with brows knit and neck craning.   Then
he called out something in an excited tone two or three
times over in his own tongue to Granville.   The Englishman stared in the same direction, but could make out
nothing definite just at first, in the full glare of the sunlight.   But the Namaqua, with a cry of joy, held up his
two fingers as before, to symbolize the two white men
and pointed with one of them to his guest, while with the
other he indicated some object in the valley, nodding
many times over.   Granville seized his meaning at once.
Could it be true, what he said in this strange, mute
language ?   Could relief be at hand ?   Could the firing
beneath show that Guy was returning ?
  As he looked and strained his eyes, peering down upon
the red plain, under the shadow of his open palm, the
objects by the water-course grew gradually clearer.
Granville could make out now that a party of natives,
armed with spears and matchlocks, was attacking some
little encampment on the bank of the dry torrent.   The
small force in the encampment was returning the **fire**

with great vigor and spirit, though apparently overpowered by the superior numbers of their swarming assailants. Even as Granville looked, their case grew more
desperate. A whole horde of black men seemed to be
making an onset on some small, white object, most jealously guarded, round which the defenders of the camp
rallied with infinite energy. At the head of the little band
of strangers, a European in a pith helmet was directing
the fire, and fighting hard himself for the precious white
object. The rest were blacks, he thought, in half-civilized
costume. Granville's heart gave a bound as the leader
sprang forth upon one approaching savage. His action,
as he leapt, stamped the man at once. There was Kelmscott in the leap. Granville knew in a second it was
indeed Guy Waring.

The Namaqua recognized him too, and pointed enthusiastically forward. Granville saw what he meant. To
the front! To the front! If there was fighting to be
done, let them help their friends. Let them go forward
and claim the great reward offered,

Next moment, with a painful thrill of shame and remorse, the Englishman saw what was the nature of the
object they were so jealously guarding. His heart stood
still within him. It was a sort of sedan chair, or invalid
litter, borne on poles by four native porters. Talk about
coals of fire! Granville Kelmscott hardly knew how to
forgive himself for his unworthy distrust. Then Guy
must have reached the coast in safety, after leaving him
in charge of the Namaqua and fighting his way through,
and now he was on his way back to the interior again, with
a sufficient escort and a palanquin to fetch him.

Even as he looked, the assailants closed in more fiercely
than ever on the faltering little band. One of them thrust
out with an assegai at Guy. In an agony of horror, Granville cried aloud where he stood. Surely, surely, they
must be crushed to earth. No arms of precision could
ever avail them against such a swarm of assailants, poured
forth over their camp as if from some human ant-hill.

" Let us run!" the sick man cried to the Namaqua,
pointing to the fight below; and the Namaqua, compre-
hending the gesture, if not the words, set forward to run
with him down the slope into the valley.

At about a hundred yards off from the crowd, Granville crouched behind a clump of thorny acacia, and sig-
naLing to the Namaqua to hide at the same time, drew
his revolver and fired point-blank at the hindmost natives.

The effect was electrical. In a moment the savages
turned and gazed around them astonished. One of their
number was hit and wounded in the leg. Granville had
aimed so purposely, to maim and terrify them. The
natives faltered and fell back. As they did so, Granville
emerged from the shelter of the acacia bush, and fired a
second shot from another point at them. At the same
instant the Namaqua raised a loud native battle cry, and
brandished his assegai. The effect was electrical. The
hostile tribe broke up in wild panic at once. They cried
in their own tongue that the Namaquas were down upon
them, under English guidance; and, quick as lightning,
they dispersed as if by magic, to hide themselves about
in the thick bush jungle.

Two seconds later Guy was wringing Granville's hand
in a fervor of gratitude. Each man had saved the other's
life. In the rapid interchange of question and answer
that followed, one point alone puzzled them both for a
minute or two.

"But why on earth didn't you leave a line to explain
what you'd done?" Granville cried, now thoroughly
ashamed of his unbelief. "If only I'd known you were
coming back to the village it would have saved me so
much distress, so much sleepless misery."

"Why, so I did," Guy answered, still thoroughly
out of breath, and stained with blood and powder. "I
tore a leaf from my note-book and gave it to the Namaqua,
explaining to him by signs that he was to let you have
it at once the moment you were conscious. Here, you, sir,"
he went on, turning round to their faithful black ally,
and holding up the note-book before his eyes to refresh
his memory, "Why didn't you give it to the gentleman
as I told you?"

The Namaqua, catching hastily at the meaning from
the mere tone of the question, as well as from Guy's instinctive and graphic imitation of the act of writing
pulled out from his waistband the last relics of a very
brown and tattered fragment of paper, on which were

still legible in pencil the half-obliterated words: My dear Granville: I find there is no chance of conveying you to the coast through the territory of the next tribe, in your present condition, unless——"

The rest was torn off. Guy looked at it dubiously. But the Namaqua, anxious to show he had followed out all instructions to the very letter, tore off the next scrap before their eyes, rolled it up between his palms into a nice, greasy pill and proceeded to offer it for Granville's acceptance. The misapprehension was too absurd. Guy went off into a hearty peal of laughter at once. The Namaqua had taken the mysterious signs for "a very great medicine," and had administered the magical paper accordingly, as he understood himself to be instructed, at fixed intervals to his unfortunate patient. That was the medicine Granville remembered having forced down his throat at the moment when he first learned, as he thought, his half-brother's treachery.

CHAPTER XXXVIII.

NEWS FROM THE CAPE.

At the Holkers' at Chetwood, one evening some days later, Cyril Waring met Elma Clifford once more, the first time in months, and had twenty minutes' talk in the tea-room alone with her. Contrary to his rule, he had gone to the Holkers' party, that night, for a man can't remain a recluse all his life, no matter how hard he tries, merely because his brother is suspected of having committed a murder. In course of time the attitude palls upon him. For the first year after Guy's sudden and mysterious disappearance indeed, Cyril refused all invitations point-blank, except from the most intimate friends. The shame and disgrace of that terrible episode weighed him down so heavily that he couldn't bear to go out in the world among unsympathetic strangers.

But the deepest sorrow wears away by degrees, and at the end of twelve months Cyril found he could mix a little more unreservedly at last among his fellow-men. The hang-dog air sat ill upon his frank, free nature. This invitation to the Holkers', too, had one special attraction; he knew it was a house where he was almost certain of meeting Elma. And since Elma insisted now on writing to him constantly—she was a self-willed young woman, was Elma, and would have her way—he really saw no reason on earth himself why he shouldn't meet her. To meet is one thing, don't you know; to marry, another. At least, so fifty generations of young people have deluded themselves under similar circumstances into believing.

Elma was in the room before him, prettier than ever, people said, in the pale red ball-dress which exactly suited her gypsylike eyes and creamy complexion. As

she entered she saw Sir Gilbert Gildersleeve with his
wife and Gwendoline standing in the corner by the big
piano. Gwendoline looked pale and preoccupied as she
had always looked since Granville Kelmscott disappeared,
leaving behind him no more definite address for love-
letters than simply Africa ; and Lady Gildersleeve was, as
usual, quite subdued and broken. But the judge himself,
consoled by his new honors, seemed, as time wore on, to
have recovered a trifle of his old blustering manner. A
knighthood had reassured him. He was talking to Mr.
Holker in a loud voice as Elma approached him from
behind.

" Yes ; a very curious coincidence," he was just saying,
in his noisy fashion, with one big, burly hand held de-
monstratively before him. " A very curious and unexplained coincidence. They both vanished into space
about the self-same time. And nothing more has ever
since been heard of them. Quite an Arabian Nights
affair in its way—the enchanted carpet sort of business,
don't you know ?—wafted through the air unawares, like
Sinbad the Sailor, or the One-eyed Calender, from London to Bagdad, or Timbuctoo, or St. Petersburg. The
other young man one understands about of course ; *he*
had sufficient reasons of his own, no doubt, for leaving a
country which had grown too warm for him. But that
Granville Kelmscott, a gentleman of means, the heir to
such a fine estate as Tilgate, should disappear into infinity,
leaving no trace behind, like a lost comet—and at the
very moment, too, when he was just about to come into
the family property—why, I call it—I call it—I call
it——"

His jaw dropped suddenly. He grew deadly pale.
Words failed his stammering tongue. Do what he would,
he couldn't finish his sentence. And yet nothing very
serious had occurred to him in any way. It was merely
that, as he uttered these words, he caught Elma Clifford's
eye, and saw lurking in it a certain gleam of deadly contempt before which the big, blustering man himself had
quailed more than once in many a Surrey drawing-room.

For Sir Gilbert Gildersleeve knew as well as if she had
told him the truth in so many words, that Elma Clifford
suspected him of being Montague Nevitt's murderer.

Elma came forward, just to break the awkward pause, and shook hands with the party at the piano coldly. Sir Gilbert tried to avoid her, but with the inherited instinct of her race, Elma cut off his retreat. She boxed him in the corner between the piano and the wall.

"I heard what you were saying just now, Sir Gilbert," she murmured low, but with marked emphasis, after a few polite commonplaces of conversation had first passed between them; "and I want to ask you one question only about the matter. *Are* you so sure as you seem of what you said this minute? Are you so sure that Mr. Guy Waring *had* sufficient reasons of his own for wishing to leave the country?"

Before that unflinching eye, the great lawyer trembled, as many a witness had trembled of old under his own cross-examination. But he tried to pass it off just at first with a little society banter. He bowed and smiled, and pretended to look arch—look arch, indeed, with that ashen, white face of his!—as he answered, with forced humor:—

"My dear young lady, Mr. Guy Waring, as I understand, is Mr. Cyril Waring's brother, and as, by the law of England, the king can do no wrong, so I suppose—"

Elma cut him short in the middle of his sentence with an imperious gesture. He had never cut short an obnoxious and obtruding barrister himself with more crushing dignity.

"Mr. Cyril Waring has nothing at all to do with the point, one way or the other," the girl said, severely "Attend to my question. What I ask is this: Why do you, a judge who may one day be called upon to try the case, venture to say, on such partial evidence, that Mr. Guy Waring had sufficient reasons of his own for leaving the country?"

Called upon to try Guy Waring's case! The judge paused, abashed. He was very much afraid of her. This girl had such a strange look about the eyes, she made him tremble. People said the Ewes women were the descendants of a witch. And there was something truly witch-like in the way Elma Clifford looked straight down into his eyes. She seemed to see into his very soul. He knew she suspected him.

He shuffled and temporized. "Well everybody says so, you know," he answered, shrugging his shoulders carelessly. "And what everybody says *must* be true . . . Besides if *he* didn't do it, who did, I wonder?"

Elma pounced upon her opportunity with a woman's quickness. "Somebody else who was at Mambury that day, no doubt," she replied, with a meaning look. "It *must* have been somebody out of the few who were at Mambury."

That home thrust told. The judge's color was livid to look upon. What could this girl mean? How on earth could she know? How had she even found out he was at Mambury at all? A terrible doubt oppressed his soul. Had Gwendoline confided his movements to Elma? He had warned his daughter time and again not to mention the fact. "For fear of misapprehension," he said, with shuffling eyes askance, it was better nobody should know he had been anywhere near Dartmoor on the day of the accident.

However, there was one consolation,—the law, the law! She could have no legal proof, and intuition goes for nothing in a court of justice. All the suspicion went against Guy Waring. And Guy Waring?—Well, Guy Waring had fled the kingdom in the very nick of time, and was skulking now—Heaven alone knew where or why —in the remotest depths of some far African diggings.

And even as he thought it, the servant opened the door, and, in the regulation footman's voice, announced, "Mr. Waring."

The judge started afresh. For one moment his senses deceived him sadly. His mind was naturally full of Guy just now; and as the servant spoke, he saw a handsome young man in evening dress coming up the long drawing-room with the very air and walk of the man he had met that eventful afternoon at the "Dukeof Devonshire" at Plym. outh. Of course it was only Cyril, and a minute later the judge saw his mistake, and remembered with a bitter smile how conscience makes cowards of us all, as he had often remarked about shaky witnesses in his admirable perorations. But Elma hadn't failed to notice either the start or its reason.

"It's only Mr. Cyril," she said pointedly; "not Mr. Guy,

Sir Gilbert. The name came very pat, though. I don't wonder it startled you."

She was crimson herself. The judge moved away, with a stealthy, uncomfortable air. He didn't half care for this uncanny young woman. A girl who can read people's thoughts like that—a girl who can play with you like a cat with a mouse, oughtn't to be allowed at large in society. She should be shut up in a cage at home, like a dangerous animal, and prevented from spying out the inmost history of families.

A little later Elma had twenty minutes' talk with Cyril alone. It was in the tea-room behind, where the light refreshments were laid out before supper. She spoke low and seriously.

" Cyril," she said, in a tone of absolute confidence (they were not engaged, of course, but still he had got to plain " Cyril " and " Elma " by this time), " I'm surer of it than ever, no matter what you say. Guy's perfectly innocent. I know it as certainly as I know my own name. I can't be mistaken. And the man who really did it is, as I told you, Sir Gilbert Gildersleeve."

" My dear child," Cyril answered (you call the girl you are in love with " my dear child," when you mean to differ from her, with an air of masculine superiority), " how on earth can that be, when, as I told you, I have Guy's confession, in writing, under his own very hand, that he really did it?"

" I don't care a pin for that," Elma cried, with a true woman's contempt for anything so unimportant as mere positive evidence. " Perhaps Sir Gilbert made him do it somehow—compelled him, or coerced him, or willed him, or something—I don't understand these new notions—or perhaps he got him into a scrape and then hadn't the courage or the manliness to get him out of it. But at any rate, I can answer for one thing, if I were to go to the stake for it,—Sir Gilbert Gildersleeve is the man who's really guilty."

As she spoke, a great shadow darkened the door of the room for a moment ominously. Sir Gilbert looked in with a lady on his arm—the inevitable dowager who refreshes herself continuously at frequent intervals through six hours of entertainment. When he saw those two *tête-à-tête*, he drew back, somewhat disconcerted.

" Don't let's go in there, Lady Knowles," he whispered to the dowager by his side. " A pair of young people discussing their hearts. We were once young ourselves. It's a pity to disturb them."

And he passed on across the hall towards the great refreshment-room opposite.

" Well, I don't know," Cyril said, bitterly, as the judge disappeared through the opposite door. " I wish I could agree with you. But I can't—I can't! The burden of it's heavier than my shoulders can bear. Guy's weak, I know, and might be led half unawares into certain sorts of crime. Yet I only knew one man ever likely to lead him; and that was poor Nevitt himself, not Sir Gilbert Gildersleeve, whom he hardly even knew to speak to."

As he paused and reflected, a servant with a salver came up and looked into Cyril's face inquiringly.

" Beg your pardon, sir," he said, hesitating, " but I think you're Mr. Waring."

" That's my name," Cyril answered, with a faint blush on his cheek. " Do you want to speak to me?"

" Yes, sir; there's half-a-crown to pay for porterage if you please. A telegram for you, sir."

Cyril pulled out the half-crown, and tore open the telegram. It's contents were indeed enough to startle him. It was dated " Cape Town," and was as brief as is the wont of cable messages at nine shillings a word:—

" Coming home immediately to repay everything and stand my trial. Kelmscott accompanies me. All well.

" GUY WARING."

Cyril looked at it with a gasp, and handed it on to Elma. Elma took it in her dainty gloved fingers, and read it through with keen eyes of absorbing interest. Cyril sighed a profound sigh. Elma glanced back at him all triumph. " I told you so," she said, in a very jubilant voice. " He wouldn't do that if he didn't *know* he was innocent."

At the very same second, a blustering voice was heard above the murmur in the hall without.

" What, half-a-crown for porterage !" it exclaimed,

in indignant tones. " Why, that's a clear imposition. The people at my house ought never to have sent it on. It's addressed to Woodlands. Unimportant, unimportant. Here, Gwendoline, take your message—some milliner's or dressmaker's appointment for to-morrow, I suppose. Half-a-crown for porterage! They'd no right to bring it."

Gwendoline took the telegram with trembling hands, tore it open all quivers, and broke into a cry of astonishment. Then she fell all at once into her father's arms. Elma understood it all. It was a similar message from Granville Kelmscott to tell the lady of his heart he was coming home to marry her.

Sir Gilbert, somewhat flustered, called for water in haste, and revived the fainting girl by bathing her temples. At last he took up the cause of the mischief himself.

As he read it, his own face turned white as death. Elma noticed that, too. And no wonder it did ; for these were the words of that unexpected message : —

" Coming home to claim you by the next mail. Guy Waring accompanies me.   GRANVILLE KELMSCOTT."

CHAPTER XXXIX.'

A GLEAM OF LIGHT.

NEXT day but one, the Companion of St. Michael and
St. George came into Craighton with evil tidings. He
had heard in the village that Sir Gilbert Gildersleeve
was ill — very seriously ill. The judge had come home
from the Holkers' the other evening much upset by the
arrival of Gwendoline's telegram.

"Though why on earth that should upset him," Mr.
Clifford continued, screwing up his small face with a
very wise air, "is more than I can conceive; for I'm sure
the Gildersleeves angled hard enough in their time to
catch young Kelmscott, by hook or by crook, for their
gawky daughter; and now that young Kelmscott tele-
graphs over to say he's coming home post haste to
marry her, Miss Gwendoline faints away, if you please, as
she reads the news, and the judge himself goes upstairs
as soon as he gets home, and takes to his bed incon-
tinently. But there, the ways of the world are really
inscrutable! What reconciles me to life every day I
grow older, is that it's so amusing! You never know
what's going to turn up next; and what you least expect
is what most often happens."

Elma, however, received his news with a very grave
face.

"Is he really ill, do you think, papa?" she asked,
somewhat anxiously; "or is he only — well — only
frightened?"

Mr. Clifford started at her with a blank, leathery face
of self-satisfied incomprehension.

"Frightened!" he repeated, solemnly; "Sir Gilbert
Gildersleeve frightened! And of Granville Kelmscott,

too! That's true wit, Elma; the juxtaposition of the incongruous. Why, what on earth has the man got to be frightened of, I should like to know? . . . No, no; he's really ill; very seriously ill. Humphreys says the case is a most peculiar one, and he's telegraphed up to town for a specialist to come down this afternoon and consult with him."

And indeed, Sir Gilbert was really very ill. This unexpected shock had wholly unmanned him. To say the truth, the judge had begun to look upon Guy Waring as practically lost, and upon the matter of Montague Nevitt's death as closed forever. Waring, no doubt, had gone to Africa (under a false name) and proceeded to the diamond fields direct, where he had probably been killed in a lucky quarrel with some brother digger, or stuck through with an assegai by some enterprising Zulu; and nobody had even taken the trouble to mention it.

It's so easy for a man to get lost in the crowd in the Dark Continent! Why, there was Granville Kelmscott, even,—a young fellow of means, and the heir of Tilgate, about whom Gwendoline was always moaning and groaning, poor girl, and wouldn't be comforted,—there was Granville Kelmscott, gone out to Africa, and, hi, presto, disappeared into space without a vapor or a trace, like a conjuror's shilling. It was all very queer; but then, queer things are the way in Africa.

To be sure, Sir Gilbert had his qualms of conscience, too, over having thus sent off Guy Waring, as he believed, to his grave in Cape Colony. He was not at heart a bad man, though he was pushing, and selfish, and self-seeking, and to a certain extent, even —of late— unscrupulous. He had his bad half-hours every now and again with his own moral consciousness. But he had learned to stifle his doubts and to keep down his terrors. After all, he had told Guy no more than the truth; and if Guy in his panic-terror chose to run away and get killed in South Africa, that was no fault of *his;* he'd only tried to warn the fellow of an impending danger. All's well that ends well; and, to-day, Guy Waring was lost or dead, while he himself was a judge, and a knight to boot, with all trace of his crime destroyed forever.

So he said to himself, rejoicing, the very day Granville Kelmscott's telegram arrived. But now that he stood face to face again with that pressing terror, his thoughts on the matter were very different. Strange to say, his first idea was this: What a disgraceful shame of that fellow Waring to come to life again thus suddenly on purpose to annoy him! He was really angry, nay, more, indignant. Such shuffling was inexcusable. If Waring meant to give himself up and stand his trial like a man, why the dickens didn't he do it immediately after the—well, the accident? What did he mean by going off for eighteen months undiscovered, and leaving one to build up fresh plans in life, like this—and then coming home on a sudden just on purpose to upset them? It was simply disgraceful. Sir Gilbert felt injured; this man Waring was wronging him. Eighteen months before he was keenly aware that he was unjustly casting a vile and hideous suspicion on an innocent person. But in the intervening period his moral sense had got largely blunted. Familiarity with the hateful plot had warped his ideas about it. Their places were reversed. Sir Gilbert was really aggrieved now that Guy Waring should turn up again, and should venture to vindicate his deeply wronged character.

The man was as good as dead. Well, and he ought to have stopped so; or else he ought never to have died at all. He ought to have kept himself continually in evidence. But to go away for eighteen months, unknown and unheard of, till one's sense of security had had time to re-establish itself, and then to turn up again like this without one minute's warning—oh, it was infamous, scandalous! The fellow must be devoid of all consideration for others. Sir Gilbert wiped his clammy brow with those ample hands. What on earth was he to do for his wife, and for Gwendoline?

And Gwendoline was so happy, too, over Granville Kelmscott's return! How could he endure that Granville Kelmscott's return should be the signal for discovering her father's sin and shame to her! If only he could have married her off before it all came out! Or if only he could die before the man was tried!—Tried! Sir Gilbert's eyes started from his head with horror. What was that Elma Clifford suggested the other night? Why

—if the man was arrested, he would be arrested at **Plymouth**, the moment he landed, and would be tried for murder at the Western Assizes And it was he himself, Sir Gilbert Gildersleeve, who was that term to take the Western Circuit.

He would be called upon to sit on the bench himself, and try Guy Waring for the murder he had himself committed!

No wonder that thought sent him ill to bed at once. He lay and tossed all night long in speechless agony and terror. It was an appalling night. Next morning he was found delirious with fever.

When the news reached Elma, she saw its full and fatal significance Cyril had stopped on for three days at the Holkers', and he came over in the course of the morning to take a walk across the fields with her. Elma was profoundly excited, Cyril could hardly see why.

" This is a terrible thing," she said, " about Sir Gilbert's illness. What I'm afraid of now is, that he may die before your brother returns. The shock must have been awful for him ; mamma noticed it every bit as much as I did ; and so did Miss Ewes. They both said at once, ' This blow will kill him !' And they both knew why, Cyril, as well as I did. It's the Ewes intuition. We've all of us got it, and we all of us say, at once and unanimously, it was Sir Gilbert Gildersleeve."

"But suppose he *did* die," Cyril asked, still sceptical, as he always was when Elma got upon her instinctive consciousness ; " what difference would that make ? If Guy's innocent, as I suppose in some way he must be, from the tone of his telegram, he'll be acquitted whether Sir Gilbert's alive or not. And if he's guilty——"

He broke off suddenly, with an awful pause ; the other alternative was too terrible to contemplate.

" But he's *not* guilty," Elma answered, with confidence. "I know it more surely now than ever. And the difficulty's this. Nobody knows the real truth, I feel certain, except Sir Gilbert Gildersleeve. And if Sir Gilbert dies unconfessed, the truth dies with him. And then—" She paused a moment. " I'm half afraid," she went on, with a doubtful sigh, " your brother's been too precipitate in coming home to face it."

"But, Elma," Cyril cried, " I can't bear to say it,—yet one must face the facts,—how on earth can he be inno-cent, when I tell you again and again he wrote to me him-self saying he really did it ? "

" You never showed me that letter," Elma answered, with a faint undercurrent of reproach in her tone.

" How could I ? " Cyril replied. " Even to *you*, Elma, there are some things a man can hardly bear to speak about."

" I have more faith than you, Cyril," Elma answered. " I've never given up believing in Guy all the time. I believe in him still—because I know he's your brother."

There was a short pause, during which neither spoke. They walked along together, looking at each other's faces with half downcast eyes, but with the not unpleasant sense of mute companionship and sympathy in a great sorrow. At last Elma spoke again.

" There was one thing in Guy's telegram," she said, "I didn't quite understand. ' Coming home immediately to repay everything.' What did he mean by that ? What has that got to with Mr. Nevitt's disappearance ? "

" Oh, that was quite another matter ! " Cyril answered, blushing deep with shame, for he couldn't bear to let Elma know Guy was a forger as well as a murderer. " That was something purely personal between us two. He—he owed me money."

Elma's keen eyes read him through at a glance. " But he said it all in one sentence," she objected, " as if the two went naturally together. Coming home immediately to repay everything, and stand my trial. Cyril, Cyril, you've held something back. I believe there's some fearful mistake here somewhere."

" You think so ? " Cyril answered, feeling more and more uncomfortable.

" I'm sure of it," Elma replied, with a thrill, reading his thoughts still deeper. " Oh, Cyril ! "—she seized his arm with a convulsive grip—" for heaven's sake, go and get it ; let me see that letter ! "

" I have it here," Cyril answered, pulling it out with some shame from Montague Nevitt's pocket-book, which he wouldn't destroy, and dared not leave about for pry-ing eyes to light upon. '' I've carried it, day and night, ever since, about with me."

Elma seized it from his hands, and sat down upon a stile, and read it through with profound attention.

At the end she handed it back, and tears stood in her eyes. " Cyril," she said, half laughing hysterically and half crying as she spoke, " you've been doing that poor fellow a deep injustice. Oh, don't you see—don't you see it? That isn't the letter of a man who has committed a murder. It's the letter of a man who has unwittingly and unwillingly done you some personal wrong, and is eager to repair it. My darling, my darling! you've mis-read it altogether. It isn't about Montague Nevitt's death at all; it's about nothing on earth but some private money matter. More than that, when it was written, Guy didn't yet know Mr. Nevitt was dead. He didn't know he was suspected. He didn't know anything. I wonder you don't see! I wish to heaven you'd shown me that letter months ago! Sir Gilbert fastened suspicion on the wrong man ; and this letter has made you accept it too easily. Guy went to Africa—that's as plain as words can put it—to make money of his own to repay what he owed you. And it's this, the purely personal and un-important charge, he's coming home to give himself up upon ! "

A light seemed to burst on Cyril's mind as she spoke. For the very first time he felt a gleam of hope. Elma was right, after all, he believed. Guy was wholly inno-cent of the great crime, and his heart-broken letter had only meant to deal with the question of the forgery.

But Cyril had heard of the murder first, and had had that most in his mind when the letter reached him ; so he interpreted it at once as referring to the capital charge, and never dreamt for a moment of its real narrower mean-ing.

That evening, when the messenger came back from " kind inquiries " at Woodlands, Elma asked, with hushed awe, how Sir Gilbert was going on.

" Very poorly, miss," the servant answered. " The doctor says he's sunk dreadful low, and the butler thinks he has something on his mind he can't get out in his wanderings. He's in a terrible bad way. They wouldn't be astonished if he don't live to morning."

So Elma went to bed that night, trembling most for the result of Sir Gilbert's illness.

CHAPTER XL.

THE BOLT FALLS.

ALL the way home on that long journey from Cape Town, as the two half-brothers lounged on deck together in their canvas chairs, Granville Kelmscott was wholly at a loss to understand what seemed to him Guy Waring's unaccountable and almost incredible levity. The man's conduct didn't in the least resemble that of a person who is returning to give himself up on a charge of wilful murder. On the contrary, Guy showed no signs of remorse or mental agony in any way ; he seemed rather elated, instead, at the pleasing thought that he was going home, with his diamonds all turned at the Cape into solid coin, to make his peace once more with his brother Cyril.

To be sure, at times, he did casually allude to some expected unpleasantness when he arrived in England ; yet he treated it, Granville noticed, as though hanging were at worst but a temporary inconvenience. Granville wondered whether, after all, he could have some complete and crushing answer to that appalling charge ; on any other supposition, his spirits and his talk were really little short of what one might expect from a madman.

And indeed, now and again, Granville did really begin to suspect that something had gone wrong somewhere with Guy Waring's intellect. The more he thought over it, the more likely did this seem, for Guy talked on with the greatest composure about his plans for the future "when this dfficulty was cleared up," as though a trial for murder were a most ordinary occurrence —an accident that might happen to any gentleman anyay.

And if so, was it possible that Guy had gone wrong in

his head *before* the affray with Montague Nevitt? That
seemed likely enough; for when Granville remembered
Guy's invariable gentleness and kindness to himself, his
devotion in sickness and in the trials of the desert, his
obvious aversion to do harm to any one, and, above all,
his heartfelt objection to shedding human blood, Granville was constrained to believe his newly-found half-
brother, if ever he committed the murder at all, must
have committed it while in a state of unsound mind, de-
serving rather of pity than of moral reprehension. He
comforted himselt, indeed, with this consoling idea: he
could never believe a Kelmscott of Tilgate, when clothed
and in his right mind, could be guilty of such a detestable and motiveless crime as the wilful murder of Montague Nevitt.

Strangely enough, moreover, the subject that seemed
most to occupy Guy Waring's mind, on the voyage home,
was not his forthcoming trial on a capital charge, but the
future distribution of the Tilgate property. Was he es-
sentially a money-grubber, Granville wondered to himself, as he had thought him at first in the diamond fields
in Barolong land? Was he incapable of thinking about
anything but filthy lucre? No; that was clearly not the
true solution of the problem, for, whenever Guy spoke
to him about the subject, it was generally to say one
and the self-same thing:—

"In this matter, I feel I can speak for Cyril as I speak
for myself. Neither of us would wish to deprive you now
of what you've always been brought up to consider as your
own. Neither of us would wish to dispossess Lady Emily. The most we would desire is this: to have our position openly acknowledged and settled before the world.
We should like it to be known we were the lawful sons
of a brave man and an honest woman. And if you wish
voluntarily to share with us some of our father's estate,
we'll be willing to enter into a reasonable arrangement
by which you yourself can retain Tilgate Park and the
mass of the property that immediately appertains to it.
I'm sure Cyril would no more wish to be grasping in
this matter than I am; and after all that you and I have
gone through together, Granville, I don't think you need
doubt the sincerity of my feelings towards you."

He spoke so sensibly, he spoke so manfully, he spoke so kindly always, with a bright gleam in those tender eyes, that Granville hardly knew what to make of his evident confidence. Surely a man couldn't be mad who could speak like that; and yet, wherever he alluded in any way to his return to England, it was always as though he ignored the gravity and heinousness of the charge brought against him. It was as though murder was an accident for which one was hardly responsible. Granville couldn't make him out at all; the fellow was an enigma to him. There was so much that was good in him; and yet, there must be so much that was bad as well. He was such a delicate, considerate, self-effacing gentleman—and yet, if one could believe what he himself more than once as good as admitted, he was a criminal, a felon, an open murderer.

Still, even so, Granville couldn't turn his back upon the brother who had seen him so bravely across the terrors of Namaqua land. He thought of how he had misjudged him once before, and how much he had repented it. Whether Guy was a murderer or not, Granville felt, the man he had saved, at least, could never forsake him.

The night before their arrival at Plymouth, Guy was in unusually high spirits. His mirth was contagious. Everybody on board was delighted at the prospect of reaching land, but Guy was more delighted and more sanguine than anybody. He was sure in his own mind this difficulty must have blown over long before now; Cyril must have explained; Nevitt must have confessed; everything must have been set right, and his own good name satisfactorily rehabilitated. For more than eighteen months he had heard nothing from England. To-morrow he would see Cyril, and account for everything. He had money to set all right—his hard-earned money, got at the risk of his own life in the dreary deserts of Barolong land. All would yet be well, and Cyril would marry, and Elma Clifford would be the mistress of nearly half the Tilgate property.

"It was all so different, Granville," he said to his friend, confidentially, as they paced the deck after supper, cigar in mouth, "when you first went out, and we didn't know one another. Then I distrusted you, and you distrusted me. We didn't understand one another's characters. But now we can settle it all as a family affair. Men who have camped out together under the open sky on the African veldt, who have run the gauntlet of Korannas and Barolong, and Namaqua, who have stood by one another in sickness and in fight, needn't be afraid of disagreeing about their money matters in England. Cyril will meet us to-morrow and talk it all over, and I'm not the least troubled about the result either for you or for him. The same blood runs in all our veins alike. Whatever you propose, he'll be ready to agree to. He's the very best fellow that ever lived, and when he hears what I have to say about you, he'll welcome you as a brother, and be as fond of you as I am."

Next morning early they reached Plymouth Harbor. As they entered the mouth of the breakwater the tender came along-side to convey them ashore. Guy looked over the bulwarks and saw Cyril waiting for him. In a fervor of delight at the sight of the green fields and the soft hills of old England,—the beautiful Hoe, and the solid stone houses, and the familiar face turned up to welcome him, —Guy waved his handkerchief round and round his head in triumph; to which demonstration Cyril, as he fancied, responded but coldly. A chill fell upon his heart. This was bad, but still, after all, he could hardly expect Cyril to know intuitively under what sinister influence he had signed that fatal check. And yet he was disappointed. His heart had jumped so hard at sight of Cyril he could hardly believe Cyril wasn't glad to see him.

As he stepped into the tender from the gangway, just ready to rush up and shake Cyril's hand fervently, a resolute-looking man by the side of the steps laid a very firm grip on his shoulder, with an air of authority.

"Guy Waring ?" he said, interrogatively.

And Guy, turning pale, answered without flinching :—

"Yes, my name's Guy Waring."

"Then you're my prisoner," the man said, in a very firm voice. "I'm an inspector of constabulary."

"On what charge ?" Guy exclaimed, half taken aback at this promptitude.

"I have a warrant against you, sir," the inspector

answered, "as you are no doubt aware, for the wilful murder of Montague Nevitt, on the 17th of August, year before last, at Mambury, in Devonshire."

The words fell upon Guy's ears with all the suddenness and crushing force of an unexpected thunderbolt. "Wilful murder!" he cried, taken aback by the charge. 'Wilful murder of Montague Nevitt at Mambury! Oh, no, you can't mean that! Montague Nevitt dead! Montague Nevitt murdered! And at Mambury, too! There *must* be some mistake somewhere."

"No, there's no mistake at all this time," the inspector said, quietly, slipping a pair of handcuffs unobtrusively into his pocket as he spoke. "If you come along with me without any unnecessary noise, we won't trouble to iron you. But you'd better say as little as possible about the charge just now, for whatever you say may be used in evidence at the trial against you."

Guy turned to Cyril with an appealing look. "Cyril," he cried, "what does all this mean? Is Nevitt dead? It's the very first word I've ever heard about it."

Cyril's heart gave a bound of wild relief at these words. The moment Guy said it, his brother knew he spoke the simple truth. "Why, Guy," he answered, with a fierce burst of joy, "then you're not a murderer after all? You're innocent! You're innocent! And for eighteen months all England has thought you guilty; and I've lived under the burden of being universally considered a murderer's brother!"

Guy looked him back in the face with those truthful gray eyes of his. "Cyril," he said, solemnly, "I'm as innocent of this charge as you or Granville Kelmscott here. I never even heard one whisper of it before. I don't know what it means. I don't know whom they want. Till this moment I thought Montague Nevitt was still alive in England."

And as he said it, Granville Kelmscott, too, saw he was speaking the truth. Impossible as he found it in his own mind to reconcile those strange words with all that Guy had said to him in the wilds of Namaqua land, he couldn't look him in the face without seeing at a glance how profound and unexpected was this sudden surprise to him.   He was right in saying, " I'm as innocent of this charge as you or Granville Kelmscott."

But the inspector only smiled a cynical smile, and answered calmly, " That's for the jury to decide.   We shall hear more of this then.   You'll be tried at assizes. Meanwhile, the less said, the sooner mended."

CHAPTER XLI.

WHAT JUDGE?

For many days, meanwhile, Sir Gilbert had hovered between life and death and Elma had watched his illness daily with profound and absorbing interest; for in her deep intuitive way she felt certain to herself that their one chance now lay in Sir Gilbert's own sense of remorse and repentance. She didn't yet know, to be sure,—what Sir Gilbert himself knew,—that if he recovered he would, in all probability, have to sit in trial on another man for the crime he had himself committed. But she did feel this, that Sir Gilbert would surely never stand by and let an innocent man die for his own transgression.

If he recovered, that was to say. But perhaps he would not recover. Perhaps his life would flicker out by degrees in the midst of his delirium, and he would go to his grave unconfessed and unforgiven. Perhaps even, for his wife's and daughter's sakes, he would shrink from re-vealing what Elma felt to be the truth, and would rest content to die, leaving Guy Waring to clear himself at the trial, as best he might, from this hateful accusation.

It would be unjust; it would be criminal; yet Sir Gilbert might do it.

Elma had a bad time, therefore, during all those long days, even before Guy returned to England. She knew his life hung by a slender thread, which Sir Gilbert Gildersleeve might cut short at any moment. But her anxiety was as nothing compared with Sir Gilbert's own. That unhappy man, a moral coward at heart, in spite of all his blustering, lay writhing in his own room now, very ill, and longing to be worse, longing to die, as the easiest way out of this impossible difficulty. For his wife's sake, for Gwendoline's sake, it was better he should die; and if only he could, he would have left Guy Waring to his fate contentedly. His anger against Guy burnt so bright now at last, that he would have sacrificed him willingly, provided he was not there himself to see and know it. What did the man mean by living on to vex him? Over and over again the unhappy judge wished himself dead, and prayed to be taken. But that powerful frame, though severely broken by the shock, seemed hardly able to yield up its life merely because its owner was anxious to part with it.

After a fortnight's severe illness, hovering all the time between hope and fear, the doctor came one day, and looked at him hard.

"How is he?' Lady Gildersleeve asked, seeing him hold his breath and consider.

To her great surprise the doctor answered, "Better against all hope, better." And, indeed, Sir Gilbert was once more convalescent. A week or two abroad, it was said, would restore him completely.

Then Elma had another terrible source of doubt. Would the doctors order Sir Gilbert abroad so long that he would be out of England when the trial took place? If so, he might miss many pricks of remorse. She must take some active steps to arouse his conscience.

Sir Gilbert himself, now recovering fast, fought hard, as well he might, for, such leave of absence. He was quite unfit, he said, to return to his judicial work so soon. Though he had said nothing about it in public before,—this was the tenor of his talk,—he was a man of profound but restrained feelings ; and he had felt, he would admit, the absence of Gwendoline's lover, especially when combined with the tragic death of Colonel Kelmscott, the father, and the memory of the unpleasantness that had once subsisted (through the Colonel's blind obstinacy) between the two houses. This sudden news of the young man's return had given him a nervous shock of which few men would have believed him capable. " You wouldn't think to look at me," Sir Gilbert said, plaintively, smoothing down his bedclothes with those elephantine hands of his, " I was the sort of man to be knocked down in this way "; and the great specialist from London, gazing at him with a smile, admitted to aimself that he certainly would not have thought it.

" Oh, nonsense, my dear sir ! " the specialist answered, however, to all his appeals. " This is the merest passing turn, I assure you. I couldn't conscientiously say you'd be unfit for duty by the time the assizes come round again. It's clear to me, on the contrary, with a physique like yours, you'll pull yourself together in something less than no time, with a week or so at Spa. Before you're due in England to put on harness again, you'll be walking miles at a stretch over those heathery hills there. Convalescence, with a man like you, is a rapid process. In a fortnight from to-day, I'll venture to guarantee, you'll be in a fit condition to swim the Channel on your back, or to take one of your famous fifty-mile tramps across the bogs of Dartmoor. I'll give you a tonic that'll set your nerves all right at once. You'll come back from Spa as fresh as a daisy."

To Spa, accordingly, Sir Gilbert went; and from Spa came trembling letters now and again between Gwendoline and Elma. Gwendoline was very anxious papa should get well soon, she said, for she wanted to be home before the Cape steamer arrived. " You know why, Elma." But Sir Gilbert didn't return before Guy's arrival in England, for all that. The papers continued to give bulletins of his health, and to speculate on the probability of his returning in time to do the Western Circuit. Elma remained in a fever of doubt and anxiety. To her, much depended now on the question of Sir Gilbert's presence or absence. For if he was indeed to try the case, she felt certain to herself, it must work upon his remorse and compel confession.

Meanwhile, preparations went on in England for Guy's approaching trial. The magistrates committed; the grand jury, of course, found a true bill; all England rang with the strange news that the man Guy Waring, the murderer of Mr. Montague Nevitt, some eighteen months before, had returned at last of his own free will, and had given himself up to take his trial. Gildersieeve was to be the judge, they said; or, if he were too ill, Atkins. Atkins was as sure as a gun to hang him, people thought, —that was Atkins' way,—and, besides, the evidence against the man, though in a sense circumstantial, was so absolutely overwhelming that acquittal seemed impossible.

Five to two was freely offered on 'Change that they'd hang him.

The case was down for first hearing at the assizes. The night before the trial Elma Clifford, who had hurried to Devonshire with her mother to see and hear all—she couldn't help it, she said ; she felt she *must* be present— Elma Clifford looked at the evening paper with a sickening sense of suspense and anxiety. A paragraph caught her eye: " We understand that, after all, Mr. Justice Gildersleeve still finds himself too unwell to return to England for the Western Assizes, and his place will, therefore, most probably be taken by Mr. Justice Atkins. The calendar is a heavy one, and includes the interesting case of Mr. Guy Waring, charged with the wilful murder of Montague Nevitt, at Mambury, in Devonshire."

Elma laid down the paper with a swimming head. Too ill to return ! She wasn't at all surprised at it. It was almost more than human nature could stand, for a man to sit as judge over another, to investigate the details of the crime he had himself committed. But the suggestion of his absence ruined her peace of mind. She couldn't sleep that night. She felt sure now there was no hope left. Guy would almost certainly be convicted of murder.

Next morning she took her seat in court, with her mother and Cyril, as soon as the assize hall was opened to the public. But her cheek was very pale, and her eyes were weary. Places had been assigned them by the courtesy of the authorities, as persons interested in the case; and Elma looked eagerly towards the door in the corner, by which, as the usher told her, the judge was to enter. There was a long interval, and the usual unseemly turmoil of laughing and talking went on among the spectators in the well below. Some of them had opera-glasses and stared about them freely. Others quizzed the counsel, the officers, and. the witnesses. Then a hush came over them, and the door opened. Cyril was merely aware of the usual formalities and of a judicial wig making its way, with slow dignity, to the vacant bench. But Elma leaned forward in a tumult of feeling. Her face all at once turned scarlet with excitement,

"What's the matter, darling?" her mother asked, in a sympathetic tone, noticing that something had profoundly stirred her.

And Elma answered with bated breath, in almost inarticulate tones, "Don't you see? Don t you see, mother? Just look at the judge! It's himself! It's Sir Gilbert!"

And so, indeed, it was. Against all hope he had come ever. At the very last mome.t a telegram had been handed to the convalescent at Spa: "Fallen from my horse. A nasty tumble. Sustained severe internal injuries. Impossible to go the Western Circuit. Relieve me if you can. Wire reply.—ATKINS."

Sir Gilbert, as he received it, had just come in from a long ride across the wild moors that stretch away from Spa towards Han, and looked the picture of health, robust and fresh and ruddy. He glowed with bodily vigor; no suspense could kill him. Refusal under such circumstances was clearly impossible. He saw he must go, or resign his post at once. So, with an agitated heart, he wired acquiescence, took the next train to Brussels and Calais, and caught the Dover boat just in time for acceptance. And now he was there to try Guy Waring for the murder of the man he himself had killed in the Tangle at Mambury.

CHAPTER XLII.

UNEXPECTED EVIDENCE.

When Sir Gilbert Gildersleeve left Spa, he left with a ruddy glow of recovered health on his bronzed, red cheek; for in spite of anxiety and repentance and doubt, the man's iron frame would somehow still assert itself. When he took his seat on the bench in court that morning, he looked so haggard and ill with fatigue and remorse that even Elma Clifford herself pitied him. A hushed whisper ran round among the spectators below that the judge wasn't fit to try the case before him, And indeed he wasn't. For it was his own trial, not Guy Waring's he was really presiding over.

He sat down in his place, a ghastly picture of pallid despair. The red color had faded altogether from his wan white cheeks. His eyes were dreamy and blood-shot with long vigil. His big hands trembled like a woman's as he opened his note-book. His mouth twitched nervously. So utter a collapse, in such a man as he was, seemed nothing short of pitiable to every spectator.

Council for the Crown stared him steadily in the face. Council for the Crown—Forbes-Ewing, Q. C.—was an old forensic enemy, who had fought many a hard battle against Gildersleeve, with scant interchange of courtesy, when both were members of the junior bar together; but now Sir Gilbert's look moved even *him* to pity. "I think, my lord," the Q. C. suggested, with a sympathetic simper, "your lordship's too ill to open court to-day. Perhaps the proceedings had better be adjourned for the present."

"No, no," the judge answered, almost testily, shaking his sleeve with impatience. "I'll have no putting off for trifles in the court where I sit. There's a capital case to come on this morning. When a man's neck's at stake,—

when a matter of life and death's at issue,— I don't like
to keep any one longer in suspense than I absolutely need.
Delay would be cruel."

As he spoke he lifted his eyes—and caught Elma Clifford's. The judge let his own drop again in speechless
agony. Elma's never flinched. Neither gave a sign;
but Elma knew, as well as Sir Gilbert knew himself, it
was his own life and death the judge was thinking of,
and not Guy Waring's.

"As you will, my lord," council for the Crown responded, demurely. "It was your lordship's convenience
we all had at heart, rather than the prisoner's"

"Eh! What's that?" the judge said, sharply, with a
suspicious frown. Then he recovered himself with a
start. For a moment he had half fancied that fellow
Forbes-Ewing meant *something* by what he said; meant
to poke innuendoes at him. But after all, it was a mere
polite form. How frightened we all are, to be sure,when,
we know we're on our trial!

The opening formalities were soon got over, and then,
amid a deep hush of breathless lips, Guy Waring, of
Staple Inn, Holborn, gentleman, was put up on his trial
for the wilful murder of Montague Nevitt, eighteen
months before, at Mambury in Devon.

Guy, standing in the dock, looked puzzled and distracted
rather than alarmed or terrified. His cheek was pale, to
be sure, and his eyes were weary; but as Elma glanced
from him hastily to the judge on the bench, she had no
hesitation in settling in her own mind which of the two
looked most, at that moment, like a detected murderer
before the faces of his accusers. Guy was calm and self-
contained. Sir Gilbert's mute agony was terrible to be-
hold. Yet,strange to say, no one else in court, save Elma,
seemed to note it as she did. People saw the judge was
was ill, but that was all. Perhaps his wig and robes
helped to hide the effect of conscious guilt—nobody sus-
pects a judge of murder; perhaps all eyes were more intent on the prisoner.

Be that as it might, counsel for the Crown opened with
a statement of what they meant to prove, set forth in
the familiar forensic fashion. They didn't pretend the
evidence against the accused was absolutely conclusive

or overwhelming in character. It was inferential only but not circumstantial —inferential in such a cumulative and convincing way as could leave no moral doubt on any intelligent mind as to the guilt of the prisoner. They would show that a close intimacy had long existed between the prisoner Waring and the deceased gentleman, Mr. Montague Nevitt. Witnesses would be called who would prove to the court that just before the murder this intimacy, owing to circumstances which could not fully be cleared up, had passed suddenly into intense enmity and open hatred. The landlord of the inn at Mambury, and other persons to be called, would speak to the fact that prisoner had followed his victim in hot blood into Devonshire, and had tracked him to the retreat where he was passing his holiday alone and incognito—had tracked him with every expression of indignant anger, and had uttered plain threats of personal violence towards him.

Nor was that all. It would be shown that on the afternoon of Waring's visit to Mambury, Mr. Nevitt, who possessed an intense love of nature in her wildest and most romantic moods—it's always counsel's cue (for the prosecution) to set the victim's character in the most amiable light, and so win the sympathy of the jury as against the accused—Mr. Nevitt, that close student of natural beauty, had strolled by himself down a certain woodland path, known as the Tangle, which led through the loneliest and leafiest quarter of Mambury Chase, along the tumbling stream described as the Mam-water. Ten minutes after he had passed the gate, a material witness would show them, the prisoner Waring presented himself, and pointedly asked whether his victim had already gone down the path before him. He was told that that was so. Thereupon the prisoner opened the gate, and followed excitedly. What happened next no living eye but the prisoner's ever saw. Montague Nevitt was not destined to issue from that wood alive. Two days later his breathless body was found, all stiff and stark, hidden among the brown bracken at the bottom of the dell, where the murderer no doubt had thrust it away out of his sight on that fatal afternoon in fear and trembling.

Half-way through the opening speech Sir Gilbert's heart beat fast and hard. He had never heard Forbes-Ewing open a case so well. The man would be hanged! He felt sure of it! He could see it! For a while the judge almost gloated over that prospect of release. What was Guy's life to him now, by the side of his wife's and Gwendoline's happiness? But as counsel uttered the words, "What happened next no living eye but the prisoner's ever saw," he looked hard at Guy. Not a quiver of remorse or of guilty knowledge passed over the young man's face. But Elma Clifford, for her part, looked at the judge on the bench. Their eyes met once more. Again Sir Gilbert's fell. Oh, heavens, how terrible! Even for Gwendoline's sake he could never stand this appalling suspense. But perhaps after all the prosecution might fail. There was still a chance left that the jury might acquit him.

So, torn by conflicting emotions, he sat there still, stiff, and motionless in his seat as an Egyptian statue.

Then counsel went on to deal in greater detail with the question of motive. There were two motives the prosecution proposed to allege: First, the known enmity of recent date between the two parties, believed to have reference to some business dispute; and secondly—here counsel dropped his voice to a very low key—he was sorry to suggest it, but the evidence bore it out—mere vulgar love of gain, the commonplace thirst after filthy lucre. They would bring witnesses to show that when Mr. Montague Nevitt was last seen alive he was in possession of a pocket-book containing a very large sum in Bank of England notes of high value; from the moment of his death that pocket-book had disappeared, and nobody knew what had since became of it. It was not upon the body when the body was found. And all their efforts to trace the missing notes, whose numbers were not known, had been unhappily unsuccessful.

Guy listened to all this impeachment in a dazed, dreamy way. He hardly knew what it meant. It appalled and chilled him. The web of circumstances was too thick for him to break. He couldn't understand it himself. And what was far worse, he could give no active assistance to his own lawyers on the question of

tne notes—which might be very important evidence
against him—without further prejudicing his case of confessing the forgery. At all hazards, he was determined
to keep that quiet now. Cyril had never spoken to a
soul of that episode, and to speak of it, as things stood,
would have been certain death to him. It would be to
suppy the one missing link of motive which the prosecution needed to complete their chain of cumulative
evidence.

It was some comfort to him to think, however, that
the secret was safe in Cyril's keeping. Cyril had all the
remaining notes, still unchanged, in his possession; and
the prosecution, knowing nothing of the forgery or its
sequel, had no clue at all as to where they came from.

But as for Sir Gilbert, he listened still, with ever-
deepening horror. His mind swayed to and fro between
hope and remorse. They were making the man guilty,
and Gwendoline would be saved! They were making
the man guilty, and a gross wrong would be perpetrated!
Great drops of sweat stood colder than ever on his burning brow. He couldn't have believed Forbes-Ewing
could have done it so well. He was weaving a close web
round an innocent man with consummate forsenic skill and
cunning.

The case went on to its second stage. Witnesses were
called, and Guy listened to them dreamily. All of them
bore out counsel's opening statement. Every man in court
felt the evidence was going very hard against the prisoner.
They'd caught the right man, that was clear—so the
spectators opined. They'd prove it to the hilt. This
fellow would swing for it.

At last the landlord of the Talbot Arms at Mambury,
shuffled slowly into the witness-box. He was a heavy,
dull man, and he gave evidence as to Nevitt's stay under
an assumed name (which counsel explained suggestively
by the deceased gentleman's profound love of retirement),
and as to Guy's angry remarks and evident indignation.
But the most sensational part of all his evidence was
that which related to the pocket-book Montague Nevitt
was carrying at the time of his death, containing notes,
he should say, for several hundred pounds, "or it murt
be thousands—and yet, again, it murn't," which had

totally disappeared since the day of the murder. Diligent
search had been made for the pocket-book everywhere
by the landlord and the police, but it had vanished into
space, "leaving not a wrack behind," as junior counsel
for the prosecution poetically phrased it.

At the words Cyril mechanically dived his hand into
his pocket, as he had done a hundred times a day before,
during these last eighteen months, to assure himself that
that most incriminating and unwelcome object was still
safely ensconced in its usual resting-place Yes, there
it was sure enough, as snug as ever! He sighed, and
pulled his hand out again nervously, with a little jerk.
Something came with it, that fell on the floor with a
jingle at his neighbor's feet. Cyril turned crimson, then
deadly pale. He snatched at the object; but his neighbor picked it up and examined it curiously. It's flap
had burst open with the force of the fall, and on the
inside the finder read in astonishment, in very plain
letters, the very name of the murdered man, "Montague
Nevitt."

Cyril held out his hand to recover it impatiently. But
the finder was too much taken back at his strange discovery to part with it so readily. It was full of money
—Bank of England notes; and through the transparent
paper of the outer-most among them, the finder could
dimly read the word "One hundred."

He rose in his place, and held the pocket-book aloft in
his hand with a triumphant gesture. Cyril tried in vain
to clutch at it. The witness turned round sharply disturbed by this incident. "What's that?" the judge
exclaimed, puckering his brows in disapprobation and
looking angrily towards the disturber.

"If you please, my lord," the innkeeper answered, letting his jaw drop slowly in almost speechless amazement, "that's the thing I was a-talking of: that's Mr.
Nevitt's pocket-book."

"Hand it up," the judge said, shortly, gazing hard
with all his eyes at the mute evidence so tendered.

The finder handed it up without note or comment.

Sir Gilbert turned the book over in blank surprise.
He was dumbfounded himself. For a minute or two he
examined it carefully, inside and out. Yes, there was no

mistake. It was really what they called it. "Montague Nevitt" was written in plain letters on the leather flap; within lay half-a-dozen engraved visiting cards, a Foreign Office passport in Nevitt's name, and thirty Bank of England notes for one hundred pounds apiece. This was, indeed, a mystery.

"Where did it come from? the judge asked, drawing a painfully deep breath, and handing it across to the jury.

And the finder answered, "If you please, my lord, the gentleman next to me pulled it out of his pocket."

"Who is he?" the judge inquired, with a sinking heart, for he himself knew perfectly well who was the unhappy possessor.

And a thrill of horror ran round the crowded court as Forbes-Ewing answered in a very distinct voice, " Mr. Cyril Waring, my lord, the brother of the prisoner."

CHAPTER XLIII.

SIR GILBERT'S TEMPTATION.

CYRIL felt all was up. Elma glanced at him trembling. This was horrible, inconceivable, inexplicable, fatal! The very stars in their courses seemed to fight against Guy. Blind chance checkmated them. No hope was left now, save in Gilbert Gildersleeve's own sense of justice.

But Sir Gilbert Gildersleeve sat there, transfixed with horror. No answering gleam now shot through his dull, glazed eye. For he alone knew that whatever made the case against the prisoner look worse made his own position each moment more awful and more intolerable.

Through the rest of the case, Cyril sat in his place like a stone figure. Counsel for the Crown generously abstained from putting him into the witness-box to give testimony against his brother. Or rather, they thought the facts themselves, as they had just come out in court, more telling for the jury than any formal evidence. The only other witness of importance was, therefore, the lad who had sat on the gate by the entrance to the Tangle. As he scrambled into the box, Sir Gilbert's anxiety grew visibly deeper and more acute than ever. For the boy was the one person who had seen him at Mambury on the day of the murder, and on the boy depended his sole chance of being recognized. At Tavistock, eighteen months before, Sir Gilbert had left the cross-examination of this witness in the hands of a junior; and the boy hadn't noticed him, sitting down among the bar with gown and wig on. But to-day, it was impossible the boy shouldn't see him; and if the boy should recognize him—why, then heaven help him!

The lad gave his evidence-in-chief with great care and deliberateness. He swore positively to Guy, and wasn't for a moment to be shaken in cross-examination. He admitted he had been mistaken at Tavistock, and confused the prisoner with Cyril,—when he saw one of them apart, —but now that he saw 'em both together before his eyes at once, why, he could take his solemn oath, as sure as fate, upon him. Guy's counsel failed utterly to elicit anything of importance, except—and here Sir Gilbert's face grew whiter than ever—except that another gentleman whom the lad didn't know had asked at the gate about the path, and gone round the other way as if to meet Mr. Nevitt.

" What sort of a gentleman ? " the cross-examiner inquired, clutching at this last straw as a mere chance diversion.

" Well, a vurry big zart o' a gentleman," witness answered, unabashed. " A vine vigger o' a man. Jest such another as thik 'un with the wig ther."

As he spoke he stared hard at the judge, a good, scrutinizing stare. Sir Gilbert quailed, and glanced instinctively, first at the boy and then at Elma. Not a spark of intelligence shone in the lad's stolid eyes. But Elma's were fixed upon him with a serpentine glare of awful fascination. " Thou art the man," they seemed to say to him mutely. Sir Gilbert in his awe was afraid to look at them. They made him wild with terror, yet they somehow fixed him. Try as he would to keep his own from meeting them, they attracted him irresistibly.

A ripple of faint laughter ran lightly through the court at the undisguised frankness of the boy's reply. The judge repressed it sternly.

" Oh, he was just such another one as his lordship, was he ? " counsel repeated, pressing the lad hard. " Now are you quite sure you remember all the people you saw that day ? Are you quite sure the other man who asked about passers-by wasn't—for example—the judge himself who's sitting here ? "

Sir Gilbert glanced up with a quick, suspicious air. It was only a shot at random,—the common advocate's trick in trying to confuse a witness over questions of identity; but to Sir Gilbert, under the circumstances, it was inexpressibly distressing. " Well, it murt' a been he," the lad answered, putting his head on one side, and surveying the judge closely with prolonged attention. "Thik un 'ad just such another pair o' 'ands as his lordship do 'ave. It murt 'a been his lordship 'urself as is zitting there."

"This goes quite beyond the bounds of decency," Sir Gilbert murmured, faintly, with a vain endeavor to hold his hands on the desk in an unconcerned attitude. "Have the kindness, Mr. Walters, to spare the bench. Attend to your examination. Observations of that sort are wholly uncalled for."

But the boy, once started, was not so easily repressed. "Why, it *was* his lordship," he went on, scanning the judge still harder. "I do mind his vurry voice. It was 'im, no doubt about it. I've zeed a zight o' people, since I zeed 'im that day; but I do mind his voice, and I do mind his 'ands, and I do mind his ve-ace the zame as if it wur yesterday. Now I come to look, blessed if it wasn't his lordship!"

Guy's counsel smiled a triumphant smile. He had carried his point. He had confused the witness. This showed how little reliance could be placed upou the boy's evidence as to personal identity. He'd identify anybody who happened to be suggested to him! But Sir Gilbert's face grew yet more deadly pale. For he saw at a glance this was no accident or mistake; the boy really remembered him. And Elma's steadfast eyes looked him through and through, with that irresistible appeal, still more earnestly than ever.

Sir Gilbert breathed again. He had been recognized to no purpose. Even this posiive identificatio fell flat upon everybody.

At last the examination and cross-examination were finished and Guy's counsel began his hopeless task of unraveling this tangled mass of suggestion and coincidence. He had no witnesses to call; the very nature of the case precluded that. All he could do was to cavil over details, to point out possible alternatives, to lay stress upon the absence of direct evidence, and to ask that the jury should give the prisoner the benefit of the doubt, if any doubt at all existed in their minds as to his guilt or innonocence. Counsel had meant when he first undertook the case to lay great stress also on the presumed absence of motive ; but after the fatal accident which resulted in the disclosure of Montague Nevitt's pocket-book, any argument on that score would have been worse than useless. Counsel elected rather to pass the episode by in discreet silence, and to risk everything on the uncertainty of the actual encounter.

At last he sat down, wiping his brow in despair, after what he felt himself to be a most feeble performance.

Then Sir Gilbert began, and in a very tremulous and failing voice summed briefly up the whole of the evidence.

Men who remembered Gildersleeve's old blustering manner stood aghast at the timidity with which the famous lawyer delivered himself on this, the first capital charge ever brought before him. He reminded the jury, in very solemn and almost warning tones, that where a human life was at stake, mere presumptive evidence should always carry very little weight with it. And the evidence here was all purely presumptive. The prosecution had shown nothing more than a physical possibility that the prisoner at the bar might have committed the murder. There was evidence of animus, it was true ; but that evidence was weak ; there was partial identification ; but that identification lay open to the serious objection that all the persons who now swore to Guy Waring's personality had sworn just as surely and confidently before to his brother Cyril's. On the whole, the judge summed up strongly in Guy's favor. He wiped his clammy brow, and looked appealingly at the bar. As the jury would hope for justice themselves, let them remember to mete out nothing but strict justice to the accused person who now stood trembling in the dock before them.

All the court stood astonished. Could this be Gildersleeve? Atkins would never have summed up like that. Atkins would have gone in point-blank for hanging him. And everybody thought Gildersleeve would hang with the best. Nobody had suspected him till then of any womanly weakness about capital punishment. There was a solemn hush as the judge ended. Then everybody saw the unhappy man was seriously ill. Great streams of sweat trickled slowly down his brow. His eyes stared in front of him. His mouth twitched horribly. He looked like a person on the point of apoplexy. The prisoner at the bar gazed hard at him and pitied him.

"He's dying hlmself, and he wants to go out with a clear conscience at last," some one suggested in a low voice at the barristers' table. The explanation served. It was whispered around the court in a hushed undertone that the judge to-day was on his very last legs, and had summed up accordingly. Late in life, he had learned to show mercy, as he hoped for it.

There was a deadly pause. The jury retired to consider their verdict. Two men remained behind in court, waiting breathless for their return. Two lives hung at issue in the balance, while the jury deliberated. Elma Clifford glanced with a terrified eye from one to the other, could hardly help pitying the guiltiest most. His look of mute suffering was so inexpressibly pathetic.

The twelve good men and true were gone for a full half-hour. Why, nobody knew. The case was as plain as a pikestaff, gossipers said in court. If he had been caught redhanded, he'd have been hanged without remorse. It was only the eighteen months and the South Africa episode that could make the jury hesitate for one moment about hanging him.

At last, a sound, a thrill, a movement by the door. Every eye was strained forward. The jury trooped back again. They took their places in silence. Sir Gilbert scanned their faces with an agonized look. It was a moment of ghastly and painful suspense. He was waiting for their verdict—on himself, and Guy Waring.

CHAPTER XLIV.

AT BAY.

ONLY two people in court doubted for one moment what the verdict would be. And those two were the pair who stood there on their trial. Sir Gilbert couldn't believe the jury would convict an innocent man of the crime he himself had half unwittingly committed. Guy Waring couldn't believe the jury would convict an innocent man of the crime he had never been guilty of. So those two doubted. To all the rest the verdict was a foregone conclusion.

Nevertheless, dead silence reigned everywhere in the court as the clerk of arraigns put the solemn question, " Gentlemen, do you find the prisoner at the bar guilty or not guilty ? "

And the foreman, clearing his throat huskily answered, in a very tremulous tone, " We find him guilty of wilful murder."

There was a long, deep pause. Every one looked at the prisoner. Guy Waring stood like one stunned by the immensity of the blow. It was an awful moment. He knew he was innocent; but he knew now the English law would hang him.

One pair of eyes in the court, however, was not fixed on Guy. Elma Clifford, at that final and supreme moment, gazed hard with all her soul at Sir Gilbert Gildersleeve. Her glance went through him. She sat like an embodied conscience before him. The judge rose slowly, his eyes riveted on hers. He was trembling with remorse, and deadlier pale than ever. An awful lividness stole over his face. His lips were contorted. His eyebrows quivered horribly. Still gazing straight at Elma, he essayed to speak. Twice he opened his parched lips. Then his voice failed him.

"I cannot accept that finding," he said at last, in a very solemn tone, battling hard for speech against some internal enemy. "I cannot accept it. Clerk, you will enter a verdict of not guilty."

A deep hum of surprise ran round the expectant court. Every mouth opened wide, and drew a long, hushed breath. Senior counsel for the Crown jumped to his feet, astonished. "But why, my lord?" he asked, tartly, thus balked of his success. "On what ground does your lordship decide to override the plain verdict of the jury?"

The pause that followed was inexpressibly terrible. Guy Waring waited for the answer in an agony of suspense. He knew what it meant now. With a rush it all occurred to him. He knew who was the murderer. But he hoped for nothing. Sir Gilbert faltered. Elma Clifford's eyes were upon him still, compelling him. "Because," he said at last, with a still more evident and physical effort, pumping the words out slowly, "I am here to administer justice, and justice I will administer. . . . This man is innocent. It was I myself who killed Montagne Nevitt that day at Mambury."

At those awful words, uttered in a tone so solemn that no one could doubt either their truth or their sincerity, a cold thrill ran responsive through the packed crowd of auditors. The silence was profound. In its midst a boy's voice burst forth all at once, directed, as it seemed, to the counsel for the Crown. "I said it was him," the voice cried, in a triumphant tone. "I knowed 'um! I knowed 'um! Thik ther's the man that axed me the way down the dell the mornin' o' the murder."

The judge turned towards the boy with a ghastly smile of enforced recognition. "You say the truth, my lad," he answered, without any attempt at concealment. "It was I who asked you. It was I who killed him. I went round by the far gate, after hearing he was there, and cutting across the wood, I met Montague Nevitt in the path by the Tangle. I went there to meet him; I went there to confront him; but not of malice prepense to murder him. I wanted to question him about a family matter. Why I needed to question him no one henceforth shall ever know. That secret, thank heaven, rests now in Montague Nevitt's grave. But when I did question him, he answered me back with so foul an aspersion upon a lady who was very near and dear to me "—the judge paused a moment; he was fighting hard for breath; something within was evidently choking him. Then he went on more excitedly—" an aspersion upon a lady whom I love more than life—an insult that no man could stand—an unspeakable foulness; and I sprang at him, the cur, in the white heat of my anger, not meaning or dreaming to hurt him seriously. I caught him by the throat." The judge held up his hands before the whole court appealingly. "Look at those hands, gentlemen," he cried, turning them about. "How could I ever know how hard and how strong they were? I only seemed to touch him. I just pushed him from my path. He fell at once at my feet—dead, dead, unexpectedly. Remember how it all came about. The medical evidence showed his heart was weak, and he died in the scuffle. How was I to know all that? I only knew this—he fell dead before me."

With a face of speechless awe, he paused and wiped his brow. Not a soul in court moved or breathed above a whisper. It was evident the judge was in a paroxysm of contrition. His face was drawn up. His whole frame quivered visibly. Even Elma pitied him.

"And then I did a grievous wrong," the judge continued once more, his voice now very thick and growing rapidly thicker. "I did a grievous wrong, for which here to-day, before all this court, I humbly ask Guy Waring's pardon. I had killed Montague Nevitt, unintentionally, unwittingly, accidentally almost, in a moment of anger, never knowing I was killing him. And if he had been a stronger or a healthier man, what little I did to him would never have killed him. I didn't mean to murder him. For that my remorse is far less poignant. But what I did after was far worse than the murder. I behaved like a sneak. I behaved like a coward. I saw suspicion was aroused against the prisoner, Guy Waring. And what did I do then? Instead of coming forward like a man, as I ought, and saying 'I did it,' and standing my trial on the charge of manslaughter, I did my best to throw further suspicion on an innocent person. I made the case look blacker and worse for Guy Waring.

I don't condone my own crime. I did it for my wife's sake and my daughter's, I admit—but I regret it now, bitterly—and am I not atoning for it? With a great humiliation, am I not amply atoning for it? I wrote an unsigned letter warning Waring at once to fly the country, as a warrant was out against him. Waring foolishly took my advice, and fled forthwith. From that day to this,"—he gazed round him appealingly—" oh, friends, I have never known one happy moment."

Guy gazed at him from the dock, where he still stood guarded by two strong policemen, and felt a fresh light break suddenly in upon him. Their positions now were almost reversed. It was he who was the accuser, and Sir Gilbert Gildersleeve, the judge in that court, who stood charged to-day on his own confession with causing the death of Montague Nevitt.

" Then it was *you*," Guy said, slowly, breaking the pause at last, " who sent me that anonymous letter at Plymouth ? "

" It was I," the judge answered, in an almost inaudible, gurgling tone. " It was I who so wronged you. Can you ever forgive me for it ? "

Guy gazed at him fixedly. He himself had suffered much. Cyril and Elma had suffered still more. But the judge, he felt sure, had suffered most of all of them. In this moment of relief this moment of vindication, this moment of triumph, he could afford to be generous. " Sir Gilbert Gildersleeve, I forgive you," he answered, slowly.

The judge gazed around him with a vacant stare. " I feel cold," he said, shivering ; " very cold, very faint, too. But I've made all right *here*," and he held out a document. " I wrote this paper in my room last night—in case of accident—confessing everything. I brought it down here, signed and witnessed, unread, intending to read it out if the verdict went against me—I mean, against Waring. . . . But I feel too weak now to read anything further. . . . I'm so cold, so cold. Take the paper, Forbes-Ewing. It's all in your line. You'll know what to do with it." He could hardly utter a word, breath failed him so fast. " This thing has killed me," he went on, mumbling. " I deserved it. I deserved it."

" How about the prisoner ? " the authority from the

jail asked, as the judge collapsed rather than sat down on the bench again.

Those words roused Sir Gilbert to full consciousness once more. The judge rose again, solemnly, in all the majesty of his ermine. " The prisoner is discharged," he said, in a loud, clear voice. "I am here to do justice— justice against myself. I enter a verdict of not guilty." Then he turned to the police. "I am your prisoner," he went on, in a broken, rambling way. "I give myself in charge for the manslaughter of Montague Nevitt. Manslaughter, not murder. Though I don't even admit myself, indeed, it was anything more than justifiable homicide."

He sank back again once more, and murmured three times in his seat, as if to himself, " Justifiable homicide! Justifiable homicide! Just—ifiable homicide!"

Somebody rose in court as he sank, and moved quickly towards him. The judge recognized him at once.

"Granville Kelmscott," he said, in a weary voice, "help me out of this. I'm very, very ill. You're a friend. I'm dying. Give me your arm! Assist me!"

CHAPTER XLV.

ALL'S WELL THAT ENDS WELL.

GRANVILLE helped him on his arm into the judge's room amid profound silence. All the court was deeply stirred. A few personal friends hurried after him eagerly. Among them were the Warings, and Mrs. Clifford and Elma.

The judge staggered to a seat, and held Granville's hand long and silently in his. Then his eye caught Elma's. He turned to her gratefully. " Thank you, young lady," he said, in a very thick voice. " You are extremely good. I forget your name. But you helped me greatly."

There was such a pathetic ring in those significant words, " I forget your name," that every eye about stood dimmed with moisture. Remorse had clearly blotted out all else now from Sir Gilbert Gildersleeve's powerful brain save the solitary memory of his great wrong-doing.

" Something's upon his mind still," Elma cried, looking hard at him. " He's dying! he's dying! But he wants to say something else before he dies, I'm certain. . . . Mr. Kelmscott, it's to you. Oh, Cyril, stand back! Mother, leave them alone! I'm sure from his eye he wants to say something to Mr. Kelmscott."

They all fell back reverently. They stood in the presence of death and of a mighty sorrow. Sir Gilbert still held Granville's hand fast bound in his own. " It'll kill her!" he muttered. " It'll kill her! I'm sure it'll kill her! She'll never get over the thought that her father was—was the cause of Montague Nevitt's death. And you'll never care to marry a girl of whom people will say, either justly or unjustly, ' She's a murderer's daughter.' . . . And that will kill her, too. For, Kelmscott, she loved you."

Granville held the dying man's hand still more gently

than ever. " Sir Gilbert," he said, leaning over him with
very tender eyes " no event on earth could ever possibly
alter Gwendoline's love for me or my love for Gwendoline. I know you can't live. This shock has been too
much for you. But if it will make you die any the hap-
pier now to know that Gwendoline and I will still be one,
I give you my sacred promise at this solemn moment, that
as soon as she likes I will marry Gwendoline." He
paused for a second. "I don't understand all this story
just yet," he went on. " But of one thing I'm certain.
The sympathy of every soul in court to-day went with
you as you spoke out the truth so manfully. The sympathy of all England will go with you to-morrow when
they come to learn of it. . . . Sir Gilbert, till this morning I never admired you, much as I love Gwendoline.
As you made that confession just now in court, I declare,
I admired you. With all the greater confidence now will
I marry your daughter."

They carried him to the judge's lodgings in the town,
and laid him there peaceably for the doctors to tend him.
For a fortnight the shadow of Gilbert Gildersleeve still
lingered on, growing feebler and feebler in intellect every
day. But the end was certain. It was softening of the
brain, and it proceeded rapidly. The horror of that unspeakable trial had wholly unnerved him. The great,
strong man cried and sobbed like a baby. Lady Gildersleeve and Gwendoline were with him all through. He
seldom spoke. When he did, it was generally to murmur those fixed words of exculpation, in a tremulous undertone, " It was my hands that did it—these great,
clumsy hands of mine—not I—not I. I never, never
meant it. It was an accident. An accident. Justifiable
homicide. . . . What I really regret is for that poor fellow Waring."

And at the end of a fortnight he died, once smiling,
with Gwendoline's hand locked tight in his own, and
Granville Kelmscott kneeling in tears by his bedside.

The Kelmscott property was settled by arrangement.
It never came into court. With the aid of the family
lawyers, the three half-brothers divided it amicably.
Guy wouldn't hear of Granville's giving up his claim to
the house and park at Tilgate. Granville was to the

manner born, he said, and brought up to expect it ; while
Cyril and he, mere waifs and strays in the world, would
be much better off, even so, with their third of the property each, than they ever before in their lives could have
counted upon. As for Cyril, he was too happy in Guy's
exculpation from the greater crime, and his frank explanation of the lesser (under Nevitt's influence), to care
very much in his own heart what became of Tilgate.

The only one man who objected to this arrangement
was Mr. Reginald Clifford, C. M. G., of Craighton. The
Companion of the Militant Saints was strongly of opinion
that Cyril Waring oughtn't to have given up his prior
claim to the family mansion, even for valuable consideration elsewhere. Mr. Clifford drew himself up to the full
height of his spare figure, and caught in the tight skin of
his mummy-like face rather tighter than before, as he delivered himself of this profound opinion. " A man should
consult his own dignity," he said, stiffly, and with great
precision ; " if he's born to assume a position in the county,
he should assume that position as a sacred duty. He
should remember that his wife and children——"

" But he hasn't got any wife, papa," Elma ventured to
interpose, with a bright little smile ; " so *that* can't count
either way."

" He hasn't a wife *at present*, to be sure ; that's perfectly true, my dear ; no wife, *at present ;* but he will
probably now, in his existing circumstances, soon obtain
one. A Man of Property should always marry. Mr.
Waring will naturally desire to ally himself to some
family of Good Position in the county ; and the lady's relations would, of course, insist——"

" Well, it doesn't matter to us, papa," Elma answered,
maliciously ; " for as far as we're concerned, you know,
you've often said that nothing on earth would ever induce you to give your consent."

The Gentleman of Good Position in the county gazed
at his daughter aghast with horror. " My dear child,"
he said, with positive alarm, " your remarks are nothing
short of revolutionary. You must remember that since
then circumstances have altered. At that time, Mr.
Waring was a painter——"

" He's a painter still, I believe," Elma put in, parenthetically. "The acquisition of property or county rank doesn't seem to have had the very slightest effect one way or the other upon his drawing or his coloring."

Her father disdained to take notice of such flippant remarks. "At that time," he repeated, solemnly, Mr. Waring was a painter, a mere ordinary painter; we know him now to be the heir and representative of a great County Family. If he were to ask you to-day——"

"But he did ask me a long time ago, you know, papa," Elma put in demurely. "And at that time, you remember, you objected to the match; so of course, as in duty bound, I at once refused him."

"And what did your father say to that, Elma?" Cyril asked, with a smile, as she narrated the whole circumstances to him some hours later.

"Oh," he only said, 'But he'll ask you again now, you may be sure, my child.' And I replied very gravely, I didn't think you would. And do you know, Cyril, I really don't think you will, either."

"Why not, Elma?"

"Because, you foolish boy, it isn't the least bit in the world necessary. This has been, all through, a comedy of errors. Tragedy enough intermixed; but still a comedy of errors. There never was really any reason on earth why either of us shouldn't have married the other. And the only thing I now regret myself is that I didn't do as I first threatened, and marry you outright, just to show my confidence in you and Guy, at the time when everybody else had turned most against you."

"Well, suppose we make up for lost time now by saying Wednesday fortnight," Cyril suggested, after a short pause, during which both of them simultaneously had been otherwise occupied.

"Oh, Cyril, that's awfully quick! It could hardly be managed. There's the dresses, and all that! And the bridesmaids to arrange about! And the invitations to issue! . . . But still, sooner than put you off any longer now—well, yes, my dear boy,—I daresay we could make it Wednesday fortnight."

THE END.

www.ingramcontent.com/pod-product-compliance
Lightning Source LLC
Chambersburg PA
CBHW020603260626
47157CB00003B/841